To my very
love + to
Cathyn 2.

The Pavements
We Walk On

Carolyn Belcher

First Published in 2016
by GWL Publishing
an imprint of Great War Literature Publishing LLP

Produced in United Kingdom

ISBN 978-1-910603-31-4 Paperback Edition

GWL Publishing
Forum House
Stirling Road
Chichester PO19 7DN
www.gwlpublishing.co.uk

Carolyn was born and grew up in South Lincolnshire in a small village called Holbeach Hurn. Her Aunt Margaret introduced her to the power of drama and theatre when she was twelve.

In 1970, with her first husband, Barry and their three children, she moved to Knotty Ash, in Liverpool. When the last of her three children started school, she took a Bachelor of Education degree in drama, dance and education. Her first teaching post was at Page Moss Comprehensive, and as a performance arts teacher, she was invited to be on the Board of trustees for The Everyman Theatre.

It was at Knowsley Community College, in 1984, where as Course Coordinator for performing arts she began writing seriously, developing scripts from student improvisations. Some of the pieces were performed at the Edinburgh Fringe Festival and two were Pick of the Day in The Scotsman.

She was one of the Founder members and first artistic director of Icarus Allsorts, a performance arts company set up to help Knowsley graduates of the performing arts, to achieve an equity card.

She took early retirement when she was fifty, and moved with her second husband, Colin, to the Maine et Loire in France in order to have more time to develop her writing.

She now lives in Suffolk where, until recently, she supplemented her pension by becoming an examiner for GCE and GCSE drama practical work. She is a volunteer at Oxfam and belongs to Write Now, the Bury St Edmunds Writers' group.

She has had several stories and poems published in magazines and anthologies, both in England and The United States, and a monologue, which was chosen to be performed at a new writing festival, in Reading. Her first novel, *Crocodiles and Angels*, was published in 2015.

Theatre still plays an important part in Carolyn's life, as do dance, gardening and entertaining family and friends.

Dedication

To Wendy

Prologue

There is a mirror in a cathedral. It is there to help visitors look at the stained glass windows without hurting their necks. Four women stop, look, sigh, and move back a few paces.

I suspect we are all peering down at the ravages of time. I hope Trevor never sees me from this angle. But, if he does, I shall be seeing all his sagging flesh and wrinkles.

Chapter One
Periods

Curiosity killed the cat.

Edith, my mother, always insisted on doing my hair even though I was eleven and perfectly capable of doing it myself. Of course she knew that I wouldn't try to tame my curly mop. I believed she thought that if she could tame my hair, she could tame me. I did try to sit still as she yanked the brush through the tangles, but it was difficult for my scalp was on fire.

"If you don't stop wriggling, Margaret, I shall tell your father I'm going to get your hair cut."

My dad thought I had beautiful hair. He wouldn't have liked it if Edith made me have it cut. He'd shown me pictures of a woman called Elizabeth Siddal. She had crinkly, red hair that looked like a mass of lit sparklers. When I wasn't in school, or anywhere near Edith, I pulled off the elastic band and set my curls free. They sprang out from my head as if to thank me and I thought, *I shall look like you, Lizzie Siddal, when I grow up.*

Yank. "Ow!" *How can I stay still? I'm not a still sort of girl. Come on, Maggie, think. What do you do in school, Miss Fidget? You hum. You hum a favourite song.*

Edith frowned. "And you can stop humming that silly song. You are not having a dog for your birthday."

3

Of course I knew this, but I couldn't stop wishing. Ideally, I would have liked a Lassie, but I guessed you had to live in the country if you had a collie dog. There weren't many sheep in Liverpool.

"Mum," I said, when the morning's torture was over. "What's the curse?"

She frowned. "Where did you hear about that?"

"Leila said she had the curse and it meant she wasn't a little girl any more, she was a woman."

"Leila said that, did she? Well I think you can stop seeing Leila; filling your head with muck... curse indeed."

"Mu-um, she's me best friend. What is it?"

"'My' not 'me', Margaret. It's for women to know and little girls to mind their own business about."

"But—"

"Don't you 'but' me. You're not too old to have your ears boxed."

"What have I said? I haven't said any dirty words. I haven't sworn. I haven't said 'God' or 'Jesus'."

"I should think not indeed. Now off you go, your father will be waiting. And don't you go annoying him about things you're not supposed to know. Just remember, curiosity killed the cat."

My curiosity was well and truly inflamed. A subject that embarrassed Edith had to be worth knowing. If any cat happened to cross my path, it had better look out.

I was never 'Margaret' to my dad, nor 'nuisance', 'naughty girl', 'nosy girl who couldn't mind her own business', nor someone whose ears needed to be boxed. I was Maggie, his daughter, and I knew he was proud of me.

"Hi, Dad. I'm ready. Are you ready?" I bounced into the back yard. I loved our jaunts together. Most Saturdays we would go out somewhere, leaving Edith and Ian, my brother, at home. Ian was three years younger than me. He was Edith's favourite.

"I would have thought you could see that I'm ready, queen." He patted his jacket pocket. "Bus fares, pipe, tobacco, that's it. Come on. We can catch the quarter past."

"Where are we going?"

"To see Uncle Charlie. We didn't go last Saturday, did we?"

Although I loved the outings with my dad, I had mixed feelings about my Uncle Charlie. If my dad left the room for any reason, Uncle Charlie rubbed his trousers where his cock was. That's what Leila called a man's dangly bit. I knew its proper name: 'penis'. My dad believed in using the correct names for things when he talked to me. I couldn't tell him what Uncle Charlie did. I was afraid he might be angry with him, might not visit him any more, and Uncle Charlie needed our visits because he lived alone. I told Leila and she giggled and said he was a dirty old man. But Uncle Charlie wasn't dirty. When he kissed me hello, he always smelt nice. It was a different smell to my dad. Dad smelt of something called Old Spice. It was an 'after shave' lotion. Uncle Charlie's smell was Imperial Leather soap. I knew the smell because it was the soap we used in our house. I guessed he didn't have any 'after shave' lotion; perhaps he couldn't afford it. He worked in a factory in Speke. Dad said he was a sweeper-upper because he had learning difficulties. Uncle Charlie couldn't read or write. My dad worked for British Rail, not as a train driver, in an office. He had friends who were train drivers. I didn't think Uncle Charlie had many friends.

He always stared at me and smiled when he rubbed himself. Sometimes, to be polite, I smiled back. At other times I looked away because I wasn't sure he was seeing me. His eyes were dreamy. Perhaps that was what I looked like when Miss Reardon told me to stop daydreaming. But I wasn't doing naughty things when I daydreamed.

I was all mixed up in my head about what was going on when Uncle Charlie rubbed himself. Enjoyment is a good thing. I enjoyed my outings with my dad. I enjoyed hanging out with Leila and Gail. So why did I feel that what Uncle Charlie was doing was naughty? And there was something else; every time he did it, my fanny tingled. It was the same tingling I felt when Ian and I played our Saturday morning games...

There was no rush on a Saturday morning. My dad wasn't going to work and we weren't going to school. Before breakfast while our parents were still in their bedroom, Ian would creep into bed with me. I'd strip off my nighty, and he his pyjamas. We'd tell each other stories, and draw the pictures for them on each other's backs with our fingers. I loved having my back tickled and scratched. Sometimes, Ian would curl around me and his small boy penis would nestle at the base of my spine. It could move of its own accord and, at times, it grew. This was when the tingling happened. I wanted Ian to rub his penis on my fanny, which made me feel like giggling because it seemed such a weird thing to want. I didn't know the proper words for women's bits and pieces then. Leila called the place between her legs her 'fanny', so I copied her.

When dad and I were safely out of Edith's eye-shot I took off my itchy, woollen hat, tugged off the elastic band, untwisted the plait and ran my fingers through my hair.

My dad shook his head. "I don't know! You, your mum and your hair. Mind you, I always think scragging hair back is like forcing boys to wear a tie. It straitjackets the wearer. But your mum has her reasons, I guess. Perhaps she's afraid you'll catch nits in school?"

"But I'm not in school now, am I?" I said, wondering if he ever asked Edith to release her hair.

He ruffled my unruly mop, but didn't reply. He rarely replied if he felt I might be tempted to say something naughty about Edith. I didn't know this, like really know. I just felt it.

Dad always talked to me as though I were an adult. He expected me to ask if I didn't understand, and he took it for granted I would remember new words and information. He never got angry with me. He was a gentle man. If I had been asked to describe my dad, I would have said that my friends wished he was their dad. I couldn't think of a better description of his character. To look at? Well he didn't have film star looks. He wasn't very tall. He was cuddly, but not fat. He had straight, brown hair, brown eyes and a smiley mouth; except when he looked serious or sad.

"What's a straitjacket?" I asked as we got on the bus.

"It's a coat with very long arms. It's used to restrain people in mental institutions if they show signs of violent behaviour. It's supposed to keep them and others safe."

I couldn't imagine how a coat with long arms would help. I pictured people running about, sleeves flailing like scythes. "That seems very dangerous, Dad. Don't the long sleeves hurt?"

"Sorry, Maggie? Hurt how?"

"Well, if I was running about with very long sleeves, they might slap other people, or I might trip over them."

Dad laughed and then his face grew serious. "The only thing that gets hurt is the patient's dignity and self esteem. The sleeves are tied behind their back, so their arms are like this." He wrapped his arms round his body. "Then the patient is taken to a padded cell, where they're locked in until they've calmed down."

"Do you think that's a good thing to do?"

"Do you, Maggie?"

From time to time, Dad answered a question with a question. Sometimes I minded, at other times I didn't. This was a not minding time because I had two pictures in my head, the first of my brother Ian when he was about three and a half. He'd been upset about something fairly stupid, like Edith tutting at him. Edith never did anything worse than 'tut' at Ian. He'd reacted violently and, when she tried to pick him up, he'd thrown himself backwards and hit his head on the table leg.

The second was of my mother in a temper. She could be a danger to herself and others when she got going. How would straitjacketing either of them do any good, that was what I wanted to know? It would probably have made them madder. I did like the idea of restraining Edith though.

I shook my head. "I think there are better ways than straitjackets, like talking calmly to people and saying nice things so they feel better, like you do with Mum when she's upset." I meant when she got mad at anything, mostly me.

"It's a humanitarian idea, Maggie, but it might not work with everyone. Some criminals are insane. They need more than calm, and kind words."

"What does humanitarian mean?"

"Being compassionate." Dad saw I was still looking puzzled. "Kind is almost what it means."

"How about aspirin? Aspirins can make you feel better."

My dad laughed. "Aspirins, your mum's cure all. There are pills which are supposed to help people in mental hospitals, they're called tranquillisers, and there's something called electroshock therapy."

"What's that?"

"A patient's brain is given electric shocks."

I gasped. "That sounds dead stupid. Electric shocks can kill you."

"These don't. The doctors have to make sure of that." He sighed. "But there are problems with all treatments, Maggie."

"Sometimes Mum gets dead mad." I glanced sideways at my dad. "But I don't think one of those jackets would help. It would make her madder."

"Um." He looked sad. I didn't want him to be sad.

"But I suppose her mad isn't the same as loony mad. It's being too cross. Aspirins help Mum's headaches but not her temper. I have to be dead careful I don't set her off again. She only takes a half. Maybe she should take the whole bottle."

"That amount of aspirin would kill her, Maggie."

I thought I'd better change the subject. My mind was pushing uncomfortable thoughts at me, like Edith dead, and the happy life my dad and I would have without her. I didn't include Ian in my thoughts. Ian had no problems with our mother. But then I decided that I was being unfair. We did have fun at times; like when she decided to teach me how to make parkin for bonfire night. I wished I could remember all the good things when she was mad at me.

The bus ride to Uncle Charlie's took three quarters of an hour; plenty of time for a conversation. Dad and I often had interesting conversations on buses. They flew about all over the place because my head was full of questions.

"Dad, what's the curse?" I said, ignoring Edith's orders.

"You remember I asked you to call a penis by its proper name?" He said very quietly, as though he didn't want anyone else to overhear what we were talking about. "I'd like you to call, the curse, by its proper name too. It's 'periods' or 'menses'. Have you ever heard of either of these words?" I shook my head. "Well, let me see how best to explain it. Where did you hear the expression 'the curse'?"

"From Leila. She told me she was a woman now because she'd got the curse. Mum said she'd filled my head with muck; I was to mind my own business, and not go round Leila's house any more."

Dad sighed, and I wondered if the curse… period, was something so bad that no one should talk about it. Perhaps it and Uncle Charlie rubbing his penis were topics to be kept hidden inside you. But if you never let them loose, how did you get to know things? And if, as Leila had said, it was about becoming a woman, not a girl, then surely I ought to know.

"A bus isn't the best place to talk about this, Maggie. When we get off, we'll pop into Newsham park and I'll tell you all about periods." He looked at his watch. "We've got plenty of time. You know what your Uncle Charlie's like if we're early, or late."

I did. He always got really upset and no matter what my dad said, Uncle Charlie believed he himself had got the time wrong, the day wrong, everything wrong. He couldn't keep still or stop talking about it.

"To think I got that wrong. I don't know, Percy, what am I like? I haven't been to the shops yet. No Fullers for your little girl. What will she think of me?" On and on, like rainwater whooshing down a drainpipe.

"Does he know we're coming?"

"Yes. Why?"

"Because when he does, he buys a Fuller's walnut cake. He knows I like them best of any cake in the world. When you don't tell him, we only get a cup of tea and a ginger biscuit." I thought that sounded a bit ungrateful. "Ginger biscuits are okay. I do like them. But they're not like scrummy walnut cake."

"I sent him the usual postcard."

"What postcard did you send?"

Uncle Charlie liked anything to do with engines; cars, steam engines, trains, aeroplanes. It didn't matter that he couldn't read, he knew that the postcard meant a 'this Saturday' visit.

"A steam train. The Duke of Gloucester. I don't think he's got that one." Dad pulled a face. "To be honest, it's a bit difficult to remember what I've sent. Still, Charlie doesn't seem to mind." Uncle Charlie had put all the postcards in albums, like other people do stamps. After tea he would pick one album for us to look at.

One day Edith had said she didn't understand why I liked going to Uncle Charlie's. I'd told her that it was because I loved Fuller's walnut cake, and looking at his postcard collection. She'd sniffed. *"A grown man collecting postcards. It's boys who do things like that. That brother of yours has never grown up, Percy."*

"Mother doesn't like Uncle Charlie, does she?"

"Why do you say that?"

"I was just thinking what she said about his postcard collection and… she and Ian never come with us to see him, do they?"

"Your mother rarely visits anyone. She's a home bird. And she thinks it's nice for you and I to have time together."

Did she? If that were true, why didn't she tell me? But Dad was right about her being a home bird. She did take us to visit our nan and granddad, occasionally. They lived in Broadgreen. Dad's parents lived in Birkenhead. We only saw them at Christmas and Easter. I liked both sets of grandparents. Nana Doreen always gave Ian and I a bit of pocket money to spend in their corner shop, and she made Wet Nellies. Ian didn't like Wet Nellies, but I did. They were stodgy, leftover bread cakes, full of dried fruit. When I was with Nana Doreen and Granddad Fred, I wondered why Edith had turned into such an uncomfortable person, not a comfy, squashy bodied person with a loud voice, who laughed a lot, like they did. Edith rarely laughed. I hoped that I would grow up like them. I was often chastised by Edith, and the teachers in school, for being too loud.

Dad and I sat on a bench by the bandstand. "Periods are to do with girls being able to have babies," he said.

"I thought only women could have babies."

"It depends how you define a woman."

"Well, Mum's a woman, and Leila said she's a woman now, so someone between the age of twelve and when you die, I suppose. Is it because I'm only eleven that I don't have periods?"

"Not necessarily. Some girls start their periods when they're eleven. Your body's telling you it's not ready to have a baby yet."

"But what are they?"

"Every month a woman's body makes eggs, and if they're not used to make a baby, they break down and are ejected by the body along with the lining of the uterus."

"What's a uterus?"

"It's a woman's womb. It's the safe place where a baby can grow."

"But is it safe after the body's ejected the lining? It might not be warm enough for a new baby to grow. My coat is lined."

Dad smiled. "Body's are wonderful, Maggie. It grows another lining."

"Wow! What a lot of work's going on in a girl's body every month."

My dad laughed. "Yes, and it's all natural. Girls who don't know about it can think they're ill when they see blood in their knickers."

"What? Blood in me knickers? Yuk"

Dad didn't correct the 'me'. "We'll get a book from the library, Maggie, then you can look at pictures of a woman's body and see how it all works."

"But how do the eggs make babies? We eat eggs. Are we eating baby chicks? I'll never want to eat an egg again if I've been eating a baby."

"No, we're not. The chickens' eggs are unfertilised. All eggs have to be fertilised to make babies."

I was becoming more and more confused. My dad fertilised the vegetables on his allotment with horse muck he got from Speke.

He must have seen how puzzled I was, for he said, "Don't worry about it now, sweetheart. When you've looked at the book it'll be clearer. And I'll be there to interpret, if there's anything you don't understand. Did Leila giggle when she told you she'd started her periods?"

"A bit; we both did. I didn't tell her I didn't know what she was going on about. So, I'm still a girl and Leila's a woman. She can make a baby, and when I start my periods I'll be able to make a baby too. But I don't want a baby, they're hard work, and they keep you awake at night. Mother told me I always kept her awake. Ian didn't, he was a very good baby."

"I don't approve of words like 'good' or 'bad' in relation to babies, Maggie. If a baby cries, it's because there's a need: food, a dirty nappy, colic. Babies are never naughty. They don't know how to be naughty. We all learn what that is, and also what good is, like we learn to talk and walk."

"Sorry, Dad."

"No need to say sorry, love. It's other people who've put ideas in your head about judging babies. Just remember, all babies are wonderful, and it's contentment in a baby that's important When I feel really hungry, I'm not contented. If I had wet underpants on, I'd feel uncomfortable. As for a pain in my tummy... Do you see?"

"Yes." I did see. It was pretty obvious really. I mean, how could a baby be bad? "Babies may be wonderful, Dad, but periods don't sound much fun. I'd prefer not to have them. I want to be an actress, or a tennis player. I bet it's difficult to be an actress or a tennis player if you have periods. Do you have to stay in bed when you have a period?"

"No."

"Then how do you stop the blood trickling down your legs? Do boys have periods as well, you know to be men?"

"Whoa Maggie, too many questions. No, only girls. Boys do go through puberty, but it's different."

"What's puberty?"

"Puberty is nature's way of changing a child into an adult."

"Oh." Then I realised something. "Of course, it has to be different for a lad, doesn't it? Men don't have breasts. Dad, how do you stop the blood staining your clothes?"

"You wear a sanitary towel. When your Mum goes shopping next, I shall ask her to get you some."

"She won't like that. And she'll be cross with me for asking you about periods. She told me not to."

"Right." He sighed. "You shouldn't really have asked me then, should you?" He looked at me in that way that told me I oughtn't to have disobeyed Edith. "But I understand why you did. Tell you what, I'll pretend I've noticed changes in you and tell her we ought to prepare you. After all, we shall all have to get used to you growing up." He gave me a hug. "Come on, time to go to Uncle Charlie's."

We got up. "Why did Leila call it, the curse?"

"I expect because her mother called it that. I'm not sure when it started, but it has a religious connection, the curse of Eve, I believe."

"I don't think Eve and the apple has anything to do with periods, Dad. I think it was knowledge."

"Good point, Maggie. As I'm not particularly religious, I don't know." Suddenly he looked mischievous. "You could always ask your mum."

"Da-ad!"

"Maggie?" He laughed. I was glad he'd been able to tease me about Edith. I knew I often made it difficult for him, and he tried to be loyal to us both.

I was grateful to my dad for being honest with me, even if the honesty wasn't always what I wanted to hear. It seemed to me that boys and men were better off than girls and women. I hated the idea of bleeding every month. It sounded painful and disgusting. My only experience of bleeding was cuts and grazes, and they were painful. As for wearing a towel between your legs, how could that be comfortable?

"What's with the bottom lip, Maggie?"

"I wish I were a boy."

"You're not the first woman who's wished that. However, all the men who fought in the two world wars, well any war, might have preferred to be women."

"Some women were involved in wars. The Amazons were."

"Yes, they were. But most women weren't involved in actual fighting."

"Horses had to fight, well not fight exactly, the men did the fighting, but the horses were in the battle. No one asked them if they wanted to go to war. I think I'll be a person who protects animals when I grow up, instead of a tennis player or actress. Then it won't matter about the periods. Do animals have periods?"

"Yes. We're here now, so no more questions until later." My dad rang the doorbell. Uncle Charlie didn't open the door and overwhelm us with his welcome. After a couple more tries, Dad used his spare key. There was no Fuller's walnut cake, no kettle filled and waiting to be put on the gas hob, no Uncle Charlie rubbing his penis. He was ill. He was so ill Dad had to run down the road to the phone box to ring for an ambulance. I stayed in the living room while Uncle Charlie wheezed upstairs.

"Pneumonia," the doctor at Broadgreen Hospital said. "He's lucky you found him when you did."

"We visit him every couple of weeks," my dad said. "I have to admit, I'm puzzled. He seemed fine the last time we saw him."

I tugged his sleeve. "Can I whisper?"

"You can tell the doctor whatever you want to tell me."

"Last week, while you were having a wee, Dad, Uncle Charlie had a coughing fit." After he'd rubbed his penis. "Dad has to go to the toilet quite often because of his kidneys."

The doctor and my dad shared a secret look, and I knew I'd said something I shouldn't have said, or something amusing.

"Have I let my tongue run away with me? Mum says I'm always letting my tongue run away with me. Sometimes she tells me that I deserve to have my mouth—"

"Maggie," said my father gently, "let the doctor go about his business."

"See?" I said to the doctor. "I told you, didn't I?"

"What's the prognosis?" asked my dad.

"Physically, your brother isn't in good shape. He's overweight, for a man of his height, and he has high blood pressure. Does he smoke?"

"Yes," I said, before my dad could answer. "He smokes a pipe. That's why his teeth are stained."

"You're a very observant young lady."

I frowned. "I'm not a young lady. I'm a working class girl. And I'm not a woman—"

"You're a working class chatterbox. Hush now."

"A very bright working class chatterbox," said the doctor. "Anyway, all these factors will make his recovery more difficult. I'm not going to pretend his condition isn't serious, but, as I said, it was fortunate you found him when you did. There is another factor. Your brother lives alone…" Again he looked at his notes. "Do you think he enjoys life enough to want to go on living? That's important."

"I don't know," said my dad.

I thought I did, but this time I didn't allow my tongue to gallop into action. I thought he enjoyed our visits. He enjoyed rubbing his penis when my dad went to the toilet. "He likes Fuller's Walnut cake with a cup of tea," I said.

Uncle Charlie didn't recover and again I was left with a head full of questions, one of which was so puzzling it made my head ache. I knew not to ask Edith for half an aspirin, however. Was it better to live with others and put up with them, as I did with Edith, or live on your own and be lonely, like Uncle Charlie?

Edith didn't want me to go to his funeral. "Funerals aren't for children," she said.

Surprisingly, my dad ignored her. "Would you like to come with me?" he asked.

Whether I really wanted to accompany him, or I said yes because Edith didn't want me to go, I wasn't sure; a bit of both, probably. I'm glad I went. I, my father and a vicar who didn't know Uncle Charlie, were the only people there.

Later, when Uncle Charlie's house was cleared out ready for new tenants, I asked Dad if I could have the postcard collection. Dad said yes, but when Edith saw it, she said they weren't suitable for a girl and she gave them to Ian. He looked at one album and then left them lying on the rug by his bed.

"Don't you want them, Ian?" she said. "I'd better put them in the bin, if you don't. I can't have them gathering dust."

"I don't want them put in the bin, Edith." My dad sounded quite stern. I thought it might be because he was still sad about Uncle Charlie's death. That was twice in the space of a few days that he had stood up to her. "I'd like you to give them back to Margaret. I think Charlie would have wanted her to have them. He didn't really know Ian."

The next day, I woke up with an ache in my lower back and when I went to the toilet there was blood on the paper.

Chapter Two
A Half Decent Kid

It is easy to be wise after the event.

At fifteen, I became infatuated with Doris Day. I knew what the word 'infatuated' meant, because when I told my dad I was in love with her, he suggested it was infatuation. I didn't want to look like Lizzie Siddal any longer. I wanted to have my hair bleached, straightened and cut short like Doris in *The Pyjama Game*. I knew that Edith, who always complained about my hair, wouldn't have allowed it, mainly to see the look of disappointment on my face. But in any case I couldn't have done it, it would have upset my dad.

One Saturday, soon after the film hit the Liverpool cinemas, I plucked up the courage to ask Edith if I could go with my friends to see it. I had a bet with myself that she would say 'no'.

Edith had her back to me. She was scraping the skin off carrots as though they'd offended her. She didn't turn round. *I'll kill her if she says no. I'll kill myself if she says no.* "No," she said.

"You don't even know what I'm going to ask."

"Whatever it is, no."

"Why?"

"Because I say so."

"Gail's mum's letting her go." I didn't mention Leila. Edith didn't like Leila or her mum. She thought Mrs Reardon was fast. *"Barmaid indeed. What sort of a job is that? I've seen her in those low cut tops. She's no better than her job. All those men leering."*

"Well your mother's not letting you go."

"But…"

"One more word out of you and you'll go to your room."

"I'm going anyway."

"You leave this room in a paddy and you won't get any tea."

"Don't want any."

Edith flung the knife in the sink, but I was out of the door before she could give me a clip round the ear.

I shoved the chair under the handle of my bedroom door and plotted. In a sanitary towel packet I'd squirrelled away money saved by not having school dinners. I would add it to my last week's pocket money. I doubted I would get any this week.

At the beginning of each week, Leila, Gail and I pooled our dinner money. We bought enough cheese and apples for the week and divided up whatever money was left over. Leila took our provisions home and brought in three apples and a portion of cheese each day. Her mum never noticed. I liked Mrs Reardon. She was fun. She taught us how to make-up our faces and paint our nails. When Edith saw my nails she sent me straight to the chemist's to buy nail polish remover and told me I was never to go to Leila's house again. Of course, I disobeyed; she said it nearly every week.

The film was being shown at our local cinema, The Gaumont, more often called 'the fleapit'. Edith didn't approve of The Gaumont. Very occasionally, when we were younger, she took us into the city centre to see a film like *Bambi*. I cried in *Bambi* and Edith told me not to be so silly, it was only a cartoon. It wasn't to me, it was real. I believed in the death of his mum, and the fire. I was terrified by the fire; all those poor animals having to flee for their lives before the flames.

I couldn't bear the idea of my friends going to the cinema without me. I needed a plan of escape, but how? A window. I would have to get back into the house via a window. If I could leave one unlatched, I ought to be able to push it up. My dad kept the cords of the sash windows well waxed so that we could open them easily. My bedroom window looked out onto the narrow part of the yard. The dining room window was under it. I shook my head; the drop was too great, even with a sheet tied to something. And how would I get back up? I couldn't leave it hanging there. The kitchen window? I would have to rely on Edith and Dad not checking to see it was shut properly. Edith always shut and latched it after she'd finished cooking; she had it open so the cooking smells wouldn't invade the house. Would she think to check later? I doubted it. I would sneak out when she was saying goodnight to Ian, and Dad was watching the football results. *Hey short-arse, this could work.* Leila had taken to calling me 'short-arse' because I was only five foot two. She was five-seven and towered over me.

I took the chair from under the handle and went downstairs, steeling myself to eat humble pie even though I wasn't very good at it. "Sorry," I said, wondering if I sounded contrite.

"Sorry? I don't think sorry is good enough." I was saved from further grovelling by Ian; he had been playing out in the alley. He rushed in, slamming the back door making both Edith and I jump. She grabbed him. Whatever had happened was secondary to dirty marks all over the kitchen lino. If I'd slammed the back door like that I'd have been for it. Golden boy didn't even get a telling off.

"Shoes off, love," was all Edith said as Ian wriggled out of her grasp.

"Jimmy's a big fat pig," he snarled, flinging himself on the doormat. "He stealed my best marble. I hate him." Jimmy was Ian's best friend.

"'Stole' not 'stealed'," said Edith. "Or did he win it?'"

"Stole. He stole my bluey. He cheated."

"Margaret, keep an eye on the veg. I'm going to see what's what here. Come along Ian."

"There's no point. He'll only say he didn't cheat." He threw his shoes in the corner by the door.

She bent down to straighten them. "Did he or didn't he cheat?"

"He must of."

"'Have' not 'of'. Next time you play marbles with Jimmy, you'll just have to win your bluey back. We can't win all the time, Ian, nor can we lose. Get your coat off and wash your hands. Then you can watch TV, if you like. Your dad's looking at the football results."

"Boring," said Ian but he did as she suggested.

Looking at the way Edith dealt with Ian, almost made me like her. Then I remembered *The Pyjama Game*.

Ian was never asked to do jobs around the house. Edith made it clear that house jobs were women's work. Normally this unfairness was enough for me to suggest he might help me to set the table, or wash up after we'd eaten. Today I let it slide. I didn't even give him a sly punch, kick, or pinch when I went into the living room to tell him that tea was ready.

Usually, having the battle with Edith over Ian and jobs gave me some sort of satisfaction, even though the result was always the same. But I couldn't risk more punishment today, nor could I behave like an angel. Edith's finely tuned antennas would have picked up abnormal behaviour, and I would have ended up back in my room with the door locked until morning. So I tried to behave a bit better than I usually did while still being a little annoying.

When Ian told Dad about his 'bluey' I teased him, not enough to cause an Edith row, just enough to get a sharp, "Margaret," with a warning look. I moaned about having to do the washing up, but I did it. And when Edith told me I hadn't got one of the pans clean enough I rewashed it, looking sulky. I was so enjoying playing my part I almost forgot to draw the net along its wire and unlatch the window after she'd left the kitchen. Later, I wondered if it was that, or my dad and *Dixon of Dock Green* that interfered with my brain to the point where I forgot so many important aspects of my imminent adventure.

I was about to start on the drying up when he came into the kitchen.

"Are you going into the yard for a smoke?" I asked.

My dad smoked a pipe. Edith wouldn't let him do it in the house. *"Filthy thing,"* she said. *"Why you want to suck that stuff into your lungs I'll never know."* If it was raining he smoked it in his shed.

"No queen, I'm not. It's almost time for Dixon. I'll have one later. Are you going to watch with me?"

Dad never presumed, even though it was something we enjoyed doing together.

In swept Edith to my rescue. She'd come down because Ian wanted a cup of cocoa. He was still upset about his 'bluey' and she thought it might help to calm him down. "No she's not, Percy. Margaret had a spat earlier. She's going to her room."

A wave of relief swept over me, followed by guilt. I kept my eyes on my chore. *Thank you Edith for being consistent.*

"But she's almost finished the washing up now, Edie and—"

"That doesn't excuse her behaviour. I'm not changing my mind, Percy."

He gave me a look that said, 'sorry love. I can't go against your mother'.

I waited until I heard Edith's feet on the stairs and the click of the living room door before unlatching the window. Then I walked upstairs, stomping a bit to show her I was peed off. I loved that expression. Leila used it all the time, 'peed off, peed off'. It was boss. I opened and shut my bedroom door a bit loudly, and then crept down again, and out of the front door. I was banking on the fact that Edith wouldn't look in on me. She rarely did now. I ran to Leila's house.

"You're late, Short Arse" she said as she opened the door.

"I'm lucky to be here at all. Edith kicked off. Have I got time to put me make-up on?"

"If you're quick."

I ran upstairs to the bathroom: powder, lipstick, eye-liner and mascara. Finally, I undid my plait and ran my fingers through my mop.

"Where's Gail?" I yelled.

"She's meeting us at the flea pit."

Suddenly the success of my plan hit me. I did a quick tap dance routine, ran downstairs and we skipped to the bus stop. Even knowing the ogre of a manager would be prowling couldn't spoil our evening and, to ice the cake, we found we had enough money for popcorn.

On the way home we sang all the songs we could remember. I was singing *Hernando's Hideaway* for the second time, as I made my way down our back alley, when I realised my mistake. I'd forgotten the yard gate. I should have gone out of the back door, left the bolt on the gate undone, slipped back in again, locked the back door and then tiptoed out the front. *What a stupid prat!*

I had two options: go round the front and face the music, or climb over the wall which was about seven foot high. I could touch the top of the wall with my fingertips. Maybe I could have jumped up and managed to hold on, but haul myself over? No chance. *Pyjama Game* music fled in the dilemma. I wanted to scream. There were empty bottles lying about. There was a broken milk crate. If it had been whole… It was then I noticed a figure coming out of a gate further down the alley. As he turned to shut it, the street light at the end, caught his face. It was Danny Murphy; he had a cigarette drooping out of his mouth. Danny wasn't someone I associated with, although he lived in our street and his sister and I went to the same school. If Edith disapproved of Leila and her mother, she hadn't got a good word to say about the Murphys.

I felt sorry for Danny's mum. There were loads of kids in their house and Mr Murphy had a temper. Danny was skinny and I reckoned he fancied himself as an Elvis lookalike, for he greased back his black hair and made an Elvis quiff at the front. He was the sort of kid who tried to look hard all the time. But there was no one else around who could help, so…

"Danny," I called, walking towards him.

"Your mum know you're out?"

I decided to be honest. "No. I'm not really snobby, you know. Edith won't let me talk to youse. Can you help me, like?"

"Edith?"

"Me mum. Can you help me?"

"Depends."

"On what?"

"On what it is you want, and what you'll do for me in return."

"Can you give me a leg up so's I can get over the wall? I've sneaked out to go the flicks and I need to sneak back in."

His grin broadened. "A leg up for a feel."

22

"A what?"

"A feel. Your tits and inside your panties."

"Bog off!" *How dare he.* I'd not even kissed a boy, let alone… I couldn't even think the words.

"I can make you," he said. "I can make you go all the way. There's no one around to hear your screams."

"You and whose army, Danny Murphy?" *Maggie, how long is it since you've been in a scrap?*

Girls were stereotyped as hair-pullers and scratchers. I punched and kicked, *used to punch and kick,* and I was quick on my feet. *Well at least you're still that.* I thought I could dodge pretty much anything that Danny threw my way, so I hoped it wasn't an idle threat. There had been nothing scientific about my fighting; I hadn't learnt boxing or anything like that. Letters home? Oh yes, there had always been letters sent home, for the scraps had rarely gone undetected. If I was unscathed, I threw them in the bin.

It was a good thing I'd chosen to wear my pedal-pushers and granddad shirt, my favourite outfit. If I'd put on my swirly skirt, I'd have been hampered by frills.

We glared at each other, then Danny lunged at me. I reckon he thought he'd be able to grab my arm, twist it behind my back and do what he wanted. I aimed a kick at his groin and twisted away as he doubled over in agony. Thanks to Leila, I knew where to hurt a lad. I turned and ran.

Back alleys are night time murky, secret places, even with the street lamp at one end. But I knew our gate because my dad had replaced the old one not so long ago. Even in the gloom it looked different. As I was making my escape I collided with a dustbin someone had left out. I hadn't noticed it before. Rubbing my legs, I realised I could use it to get me up and over our wall. I reckoned I might have enough time before Danny had sufficiently recovered to give chase. It was my only option. I hauled the empty bin to our gate and climbed onto it. If night time alleys were gloomy places, back yards were black holes. Poised on top of the wall, I couldn't remember if there were any obstacles, like pots, to be avoided.

Come on Maggie, use your brain. Our bin was to the left of the gate behind a fencing panel. Edith had made my dad construct it so she didn't have to look at the bin all the time. The other side was my dad's shed. *There's nothing in front of the gate, is there?*

"Think you can get away, cow?" I felt a hand grab my foot so I launched myself forward. I had to, or I'd be dragged into the muck of the alley and raped by a sixteen year-old thug. There was a loud clang as I landed on the metal bin and rolled onto the ground.

"Ow!" I would have a few bruises in the morning, otherwise I was okay. But the noise!

My dad and Edith's bedroom was at the front of the house. Mine was in the middle, then there was the bathroom, and Ian's was at the back. I didn't know whether the clang had been loud enough to force its way through all those walls to my parents' bedroom. Ian slept like one dead. The atom bomb wouldn't have woken him. I stayed where I was for a few minutes. Danny must have given up. He hadn't been foolish enough to follow me into the yard, not after all the noise I'd made. If guardian angels, or fairy godmothers existed, then mine had been with me that evening.

I was as resourceful as Doris Day. I felt my way over to the window and pushed. It resisted. *Oh no, surely... It's stiff, Maggie. They rarely open it... Edith always opens it when she's cooking. Hell!* I pushed harder. I wanted to break the bloody thing. I wanted to cry. Maggie Doris Day was fast turning into a soggy Wet Nellie. What was I going to do? Sleep in the yard? I couldn't even get into the shed. Dad always kept it locked and the key was in the kitchen. It was the only part of our home that was truly his. And what would I do in the morning? *Der!*

I grabbed some earth out of a terracotta plant pot. Just as I was about to launch it at Ian's window, without any hope of waking him, I heard the back door opening. That was it, defeat. I had to resign myself to the tirade and whatever punishment Edith decided to give me.

"Maggie?" It was my dad's voice.

"Dad?" A wave of relief threatened to knock me over. I ran to the door. "I'm sorry. I know I've been deceitful and all that, but it was *The Pyjama Game*, and I'd been saving up for ages."

"Shh! Your mother's fast asleep. I'm surprised that clang didn't wake her up. It was as loud as the whole timpani section of the Liverpool Philharmonic orchestra."

I knew about orchestras because my dad had taken Ian and I to a concert for children where we had been introduced to the instruments. Afterwards they'd played *Carnival of the Animals*.

"Have you hurt yourself?"

"I'm alright. Just a scrape and a few bruises."

"You were lucky. You could have broken something. Pity you didn't try the gate. I left it, and the back door unlocked."

"I didn't know, did I?"

"Come on in. I would make you a mug of cocoa but we don't want to tempt fate, do we? Your clothes are filthy, love."

"I'll shove them under my bed and take them to Leila's on Monday."

Leila had to do her own washing. Her mum wouldn't notice one more pair of pedal-pushers and one more shirt on the line. I'd have to do them by hand but that was better than discovery. Edith was now the proud possessor of a washing machine. It had an electric mangle. She'd warned Ian and I not to go near it, as if it was some snarling, wild animal.

"I know you two," she'd said. *"You'll get your fingers caught in that roller."*

I'd have liked to tell my dad about my escape from Danny, but he wouldn't have been able to do anything about it, because if he had, my escapade would have reached Edith's ears.

"I'm not going to tell your mother what you've been up to," he said. "But I want a promise that you won't try anything like this again."

"I—"

He shook his head. "I mean it, Maggie."

I hung my head. "I promise."

"That's my girl."

I wasn't sure that I could keep the promise, so I crossed my fingers behind my back.

I doubted that Danny would attempt anything during the day and, despite a false promise, I wasn't about to sneak out at night again, for a long time. I was wrong.

In the nineteen fifties, in England, there was a variety of ways children could be educated. I went to New Heys High School, my brother Ian went to Quarry Bank Grammar School. Danny went to the Catholic Secondary School.

Danny didn't attempt to sexually assault me. He took to hanging about outside the school at going home time and shouting out for all to hear, 'tart', 'cock teaser', 'bitch', 'slag'. Then the whispering campaign started. Pupils I didn't know stared at me, nudged each other and giggled.

"It's Neave," said Gail.

"You'll have to deal with her, Maggie," said Leila.

"I haven't had a fight in school since fourth year and I'm not about to have one now. I've got you two to stick up for me. I don't need no agro."

But then Neave started passing notes round the class, one of which was intercepted by Mr Davis, the geography teacher.

'Margaret Turner is a tart she's had sex wiv evry lad in our street you doan have to pay her she begs for it.'

Neave and I were taken to see the Head. She read the note. You could see she was angry from the way her mouth tightened into a thin line.

"I don't believe you wrote this, Neave. You wouldn't be at this school with spelling and handwriting like that. Who did write it?"

Neave stared at the wall behind the Head's desk.

"Passing notes in class is against school rules. Why did you do it?"

"Ask her."

"No. I'm asking you."

Silence. Then she looked down. "I did it for me brother, Danny, 'cause of what she did to him."

"Where does he go to school?"

"The Sec. Mod. Miss."

"I'm giving you a week of detentions, Neave. I shall inform your parents that you will be kept behind in school, every day next week."

"She kicked our Danny in the balls, Miss," said Neave.

"Why did I do that, eh? He was trying to rape me, Miss."

"I don't want to hear any more. Borstal's what your brother deserves. I shall be ringing the Headmaster of the secondary school to tell him what Daniel has been up to. He will probably be expelled. As for you, your first detention task will be to write a letter of apology to Margaret."

Danny was expelled that afternoon, and when his dad found out, Danny ended up in casualty with a broken nose and fractured collar bone. Neave fared better. She got a thick lip.

The next day, after school had finished, I was in the middle of doing my homework when there was a knock at the door. Ian went to open it. Mrs Murphy pushed past him, dragging Danny with her.

"See," she yelled. "See what your daughter's done?"

Edith looked puzzled. No letter had come home with me to say I'd been involved in a fight. I was free from cuts and bruises, as far as Edith knew; she hadn't seen my knees or my shoulder.

"My Danny's got expelled because of her."

"Margaret, can you explain what's going on here?"

Before I could get a word out, and I had no idea what that word was going to be, Ian said, "Danny's been telling lies about our Maggie. It's all up and down our street. Jimmy and me have said it's fibs."

"And what were the lies, pray?" Edith never took her eyes off Mrs Murphy's face.

Ian told her everything he'd heard. Fortunately for me, he didn't know *The Pyjama Game* story that had preceded it. But would Danny have told his mother? Would it all come out now?

Edith could have beaten the Head in any contest regarding thin lined mouths in anger. While she was listening, she pulled her lips into her mouth so far you couldn't see them. She drew herself up to her full five feet four inches and said, "Your…" There was a pause as though she didn't want to say the word 'son'… "Your son got what he deserved."

"What?" screamed Mrs Murphy. She pushed Danny forward. "He deserved this?"

"My daughter didn't deserve to be called a tart who would let boys have sex with her, and we cannot be held to account for the way your husband behaves. I want you to leave now. If you don't, I shall call the police." We were one of the few houses in our road with a phone. They left.

It was Dad's bowls evening. I didn't know if I was glad he wasn't at home, or not. I looked at Edith. Ian looked at the two of us. I couldn't tell what either he or she were thinking.

"Finish your homework, Margaret. I'm going to have a talk with your father when he comes in," was all she said.

When I was about to get ready for bed, she called me into the sitting room. "There are some Saturday jobs going in Woolworths on Allerton Road, Margaret. Your dad and I think you should go for one. If you get it, it will stand you in good stead for when you leave school."

"But I want to go to college. I'm getting good grades. I should get enough O-levels to let me stay on at school."

She ignored what I said. "I shall get a form tomorrow."

I argued. I pleaded. I asked my dad to stick up for me, knowing he didn't have the necessary weapons to defeat Edith once she'd made up her mind.

So, that was that. Any dreams I'd had of becoming a teacher sank in the stew of my mother's decision. I was to work in Woolworths on Saturdays, and go for a full time post in a shop, in July.

Danny ran away from home. Two houses where, in one way or another, children suffered because of a parent. Maybe, in different circumstances Danny would have been a half-decent kid.

Chapter Three
I am better than Pick-n-Mix

Anything for a quiet life...

I was pissed off. A new word from Leila. She'd got bored with 'peed off'. 'Peed off' was for children, so she said. At home, the word stayed in my mind. It didn't spatter out. It meant urine, the same as peed off, but sounded more grown-up, somehow. Then there was fuck, shit, twat, bollocks and arsehole. Leila knew them all.

"Me mum says the men who come in the pub use those words all the time."

We whispered the words to each other, and giggled about them in tea-breaks.

Who was I pissed off with? Edith, who else? I was pissed off with the way she had interfered in my life, stopping me from going to college. I couldn't let it go. Questions I couldn't ask lay stagnating in my mind. Was it because she hated me? Was it because she hadn't been given the chance when she was young? Was it to do with some psychological need to control me, my dad and Ian? Was it? Was it? Was it?

My dad was the breadwinner. At home he had allocated duties and permitted pleasures. He was allowed to smoke his pipe, but only in the yard. He was allowed to play darts for the Edge Lane office team. He was allowed to watch certain programmes on the television and he used to be allowed to take me out for the day on Saturdays. That had been wrested from him because I had to work in Woolworths. He never complained.

In different ways she controlled Ian and me. Maybe she believed that if she didn't rule us all in some way, her world would spin out of control.

If Ian inadvertently disobeyed her, his punishment would be a mild reprimand. If Dad did something wrong, a forgetting crime usually, she put him in Coventry. Sometimes I wondered if he welcomed the frozen silence.

My punishment was Woolworths for I had been offered a permanent job. It was a five year sentence as I was under Edith's rule until I was twenty-one. But I was not going to let her make me into a comfy cardy she could wrap round her body when she was cold, when it suited her. If I were a woollen, I'd be a scratchy one like mohair; seemingly soft when first put on but irritating as the hours passed.

Dad and Leila persuaded me that it wouldn't be so bad; a bit of money to spend after the couple of quid I had to give Edith for my keep. He also said that if I was really serious about training to be a teacher, I could do my A-levels at night school then go to college when I turned twenty-one, when she couldn't stop me. It was a raft to cling to; it helped me to forgive him for his philosophy of 'anything for a quiet life'.

I chose to study English Literature and History A-levels. My favourite, of the two was English Literature. When we wrote essays we had to use quotations. Some of them, I knew, I would remember all my life. One, that seemed particularly apposite – I was learning so many new words, swear words from Leila and erudite words at night school – was from *St Joan*, by George Bernard Shaw.

'Perpetual imprisonment? Am I not then to be set free? Light your fire, do you think I dread it as much as the life of a rat in a hole?'

Before night-school I'd felt like a rat in a hole and I'd dreamed of coming out and biting Edith. She had forced the Maggie with aspirations to become a teacher, to wait five years instead of two to start her training. At sixteen, five years seemed a lifetime.

In infant school we used to play a game called 'keeper of the keys'. The blindfolded keeper placed a bunch of keys under his or her chair. One pupil at a time had to try to steal them. If the keeper pointed directly at you, you were out. If you managed to get back to your chair with the keys, you won, and became the next keeper. I used to enjoy the game. If I got my A-levels when I was eighteen, there would be three more years of Pick-n-Mix and no study to challenge my bored brain. I had to try to steal the keys around results time, or go mad. But a gorgon would be sitting on the chair, not a fellow pupil.

The first time I thought of Edith as a gorgon was when were doing Greek mythology in junior school. Medusa was a gorgon. She had snakes in her hair and, if you looked at her, she could turn you into stone. Another gorgon had a loud roar and sharp fangs. Both descriptions seemed wonderfully apt for Edith. If I argued with her, she would stare at me and my body would petrify. It affected my arms first. They became heavy, then stiff and I knew I wouldn't be able to escape the roar and the fangs.

I didn't know what had turned her into a gorgon. She'd been an attractive woman when she and my dad got married. Sometimes, when I was younger and was sent to my bedroom, I would creep into their room, open the cupboard and take their wedding photo album off the shelf where it lay among old electricity bills and other items connected to running a house. I was always surprised by what I saw. She had red hair, like mine, which tangled around her face. I only ever remember her with it scragged back. Perhaps it was a workplace, like Woolworths, that had soured Edith. Perhaps she'd had to deal with a manager like Arnold Taylor and that had convinced her that she had to be the one in control... of everyone in her life. Of course, I never dared ask her.

Arnold Taylor was a groper, a slime-ball. We had to find ways of making sure we were never alone with him. He forced kisses on the girls under his supervision, and was a bottom and nipple pincher, possibly worse if he decided he had been given any encouragement.

One day, after I'd been to the toilet, he sneaked up behind me and, before I knew it, caught me, pinioned me against the wall, stuck his foul smelling mouth on mine and started massaging my breasts.

"Open your mouth," he hissed. "Let me tongue-kiss you. You'll like it."

There was the sound of a door shutting and footsteps, at first far away and then getting nearer.

He released me and stepped back. "Don't you say anything to anyone, Margaret. I'll get you the sack if you do. It's not a tea-break and you're not allowed to go to the wash-room unless you're on a tea break."

Shock time for Mr Molester. "You are if you've got your period. I've read me rights, Mr Taylor. And if you ever try this on again, I'll tell me boyfriend. In fact I might tell him anyway. He's a bouncer at The Cavern." *Did they have bouncers at The Cavern?*

It worked. He backed away mouthing, "No need for that, Margaret. I was just being friendly, like." He ignored me after that.

When I told Leila what had happened, she clapped me on the back. "Bloody brill, Short-Arse. That's two of us who've sorted the turd. Me with action, you with words."

"What did you do?"

"Brought me shoe all the way down his shin and stamped on his foot with me stiletto. Didn't you notice him limping a couple of weeks back? I'll teach yer, it's dead useful if a lad tries it on and you don't want him to."

"Cool. Mr Molester ought to be reported though. I reckon we shouldn't be so scared of losing our jobs. He didn't sack you, did he? Let's call a lunch hour meeting of the girls. The older women ought to be able to look after themselves."

"And say what?"

"We could talk about different ways of dealing with him. We could all have a lesson on stiletto stamping."

And we did. Turd Molester's reign came to an end.

Trevor, my real boyfriend, was one of the Woolworth's Saturday staff. On the other six days he was attempting to find a toehold in the world of contemporary music. Nobody knew I had a boyfriend. In work we pretended we didn't like each other. This started with a 'Leila bet' on our first date at the ice skating rink.

Mac and Trevor worked in stores together. They didn't have a lot in common, except for a dry sense of humour and cricket. They both played for a local team. Trevor told Mac he fancied me. Mac told Leila; they'd been going steady for three weeks, and she told me. I sent the message back down the line that the fancying was mutual.

"Good thing those two are in the storeroom and we're on the shop floor," said Leila. "We'd have complaints from customers, else."

"Why?" I asked.

"Lustful looks and sly kisses."

"You and Mac might," I said. "We wouldn't."

"I bet you a quid, you can't pretend to dislike each other in work."

"You're on," I said.

"You won't be able to keep it up. Someone will see a look or a brush—"

"A brush?"

"You know, brushing past each other deliberately. Touching hands when you think no one will notice."

Little did she know she was giving me clues what not to do. Trevor and I got so good at it that there were times, out of work, when we had to check that we did still fancy each other. We won, and continued to play. Strangely, it added spice to our relationship.

My dad liked Trevor. Trevor liked my dad. Edith didn't like Trevor. Trevor didn't like Edith. I suspected that she had determined she wouldn't like him even before she met him. Trevor wanted to like her. Their first meeting sealed that he wouldn't.

Trevor and my dad shook hands. They smiled at each other. Trevor and Edith eyed each other up. Trevor had a bunch of carnations for her. He held them out. She made no move to take them so he laid them on the table. My dad went to find a vase.

"Not the cut glass one. Get the old green thing," Edith called.

She had declared war and I hated her for her rudeness. Later, Trevor told me he'd got her measure and I wasn't to be upset. "I can give as good as she can," he said.

He asked me to marry him on the day I got my A-level results. I was a wee bit disappointed that I didn't get straight As. I got an A in English Literature, B in History and C in General Studies. I wasn't too bothered about the General Studies. I hadn't worked for it in the same way I had my other two subjects. Politeness dictated that he asked my dad for my hand. He was delighted. Edith sniffed and said that we couldn't get married until I came of age.

"Are you going to force us to live in sin, Mother?" I said, love making me bold.

"You wouldn't."

"Yes, I would. We've found a flat."

"Say something, Percy."

"I have, Edie. I've given my permission."

Perhaps having another man, an ally, present made my dad bold? It didn't protect him from the gorgon stare. I was protected as Trevor and I were holding hands.

The next difficult moment occurred when I told her we were going to get married in a registry office.

"You won't be properly married if you're not married in church," she said.

"There's no point, Mother. Trevor's an atheist and I'm an agnostic."

"And what do those two words mean when they're at home?"

"Trevor doesn't believe in God and I don't know if I do, or not."

"I've brought you up to go to church every Sunday."

"That doesn't mean anything, Mother." Only that, as a child, I was bored by the sermons, and as an adult, found some of the people in the congregation, unchristian in their attitude and behaviour.

"Well I shan't come to the wedding," she said.

I was relieved. How many girls could say that?

Of our two families, Dad came; Katy, Trevor's mum came, his sister Ruth came, and his Aunty Molly.

Molly was older than Katy. She wasn't what people described as the brightest button in the box. She was a spinster, having lived at home until hers and Katy's parents died. By then it was apparent that she had a memory problem and she moved into sheltered accommodation. Six months before the wedding, there was a fire in the block of flats where she lived: another resident had left an iron on when she went out. So, Molly went to stay with Katy while the repair work was being done. They discovered they liked living together. A happy outcome, you could say.

Trevor didn't have a dad who would come or not, according to his principles. His dad had gone to work one day, as usual, but failed to return in the evening. Katy received a letter the following day, just before she was going to inform the police that her husband was missing, to say that he had been offered a job abroad, and it was better for him not to be saddled with a wife and two children.

Molly wanted to be a bridesmaid, and was dreadfully upset when I told her there weren't going to be any. "My friends Leila and Gail are going to be witnesses, Molly. You and Katy are the chief guests. Would you like me to come with you to look for an outfit?"

"Katy's going to make my dress," said Molly. "I'm going to have a pink, shiny dress. That's what bridesmaids wear."

I had forgotten Katy was a dressmaker. "That will be lovely, Molly."

Katy winked at me. "I was hoping you might want me to make your wedding dress," she said.

"Would you? That would be great."

"Tell you what, let's the three of us go into town to George Henry Lees to get the material. We can have a bite to eat in their restaurant afterwards, my treat."

The excursion was a Molly fun day. If I'd had any thoughts about what colour dress I would wear, or what style it should be, I forgot them. Molly dictated and I found that I was easily persuaded.

"Not white, Maggie," she kept saying. "You don't want to be like all the other… all the other… girls who…" She turned to Katy. "What will Maggie be?"

"A bride."

Molly smiled. "That's it. The word just wouldn't come into my head."

And so it was that I wore a creamy gold, knee length, full skirted dress with a lace, copper coloured, bolero. As for Molly? Perhaps she was one of the first mini-skirted women in Liverpool?

And the dress was pink and very shiny.

The flat Trevor and I had found, was a spit from Sefton Park. Every fine working day, I walked across the park and down Queen's Drive to Woolworths on Allerton Road. If it was inclement, I got the bus.

The flat was small, but not too small to accommodate a piano; Trevor needed his piano. The more he improvised and scribbled down notes on manuscript paper, the more frustrated with my 'same every day' job I became. He was in the process of fulfilling his dream to become a recognised composer of contemporary, minimalist music, whereas I was stagnating. In an age where men were still the main breadwinners, I was one of the exceptions. Love, not Edith, had snared me. The fact that I had walked freely into the trap didn't stop me moaning.

"I'm better than 'Pick-n-Mix'," I groaned, more or less every day.

One day Trevor flung down his pencil. "For god's sake, Maggie, stop moaning and do something about it."

"Do what?"

"Go to teacher training college. You've got your A-levels. What's stopping you?"

"How can I? We've got the rent to pay, the rates, the lecky, and then there's food…"

"We'll manage. You'll be eligible for a grant, and we could both work Saturdays. I might even get some commissions. You are better than 'Pick-n-Mix'."

"It's a three year course, you know. That's a frigging long time to manage on peanuts. And, if I resign my job, will they let me work on a Saturday?"

"Look, I can't say yes, for certain. But you're a good worker and you rarely need a day off, do you?"

"What about perv? No hang on, he's going isn't he? He's being transferred to Bootle. It'll be up to a new manager. And you really think we could manage?"

Trevor shrugged. "We'll see."

The following Sunday I told Dad and Edith that I'd applied to go to teacher training college. Ian was out. His former arch marbles' enemy, Jimmy, had invited him for tea. Afterwards they were going to The Cavern. I knew. Edith did not. Trevor had gone to see Katy.

"I can't believe what I'm hearing," Edith said. "Such nonsense. College indeed. I thought—"

"I think it's a good idea," said my dad. "Maggie's got brains. She ought to use them." He put his hand, gently, on her arm. She shook it off.

"She did use them, with your help, at Night School. And now look what you've done. Put grand ideas into her head. At Woolworths she gets good money for using them, which is more than she'll get in college.

"How are you going to survive, that's what I want to know? I'm not having your dad helping you again. And don't look at me like that. I know he gave you the deposit for that flat. You would go and get married. We told you to wait, but—"

"I didn't give her any money," said Dad. "You should know I wouldn't do anything like that without consulting you, Edie. It's not my way. I told her to follow her heart, and I think she should do that now."

"Well someone must have coughed up."

"It wasn't me."

"It was Katy, Mother."

Edith opened her mouth and shut it again. I imagined all the cutting remarks she might have said.

"What does Trevor say?" asked my dad.

"Why do we want to know what Trevor says? Until he gets himself off his backside and starts earning some money, what he says is irrelevant."

Before I could explode, my dad said, "Not to me, it isn't, Edie. What did he say, Maggie?"

Edith gave him her basilisk stare. I imagined that he would be in for a tirade, followed by Coventry after I left. My treacherous mind couldn't help thinking, *why now, Dad? Why didn't you have the courage to stick up for me when I was sixteen?* Then love for him swooped in. If I had stayed on at school I wouldn't have met Trevor. Maybe Leila and I would have drifted apart? I decided I would ask him to come home with me for a couple of hours. Give her time to calm down.

"He wants me to do what's best for me. I ought to be able to get a grant, and do a Saturday job."

"You see," said Edith triumphantly, "he's not going to contribute, is he? He'll just keep asking his doting mother for subs."

"I think you've forgotten something, Mother. Trevor does contribute; he works in Woolies on a Saturday; that's how we met, and—" I had been going to add, that one of his pieces had been chosen for a festival of contemporary music in New Brighton, but it was chosen, not commissioned; no fee.

She interrupted: "More's the pity. So, you'll be sponging off the state like all the other layabouts, then."

"Students aren't layabouts. They work very hard. Anyone who goes to college is eligible for a grant. Trevor works at composing. That's his job. That's who he is. The Trevor I know would die if he did anything else."

"Don't be such a drama queen, Margaret. Of course he wouldn't die. We're ordinary working class folk, and the sooner you and Trevor get that into your pipe-dream heads, the better."

Pipe-dream heads! What a fantastic image. Edith had surprised me. She could write poetry if she... perhaps she had, when she was younger?

"It wouldn't be so bad if he composed music people wanted to listen to, instead of all that plink-plonk scratchy stuff."

My stomach lurched. Not only had I admired her turn of phrase, we'd agreed on something. However hard I tried, I couldn't like Trevor's music, but I'd have cut out my tongue rather than say so. I changed the subject before I could tell her something that would return to haunt me.

"Dad, would you come home with me? I'd appreciate your help with preparation for my interview."

"Don't be late for tea," was all Edith said.

If he saw through my ruse, he didn't say. Trevor was there when we got in. Dad and he spent a couple of hours together dissecting England's test series' results. My interview wasn't mentioned.

A month later, as I was putting carnations into a bucket by the till, I felt a strong urge to give in my notice, but I couldn't; I hadn't received a letter of acceptance, or rejection. I was still anxious that I might have been rejected because of the way I'd spoken to the principal at my interview.

Chapter Four
The Interview

Engage brain before opening mouth.
And don't count your chickens before they are hatched.

An interview. I had been invited to an interview. I didn't know whether I was excited or nervous. I was certainly in a tizzy.

"Wear your… your… bride dress, Maggie," advised Molly. "It will bring you luck."

I felt like laughing but that would have been unkind. I said I'd think about it. What I did wear was a simple lime green linen shift, that I'd bought from Paddy's market.

At the college reception I was advised to go to the visitors' lounge. There, eyeing each other up, silent through nerves, were sixteen hopefuls waiting in a room I never revisited. The chairs were arranged in a square around the walls. I eyed up the other hopefuls and sat down next to a mermaid. That is what I saw when I looked at Angela; of course I didn't know her name then. Two minutes later a mouse walked in. I thought that because her dress was mouse brown with cream embroidery on it. Her shoes were brown, and her fawn hair was caught up in a ponytail. She was like Beatrix Potter's Mrs Tittlemouse. She wasn't beautiful, like the mermaid, but there was something arresting about her. She had poise. She sat in the spare chair next to me.

"My name's Margaret," I said. "But I prefer to be called Maggie."

The mouse laughed. "My name's Deborah, and I prefer to be called Debbie."

Debbie had a 'woolyback' accent. I guessed she was from St Helens or Wigan. "I love your dress," I said.

"It's not mine. It's my sister Allie's. She lent it to me for good luck. She got it from Paddy's market."

"Bloody-hell! What a coincidence. That's where I got mine. I get all my clothes from Paddy's market or jumble sales."

"So does Allie. Normally, I wear jeans, but I couldn't today, could I?"

The mermaid on the other side of me said, "So do I. I'm Angela, by the way, and I don't like being called Angie. Ange is okay if you must shorten it." She had a posh voice. "Excuse me a mo." She got up and counted heads. "I think I've introduced myself to everyone. I'll be around all day if you need any help."

I guessed she was a student in her second or third year. When she sat down, she drew her chair closer to mine.

It was at this point the comedy started. The visitors' room door opened and a story book granny appeared. She had fluffy white hair, spectacles and a round, comfy body. The only thing she didn't have was a bag of knitting. The voice was so far removed from the image, I had to blink to make sure it was she who had spoken. I wanted to laugh. *Think Edith,* I admonished myself.

"Doctor Rosthwaite," she barked, like any practised sergeant major on a parade ground. "Got to give you the once over. Make sure you're up to the course and, if you pass it, teaching. When you come into the medical room, strip off, bra and pants."

"Where's the medical room?" another prospective student asked.

"Next to this one. First door on the left. Come in alphabetical order. The list's on the notice board." She pointed to the wall by the door. "Amanda Abbott, you're first, then Carol Barker." She left.

"What can be so strenuous about learning to teach English and History? Are we expected to re-enact historical battles?" I asked.

"Wednesday afternoons are strenuous; you have to do a physical activity. And if you've chosen any of the sciences or humanities, so are the field trips," said Angela.

"So I was right," I said.

"Right about what?"

"That you must be in your second or third year, so know the ropes."

"Yes and no. I should be in my second year, come October, but I have to repeat my first one. Sorry, I guess I didn't make that clear when I spoke to everyone."

I wondered why she had to repeat her first year, but didn't like to ask. "That's okay. Did the sergeant major, granny mean we're to take off all our clothes, in here, like?"

Angela and Debbie laughed. "No. When you go in, you strip down to your bra and pants. Is your name Margaret Harvey, and yours Deborah Willis by any chance?"

"Yes," we both said and I added, "Why?"

"Because I'm your mother."

"I don't think you are." I said. "My mother's a gorgon, and she looks nothing like you." *Once upon a time she looked like me.* The sadness I felt whenever her photo image came to mind, floated round my head.

"Your college one. That's the name Dawn Rose dreamt up for second and third year mentors."

"I thought you said you were going to be repeating your first year?"

"I did. But for some reason they decided I should still be a mother."

"Well I warn you, I don't like being bossed. Who's Dawn Rose?"

"The deputy principal. I'm not in the bossing game, just the helping game."

"Why do we have to take off our clothes? What is she checking us for?" said Debbie.

"Lice and nits."

"What?" Debbie and I spoke together.

Angela laughed. "None of the students are really sure why. We think it's some sort of duty of care thing like having college mothers."

"What sports are on offer?" I said, thinking that I hadn't bargained for having to play something.

"Hockey, lacrosse, netball, soccer… almost any sport you can think of. Oh, and gymnastics and contemporary dance. I don't do a sport. I do contemporary dance."

I wonder what contemporary dance is? It has to be dance of today. But what is it? Pity it isn't tap. Still, any form of dance will be fun. If you get in, Margaret. Don't count your chickens. "I think I'll do dance." *Bloody hell! Did you listen to yourself just now? No, because you're still at it.*

"Me too," said Debbie. "I used to be quite good at gymnastics when I was at junior school. I'm not sure I want to do that again. Something new would be exciting."

"Is there a drama club?"

"Yes. Monday evenings."

Mondays, great. On Mondays Trevor met my dad for a drink. A new 'allowed' outing for my dad. Edith had started going to see Nan and Granddad on Monday evenings.

"Are you mum to all the students in this room, if they get in, like?"

She grimaced. "No, just you two. There are some duties that are passed round, like being here today in case anyone needs anything, or gets lost. All second years have a quota of first years to look after. It's a nice idea; saves students feeling lost in their first term. Oh, the reason I won't be in my second year come October is because I was ill last term, with glandular fever."

"I don't wear a bra. My breasts aren't big enough to bother with one," said Debbie. "Will it matter?"

"I wish I didn't have to wear a bra." Angela and I spoke together.

"I'm sure it won't matter," said Angela. "Why should it?"

Debbie shrugged. "I don't know. I just wondered. I really want to get in. I've set my heart on it. It's because of my sister, you see, she's deaf. My parents took her out of school because the education she was offered was so undemanding. Allie's very bright and she's good at sport. When I've finished training, I want to teach in a special school."

"This bit isn't part of the interview. Dr Rosthwaite's a physiologist Macker uses to check backs and feet."

"Macker?" said Debbie.

"Miss Mackenzie, the principal. Dr Rosthwaite is 'Rozzers'."

The granny, sergeant major had a Ph.D., in physiology and, by the time she finished with me, I felt as though I'd done a workshop in contortion techniques. She called me 'my child' and told me she was going to give me some exercises to strengthen my back.

"You're quite tight here," she poked my lumbar region. "You should do these exercises every morning. If you ever want to have a baby, they will help strengthen your muscles for the birth."

I wanted to say, *'do you exercise that comfy body of yours every morning?'* or, *'I get quite enough exercise having sex every day.'* And that made me want to giggle. Luckily I was getting dressed, so she didn't see the grin on my face.

I didn't see Angela or Debbie again until lunch. After the session with Rozzers, I had an interview with Macker. She was a bit like a digestive biscuit, hard to swallow unless you dunked it in a cup of tea. I don't like digestive biscuits and I didn't warm to her. She gave nothing of herself and seemed little interested in anything I might have had to say. She sat, expressionless, behind a mahogany desk, in a room as bland as she was. The only time emotion stirred her, was when I told her that I couldn't accept living in halls for the first year.

"But it's a rule, Mrs Harvey," she said with a look of astonishment on her face. A prospective student was questioning rules? "All first years live on campus. We are in loco parentis."

Oh god, Maggie. This is the second time this morning that you've had to swallow laughter. Stop imagining Trevor's face when you tell him you'll be absent for ten weeks at a time.

"Well you can't be 'in loco parentis' of me, Miss Mackenzie. I'm afraid my husband might see my living in college as grounds for divorce." That sounded polite enough, with a touch of humour. "As you must have noticed, I'm *Mrs*. Harvey, not Miss."

"We can't make an exception for one student. You can apply for two exiats per term."

Exiats? Had I walked into an Enid Blyton novel? I heard Trevor shouting, *'Fight her Maggie. Get George on her. Get Timmy the dog.'* The words rebounded off the beige wall behind her head.

"I'm not prepared to 'live in', Miss Mackenzie." *Trevor and I have sex every day.* "If that's an obstacle to my being accepted, I shall have to reconsider the offers I've had from the other colleges." I crossed my fingers for the blatant lie.

"Um." She frowned. "I think that will be all, Mrs Harvey. Good morning."

I swept out; if you can sweep in a shift.

Angela and Debbie were already in the refectory. Angela performed an elaborate mime to tell me to join them after I'd got my food. I mimed back, yes, chose a ham and cheese salad and went over to their table

"Macker, or whatever her name is, is out the ark, isn't she?" I said. "She knew I was married, she had me frigging form on her desk and she called me 'Mrs Harvey'. Then she said that all first years had to live in halls. I was gob-smacked. *'Those are the rules Mrs. Harvey. We can't make an exception for you.'* I told her my divorce would be on her conscience. Exiat indeed. I bet they have exiats at Liverpool College. If I'm not accepted, I shall have to try the other colleges. I don't want to now I've met you two."

"So that's two of us on the reject list then," said Debbie. "Me with no bra, and you refusing to obey Macker's rule. You were right about Dr Rossthwaite being nice. She gave me a kindly lecture on the advisability of supporting breasts, and told me I was too thin.

"I told her I'd always been skinny, but I was as strong as a horse and had an enormous appetite. I didn't tell her I was a veggie though."

"Don't worry," said our mother. "You'll both get in. Everyone here today will get in. The government are desperate for more teachers."

"Thanks. That makes me feel great. Why did Macker keep saying 'we'? Is it another example of snobbery, you know, the 'royal we'?"

"No. She and Dawn Rose, the Deputy Principal are joined at the hip."

"I saw her name on the board outside Macker's room. Dawn Rose… Is she the Dawn Rose of 'mother' fame?"

"There couldn't be two Dawn Roses in one institution, could there? One's quite enough."

"I kept seeing Macker as a digestive biscuit. What's Dawn Rose like?"

"If we're talking biscuits, a ratafia. She's posh."

"I don't like digestives and I've never had a ratafia. Are you sure you haven't made it up?"

"It's an almond biscuit. You have it with dry sherry."

"Bloody hell, ratafia biscuits and dry sherry. You're posh school posh, aren't you?" I said.

Angela grinned. "And you're a scally."

"And I'm a woolly-back," said Debbie.

"Musketeer-esses," I said.

On the bus home, I wondered if they hoped we'd be together in October. I certainly did.

July the thirtieth, the day that would be forever etched in my mind. The letter was waiting for me on the work surface just in front of the kettle so I wouldn't miss it when I got in from work. I picked it up, turned it over and stared at it.

"Are you trying to divine what it says?" said Trevor. He was walking round our living room tapping the furniture with a conductor's baton. I didn't ask why. He often did odd things like that. I suspected it would be that he was listening to different sounds he might weave into a composition.

"I daren't open it. I keep seeing Edith's smug face when she finds out I've been rejected."

"Do you want me to open it?"

"Yes please." My voice was like a droopy bottom lip.

"Your mother's right about one thing, you are a drama queen. Give it here then."

"I'll put the kettle on while you read the bad news."

I heard the envelope being ripped open. "Better make it hot and sweet."

"I knew it," I wailed. "They've turned me down 'cause I wouldn't live in, haven't they?"

"No, they've—"

"You fuck-face, give it here."

"Language, Harvey!" Trevor, holding it aloft, ducked away from me. Trevor was six foot one, I was five foot two. "I'll give it to you if you give me a kiss."

"Shan't." I jumped up to try to snatch it.

He grabbed my arms, pinioned them behind my back and kissed me. "Clever girl," he breathed into my mouth.

I snatched the letter, scanned it and danced round the flat. "Now I can give in my notice," I shouted.

"Not till the first of September, sweetheart. It wouldn't be a good idea. We're going to have to try and save."

"Poo. Never mind, I can tell all me friends and Dad and—"

"Careful, idiot. You'll knock something over."

"Then you, my cricketing husband, can catch it before it crashes to the floor. Or, you could use the sound of the crash in your latest—"

"Don't you dare say 'plink-plonk'. I'll catch you." He chased me into the bedroom.

"I didn't know you knew—"

"I know everything. I'm inside your mind, Harvey."

He pushed me onto the bed, covered my face and neck with kisses, eased my skirt up to my waist, pulled down my knickers, loosened his trousers, pulled them and his y-fronts down, and eased himself inside me. I was already wet.

"This is what married couples do, Macker," I yelled as we moved to the rhythm of the bed springs. "They fuck." I grabbed Trevor's arm. "Before you spurt, you'd better put a johnny on. I haven't got my cap in and we don't want to make babies, do we?"

"Shit no." He pulled out. I slid down his body, took his penis in my mouth and sucked it right down my throat.

"No more," Trevor moaned. He grabbed a Durex from his bedside cabinet drawer and rolled it on.

Later, as we lay entwined, I said, "I've been thinking of going to family planning to talk about the pill. I hate having to put in me Dutch cap, just in case. It takes any spontaneity away, and johnnies aren't much fun for you, are they?"

"I certainly prefer sex when you've got your cap in, but I can see why it's a bore for you. What about the side effects of the pill?"

"That's what I want to have a chat about before I make up me mind. Do you want to come with me?"

"I…"

I could see his unspoken words. *'That would mean taking time off from working on my latest composition.'*

"You don't have to. I'm a big girl, I can go on me own."

"No, you're not a big girl, you're a red, furry animal." He stroked my pubic hair. "Except your pubes aren't furry. They're coarse and springy."

"Is that surprising? My head hair's coarse and springy. Edith tried to tame the spring, but she couldn't. Food! I'm so hungry I could eat your penis. Penis for our evening meal. Do you want your penis deep fried in batter, grilled or roasted? How about curried penis?"

"Stop it, Maggie. I shall have a hernia laughing."

"Um, interesting, that. A laughing hernia instead of a laughing hyena. What are we eating?"

Trevor was a very good cook. He did the evening meal during the week. We usually had fish and chips or a Chinese take-away on a Friday, and we went to the Brook House with Leila and Mac on a Saturday, except when Mac or Trevor had away matches. I cooked on Sundays if we didn't go to my parents' or Katy's.

"We've got spag bol."

"Oh no! Not worms again."

"You monster. You love my spag bol."

I did. And I loved my prospective future. "I can't wait to tell Leila." *Will she be thrilled for me? Yes, of course she will, but…* "Oh!"

"What now?"

"I can't go to college."

"Are you mad?"

I sank back onto the bed. "I can't go because I'm a Woolies' snob. I've been saying and saying, 'I'm better than Pick-n-Mix'. That's saying

I'm better than Leila. How could I even think that?" I wailed as my college dream sank into the mattress.

Trevor sat up. "Do you want me to give you a good shaking? What a load of rubbish. Do you think, when you're with Leila, that you're better than her?" I shook my head. "Will you stay friends, do you think?" I nodded. I couldn't imagine a world without Leila's friendship.

"So, you red headed drama queen idiot, all jobs are important, and we should value them for what they are. At the moment, you and Leila are in the service industry. She's going to continue to stay in it, so are you on a Saturday, if the new manager lets you. Society needs all its workers."

I grimaced. "I'm not sure anyone needs Edith!"

"I do."

It was my turn to say, "What?"

"You wouldn't be here if it weren't for your spirited mother."

"'Spirited' isn't a word I'd use for her. Bloody minded more like. You'll have to help me remember to take it, if we decide it's a good idea."

Trevor looked puzzled. "You've lost me, take what?"

"The pill, dozy."

"Me, dozy? It was you who changed the subject. I suggest you leave the packet by the toothpaste with your mascara. Then you'll always remember!"

"Why does it irritate you that I leave my mascara there?"

"I'm convinced that if I come home tipsy, one day, I shall clean my teeth with it. I reckon you could go out with no knickers on, as long as your eyes were mascaraed and your ears ringed."

"I reckon I could too. You know I don't have eyelashes unless I mascara them. And I do try to remember to put it away. I always seem to be in such a rush"

"You know my answer to that."

"We're so different, aren't we? I sometimes wonder how we hit it off. You're a thoughtful slowcoach. I'm a spontaneous rush."

"I am not a slowcoach, bitch. Seriously, that's why we hit it off. We compliment each other. You make me more spontaneous. I calm you down."

"Well at least neither of us are digestives. I wonder if digestive biscuits have sex?"

"Now you've lost me again."

"Miss Mackenzie. I told you she was as dry as a digestive. Do keep up, Watson. I think she'd be terrified of willies."

"She could be a lesbian."

"Maybe? No, I think she's an abstainer. So she wouldn't know what she was asking of a warm blooded male and female by keeping them apart for weeks on end, would she?"

"I could always offer—"

"If you did, I'd get Edith onto you."

"Ah! A fate worse than—"

"Having sex with a digestive biscuit, I should think. Do we have enough money to go out and celebrate after spag bol?"

"We could always invite your dad to join us. Then he'd pay."

"Oooh that's a Moriarty suggestion, Watson."

"Yes. Good though, eh?"

"No. How would he explain the phone call to the gorgon?"

"Ah! He might come anyway."

"If he doesn't have a darts' match, he might. However, just in case he doesn't, do we have any money?"

"Enough for one drink each, as long as we both have a shandy... not very exciting. You know what, Maggie, we shan't be able to have a take-away every Friday from October on, and I shan't be able to go to the pub with your dad on a Monday either."

"Do you mind?"

"I'll be sad not to see your dad every week. But he's got his friends from the club to talk to. And I was getting bored with Friday's fish and chips or Chinese, if I'm honest."

"I think he'd be sad not to see you. I reckon we'll need to have a chat with him.

"I'm not sponging off your dad."

I sighed. "Okay. But what about Saturdays? We meet Leila and Mac at Brook House on Saturdays."

"There have to be changes, Maggie: cause, effect. The cause is worth it. Once you're qualified, you'll be able to keep me in the manner I've become used to!"

"I don't know what you think teachers earn."

"More than Woolies' employees. Re Mac and Leila, we could still meet, but in each other's houses; maybe have a meal together. Eating and drinking at home's cheaper than eating in a restaurant. I'm quite happy to cook. But we'll probably have to cut our get-togethers down to twice a month, once at ours, once at theirs."

"If I know Leila, she'll say come to theirs all the time. I bet I'll have loads of homework. God, Trevor, do you think I'm up to it?"

"Course you are. You'll be writing an essay on Shakespearian sonnets, while I compose—"

"Plink-plonk." I couldn't resist it.

He threw a cushion at me and... deja-vu!

We ate late. We did ring my dad, and he did join us at the pub. He insisted on buying a couple of rounds to christen my fresh start. Trevor couldn't resist winking at me.

Chapter Five
Magic Mushrooms

Life is either a daring adventure or nothing.

In nineteen fifty-eight there was a huge expansion of teacher training places. The government wanted to reduce class sizes, both in the primary and secondary sector. Colleges began to offer three year undergraduate training courses. By nineteen sixty-one, when I started college, some of the teething problems had been sorted out: some, but not all, especially where colleges were for women students only. On the eve of my first day at college, there was a fire alarm practice. Some wasteful time was spent searching for a Margaret Harvey. Angela and Debbie chose to join in the hunt. It was when Dawn Rose talked about having to phone the police that Angela explained who I was and where I would be.

Apparently, Dawn Rose said, "Why didn't you tell us before?"

To which Angela replied, "To make a point, Miss Rose. It's daft to expect married women to live in college. Rules can be changed. It's the nineteen sixties, not the nineteen hundreds."

Then Dawn Rose said, "Um. It isn't that easy to change rules, you know. We would have to table it at the next staff meeting. Then it would have to go before the board of governors. But, I do see your point. I'll talk to Miss Mackenzie."

In the first and second year at our college, everyone studied three subjects. For me, it was English, History and Education. All students had to attend lectures and seminars on Education.

English was divided into language and literature. History, as in A-level, looked at different periods, themes and events. In year three, you chose which was to be your major and which your minor. Even though I enjoyed History, I knew English would be my major. Education still took up a third of our time, and in the Easter term there was a long spell in a school on teaching practice.

The weeks of the first term passed in what seemed like a blink. I enjoyed, almost without reservation, everything about the course. The slight reservation? English language, although I understood why we studied it. My brain seemed to be exploding with knowledge.

When we read *Look Back In Anger*, I was a little taken aback by Jimmy and Alison's animal pretence game. It was as though John Osborne had spied on Trevor and I. Jimmy Porter, the main male protagonist was a complicated shit. I couldn't think of any other words as apt as those to describe him and I couldn't understand why Alison was such a doormat. Eunice, one of the English lecturers, organised a screening of the film in one of the lecture theatres to help us understand the complexity of the relationships. Richard Burton played Jimmy and Mary Ure, Alison. It did help. At last I understood why Alison had fallen for him; that brooding anger, tempered by good looks and charisma were very attractive. Why she allowed him to treat her as he did was still a puzzle. Why didn't she stand up to him? It was a question I kept asking myself.

"You don't think Trevor would ever behave like that?" said Debbie when I told her and Angela about Jimmy and Alison.

"I can't imagine a situation where he would. And if he did, I can't imagine me letting him get away with it."

"I can't either. You terrify me, Maggie," said Angela.

"You what?" I said, and put on my hard scouse face. "You want a fist in your gob?"

Joke words. Pretend anger. Would I ever find myself in a situation where my confidence was undermined? After all, I didn't have to look further than my childhood home for an example of unfair control and someone I loved and respected who couldn't deal with it. My dad had allowed Edith to rule us, and him. I did blame him, for a while, especially when he didn't support me in wanting to stay on at school. But, I wouldn't have met Trevor, Debbie or Angela, if I had. My life was richer because of them.

Round and round the rugged rocks...

My two worlds did and didn't mix. I tended to keep college life, college friends separate from my childhood friends. Leila, Mac, Trevor and I still got together on a Saturday evening, but once a fortnight, either at their flat or at ours. As it turned out, none of us could afford to go out. Leila and Mac were saving to get married. We were struggling to make ends meet. Gail, apart from birthday and Christmas cards had faded from our lives. She had married and moved to Newcastle-on-Tyne.

The men talked sport; Leila and I reminisced or looked to the future. One Saturday, while we were doing the washing up, she told me a secret; one she made me promise to keep. She was pregnant, a one night stand after Gail's hen party.

"But I was with you on that night out," I said. "I don't remember you going off with anyone."

"We were so pissed, Maggie. What am I going to do? I'll have to have an abortion. You'll come with me, won't you? And you won't—"

"Of course I won't. But you can't have an abortion, Leila. It's illegal and it's not safe. You know it's not safe."

She burst into tears. "What am I going to do?"

"You and Mac? I imagine you have regular sex?" She nodded, tears still streaming. "Then you tell him you're pregnant and you keep quiet."

"But what if the baby looks nothing like me or Mac?"

"These things do happen in families. You say, 'doesn't he or she look just like Aunty or Uncle so and so?' You play it cool, Leila. Do you remember what your one night stand looked like? I bet you don't even remember if the sex was good or not."

"I remember being freezing cold. Okay, I'll do it. You're still me friend, aren't yer?"

"Course I am, you big Nellie. I love the bones of you."

I did. And I knew I would support her through whatever happened. It wouldn't be an easy pregnancy, mentally, for I imagined that the anxiety about what the baby would look like would continue to haunt Leila. At least Mac had a steady job in a car factory; the same one where my uncle Charlie had worked.

Leila's dilemma made me think about what I would do if Trevor and I had a pregnancy accident. I knew that I didn't want children yet. I wasn't sure that Trevor would ever want them. The only discussion we'd had was in relation to the enjoyment of sex, and how the pill might be our way forward. Jokingly, Trevor had suggested that I kept the packet of pills on the shelf above the basin in the bathroom, alongside my mascara. Of course I didn't. It was in the drawer of my bedside cabinet. Because of Leila's situation I thought that maybe I ought to take up his suggestion, joke or not. If he asked why, I could tell him... tell him what? I didn't lie to my husband. No, I'd just have to carry on with what I did now and be especially vigilant. My children were the subjects on my course and I enjoyed nurturing them. They had been babies when I took my A-levels. Education was a baby now. English and History were toddlers.

Until I started my course I had no idea that education, as a subject, existed; I thought teachers taught and children learnt. I had embarked on a journey into a new world where I was expected to study the history of education, educational philosophy, child development and educational psychology. I became familiar with educationalists like Jerome S Bruner, Piaget and Chomsky.

The dance and drama clubs were more ventures into unknown territories. I'd been a film fanatic all my life, particularly musicals, but I'd never been to see a play. The drama club not only put on plays, it also arranged for members to go to the theatre.

The first play I saw was *The Country Wife*. It was a Restoration comedy by William Wycherley. I could see how important something called 'comic timing' was. A joke or innuendo could succeed or fail according to the actor's ability in this technical skill. Film stars made acting seem so effortless, but it was aided by takes and editing. In a theatrical performance, yes there were rehearsals, but after that it was you and the audience. How scary was that?

Every Wednesday, I moaned about what Dance club was doing to my body. I demanded hot baths and massages. "It's not fair," I wailed. "Debbie's done gym since she was a tot. Angela seems to be double jointed and I'm a frigging duck billed platypus. The positions Patsy expects me to contort my body into are impossible and excruciating. My back hurts. My hips hurt. She has us sitting on the floor with our legs apart. Angela and Debbie can get theirs like this..." I demonstrated with my arms. "Me? I'm lucky if I can do this. Today she came over to me, sat down opposite, put her feet inside my legs, told me to sit up straight, then she pushed. She's a sadist Trevor."

"Don't go to dance club any more then."

"And do sport or gymnastics instead? No way. It's the best of three evils. Besides, my mates are there, aren't they? And now Angela and I have agreed to be in Debbie's choreography for the dance club's performance at the end of October. Why she's even considered having a duck billed platypus in her choreography is a puzzle.

"I reckon Patsy must think she's going to be an artistic director of a company like Ballet Rambert, the way she treats us. 'You must be professional,' she yells, flapping her arms like a swan about to take off. In vain do I tell her that dance is a hobby and that I'm a trainee English and History teacher, not a fledgling contemporary dancer."

In any relationship, where the two people have demanding career lives there can be a clash of engagements. Trevor and I had one such clash that October. His concert and our dance performance were scheduled for the same night. I wouldn't be able to hear his latest plink-plonk composition. He wouldn't be able to see his duck billed platypus of a wife dancing. The sod's law bit was this was a concert to which I would have liked to go. While he was composing the symphony, I heard references to Liverpool; hints of Jerry and the Pacemakers, The Beatles, other well known Scousers. I even thought I heard, 'come on you reds,' at one point. I was intrigued and now I wouldn't hear the finished piece.

On the eve of our dress rehearsal, Katy rang. She had a dripping tap in the kitchen. She had tried to change the washer, but couldn't get at it as the joint had furred up.

"No problem, Mum," I heard Trevor say. "I'll come straight over." He made an 'I'm sorry' face at me. When he put the phone down he said, "She'd have done it herself but she can't get at it. I'll be as quick as I can."

"Can't it wait until tomorrow?"

"No, Maggie. If I don't help her today, I can't do it until Sunday. I don't want to leave her with a dripping tap for three days. She's nervous that the washer will go completely. Come with me."

I loved Trevor's mother almost as much as I loved my dad. She was kind, generous and thought well of the whole world and his wife. I also loved Molly, but she was a chatterer. Most of what she prattled on about was mundane. Normally, I let most of it wash over me, but I knew I couldn't deal with 'mundane' this evening, and I didn't want to be unkind. It would be alright for Trevor, whatever she was like, as he was going to immerse himself in a 'dripping tap' job.

"I can't, really I can't. I ought to rehearse." As I said 'rehearse', my stomach clenched in a griping pain.

"Is that a good idea without the others? What about your cues?"

"I've got music cues, and I need to be a perfect duck billed platypus." I tried to smile, and failed.

I did have music cues, but he was right about needing the others, and after he left, I drifted miserably round the flat, admonishing myself for being such a butterfly-ridden coward.

"Eat, Maggie. You have to eat. Have a glass of wine and make yourself an omelette." I knew there was a small amount of wine left from the weekend, not enough for the two of us, so it wouldn't matter that I had it. Besides, Trevor would be offered a couple of bottles of beer by Katy. Gander. Goose. When I went to get the eggs out of the fridge, I saw the small polythene bag full of magic mushrooms. I knew what they were. At this time of the year you could find them in parks all over Liverpool. What were they doing in our fridge? Trevor and I didn't indulge in drugs.

Not true, Maggie. We all indulge in some drugs; caffeine is a drug. The glass of wine you're about to drink is a drug. Paracetamol... I could have gone on.

I wasn't sure about the effects of any drugs like cocaine, opium, LSD or magic mushrooms, but my hand suddenly seemed to have a will of its own, for I found I'd taken the bag of magic mushrooms out of the fridge instead of the box of eggs.

Surely you're not thinking of trying them, Maggie? A few, just a few; they could help.

I had no idea how many to take. They were so small. I shook a few out into my hand, re-sealed the bag and put it back in the fridge. Lying there, they didn't look too appetising. Before I could change my mind, I ate them. Gritty earth, that was what they felt like in my mouth. They certainly didn't taste of mushrooms. I took the eggs out of the fridge, made a cheese omelette, drank my glass of wine, and waited.

Half an hour drifted by. My jitteriness was slightly dulled by the wine, but that was all. No magical effects. I decided to have a piping hot bath and try to finish *A Clockwork Orange*. I liked reading in the bath. I had a critical essay to do the following week.

It was when I was trying to focus on the text that it started. The words began to dance. I don't mean they became blurred, like when you've had too much to drink; I'd only had one glass, well, barely one; I mean they danced about. I rubbed my eyes. It did no good. They danced off the page and round the bathroom. The word 'but' was doing an arabesque on the hot tap. 'Three sins' were up on the ceiling doing a cha-cha-cha, or that's what it looked like. All the words finally landed up in the corner by the basin, where they were engulfed by my clothes. They seemed to be shouting 'Droog' at each other.

It was then I noticed some green frogs jumping up at the door, which of course was closed. After a few goes, as one they stopped, turned and hopped across the lino towards the bath. I scrambled out just as they jumped in. It was very noisy what with the croaking frogs who were hopping in and out of the bath, and the dancing letters, who were chattering. Okay, their noise was muffled by my clothes but... I grabbed my towel and ran into the bedroom. Too late, I remembered *A Clockwork Orange*. Had the frogs tipped it into the bath? I ran back to the bathroom. There it was, under the water, as I feared. I would have to buy a replacement copy; it was a college library book. Trevor wasn't going to be too pleased about that.

I put on my pyjamas, and made for the telephone. I needed to talk to someone. I rang Leila.

"Hi queen," I said, and then I started to giggle, and once I started, I couldn't stop.

"Maggie?"

"I think so, but I'm not sure. I was Maggie earlier this evening."

"Are you drunk?"

"No. I've only had three quarters of a glass of wine. How are you, girl?"

"I'm fine. And if you're not drunk, you're frigging something."

"I know. It's just so funny. I shall get kicked out of college because of these cute little Disney frogs, you know the sort, cartoon ones like in *Snow White* and *Cinderella?* Well, they've only gone and knocked *A Clockwork Orange* into the bath, and it's a frigging library book. I didn't fancy staying there with the frogs in case they pooed and weed in the water? Shit Leila, it's just so... whoops, me legs won't hold me up any more."

I collapsed on the floor. "Oh fuck! I've wet me knickers."

"What the hell have you taken? You've not taken LSD, have you?"

"No, oh my god, no. Oh-oh, the frogs have joined me in here."

"Is Trevor there with you? Has he taken—"

"Magic mushrooms? No, he's at Katy's, mending a dripping tap. They tasted yukky, but... Oh god my tummy hurts with laughing."

"I'm coming right over. Drink some water and sit down."

"I am sitting down. Are you sure you want to come over? I think I smell of wee."

"Well I better get you cleaned up before Trevor gets home. It's your dance performance tomorrow evening, you idiot."

"So it is. But I'll be fine. *There once was a duck billed dancer.*
With feathers all...

"Who ruined her friend's choreography." I wailed. "What have I done, Leila? I am such a... whoops, I think I'm going to puke as well as pee. That's good alliteration. Puke and pee. We have to do things like alliteration in English."

When Leila rang the bell, I crawled through the sitting room and into the hall where I hauled myself up and, after several tries, managed to open the door. Leila took one look at me and dragged me back into the bathroom. I talked, non stop, for I knew I could solve all the world's problems.

"That Mac's got it wrong. Not your Mac, MacMillan, Mac. We had it just as good in the fifties, didn't we? Apart from Suez. That was bloody awful. Debbie wants us to join CND. I think we should. We could all... Oh, the frogs have gone. Thank the Lord for that. Why do we say 'thank the Lord' when we don't believe in him?"

Another fit of the giggles overtook me. Leila stripped off all my clothes, helped me into the bath and shoved the shower attachment onto the taps. Then she hosed me down.

"Oh Leila," I snorted. "I feel like a dog who's rolled in the mud, and it's just so funny. Trevor's playing waterworks at his mum's and you're playing waterworks here, with me. The curtains are cascading like some giant waterfall, down the windows. Plus I must have left the taps running in the bath. Look at all the water trickling under the door. Oh, the frogs are back. Aren't they sweet?" I clutched Leila's arm. "What am I going to do about Debbie's choreography?"

I wailed. "Poor Debbie. She shouldn't have included me in it. She knows I can't dance. Well I can, but not well. Did I tell you, Patsy said I looked like—"

"A duck billed platypus. Yes you did. Come on, out of the bath with you." Leila wrapped a towel around me. "Can you manage to dry yourself?"

"Course I can." Another fit of giggles overcame me. "Perhaps I'll dance like a frog now. I wonder what Patsy will call me then? *'There's no such word as can't, Maggie, only won't.'* Only I can't, Patsy. It isn't a case of won't. My body can't get into those positions. I'd like to see her try to read *A Clockwork Orange* when all the words dance off the page. Perhaps they want to be in Debbie's choreography? They'd be a bloody sight better than me. Do you know, the sins danced on the ceiling. She can't do that, or was it the trons, no trogs, no stupid, droogs."

"I'm going to get you a glass of water."

"Hey!" I called after her. "I'm going to tell you a secret. Trevor calls me a barbarian. He says only barbarians put vinegar on their chips. I tell him he's not a proper Scouser 'cause he doesn't. Oh Leila, I am so sorry. I am such a bitch. I never asked you if you were okay now? Like, is Mac pleased about the baby… You know." I pointed to her stomach. "Have you stopped having morning sickness?"

"Yes," said Leila. "I feel great now. Mac and I are fine about the baby. It's you who aren't fine, Short Arse. Do you think the m-m effect is wearing off yet?"

I walked through to the living room, still with my towel wrapped around me. The frogs were hiding under the table which was strewn with Trevor's music. The notes started to rise off the manuscript paper and dance, tunelessly round the room. "Trevor is going to be furious," I wailed. "I've ruined the score."

"It's not ruined," said Leila. And plonked herself on the couch.

He arrived back at midnight as I was crooning into a wooden spoon microphone to the tune the notes were playing.

Leila told him what I'd done. "She's having a pretty normal reaction to the mushrooms, I'd say. Hallucinations, giggles, misery and power. Who do they belong to?"

"Lenny."

"I might have guessed. How is the old fart?'

"Up to his ears in motor bike grease and oil. The business seems to be doing well. I think people know he loves engines and therefore they trust him."

"Why have you got the m-m's in your fridge?"

"Because his wife would go apeshit if she knew he had any."

Leila nodded. "She would, wouldn't she? It's always been a puzzle to me why he married such a prim and proper girl. I didn't know you swore, Trevor. In all the years I've known you, I don't think I've ever heard you swear before."

Trevor rubbed his head. "I don't, well not in front of women friends. I don't know why I did, just then. Lenny swears all the time, doesn't he? Perhaps thinking about him brought out the swearwords."

"We're all hypocrites. I swear a lot, but never in front of Mac. Will Lenny go apeshit if he knows Maggie's eaten some?"

"I doubt it. Apart from his rather stormy relationship with Jen, he's so laid back, he's almost horizontal."

"Right, I'm off. Good luck, Doris. Sock it to us tomorrow."

I stopped singing. "Doris? I thought I was Shor… Oh, I get it. Those were the frigging days, weren't they? Hello, my darling husband. Warning. Don't go in the bathroom. It's full of frogs. They were under the table but I think they got a monk on when your notes started to dance round the room. The frogs are very cute, but a bit frisky. Oh, and there are words dancing all over the place too, so it's a bit crowded just now. To cap it all, I'm going to have to buy another copy of *A Clockwork Orange*. The frogs threw it in the bath."

Leila shook her head and pointed to the intact copy of the book on the coffee table. She had retrieved it from the edge of the bath before hosing me down. She hugged us both and put on her coat.

"Oh god! Your score. The notes. Where are they? They were dancing round the room, playing *Secret Love*, a moment ago."

"Thanks for coming round, love." Trevor said, shaking his head.

Leila shrugged. "It's what friends are for, isn't it? Byeee."

"And what are we going to do with you then, you daft madam? I don't suppose you know how many you've eaten."

I think I shook my head. I wasn't sure because laughter had me in its clutches again.

At four in the morning, I began to feel more like the Maggie I knew. Trevor and I subsided into bed, and it really was a case of head hitting pillow, for the next thing I knew was the alarm telling me it was Duck-billed Platypus day. I felt like one of those frogs, only squashed.

"Why did you do it, love?"

"I don't know. Scared. On my own. Feeling sorry for myself. You name it. I wish I hadn't. I feel shit."

"So do I. I really wanted to be on the ball today."

"Me too. I'm sorry. See you later."

His kiss, and 'good luck' were grudging. That he didn't say, 'Maggie, my concert is more important than your dance performance, it could mean another commission, more money,' was something, I supposed. I deserved it. But I hoped he would forgive my lunacy and we would laugh later.

On my walk through Sefton park, I breathed deeply, trying to get as much park-fresh air into my lungs and bloodstream as possible, but I couldn't help replaying my experience of the night before. Why frogs and dancing words, in particular? Yes, there were other things but they had dominated my experience. Did everyone who ate magic mushrooms spend the night with frogs and dancing words, or was there something in my psyche that had conjured them?

Why had I believed that *A Clockwork Orange* had been pushed into the bath by the frogs? As I had no intention of ever indulging again, I guessed these questions would remain unresolved. I could ask Lenny, I supposed. I shook my head.

Chapter Six
Bill

Every cloud has a silver lining.

At the dress rehearsal, I was as nervous as a rabbit caught by the eyes of a fox

"Whatever's the matter with you?" said Angela, as we climbed up the steps onto the stage.

"You look as though you've spent the night wrestling with monsters."

I laughed. Bravado. It was a false laugh, for she didn't know how near the truth she was. "Frogs," I said. "I was wrestling with frogs. It's a long story."

Debbie hadn't arrived yet. Did I start the story and then tell it all over again when she came, or stall Angela? As though I'd conjured her up, Debbie danced in.

"Did either of you pick up my tape, yesterday? It's not in my bag. God, I'm so excited, I can't wait to get cracking."

"Did you leave it in the machine?" Angela went over to the tape deck. "Here, is this yours?" She handed the tape to Debbie. "While we're changing, Maggie's got a story to tell us."

"About frogs."

Debbie looked at me for the first time. "You look dreadful, Maggie. Are you ill?"

"No, it's just that…" I launched into the story. Before I was half way through, they were crying with laughter.

"Jesus, Maggie. You never cease to amaze me," said Angela.

"Well, I'm not going to treat you lightly just because you've only had three hours sleep and played with frogs for most of the night," said Debbie. "You both ready for warm-up?"

I groaned. "You're not going to make us do sparklers and antelopes, are you? I hate frigging travels at the best of times. I'll be sick if I have to do them now."

"Language, Scouse," said Angela. "Or like your mother, I shall be forced to wash your mouth out—"

"You and whose army?"

"At a guess, an army of frogs."

"Below the belt—"

"Can we please get on," shouted Debbie. We turned and looked at her. "Sorry. I'm nervous as well as excited. My whole family's coming to watch. I want it to be perfect."

Perfect? How will I be perfect? Pigs really will fly.

"And yes, I am going to include travels, Maggie. A warm up has to include everything, otherwise the body isn't warmed up properly."

"Now you sound like Patsy."

"I do not… Do I? Do you know I was thinking last night, I'm so glad I've discovered dance. I think my body's been missing the sheer joy of moving, without my realising it. Yes I've played netball and tennis, but it's not the same. The body feels different."

"Don't I know it," I said.

"Patsy should stop treating us like a professional company. I don't know where she's got this attitude from. We're not a professional company, we're a dance club and therefore amateurs," said Angela.

"I know," I said. "One Duck-Billed Platypus day she admitted she'd been told by her dance teacher that any performance had to be as professional as possible, otherwise there shouldn't be a charge for tickets; she was eight at the time. They put on shows at *The Neptune*. Debbie, dear woolyback Debbie, this Duck-Billed Platypus's bones ache, and she doesn't want to do any bouncy things."

"Tough! It's not my fault you've magic mushroomed yourself into this state. Right, full body stretches." She started the tape. "Five, six, seven, eight…"

That I didn't puke all over the floor had to be a minor miracle. But I didn't. I survived. When it came to little jumps she said, "Quarter turns, half turns, then full turns and don't forget to whip your head round."

"If I whip my head round, I shall be in traction for a week," I said.

"If you don't stop moaning, Debs and I will throw you in the lake," said Angela.

"What lake?"

"I don't know. The nearest lake. Sefton Park lake. You can join your froggy friends."

"You're not going to let me forget my episode, are you?"

"Too right I'm not. It's blackmailing material for—"

"Excuse me." A man walked into the theatre, wheeling a trolley full of plants in pots of all different sizes, and vases of flowers. "I was told the theatre would be empty."

"Well, obviously it isn't," said Debbie.

"I've got to fill the place with plants."

"Why?"

"Some sort of presentation?"

"It can't be the Cert Ed presentation, that's in July," said Angela. "I bet the bursar's hired out the theatre. Some money making scheme because of funding cuts, no doubt."

"And where are we supposed to rehearse?" asked Debbie. "Just a minute. When is this presentation? If you're filling the place with flowers today… Bloody hell, it's tonight, isn't it?"

The man looked uncomfortable.

"Have you, perhaps, made a mistake with the venue or the day?" I asked.

He pulled a sheet of paper out of his overalls' pocket, looked at it and shook his head. "My instructions, or at least the nursery's instructions."

"Let's see," said Angela. "Whoops, major cock up. Great. The theatre's been double-booked. I bet Patsy doesn't know."

We looked at each other.

"What do we do?" I said.

"While you three are deciding what to do, can I start setting these up?" asked the man.

"No," snapped Debbie. "Not till we've finished our rehearsal. Sorry, I know it's not your fault. You can watch if you want. Give us your opinion, then—"

"Debbie," I wailed. "What's the point? There isn't going to be a dance performance." In my state, warm-up was bad enough, without having to dance in front of a stranger.

"Maggie's right, Debbie. There won't be a show," said Angela.

"There will. Patsy will sort it. She'll be here at eleven for her rehearsal. There's nothing we can do just now, so we might as well carry on." She turned again to the man. "You sit over there." She indicated the tiered seating. "We can't finish warm-up now, there isn't time. We'll help you put all the pots and vases in place afterwards."

"Mice aren't supposed to be tyrants," I grumbled.

Considering everything, I acquitted myself not too badly. I knew I would never be a good dancer; I certainly wasn't on top form because of my escapade, but I remembered what I had to do and I didn't make a mistake.

"Well?" Debbie said to the man, after we finished.

"It's good," said the man.

"What's the 'but'?" I asked.

"How did you know there was a 'but'?" he said.

"Your voice suggested a 'but'."

"In my opinion, and it is just my opinion, it lacks drama. It's very lyrical and I like that but... look, I know plants not dance. You have showy plants like dahlias. They're all drama. Then you have lyrical plants like Astrantia. They're like old fashioned tapestries, subtle, calm, no drama. In a garden you need some plants that combine the two, like lupins and delphiniums. They're subtle and dramatic. Can you play me the tape again, please?" There was a pause while Debbie rewound the tape. "See, there, in the beginning section. Don't you think it's demanding a dramatic response? That passage is repeated later."

Debbie was gazing at this gardener in astonishment. No, we were all gazing at him in astonishment. He blushed. "I'm sorry. I didn't mean to be impertinent."

"I didn't feel you were being impertinent," said Debbie. "You've really helped me, thank you. But is it too late? Have I time…?"

Afterwards, I decided that that was the moment Debbie fell in love with the trolley man.

"My god, a nursery man who talks about lyricism. We ought to kidnap him. There aren't many cultivated men around here," said Angela.

"Don't take any notice of her, trolley man. We can't keep calling you that. What's your name?" I said

"Bill."

"I've got an idea, Bill' said Debbie.

I groaned. "My belly wants a hot water bottle."

"Your belly? I thought it was your head that was messed up?" said Angela.

"Everything's messed up. I'm a mushroom mess."

"This won't take long, promise." Debbie looked at her watch. "We've got thirty minutes before Patsy arrives. We'll go through it one more time with my new idea. Maggie and Angela you enter, pushing a trolley. We can borrow one of the refectory ones for the performance, but we'll use this one for now."

"I don't know what you're planning to do, Debbie, but refec. trolleys are nothing like this one." said Angela.

"True." Debbie frowned.

"I reckon you could borrow this one," Bill said. "Obviously I'd have to ask the boss, but—"

"You angel," said Debbie. "Right, where does this lot have to go?"

He looked at his piece of paper again. "The five tubs are for the back of the stage. One vase is to go on a table. The other on a pedestal.

The table and the pedestal are backstage. The ones for the side of the stage and the auditorium are in the foyer."

"Okay. We can put the tubs in place, They shouldn't be in our way. Come on you lot, let's get shifting. The vases will have to go on the floor for the time being. We'll help with the others later. No point in bringing them through until we know which event is going to happen."

I do, and I bet Angela does. What cloud cuckoo land is Debbie on?

"You can't do that," said Bill. "They're very heavy."

"We can if we carry them between us. We're dancers, we've got muscles."

"I am not a dancer," I said, "and I haven't got muscles."

"No, you're a moaner," said Angela.

When the pots were in place, Debbie said, "Now we've got to get the trolley onto the stage." The four of us carried it up the stairs. "Okay, back in your seat, Bill." She grinned at him. "You two use exactly the same travel but with the trolley, okay?"

"The swooping turn, followed by the side faint, like this?' said Angela.

Debbie nodded. We practised. The swooping turns took us away from the trolley, then we ran back towards it, grabbed hold, pushed it forward and sank into a sidewards faint.

"Now repeat the sequence," said Debbie. She clapped her hands. "That looks great. Okay. Take the trolley back and start again. I'm going to join in."

On the second side faint to the floor, Debbie ran in and did a neat cartwheel over the trolley; or it would have been if the wheel brakes had been put on. As it was, the trolley skidded off and Debbie crashed to the floor.

We rushed over to help her up, Bill ran down from his seat and up the stage stairs. Debbie sat up. "I'm okay," she said. "Was that dramatic enough?" As she tried to get up she went white. "The pain… my ankle. I feel sick."

"Ambulance," Angela said.

"Quicker if I take her in the van," said Bill.

It made sense. Bill picked her up as though she were a precious piece of china and carried her to the van just as Patsy arrived. Angela explained what had happened and why the foyer and back of the stage were full of pots of flowers while we settled Debbie in the front seat. Angela and I climbed in the back and sat on a couple of sacks. Bill drove as though his cargo would fragment if he went too fast. We knew before Debbie came out with her leg in plaster that she'd broken her ankle. The concert was postponed until just before the Christmas holiday. Patsy told us that the bursar was oily in his apologies.

Out of some adversities come blessings. The three of us, Debbie on crutches, went to Trevor's concert. For the first time, my college life merged with my home and erstwhile working life, as everyone, bar Edith, came to support him. I didn't know what the others thought of his Liverpool symphony, but I really liked it, as I had expected I would from the odd bits of piano experimentation I'd heard.

When it came to December, our dance performance also went well. Debbie couldn't perform as her ankle, though mended, wasn't strong enough. Patsy took over her role. The digestive biscuit and Dawn Rose attended. They delighted Patsy by telling her how professional all the choreographies were.

In the Easter Term, we were due to be sent out on our first teaching practice. Before we broke up for Christmas, we were told which school would be honoured with our presence, and who our tutor would be.

I discovered that I had been given a catholic secondary modern school in Bootle and Dawn Rose for my tutor. To say I was not too happy at the latter was an understatement.

"Why do I get Dawn Rose for teaching practice? Why not one of my subject tutors?" I asked Angela.

"Because this is more of an observation TP," said Angela. "You won't teach many lessons, and she'll only come out to the school once, maybe twice. She has to check on your punctuality, politeness, things like that, and chat to you about what you've learned. She might watch a lesson in your second week, if you get to teach one, but she might not. You'll get one of your subject tutors for your second year TP, and for your final one."

"Never mind talking boring college stuff. Guess what? I've got a date with Bill, this evening," said Debbie.

"Bill?" I said. "Trolley man, Bill? Knight to the rescue, Bill?"

"Yes. We're going to see *La Dolce Vita*."

"He took long enough to get round to it, didn't he? It was obvious he fancied you on ankle accident day."

"He was going out with someone else then. He told me that he'd been trying to tell her it was over, but couldn't pluck up the courage. Then she dumped him."

"Lucky or what? *La Dolce Vita!* Get you!"

"You're a one to talk with your *Look Back In Anger*, your *Country Wife* and your Shakespeare."

"All British, not arty-farty foreign."

"Take no notice of her, Debbie. Where's it on?" asked Angela.

"Bill belongs to the film club at the Uni., don't ask me how or why. After it, we're going for a meal in the Philharmonic dining rooms."

"Wow, is he treating you?" I said.

"Certainly not. We're going Dutch. I don't want him to get any ideas."

"How can you afford to eat out in The Philharmonic Dining Rooms?" asked Angela. "Unless I ask my folks for a sub, I can't even afford fish and chips as a treat."

"It's not that expensive. And I've still got some of my birthday money stashed away."

"You sound like Eunice with your 'any ideas' nonsense," I said.

"Nonsense? It isn't nonsense to pay your way when you go out with a man for the first time. It says I can't be bought," said Debbie. "Anyway, I hope I don't sound like her. She's scary."

"She is and she isn't. Last tutorial, when we were discussing *Room At The Top*, she said, 'Remember girls, men only want one thing from women: sex,' and then she grinned. 'And what they can't cope with is, that it's all I want from them too.' She's outrageous."

"But that's not what I'm saying. I think her way of looking at men is warped. I just want Bill to know that I don't want sex with him, yet. I want to get to know him. So, I'm not like Eunice at all."

Eunice was one of our English lecturers and the tutor I was hoping would have been assigned to me for teaching practice. We'd never met anyone like her. She aired her philosophy on life in almost every tutorial and was often embarrassingly frank. She kept nothing about her personal life private. She wasn't overly keen on men, but she loved sex, or said she did; especially in slippery, black satin sheets. Her bedroom was decorated with black and white toile de jouy wallpaper, and there were curtains of the same pattern. Women had to endure men in order to enjoy sex, unless you were a lesbian which she wasn't. She had been to bed with a woman, and apparently the sex was good, but she missed the smell of a man and the thrust of a penis; that was how she described it. Apparently vibrators were a good substitute but not as exciting.

Men were necessary for procreation, but after the sperm joined with the egg, they were expendable. As a parent, all they did was get in the way. Children were much better off being brought up by their mothers. *Not my mother,* I thought.

I was nineteen going on twenty, married, and in love with my husband. I also loved and admired my father, well his mind, anyway. I didn't agree with Eunice, but I was fascinated by her philosophy.

She wasn't afraid of using swear words. "They're only words like any others," she said. "As with all words, it depends how you use them. Our world is full of words and we shouldn't be afraid of them. If you get the opportunity, go and see the film about Lenny Bruce."

That was how I'd felt from the moment Leila had taught Gail and I 'peed' and started calling me 'short-arse'. It irritated me that every time I even thought a swear word I heard Edith say, *'I shall wash your mouth out with soap and water, Maggie.'* To my mind, swear words had a place, but, I also thought that we had a rich language, and to use a swear word to replace an adjective showed a paucity of vocabulary.

"Yeh, but…" Yeh but what? I didn't know where my 'yeh, but' was going. "Look it's great that you're going out with Bill, Debs. Now, can we concentrate on helping me impress Miss Sugar Knickers."

Angela and Debbie collapsed with laughter. "Miss who?" Angela screeched.

"Dawn Rose. I just thought of it. Suits her, doesn't it?"

She was almost the exact opposite of Eunice; a woman out of her time. She floated everywhere in a haze of gossamer fabric. Like the Queen, we could never imagine her burping, farting or shitting. She glowed rather than perspired and she wouldn't know what a sweat was, even if she saw horses at the end of a race. I couldn't imagine what a staff meeting was like with Digestive Biscuit, Sugar Knickers and Eunice all in the same room.

Before we knew it, the first term was over and Christmas was upon us. Trevor and I decided we couldn't face an all day full family affair; our flat was too small.

Then we discovered that Katy and Molly had been invited to Trevor's sister's home. She lived on Egremont promenade, in Walleey. "You two come on Boxing Day," she said when she rang us up to tell us.

That left my family. Duty told me I had to see them. Love told me I wanted to see my dad. My brother still lived at home. The last time I saw him, he told me he had a girlfriend, and that they were going steady.

"Why don't we invite them to ours for Christmas lunch?" said Trevor.

"We don't have enough money to buy all the food.'

"Oh, but we do. I've been a bit sneaky." Trevor had been the house-husband from the start of our marriage. He was a very good cook. "Look." He showed me a book of Co-op stamps. "I've been collecting them since September. There's enough for all the food. I bet your dad would bring along some booze. We know we'll have mince pies from Mum, and… another secret, close your eyes… Da-da." I opened them.

He was holding a pudding basin covered with a cloth. "I made it. I went to the library to find a recipe. So we're laughing."

I was astonished. "Why you sneaky, amazing man. The next time Eunice tells us that the only use men have is to sexually please us, I shall relate my Christmas story."

Trevor put down the pudding and grabbed me. "But she's right about us just wanting sex from women, well one woman in my case," he said as he pushed me towards the bedroom.

"No, on the couch. I want to fuck on the couch."

"Did you say 'fuck', Margaret Harvey?"

"I did. And I'm pissed off with thinking about having my mouth scoured. Also," I grinned, "I shall think, that's where we fucked, when Edith sits on it, on Christmas Day."

I never knew why people bothered to sing about snow at Christmas, in Liverpool. Wind and wet, yes. Snow no. But this holiday was crisp and icily cold, so although the only snow was the canned stuff I sprayed onto the Christmas tree. Outside trees, bushes and plants sparkled with frost.

Teaching practice, or teaching observation as it ought to have been called, began the day after the new college term started. On my first day in the school, Paula, the teacher in charge of students, advised me to make all the lessons fun. "If they learn anything, it'll be a bonus," she said. "They're not very motivated."

"Which teacher will I be shadowing?"

"Me."

"But you're a PE teacher."

"Yes. This TP is about teaching skills, not a subject. I assumed your TP tutor would have told you that."

No one had told us anything. We had been given an A4 sheet of general instructions, but it was about dress code, punctuality, and making sure we didn't sit on an assigned chair in the staffroom. Apparently teachers always sat in the same chairs and got upset if an outsider usurped one.

I fibbed. "My friends mentioned it. I was off when Miss Rose wanted to see me and then she couldn't rearrange. I just wanted to check, you know, make sure I knew I was on the right lines. I think I'm a bit of a 'check twice' person." *Thank you Dad.* I heard his advice from my childhood. *'Always double check Maggie, especially in practical jobs where a mistake could either ruin what you're doing or cause an accident.'*

Paula gave me a funny look. Were nerves making me too talkative?

"I guess I'm a bit nervous, as it's the first TP." That sounded okay. "After all, some schools might have different expectations from others."

"No. We're all expected to sing from the same hymn sheet."

Ah. A religious metaphor. I'm in a catholic school. I must remember that; mind my 'Oh god's'.

"I noticed that you put on your form that you belong to a dance and a drama club. When you take a PE lesson, you could give it a dance or drama slant, if you want."

"So although it's an observation TP, I will some teach lessons?"

"One or two in the second week, to give you a taste of what it's like."

I would plan a dance lesson. I'd no experience of PE. *Thank goodness for the warm-ups Patsy made us do. I'll have to choose ones that don't make me look like a duck-billed platypus though.*

In the first week I watched. In the second week I taught three lessons.

"Most interesting, Margaret," said Dawn Rose when she made her first and only appearance. "Dance with a dramatic theme. The pupils seemed to appreciate something different. You kept their attention all the way through the lesson. However, when you teach dance, you do need to think about rhythm. You ought to do a rhythmic warm up, using your voice to help them."

"I'm not sure what you mean?" I said. "Dance isn't an option in college for us, Miss Rose, just for PE students. I belong to the dance club, as you know. I don't intend to use dance in an English lesson. That's what I aim to teach, and possibly some history."

"Yes, I know that. But as you so obviously enjoy doing dance, you may want to run dance clubs when you get a job."

I doubted it. Clubs were extra-curricular activities. I was pretty sure I'd want to go home to Trevor.

She got up, and began to clap her hands and chant, "Ta ta tee, ta ta taa, ta ta taa taa taa, ta ta tee, ta ta taa, ta ta taa."

I didn't know where to look. Disbelief was warring with the desire to giggle. I could not 'ta, ta, ta,' in this school. I doubted that it would be possible to 'ta, ta, ta,' in any school on Merseyside.

"I didn't know you were a modern dance teacher, Miss Rose."

"Oh yes." A dreamy look came into her eyes. "I trained, as a mature student, at the centre Rudolph Laban set up in Manchester. We call it contemporary dance, rather than modern. Modern's more to do with dance in musicals and shows; still wonderful, of course. Sadly I had to give up dancing: a skiing accident. I had to give up tennis too. Miss Mackenzie gave me the opportunity to establish dance as part of the PE curriculum. We're old friends. She was an excellent tennis player. We were in the doubles together in various tournaments. Now, where dance is concerned, I'm theory. Judy is practical work."

A grudging respect for Sugar Knickers crept into my head. But I knew I couldn't cope with 'ta, ta, ta'.

"Are you coming to see me again, Miss Rose?"

"No. We only visit once in the first TP. Goodbye, dear."

"Sugar knickers is okay, you know," I told Debbie and Angela. "She suggested I start dance and drama clubs in the school where I get a job."

"If you get a job," said Angela.

"If we get a job," said Debbie.

"If we pass the course," I said.

Chapter Seven
I want this baby

Procrastination is the thief of time.

In June nineteen sixty-four I became a qualified teacher. Angela, Debbie and I, alongside the other teachers of the future, trooped up onto the stage to receive the certificates to say we had passed the course. They were presented by the Dean of Liverpool University. It was the same stage where Debbie had broken her ankle in our first term. The years had flown by and with them Woolworths' Maggie; I had changed. Yes, I was still a working class Scouser in many ways, but I was now middle class because of the education I had received at college, and because of the people with whom I had associated.

We are all people of many hats. Few wear only one or two. I could put on and take off my various hats with a flick of my wrist, according to the environment and the people in it.

Certificate day was a day of joy and sadness. Joy that we had all passed. Sadness that Allie, Debbie's sister wasn't with us to share her achievement. If Allie had lived, she would have been in her first year at college or university, being two years younger than Debbie. Although Bill had done much to ameliorate Debbie's grief, anyone could sense it still wrapped her in a grey cloud from time to time. She had become an avid anti drink-driving activist, and politically active in other ways, having joined Friends of the Earth and CND.

I got a job in Kirkby, and Angela in West Derby. Debbie? Debbie married Bill, and had a baby.

Originally, Kirkby had been a small Lancashire town in its own right. But after the Second World War it had grown exponentially because Liverpool had suffered such severe bombing. New estates were needed to house the homeless, so it had become a dormitory town. The school where I was to be a probationary teacher was one of the first comprehensives in England.

As a probationary teacher I was monitored by the Heads of English and History, and every so often, an adviser would come in to see me. I passed my probationary year, and felt as though I was in safe waters, swimming confidently forward until…

Oh god, I'm pregnant. I'm pregnant. Oh God! I felt as though the breath was being sucked out of my body. Then, as it percolated back in through my nose, my mouth the pores of my skin, I felt… complete. How could I feel this satisfied when we couldn't afford for me to be pregnant? Round and round I went in ever decreasing circles to a centre that shouted, "Maggie Harvey you are pregnant, and fuck me girl, you want this baby." Once I'd landed there I wanted to share the news and my found joy with the man I loved. But every time I thought of telling him, I saw anger, not pleasure, on his face, and I quaked.

Becoming a well known composer was Trevor's aim, his raison d'être. He had no other. Becoming a father? We'd never discussed having children. I'd intuited that children weren't part of his plan. He had encouraged me to become a teacher, but it was a sparrow's egg of an ambition beside his eagle's. He didn't know I wanted to be a mother. Until test positive, *I* didn't know I wanted to be a mother. How would we manage? I pushed that question away. I couldn't deal with it. But Maggie being Maggie, I had to tell someone, lots of some-ones. Soon everyone knew but Trevor and Edith.

I'm lumping Trevor and Edith together? Wrong. Sinful. You don't believe in sin, Maggie. Sin is to do with religion. But it is wrong, not telling both of them is wrong. Dad will tell Edith. She'll make a face and, when she sees me, give me a piece of her mind which I know already as I've heard it so many times before.

'You're going to get married? Is that man going to get off his backside and earn some money? You're going to college? Is that man…? You're pregnant? Is that man…?'

Angela understood my reticence to tell Trevor, but she advised me to do it before I started to show. She had known, from before their marriage, that Dave didn't want children, had accepted it because she wanted to be with him, more than to be a mother.

Angela had met Dave at a cricket club dance at the end of our first year in college. I'd invited her. I would have invited Debbie as well, but she'd gone to Ireland, with her family. Angela and Dave started going out with each other, going steady, almost immediately, and I don't think either of them went out with anyone else. They got married in Southport in the September after we graduated.

Debbie and Bill had got married, in the Easter holiday of our final year. She had been two months pregnant. I thought she might have been annoyed with herself for not taking precautions, as it meant she couldn't apply for teaching jobs and, as we all knew, her ambition had been to teach in a school for handicapped children.

She couldn't understand my fears about telling Trevor. "He'll be delighted," she said. "You'll see."

Leila was pregnant again. Once set on birth course not abortion course, she had sailed through her 'one night stand' pregnancy. I sometimes believed she had willed the baby to look like her. Was it that two close friends having children influenced my feeling of, not just acceptance of my state, but euphoria? Both urged me to tell Trevor. So did Katy. It seemed that all the world and his wife was waiting for me to act. Indeed, I was surprised that Katy wasn't upset by my behaviour. If she was, she didn't show it.

My dad was the most forthright. I had called in to see him on my way home from work. I knew Edith would be out. It was her afternoon for helping my gran and granddad.

"It's Trevor's right to know, Maggie," he said. "He'll be mortified, and justifiably angry if he suspects the whole world knew before him. I'm surprised at you."

"Not the whole world, Dad. I haven't told Mother."

"Now you're splitting hairs. I want you to tell him as soon as you get home."

What I hadn't told my dad; what I couldn't tell him was, that once Trevor knew... *Where the hell am I going with this? Abortion is illegal, Maggie. Trevor wouldn't... but what will he do? Say our marriage is over?* I knew that it was this persistent thought that prevented me from telling him. My mind, my body, revolted at the idea. I thought about the conversation I'd had with Leila. How could I be thinking of doing what I'd advised her not to do? It was simple. I could if it meant losing Trevor. An abortion would mean lying to my friends, my dad. I'd have to tell them I'd had a miscarriage. *For god's sake Maggie, you could die. That's what you told Leila. Women died when they went to a back street abortionist. And where are you going to find the money?*

I had been able to keep it a secret from Trevor because I didn't have any pregnancy symptoms, like morning sickness. I still wanted sex. I was still slim. I knew some pregnant women went off intercourse when they were first pregnant. So I kept on delaying, even though at the same time I was telling myself that we had to make a decision together about the fate of our baby. It was only a foetus now, our embryo baby; our baby. Surely he wouldn't want to flush our baby away. And, how would I feel about him if he told me he did? But I knew my dad was right. I had to tell him.

As I walked through the park, I practised what I had to say. *'Trevor, I've got something to tell you. I'm...'* No. *'Trevor, we're going to have a baby...'* No. *'Trevor, how would you like to be...?' 'Trevor, what would you think if...?'*

"Trevor, I'm pregnant."

He froze mid pen stroke. *Oh god!* Eventually he said just two words, "How come?"

Was that better than aggressive negatives? Would he shout at me when I told him how?

"I forgot to take the pill one day, a couple of months ago." *Nearly four months, Maggie.* "When we went to Mac and Leila's party, you remember?" He must remember. Mac almost caught us fucking in their bedroom. "I thought just missing one wouldn't matter."

"How far gone are you?" *No anger, not yet anyway.*

"Three months, give or take a couple of days."

"How do you… you've had no morning sickness?"

"Some women do, some women don't, Trevor. I'm a don't. I suspected I was pregnant when my boobs started itching and I missed my second period, so I went to the doctors."

"Why didn't you tell me then?" *Still no anger. He's being very calm, matter of fact. Too calm.*

"I don't know, Trevor. I'm sorry. I was dead nervous. I mean, I knew, well suspected you didn't want a baby. You know, like Dave. I've been through such see-saw emotions. Wanting the baby. Not wanting the baby. Wondering how we could we afford the baby? I know I should have told you before, like. Please don't be angry." *He's chewing his pencil, one of his worry habits.*

"I'm not angry. Hurt a little." *He hasn't asked me if anyone else knows.* "So what do you want to do?"

Not 'we'. "The only thing we can do; keep the baby. Abortion is illegal. I was hoping you'd feel the same."

"Right." He put down the pencil, got up, and came over to me. *He's not going to hit me, is he? Make me fall, miscarry? You stupid drama queen, Margaret Harvey. Trevor, hit you? That's an awful thing to think.*

He put his hand on my stomach. "Well, you interrupter of our peaceful life are you going to be a boy or a girl? We could have you adopted." I felt as though he'd punched me in the stomach. "But, even though a baby hasn't been part of the plan, we can't do that, can we? We shall have to think about how we're going to manage."

I nearly cried with relief. "I'll get maternity leave—"

"Is that paid maternity leave, Maggie?"

"Yes, eighteen weeks, I think. I'm not sure about that. I'll find out. Would you be prepared to look after our baby when I go back to work?" I stressed the 'our'.

"Look after the baby? And what about my work?"

He didn't take up the 'our'. 'The' baby… "Baby's sleep a lot. I'll express enough milk—"

"Are you sure you haven't thought it all through?"

"No. I'm making it up as we talk."

"Maggie!"

"Well, of course I've done some thinking. I couldn't help it, could I?"

"Well I'm not sure about being a baby minder. What about your parents? Couldn't—"

"My dad, maybe, Edith, never. Surely you wouldn't be happy to hand our baby over to her? I know she'll have to see the baby, but I couldn't trust her to look after…" *Do I say 'it', 'him' or 'her'?* "Katy, deffo. But we can't assume any one of them'll want to baby mind any more than you do."

Trevor moved away. "I didn't say I didn't want to. I said I wasn't sure. I need to think about this, Maggie. It's…"

I saw him struggling for words and I felt sure he wanted to say, 'a bombshell' or 'a catastrophe'. I wished he could be pleased for us.

"I'm going out for a bit of fresh air. I'd just about finished what I'd planned for today. Perhaps you could make the meal this evening?" He put on his coat and left.

I ate alone, the shepherd's pie congealing in the dish. Afterwards, I went to the phone box. I phoned my dad and Debbie. She told me not to worry. Trevor would soon get used to the idea. But would he? I was in bed when he got in at eleven.

He was tipsy, not drunk, amorously tipsy. We made love. He held me and said, "I will look after the baby, if it's what we need to do, Maggie. It'll be fine. I'm sure Katy and Molly will want to be involved somehow, and you never know, your mum might be so thrilled that she'll be a great granny pussy cat not a gorgon."

All those words tell me it's not what he wants. But I knew it, didn't I? No matter what anyone else said, I knew having children had never figured in Trevor's plans for… himself, not ourselves.

Shit, how are we going to be able to afford things like a pram? I hope I'm right about the sleeping part. I was a fractious baby, Ian an angel. Our baby has to be an Ian, not a Maggie. What was Trevor like as a baby?

Shit! How are we going to be able to afford other baby equipment? You beg, borrow and steal, Maggie. Well, maybe not steal. Your baby doesn't deserve a jailbird for a mother. Babies have slept in drawers before now. These thoughts mustn't be shared with Trevor. No worry, no pressure.

When do I tell them at school?

Dad didn't tell me how Edith received the news. I went round to see them the Sunday after I'd told Trevor. He didn't come with me. He went to see Katy and Molly, to tell them. The webs we weave. I kept my fingers crossed, metaphorically, that Katy wouldn't let slip that she knew already.

Edith greeted me at the door with a look of triumph on her face. "So much for wasting your time at college, my girl. And that husband of yours will have to get a job now."

I knew it. Oh god it's so boring that she does what I expect. "No, Mother. I'm going back to work and Trevor's going to look after the baby."

It floored her. All she managed was, "Well!"

"That sounds like a sensible idea, Maggie. And we—"

"No. You've made your bed, my girl, you'll have to lie in it," said Edith.

It was no more than I expected. When Dad walked me to the bus stop he said, "A penny to a pinch of salt she'll come round once her grandchild's born."

I didn't want to hurt him by saying I didn't care if she came round, or not. "You'll be a lovely granddad," is what I said.

Trevor assumed that I would be able to carry on as normal. And this was what I wanted. If he wasn't overjoyed about the pregnancy, he was supportive. He encouraged me to go to antenatal classes and said he wanted to be present at our baby's birth. I tried hard not to show how pleased I was.

The next day, after work, I went to the surgery to tell the doctor I wanted a home birth and find out when the antenatal clinics were. There were two, one on Wednesdays at three-thirty, this was followed by a relaxation and exercise class. The other was on Fridays from four-thirty until six. The midwife, Beverly, told me to try to come to both. I went to see the Head to find out if I could leave school at three on Wednesdays. It was fortunate that the last lesson was a free one for me, so all it meant was that I couldn't be put down as a substitute. He was agreeable, but said if there was an illness epidemic, I might have to forego one clinic.

At the second session, I met a woman called Einna. *Odd name, Einna,* I thought. We were next to each other in the relaxation and exercise class.

One woman, she was big and must have been near her due date, farted during a particular exercise. Then, all round the room I heard small puffs of expelled air. I caught the eye of the woman next to me and we both subsided into muffled giggles.

"Where do you live?" I asked her as we were putting on our coats.

"Ferndale Road," she said.

"Not far from me, then. I live just off Lark Lane, Hadassah Grove. Do you fancy coming back to mine for a cuppa? I can still drink tea… coffee, yuk."

"I'm the same."

"What do you do?" I asked her.

"I'm just a housewife. John, my husband's a bit old fashioned where women and work are concerned, even more so now I'm pregnant. But… oh, it's a long story. I won't bore you with it just now."

I didn't press her as she looked… sort of shut off, sad.

"What does John do?"

"Teaches PE."

"Trevor's a musician. He wants to be a well known composer, like someone called Steve Reich. I'm not sure I like the music he composes. It's very modern. You might have to put up with a bit of plink-plonk. That's what I call it… sometimes to his face as a tease. I do like some of his pieces. His Liverpool Symphony, for example."

"I prefer the romantic composers, like Beethoven, Richard Strauss and Bruch, but I do like some contemporary ones. Have you heard of Peter Maxwell Davies or Harrison Birtwhistle?"

"Yes. They're okay. I think I need tunes in music. As a kid I loved the films of Doris Day. I still like musicals."

"So do I, some. My favourite's *West Side Story*. Do you work?"

"I have to. I'm the breadwinner. But 'have to' isn't fair. I like my work. I'm a teacher – English and History. Where does John teach?"

"Saint Cuthbert's."

"I teach in Kirkby."

I related some of the week's comic incidents and soon the cloud that had been hovering over Einna's head floated off in our shared laughter.

"Our school is divided into houses. I'm in Wordsworth House. Its Head is a man called Clem Williams. I think he knows every cliché under the sun. His favourites at the moment are 'acid test', 'above board', and 'actions speak louder than words'. I bet you can imagine how he uses them."

"He should get together with John and my sister. I'm being driven mad with their clichés. 'Don't forget you have to eat for two. Don't lift, you could damage the baby. Don't stretch. Have lots of rest now, while you still can. Don't drink alcohol. Don't drink tea or coffee.' I feel as though the 'don'ts' are going to smother me."

"Trevor doesn't molly-coddle me, thank goodness." I unlocked the door to our flat. Trevor was at the dining table, surrounded by manuscript paper. "Hi, love. You want a cuppa? This is Einna. Our babies are due the same week."

"Unusual name," He got up. "I've just got to finish this, so if you'll excuse me—"

"You'll go into the bedroom while we have a natter?"

"Yes. I've just had a cuppa." He planted a kiss on the top of my head and left the room.

"Put your coat on a chair, Einna. And that reminds me, I meant to ask you before, why 'Einna'?"

"Are you sure you want to know, it's a rather long story. All my stories seem to be long ones. In a way it's related to the other one."

"Don't tell me if you don't want to."

"No, it's okay. I'll do the short version. My mother gave me to my sister, Annie, when I was a baby. Even my name is hers; it's Annie spelt backwards. I don't know how they managed the baby bit. I suppose Pearl had to look after me while Annie was at school and then when she came home…"

Einna paused, as though searching for something she couldn't find. She shrugged. "I'll never know that bit."

I wanted to say, 'you could ask Annie'. The look on her face prevented me.

"Children get bored of toys, don't they? Or they grow out of them. Annie didn't get bored of me because I wasn't a doll. I grew. She grew. She enjoyed bossing me about and punishing me. Pearl did nothing to stop her."

"Shit," I said when she had finished. "Didn't the teachers notice the bruising when you changed for gym?"

She pulled a face. "If they did, they didn't say anything. Don't forget, there was no Children's Act in the fifties. At least I've escaped. I did have older role models who cared about me, my Aunt Ruby and Uncle Charles. There was also a woman called Jean. She was my friend."

She told me about Jean and Matilda, the last hut along the beach at Hunstanton, "My sanctuary. I'm not religious, Maggie, but I've always thought of her, Uncle Charles and Aunty Ruby as guardian angels. I held on to their love."

"I had my dad and my friends So we both had mothers who didn't mother us. Well, in my case, not as a mother should." It struck me that Einna hadn't mentioned any friends of her own age. I supposed Pearl and Annie wouldn't have allowed friends in the house. *Should I ask?* "What about school friends?"

"I had friends, in school but not a friend, friend, if you see what I mean? I wasn't allowed to bring friends home."

I was right.

"This is the first time I've told anyone about my childhood." She seemed to be studying my face. "I learnt to lie, Maggie. There was a spider behind a picture in my room. I pretended I was that spider, and the lie webs I spun were to keep me safe. Looking back I know it was a survival strategy. I used to pretend I went to Jean's house to play. Neither Pearl nor Annie were curious enough to ask about her, or check up where I went. It wasn't a house I went to."

She told how she'd met Jean and Nelson and how Jean had died of cancer. I gave her a hug. "Thank you for feeling you could confide in me. Everyone lies, you know. Lies aren't necessarily bad." Something told me it was time to change the subject. "Hey Einna, you know your problem with your husband's attitude to your pregnancy?" She nodded. "Why not see if he'll go with you to your next appointment with your midwife. Is it Bev?"

"Yes."

"She's mine too. I feel I can say anything to her. She's brill. Tell her you're drowning in clichés. I bet she'll soon sort John out. And next week I'll introduce you to my erstwhile college friends, Debbie and Angela. I'm not sure, now I've said it, that 'erstwhile' is the right word, because they're still my friends. Debbie's a little brown mouse and Angela's a mermaid. You'll see why when you meet them."

"And you're—"

"What do you mean?"

"Mermaid, mouse, and…"

"Oh, Lizzie Siddal."

"I knew you were going to say that. As soon as I saw *Pandora* in The Lady Lever gallery, I felt like I'd seen her, live, somewhere."

It wasn't just a mutual circumstance that pushed us into friendship. We clicked, in much the same way that Debbie, Angela and I had clicked when we first met. Sometimes it happens like that. Other times it can take a long time to get to know someone.

Her stories of how Annie, her sister had bullied her, and Pearl, her mother had allowed it, made me angry and sad. Whatever Edith had done to try to get me to behave as she wanted, she had never been as horrid as those two evil witches. Nevertheless, I couldn't help remembering some of the more difficult conversations I'd had with the gorgon.

"Did you hear what I said, Margaret?"

"Yes, Mother." I always crossed two fingers behind my back. Why did I do that?

She was never content with one, 'Yes, Mother'. *"Let me hear you say it again?"*

"Yes Mother." Four fingers.

"Louder, Margaret."

"Yes Mother." Six fingers

"Look me in the eyes when you say it."

She knew, I'm sure she knew, that I didn't want to look her in the eyes. I crossed all my fingers and squinted at her. Later, when I was a teenager, it was the 'v' sign. Why she didn't make me show my hands, I don't know.

"I've told you my story. It's your turn," said Einna. "Why do you describe your mum as a gorgon?"

"Because of her basilisk stare. It all started when I learnt about Medusa in junior school. I was convinced Edith was like her and was capable of turning me to stone when she was angry with me."

"And you never call her 'Mum' or 'Mummy' when you're thinking or talking about her?"

"No."

"I would have loved to have a mother I could call, 'Mum' or 'Mummy'. I still fantasise about it. They say, forgiveness makes the forgiver feel better. Do you think it does? I find it hard to think of forgiving Pearl and Annie."

I shrugged. "It's odd. I have things I find hard to forgive Edith for, but the odd thing is, she sort of did me a favour."

"How?"

"The people I've met and love because she didn't let me stay on at school."

"Ah! Maybe now I've met you, I'll begin to think like that."

After she had gone home, I found that the forgiveness issue would keep crawling about in my mind. How could you forgive someone who

88

continued to hurt you? If you turned the other cheek, weren't you colluding in unacceptable behaviour? And didn't forgiveness have a price, usually. Would forgiving Pearl and Annie get rid of the haunted look in Einna's eyes; a look that made her seem as though she were being troubled by ghosts? However difficult I found Edith, at least she acknowledged me as her daughter. Many children are given up for adoption but few live in the same house as their mother, and can't call her 'Mum', 'Mummy', 'Mother'.

> *Annie was a crocodile.*
> *Edith was a gorgon.*
> *Would Annie crocodile*
> *eat up Edith gorgon*
> *with her terrible teeth?*
> *Or would Edith gorgon*
> *turn Annie crocodile*
> *into stone with*
> *her basilisk stare?*

Einna gave me the poem after our antenatal class the following week, and she told me she had managed to persuade John to go with her to see Bev.

One Friday, in January, Trevor asked me if I could do the weekend food shopping on the way home. He had a meeting with a group of young musicians who wanted to commission a new piece for a concert in March.

I got off the bus in Allerton Road. I decided that, after I'd shopped, I would walk home via my park; that was how I saw Sefton Park. I allowed other people to enjoy it. That Friday, however, there was a cruel breeze, and I struggled to fasten the buttons on my coat.

Hey baby. I might have to ask your Nana Katy to make my coat bigger, somehow. You're beginning to grow, aren't you? She's a whiz with a sewing machine. She made my wedding dress. I can't afford a new coat, especially one I'll only wear for a couple of months. I suppose I might find one at a jumble sale or Paddy's Market. I wonder if you'll like jumble sales? Angela, Debbie and I are addicted to them. We're going to take Einna to one soon. Somehow, I don't imagine she's ever been to a jumble sale. Pearl wouldn't have allowed any jumble sale clothes in the house. I don't think she and John are as strapped for cash as we are; John must be further up the incremental scale than I. But… well it's also the fun of the bargain hunt.

Trevor and I managed quite well on my salary; teachers were not well paid. But then we had got used to having very little when I was a student. There was no money left at the end of a month for luxuries, and we rarely bought expensive meat or fish. I was considering whether to buy liver, cod for a fish pie, or vegetables for a vegetarian crumble, as Trevor hadn't told me what he wanted to cook for our evening meal, when I noticed an old man, shuffling along the pavement in his pyjamas. He looked blue with cold. What surprised me was, that people passing by were ignoring him. I touched his arm, hoping he wouldn't be too surprised. He didn't jump. He merely stopped his shuffle and looked at me.

"You're not from the hospital, are you?" he said.

"No. Were you hoping I was? Are you lost, Mr…?"

"No. I'm going home. I told them yesterday I wanted to go home."

"And they said, no?"

He nodded. "They said I could go home when I was better. I am better. I don't think I was ever ill."

"Well you will be if we don't get you somewhere warm, the wind's perishing, Mr…?"

"My home's warm."

"I tell you what, we'll pop into the bakers. I've got to buy a loaf of bread. It's lovely and warm in there." I could ask Mrs Murray to phone the hospital. By now, I wasn't sure if he'd forgotten his name, or didn't want to tell me.

Mrs Murray, church goer that she was – I knew this because I'd heard her talking to another customer, a fellow parishioner of St Stephens, about the vicar's sermons – said, "I don't want him in here. He smells. It'll put customers off."

"So this is what Christian charity looks like it, does it? If he dies of pneumonia, you will be partly culpable." I said, wondering if Mrs Murray knew the meaning of the word? "You'll smell like him, one day. We all will. It's an old age smell. I shan't be buying bread from here any more." I hoped she wouldn't say that I wouldn't put her out of business if I didn't, for we only bought two loaves a week.

I took the man's arm. "Look, I can't keep calling you 'man'. I'm going to call you Albert. You suit Albert. Is that okay?" He didn't reply. I took off my coat and draped it around his shoulders.

"Ta, queen," he said.

By the time we'd tried three more shops I was shivering. We received similar responses in each one. The milk of human kindness wasn't much in evidence in Allerton Road that afternoon.

Is it worth trying our bank? The manager seems like a kind man. Oh give it a go, Maggie. Trevor won't like it if we have to change banks as well as shops, but… We went in.

"This isn't my home, queen," said the man I'd called Albert. His and my teeth were chattering.

"I know it isn't. I'm hoping they will telephone the hospital for us and—"

"I don't need no hospital, girl."

"Well, maybe they'll send an ambulance to take you home. Please," I said to a young woman at the counter, "could Albert—"

"Who's Albert?" said the man. "My name's Henry."

Ah. I still thought he looked like an Albert. "Please, could I leave Henry here, in the warm, while I run to the hospital—"

"What, Sefton General?" said the young woman, not wrinkling her nose in disgust. "I can't have you doing that, not in your condition."

Normally that would have annoyed me. What was my 'condition'? I was pregnant, not ill. But today, no. I was happy to accept whatever she was planning to do.

She disappeared for a moment, then returned and let herself out from behind the counter. She was carrying a chair. "You sit down, Henry. Goodness me, you're frozen. I won't be a mo." She disappeared again, then came back with a rug. "My car rug," she said. "I'm going to put the kettle on and phone the hospital. You sit there by the radiator." She wrapped the rug round Henry's shoulders and gave me back my coat. "Here," she said. "You'd better put this back on. You look perished as well. Tea or coffee?"

"Are you sure it will be okay with Mr Jamieson?"

"He'll be fine as long as I make him one too. I'll phone the hospital while the kettle's boiling. Luckily we aren't inundated with customers at the moment. Perhaps they poked their noses out of their front doors and were blown back inside by the wind."

"It wasn't as bad when I got off the bus," I said.

A few minutes later she appeared with two steaming cups of tea and a plate of ginger biscuits. "They said thirty minutes. You getting a bit warmer, Henry?"

Henry nodded, his mouth full of ginger crumbs. "This is a nice place you've brought me to," he mumbled. "And you make a nice cuppa, queen."

When the ambulance arrived, Henry greeted the driver as though he were a long lost friend. "He's always doing this," the driver said. "It's a wonder he hasn't caught his death before now. You cost the NHS a pretty penny, don't you, Henry?"

Later, when I related the story to Trevor, he said, "I'm glad you told those prejudiced bigots what you thought. We'll use the shops up the Rose Lane end from now on. Fish and chips for our evening meal it is, then?"

"Great, if you get them. I've not yet defrosted, and I'm whacked."

"Is that the wobbly bottom lip I see?"

"Yes, it bloody well is."

"You won't be able to swear in front of the sprog, Maggie."

"I know. I've got to get all my swearing out the way before May. Shall we call the baby—"

"No, if you're going to say Henry. If it's a boy, I'd like to call him Stuart. Your dad—"

I frowned. "My dad's name is Percy, you know that."

"I thought his second name was Stuart? It would be a bit old fashioned to have a kid named Percy, today. But Stuart? Yes, I like Stuart."

Of course my dad's second name was Stuart. How could I have forgotten that?

"And Derek after my grandfather. If it's a girl, Alice after my mum and Louise after your gran."

"Your mum's name is Katy."

"Katy Alice. I prefer Alice to Katy."

Even though I'm not having a say in our baby's name, I'm happy Trevor is participating. It makes it seem as though he does think about the baby, sometimes. Also, I can't help feeling, how sad it is that we both know I wouldn't want a daughter named after Edith, and he wouldn't want a son named after the father who had abandoned him, Katy and his sister, Ruth.

He went to the door. "Can we afford fish and chips?" I asked.

He fished in his pocket. "Yes."

"That's a relief. I know it's not far to the chippy, Trevor, but you'd better put your coat on or you'll perish."

"You know I don't feel the cold, bossy boots."

Later, as we were eating our meal, he said, "You haven't forgotten it's the concert this Friday, have you?"

"As if. We're all coming."

"All?"

I reeled off the names. "Leila and Mac, Angela and Dave, Debbie and Bill, Kate and Molly, my dad. Sophie is going to stay with Debbie's parents for the weekend, so Bill and Debbie can decorate the third bedroom for her. The baby will have her old room."

Trevor ran his fingers through his hair, a habit of agitation. "Lucky them. Are you going to mention the concert to Einna?""

"Do you think I should?"

"Up to you. She's a musician, isn't she?"

"A violinist. But not a pro."

"But she knows about music."

"I guess so."

"I think I'd like her to come. Her opinion could be really useful. I bet none of your other friends like the music. You don't, not really."

"I've always been honest, haven't I? I prefer music that's more tuneful. But I can appreciate it, especially your more dramatic compositions, like The Liverpool Symphony. And they're your friends too, Trevor."

"I think of them as your friends and mine by default."

The piece we were going to hear was a concerto called, *So You Think You're Not Racist* and the bits I'd heard him trying out on the piano did sound dramatic. "Is the orchestra playing the Liverpool Symphony as well as your new piece?"

"No. The concert's not just my music; I'm sure I told you that?"

"A pity. I love that one. You should dedicate the concerto to the shopkeepers on Allerton Road."

He laughed. "I would if it wouldn't offend all the ones who wouldn't have behaved like that. And they weren't being racist, were they? More smellist."

"I bet they're racist as well. But I doubt they'd come to a concert of contemporary music. Is that 'ist'?"

Trevor shrugged. "I suppose it might be. It's true though."

Leila and Mac had to go straight home after the concert; their babysitter could only stay until nine-thirty. The rest of us went into town for a Chinese meal: Dave and Angela's treat because they'd had a small win on the pools. John didn't want to accept their hospitality because he'd only just met them. Angela told him not to be so English.

"You'll know us by the end of the evening. And Einna knows us. We'll have a banquet, I've never had one before."

None of us had. The restaurant served it with pots of jasmine tea, which they kept replenishing. The men had beer as well.

We alcohol free women failed to notice the effect we were having on our men. As the meal progressed, we got louder, and despite alcohol, they got quieter. Soon we were laughing with tears in our eyes. Einna, Debbie and I had to escape to the ladies; the late pregnancy bladder effect.

"What a lovely end to the evening," I said to Trevor, as we were getting ready for bed.

"You and your friends are very loud when you're all together. You're like an unruly gang, a monstrous regiment of women. John Knox would have been terrified of you, even though it was Queens he was referring to rather than the whole female sex. I suppose he must have meant Mary, Queen of Scots and Elizabeth, Queen of England."

"I wonder if that's where calling women 'queens' in Liverpool, comes from? Some comic knew about the monstrous regiment and why John Knox used the phrase. I gather you used it, not intending to be complimentary?"

"Cap fits, Maggie? We men couldn't get a word in edgeways."

"Okay, we may have been a bit loud," *Why do I want to mollify him? Is Debbie mollifying Bill? Is Angela mollifying Dave?* I changed the subject. "I thought the concerto was very dramatic, Trevor."

He decided to accept the change. "It went well. Max told me the musicians enjoyed playing it."

"That's good after the fractious rehearsals you had sometimes. Do you think they'll commission another piece?"

"I hope so. The fee I got will buy a playpen."

"A playpen?" Caged animals, that's what came to mind. But I wasn't going to be looking after our child.

"Well we won't need that yet, and we can go to *Babe* when we do." *Babe* was a nearly new shop aimed at parents-to-be.

I still found it difficult to picture us with a baby and wondered if all first time mums felt as I did. It didn't seem right to include first time dads, as I suspected that Trevor wasn't a normal father-to-be. We had seemed complete, as a couple. How would we be as a threesome?

When I thought about the actuality of our baby, one image kept recurring in my mind. It was of he or she in a pram in the garden, gazing up at the dappling light through the Rowan Ash leaves. Ours was a ground-floor flat, and we had use of the garden, such as it was, a path, some grass – you couldn't call it a lawn – and a Rowan Ash tree. It was a utility garden, useful for the washing, and a baby in a pram.

Einna had her baby, Claire, two weeks before 'sprog' was born; that is what I called the baby when it began to kick. John's mum, May, was present at Claire's birth. John, unlike Trevor, said he couldn't face it. Ten days after my due date I was still as big as a hippo, and fed up with flatulence and nights interrupted by sprog's dance.

By now, Einna had become a fixed member of the monstrous regiment of women. We had chattered and giggled our way through the remaining months of our pregnancies, both of us burgeoningly healthy.

Einna had Claire at home. It was beginning to look as though I wouldn't be so lucky.

"If the baby doesn't come by the weekend, Maggie, I'm afraid you'll have to go into hospital to be induced," said Bev.

Words I didn't want to hear. I had set my heart on a natural, home birth. Then, as if answering a prayer, Molly gave me some women's magazines she had finished with. In one there was an article about babies who seemed to want to stay in the safety of the womb. It suggested that you could encourage the birth through a concoction of orange juice, bicarbonate of soda and castor oil. What I failed to read was the dosage: one table spoon. I mixed the ingredients and drank what amounted to the whole bottle, forgetting we had invited the extended gang for dinner. Einna and John brought Claire in her carry-cot. Debbie's parents were minding Sophie.

Trevor had made two vegetable crumbles, one with grated cheddar cheese on top, the other without, in deference to vegan Debbie and Bill. Their crumble topping was made with margarine rather than butter. They were followed by a green salad, and then a rich and creamy rice pudding and fruit salad. Our friends provided wine and beer. Debbie and I drank water. Einna allowed herself half a glass of wine as she was breast feeding. John pulled a face.

As Trevor and I were about to clear away the dishes I had a sharp pain, followed by water trickling down my legs. "Oh god!" I said.

"What's up?" asked Angela.

"My waters have broken, and…" I doubled over as a pain hit me. It wasn't a contraction. I ran for the bathroom.

Later, Einna told me that a study of the faces around the table, would have intrigued any psychiatrist; a variety of emotions were frozen in the moment: disgust, wonder, concern, terror. Trevor seemed paralysed. Einna had to nudge him into action.

"Ring Bev, Trevor," she said. "I'll help Maggie." She also ran into the bathroom.

Angela took over clearing away the dishes and Debbie found a floor cloth and bucket and wiped up the birth water.

Apparently John's face was particularly intriguing. It shifted between horror and wonder; perhaps because he had adamantly refused to take part in Claire's birth, and because his wife had taken charge. Debbie told me this later.

"Tonight, you're a wonderful monstrous regiment," said Trevor as he dialled Bev's number.

"Is there anything I can do?" asked Bill. "I would say, John, Dave and I, but John's looking green around the gills."

"Am I?" said John. "Actually, I'm okay. I can help."

"Hot water, please" said Debbie. "I guess, it would be great if you could finish clearing away, do the washing up and then make tea or coffee. Is that possible?"

"Of course it is," said Bill. "Who'd have thought a dinner party would have turned into a birthing party?"

"I hope you haven't got a D and V virus," said Einna who was kneeling by the loo rubbing my back. Debbie and Angela were now sitting on the edge of the bath. "That would be more than bad luck."

"My birth cocktail, I think." Between bouts of pain and possible contractions I told them what the cocktail had consisted of.

"You dozy woman."

"You daft mare."

"You never cease to amaze me."

My three friends spoke at once.

"God, Maggie. I hope Sprog hasn't slipped out down the loo along with the poo," said Angela. "Hey, a birth poem."

That was it. Giggles engulfed us and soon we were crying with laughter.

"I didn't want to go into hospital," I spluttered.

"Never mind hospital, have you finished pooing?" said Einna.

"I think so. Whoops no. Bloody hell, Einna. I've no idea what's what."

Bev arrived, with a trainee midwife, just as Angela, Debbie and Einna were getting me onto the bed. Debbie had found the birthing pack and put the rubber sheet over the blankets, with a clean white cotton one on top. Then they all, including Trevor, helped me to control my breathing and pushing, which I have to say didn't amount to much, as sprog arrived with a whoosh. Indeed such a whoosh that when I asked the five women and Trevor whether our baby was a boy or a girl, they didn't know.

When everyone but the two midwives had gone home, Trevor picked up our son, Stuart Derek and looked at him properly. "He's... he's... funny. He looks like a miniature you."

"Well thanks," I said, looking at the red, wrinkled baby. "I think he looks like Henry."

"Henry?"

"The escapee from Sefton General. Claire doesn't look like this."

"Nor will Stuart, in a day or two. You'll see," said Bev.

"Ow," I squeaked. "I'm having another contraction. What's going on? I'm not having twins, am I?" At no antenatal had anyone mentioned twins.

Beverly laughed. "Tell Maggie what's happening, Shamira."

"It's your body expelling the afterbirth."

Neither Einna nor Debbie had mentioned follow on pains to expel the afterbirth. But, when I was cleaned up and Trevor handed Stuart to me, I felt a glow starting somewhere deep inside me, the love that turns a woman into a tigress.

"You red, wrinkled darling," I said. I held my other arm out to Trevor and he lay down beside me. The little old man that was Stuart, looked at us both, and I could have sworn he smiled.

Of course Bev was right. In a couple of days the redness and the wrinkles disappeared, as though they'd been ironed away.

"Once upon a time we were two, and now we're three, and I think it's going to be alright," said Trevor.

Chapter Eight
Colditz

Necessity is the mother of invention.

It wasn't so much a battle that was lost and won; when I went back to work in the September, I felt I'd lost and won. I'd won motherhood. I'd lost Trevor. It wasn't immediately apparent, for we were both at home with Stuart and I made sure Trevor had plenty of time for composing. But when my maternity leave finished, Trevor and Stuart were together, on their own and I felt as though I was a piece of elastic, stretched taut between them and school.

Anxiety was my constant state of mind. When I should have been concentrating on a lesson, my thoughts would turn towards my son and husband. I wondered if I'd be faced with a contented man and smiley baby when I got home? The man, because he'd had chunks of time at his disposal. The baby because he was well fed, dry, no nappy rash and no teeth pushing up through tender gums. Or would I see a man and baby, both red cheeked and upset?

I rang every lunch time to check how they were, but as all my women friends said, why? What was I going to do about it? Trevor had to get on with it just as other carer parents, all over the world, who couldn't afford nannies or au-pairs, had to get on with it. But in the nineteen sixties it wasn't usual for a man to be the baby minder. The hopeful composer didn't care that he wasn't the norm, any more than he cared about me being the breadwinner. All he minded was having enough time to compose, arrange and rehearse. The rehearsals were the easiest part of his work to manage as Stuart loved the fuss made of him by the musicians. He also loved the cacophony of sound in the rehearsal.

Occasionally, Einna called round to see Trevor and Stuart, as did Debbie, who had a part-time job at St Paul's school for the blind so she could spend time with Sophie, who was two and Jacob, who was three months. Debbie's parents looked after the children when Debbie was in work. Her energy amazed me. She never seemed tired. I seemed to feel tired all the time. But I was determined to carry on, job, being a wife and mum, and seeing friends. *How do people cope if they have a colicky baby? Stuart's a good baby. Not 'good', Maggie. Remember what your dad told you all those years ago?*

"How's Trevor coping?" I asked my friendly spies.

"Fine," both women said independently.

"Stuart was asleep and Trevor happily working."

"Stuart was outside in his pram, watching leaves dancing in the sunshine."

"Stuart was in the playpen, asleep. Stuart was... Stuart..."

"Please tell your friends not to call round," Trevor said, one day. "It's very nice of them, but it always seems to happen when I've just managed to grab a few moments to myself."

"Surely you're big enough and ugly enough to tell them? They're your friends too."

"Why do you feel the need to say that?"

"Because they are, and you keep saying, 'your friends'."

"It's not relevant to what I'm saying, Maggie. I don't want to be rude to Debbie and Einna. As I said, it's nice of them to call."

"Especially when Einna takes Stuart off your hands." She sometimes took both him and Claire to the park, one each end of the pram.

"Why are you being contentious?"

"I'm frazzled." *As well as tired.* It had been a B3 day. I always felt as though I'd been wrestling in mud on B3 days.

"And you think I'm not?"

We stared at each other.

"I don't want to quarrel, Maggie."

"Nor do I."

Nor did I. I wanted to enjoy being a wife, a mother and a teacher. Was that too much to expect? Perhaps in nineteen sixties Britain, before Germaine Greer had written *The Female Eunuch*, where women were, in the main still considered as housewives and mothers, it was. We were not driving down a road together. We rattled along. And sometimes the rattle was gentle, almost non-existent, at other times it was a destabilising rattle which almost rocked us off the road. Would I have done anything different if I could have seen what was going to happen in 1968 when the tyrannical twos de-stabilised our rattle existence? Who knows? If I had known, would I have asked Edith and my dad to mind Stuart on a more regular basis? I couldn't deny Edith loved Stuart. She had gone quite dewy eyed the first time she'd seen him and hidden it by telling me that pink babygros were for girls.

"Einna gave them to me. Claire's out-grown them. We can't afford new, Mother, and I don't think Stuart knows his colours yet."

"No need to be clever, Margaret." She picked Stuart up.

I just stopped myself telling her to be careful of his head. "Look," she said. "He's smiling at me. He knows I'm his nana." She looked at me with eyes that dared me to say, 'You know it's wind, Mother'.

Envy turned my blood green. As it had been with Ian, so it would be with Stuart and the only way I could prevent it was by not allowing her to see him; not allowing my dad to… That wasn't acceptable. I wanted Stuart to get to know his granddad.

One Friday evening, Angela rang me and suggested that the gang had a day out together and I realised that I hadn't laughed, not knickers' wetting laughter, for months.

"May is going to have Claire," said Angela, because John is playing rugby, of course, and Bill's happy to look after Sophie and Jacob."

"I can't ask Trevor to mind Stuart again. The weekends are the only time he has to himself."

"Your mum and dad?"

My parents? Could I ask my parents? A day out with the gang. Was it worth bending my resolve? Yes.

The pause at the other end of the phone was so long, I thought Edith was going to say 'no'. I learnt later, from my dad, that she was overcome with happiness, but couldn't bring herself to admit it. *Hey Maggie, don't start feeling guilty. Yes you've been punishing her for the way she brought you up, and her negativity towards Trevor, but there are two people in this equation. There are always two. Can I bring myself to say 'thank you' to her?*

The following day, Saturday, we went to Paddy's market. I did wonder if tiredness would prevent me from enjoying our jaunt. But the gang together worked its magic. Tiredness lifted off me like a November the fifth rocket. I bought some red and silver imitation crocodile shoes, with heels as high as Everest. Angela bought some cowboy style boots and a riding crop, Debbie, a rust coloured suede jacket with a fringed hem and Einna a long, black faux Astrakhan coat.

"Why the riding crop?" Debbie asked.

"It's for my mum. She needs to protect herself and Fluff when she's on heat."

"Fluff? Fluff just doesn't sound like a name your mother would choose. Bonzo, Tia, Bruce, Freya, yes. But Fluff?"

"Mum didn't know what to call her. We'd always had Labradors before. We don't even know why she chose a Yorkie. She said, 'It's just a bit of fluff, Alec.' And the name stuck. I'm hungry. Anyone else hungry?"

"You're always hungry," I said. "And you never put on any weight."

We had hot dogs off a 'greasy spoon' stall, except for Debbie – she had brought sandwiches with her – and took the bus into the city centre for the afternoon. It was liberatingly wonderful.

In George Henry Lee's silver service restaurant, where we needed – 'needed' being the operative word – restorative tea, I decided the moment had come for me to ask the gang for advice.

"Before Stuart," I said, sipping proper, leaf tea, "I reckon I was an imaginative teacher. I certainly enjoyed my work. Now, I feel as though I've lost my way. I don't have a problem with the top stream kids. They just get on with things. I can use past lesson plans on them and it doesn't matter, but with a class like B3, I'm floundering."

"You've got to give yourself time," said Debbie.

"I don't feel I've got time," I said, as I took a bite of coffee and walnut cake. "I'm supposed to instil a love of literature in fourteen lads who don't want to read or write because they'd rather be playing football, and sixteen girls who would rather read a woman's magazine than any of the books we're supposed to be reading. I just feel as though they've defeated me."

My friends were sympathetic but couldn't come up with a solution to my problem; really, I shouldn't have expected one.

Perhaps it was the word 'defeat'? Perhaps it was the gang day out, but from that café moment I knew I had to do something dramatic to claim the attention of those pupils. I couldn't let their boyish antipathy and girlish apathy beat me, nor could I blame Trevor and Stuart.

On the way home, on the bus the following Monday, I had an idea. Maybe it was the grey day and the grey tower blocks of the Bluebell Estate that said 'prison camp'? Whatever it was, I felt like dancing down the aisle to kiss the driver.

"You know I've been driven hairless by B3, Trevor?" I said as I bounced into our flat, scooped Stuart out of the playpen and smothered him in kisses.

"I know you've taken B3 out on me and been abjectly sorry afterwards," said Trevor. "As far as I can see you've still got a full head of hair." He did not look up from his score.

Hey, I've just noticed, my menfolk are happy. "You're not even looking at me," I said.

"Give me two minutes and I'll put this away… promise. Tell you what, put the kettle on. Stuart's bottle needs warming up and I need a cuppa. I expect you could do with one, too. Then I'll check to see if you're bald, okay? I bet, that at this very moment, Stuart has his fingers tangled in your mop. Am I right?"

He was. It was part of his 'welcome home Mummy' routine. This was usually followed by demands for a drink and a rusk. When we were sitting on Katy's couch – Katy's because she had given it to us after she'd bought a new one – sipping builder's tea, I told him my idea.

"A prisoner of war camp? That's crazy."

"No, listen. It'll work. I know it will. The boys subvert every lesson and the girls don't say a word. Nothing I prepare pleases them."

"But why escape from Colditz?"

"We're supposed to be reading *The Prisoner Of Zenda*. I thought, if I introduced the idea of prison life, in a different way, they might make more of an effort with the book. Please say you'll help me make the tape."

Stuart dropped his empty bottle on the rug and fell asleep in my lap. He started to make wooffly snoring noises. I laughed. "Oh Trevor, he sounds just like I imagine Tigger would sound. You could tape his baby snores for one of your pieces."

"I might just do that." Trevor stroked his son's head. "He and I have had a good day. This morning he was very happy with his bricks and then his post-box. After lunch, we went shopping and by the time we got back here, he'd fallen asleep in his pushchair, so breadwinner, I've had a productive day. I've drafted one movement of the piece for the string quartet. What do you want on your Colditz tape?"

"Storms, war sounds, and you barking orders in German. You see? Your O-level German will come in useful."

"Not much to ask for a doomed project."

Stuart woke up, stretched in the way of all baby animals. "Down, Mama," he said, wriggling off my lap. He pointed to his train set. "Me crash."

"Why do you want to crash your trains, sweetheart? It's dangerous if trains come off—" It was then I noticed Trevor looking guilty. "What?"

"We practised crashing yesterday."

"Why?"

"Well, I was listening to the sound the trains made on the wooden rails, and Stuart doing his woo-wooing and I suddenly knew that I wanted those sounds in the piece." He shrugged. "It sort of followed on from that." He got up and went over to his tape recorder. "You can listen to a bit, if you like."

He switched it on. The sounds were mesmeric, so much so that I jumped when the crash occurred. It was echoed by Stuart shouting, "Crash," the delight evident in his voice.

"That's brill, Trevor."

"You like it?" Trevor sounded astonished.

"I do as sound effects. Whether I'll like it in a composition… You could do some more taping of train crashes for me."

"Leave it with me. Okay, Tigger, let's set up a track for crashes. It's a good thing his trains are robust."

"Not Tigger," said Stuart.

"Oh yes you are. You're a bouncy Tigger."

When he was noisily engaged in crashing two of his engines, I said, "My classroom is like a prisoner of war camp, as it is. Everything about it is grey."

"Problem, Maggie. There weren't any female prisoners of war in places like Colditz."

"That's the dramatic licence bit. You'll need to sound as if you're barking out orders. If the kids don't obey, they'll be punished, like sitting on the floor with their hands on their heads."

"What makes you think they'll go along with any of it?"

"I don't know. Intuition? They don't have drama, as a lesson, in the school. I just feel they might go for it. If they don't, I'm no worse off, am I?"

Stuart left off crashing his trains, picked up his miffy, an old muslin nappy he used as a comforter and wrapped them up in it. "All better,' he said.

"That sounded just like Molly. Kids learning to talk are little parrots, aren't they?"

"Yes. This is 'be careful' time."

"I don't swear in front of him. I haven't since he was born." Trevor just looked at me. "I haven't."

"Anything you say, Maggie."

"You." I hit him with a cushion.

Stuart looked at us in astonishment, and then shouted, "'Gain."

"In a minute, sweetheart. You and I will both hit Daddy with cushions."

"That's cruelty to composers. Come on, let's explore your idea a bit more."

"It might be better if they have to sit under a table, rather than with their hands on their heads. I shan't speak. I'll just flick a riding crop on my boots. Riding crop, I need a riding crop. I'll ring Angela to see if I can borrow hers. She bought one at Paddy's market, last Saturday. It's for her mum. She needs it to ward off sex starved dogs. I'll borrow her jodhpurs and one of Debbie's brown shirts"

"But a riding crop sounds more like some landed-gentry hunting scene, or a kinky brothel, Maggie."

"Will you stop rubbishing my idea."

"I just want you to think everything through. Especially as you're asking for my help."

"Sorry. Just say yes or no, please. If you say no, I'll have to ask Dave or Bill to make the tape." Then I giggled. I couldn't help it, the thought of soft spoken Bill with his wooly-back accent barking out orders was too silly.

"What?"

"Bill being a German officer."

"I'll do it, but I bet you it won't work."

"A quid?"

"A fiver."

"A fiver? You gambler! That's a week's housekeeping. Oh, okay."

When I rang Angela she said, "You ought to be locked up, not let loose on the innocents of Kirkby. Luckily Whisky's not on heat yet."

"Whisky? I thought your mum's dog was called Fluff?"

"Mum decided she couldn't stand yelling 'Fluff' out the back door when she wanted her to come in, any longer. Dad chose Whisky. Mum calls her Wizzy, because she's so quick on her feet. Mum rang me up yesterday and told me Wizzy's learnt to catch a tennis ball now."

"She sounds a fun dog."

"Yes, at the moment. The Labrador we had when we were kids was disgusting. He was called Shorty; I've no idea why. When he got old he had these running sores all over his legs. Yuk!"

I agreed with Angela. That did sound disgusting. Also the poor dog must have been in pain.

Trevor had a week to sort out the tape and it was amazing, considering he was so doubtful of the success of my project. As well as howling wind and barked orders, he'd added noises that sounded like machine gun fire, and hands running along wire mesh fences. He was so pleased with it, he said he wanted to include it in the piece he'd been composing.

"I thought you'd finished that."

"I said I'd drafted the first movement. I thought you weren't listening. In any case, there's always room for new ideas."

On Colditz Day, I didn't go to the staffroom at break. I transformed the classroom into a prison camp. I upended the tables to form a wall, keeping one aside. I put it in a corner. It would serve as solitary confinement. I stacked the chairs into a tower on one end of the table wall. Then I set up the tape and waited.

The lads bounded in first, riot alight in their faces. The girls slouched in. As soon as they saw me they stopped, 'what's this?' plain in their eyes. I let the tape speak for me. Through the howling wind, I and they heard, 'Achtung! Get in line, now!'.

The girls put their bags by the chair tower and sat, cross legged, on the floor, almost as though they knew this was their allotted place. There were whispers and shrugs. I was beginning to think I'd lost the bet; another failure.

"Miss, what's the uniform, Miss?" said one of the girls.

The others shushed her. I didn't reply.

"Nazi," said a boy. "That's what she looks like."

"I don't think so. I think she looks like a meff."

They stared at me. I stared back. Then, the lads went into a huddle. I tapped the whip on the side of one boot. There was a hum of whispering under the variety of sounds Trevor had created. One lad broke away from the group and ran over to the cupboard in the corner. He opened the door, and rummaged about. I wondered what he was hunting for. While my attention was on him, the rest of the boys rushed me and grabbed my arms.

"You'll be for it," said one of the girls.

Her name was Mandy. She was an unusual girl, but not a victim, a loner. Her parents were elderly and she was their only child.

"We're not allowed to get hold of teachers."

"Shut it, Meff," said a lad called Jonno.

"I'm not a meff," said Mandy. "Just because I go to Mrs Melia to get me reading better, doesn't make me a meff. Bet I can read better than you, now."

"Get you later, Meff."

"No you won't, 'cause you'll be in Tommo's room."

Tommo was the Headmaster, Mr Thompson.

"Found some," yelled the lad in charge of the cupboard search. He ran over with a ball of thick string. "Eh, youse lot, the frigging cupboard's almost empty. I reckon we should put Miss in it, don't you?" He grinned.

I very nearly dropped my chosen role to admonish him for swearing and to tell him it really wasn't a good idea. I managed not to. It could be said that swearing was part of the drama and therefore allowed. As for binding me hand and foot and shutting me in a cupboard, I didn't believe they would actually do it.

"Brill!" said Terry Bailey, nickname, Tegsy.

"Don't be fucking idiots," said Jonno. "Meff's right. We'd get sent to Tommo. We'd get expelled and me dad would kill me. We'll tie her hands behind her back and then…" He looked around. "You, Nazi, sit on the floor." I obeyed. "And you, Tegsy, tie her feet to a table leg. Are there any rags or anything in that cupboard, Scotty?"

Scotty went back to the cupboard. "Yeh," he yelled. "There's a mingy scarf. Will that do?"

"Boss." Jonno blindfolded me with it. It did stink, a bit, but mainly of being stuffed in a cupboard for goodness knows how long.

"Youse lot are off your trolleys if you think Tommo won't go mad," said Mandy. The other girls giggled.

This wasn't the plan that had been fizzing in my mind ever since I'd got the idea. However, it was drama, a drama they were controlling. And even if they didn't then enjoy reading *The Prisoner Of Zenda*, I reckoned I might be able to squeeze some creative writing out of some of them.

"Youse lot," I heard one lad say. "Give us ten, then you can free her, if you want."

Ten to do what? Make some sort of tunnel?

I heard the sound of scraping chairs, footsteps and a door closing, then silence, except for Trevor's tape.

Wow, they've escaped from Colditz. Is that good? Possibly not. Pupils weren't allowed to roam the school during lessons. Could I free myself? I was sitting on my tied hands. My feet? I couldn't move my feet. Someone was good at knots.

Thoughts tumbled about in my head, each one dismissed and left lying in a heap. Yell for help? Would anyone hear, and if they did, how stupid would I look? Where had the class gone? It was that thought that kept tripping me up leaving me winded, for too late I remembered the note in my pigeon hole about the feud with St Austin's. *'On no account let pupils leave the school premises.'* On no account... That's what had happened, hadn't it? They hadn't just escaped from Colditz. They'd escaped from the school to terrorise pupils from St Austin's. *Oh god!* If I could have put my head in my hands, I would have done.

How long would it be before someone missed me? Lunch time? All day? Would everyone go home at the end of the day, leaving me alone with the ghosts? One of the cleaners would find me. Frank, the caretaker would find me. *Help! Please don't let Frank find me.*

I'd be disciplined. I might get the sack. No, not the sack. I read somewhere that a teacher could only get the sack for having sex with a pupil, consensual or rape, or falsifying the register.

"Miss," I heard a whisper. It wasn't the wind on the tape, was it? I did hear someone whisper, 'Miss', didn't I?

"Are you okay, Miss? I think the ten minutes is up, Miss."

"Who's that?" I whispered back. *Why am I whispering?*

"Mandy, Miss."

Oh, thank goodness. Mandy may have to go to Miss Melia for reading, but she's a sensible girl. It's a pity the education system doesn't rate common sense. "Can you untie me please, Mandy?"

"Yes, Miss. I'll try. I'm not that good at untying knots, Miss, but I'll have a go".

Hearts do sink. Mine was pushing its way through the lino tiles. "Okay. If you can manage to loosen the string, I might be able to do the rest."

"I'll take your blindfold off first, Miss. Then, if I do your feet Miss, you'll be able to stand. and I can have a look at your hands, Miss. Can you bend your head please, Miss?"

She whipped off the scarf. Then it seemed like an age before she managed to untie the string binding my feet to a table leg. That left my hands.

"The knots are really tight, Miss. I can't get them undone."

"Tell you what, Mandy. There are scissors in my bag. You can cut the string."

"Pupils aren't allowed to go into teachers' bags Miss."

"This is an emergency Mandy. I'm giving you permission."

String cut, I rubbed my wrists.

"That was good, wasn't it, Miss? Didn't I do well? I like Bruce Forsythe, Miss."

"Have the lads gone out of the school grounds, Mandy?"

"What would they do that for, Miss? They've gone to play footy, Miss and the girls are having a smoke in the toilets."

"How do you know?"

She shrugged. "It's what they do, Miss."

"And you didn't want to go with them?"

"No, Miss. They're not me friends, Miss. Megan's me best friend, Miss. She's in Miss Melia's group with me, Miss."

"So they're definitely still in school."

"Yes, Miss. They seem like big bullies, Miss, but they're not really. They just act big. They'd be dead scared they'd get caught. You can't get out the school gates without being seen, Miss."

Of course they would have been seen. What a Madam Panic I am, and how sensible Mandy is. "But they'll have been seen on the field."

"No one takes no notice of boys on the field, Miss. There are always boys playing footy. It's all they ever do, isn't it, Miss?"

She was right. I wouldn't think it was unusual to see lads playing football.

So, should I round them up? No, someone would, in all probability, notice that. But I could explain it away by saying I'd sent them out for a game as part of the lesson. Would anyone believe me? I'd often moaned about B3 in our staffroom.

The door of the classroom opened. The girls slouched in. "You freed her," said Julie Morris.

"Yes," said Mandy.

"Why?"

"Cause Jonno said to, after ten."

That seemed to floor Julie. "Are we in trouble, Miss?"

How ought I to play this? "Well—"

"It's what prisoners do, innit Miss? They try to escape. I saw a film about it, once," said Mandy.

"And play footy?" Julie sounded scathing.

"Yeh. They had to play footy for exercise."

"Go the bogs to—"

Surely she's not going to admit to smoking. "That's enough, Julie. I'm not going to punish anyone. All you were doing was participating in the drama."

Julie looked as though she would like to say that going to the toilets for a fag wasn't joining in anything. But she couldn't. Instead she said, "Why didn't you escape then, Mandy?"

"In the film, one prisoner got hurt. I wanted to be him."

"I bet he didn't free a German guard."

"No. But the prisoners in the film didn't capture a guard neither,' said Mandy. "We was pretending, wasn't we, Miss?"

"Yes, and I think we all pretended very well. Anyway, I'm glad you came back before the end of the lesson, I wanted to have a chat about how you—"

"Shall I go and get the boys, Miss?"

I looked at the classroom clock. There was fifteen minutes to the bell. "Thank you Julie. That would be helpful."

"Can I go too, Miss?" It was Paula, Julie's shadow.

"No, Paula. Off you go Julie."

"Are you going to put them in detention, Miss?" said Mandy.

"No. In next week's lesson, there'll be reprisals."

"What's them, Miss?" asked Paula.

"Getting back at someone and punishing them."

"Can I be a guard, Miss?" asked Lorraine Murphy.

I couldn't believe it, it wasn't just taking off, it was flying Not in the way I'd planned, but… stuff *The Prisoner of Zenda*. We'd write our own story. I'd encourage the girls to be guards in control of punishments. The following week I'd start with the boys' capture. In they bounced, full of bravado.

Before they had a chance to say anything, Paula said, "Miss isn't going to punish youse."

"Of course not," I said. "You did what prisoners do. It was brilliant." The lads looked totally nonplussed. "In a minute or two, we'll put the classroom back to normal. Next week you can set it up. You might have better ideas as to how a prisoner of war camp would look."

"We're going to do it again next week, Miss?" said Jonno.

"Yes, but not the escape part. We're going to do the bit that follows it. What punishment do you think the guards would give?"

"There's only one guard, Miss: you."

"There will be other guards next week, won't there girls?"

"Yeh," said Lorraine. "We'll be dead bad guards."

"Executions," said a lad called Steve. "We'd be put up against a wall and shot."

"My granddad told me about prisoners playing footy with the German guards," said Jonno.

"It's a lesson we all need to learn. Ordinary people don't necessarily want to fight ordinary people from other countries. They're made to by those in power."

"I bet lots of Germans didn't want to fight, did they, Miss? I'd like to be a German guard," said Julie. "I've got a German-pen friend. I shall be a nice guard."

As more girls clamoured to be Germans, nice and nasty, the bell for school dinner went and a 'wow' hit me in the face. No one rushed for the door. They were in charge and ideas were bouncing off the walls. I almost had to push them out of the classroom. *That'll teach you to have no faith in my ideas, Trevor.* But his tape was wonderful, so I'd treat us to several bottles… No, we'd treat Leila and Rob to an evening at their local.

"See you at the gala, Miss," said Julie.

Gala? Oh no! The bloody swimming gala. In the excitement of preparing for Colditz, I'd forgotten the swimming gala and the ritual of staff being pushed into the pool, fully clothed.

"Yes, Julie." *Can I wriggle out of it?* No. Mr Thompson demanded full attendance from his staff on occasions like this.

Later that day, during afternoon break, Clem approached me. "Did I see some B3 lads out on the field when they should have been with you, Maggie?"

Shit! I might have known, 'see everything Clem' would have noticed. "You did, Clem," I said as nonchalantly as I could. "It was part of the drama we were engaged in on the theme of escape."

"You oughtn't to—"

"Don't be so stuffy, Clem. Trust is what these kids need."

"Yes, well, we don't all think like that. You haven't forgotten the swimming gala after school, have you?"

"Yes, I had, so I haven't got a change of clothes. Bit of a bore going home on the bus, sopping wet, but I expect my mac will—"

"I can give you a lift, if you like?"

I looked at him in surprise. One moment stuffy as a shut up room, the next helpful.

"Thank you. That would be great."

"Don't want you catching your death."

Another shock. Clem sounded almost normal. "Perhaps you could ask Frank for a bin-bag for my car seat?"

"Of course." *Not on his life! I'll ask Lorraine.* Lorraine cleaned the staffroom. When I took drama club, we had a cup of tea and a chat. It had been agreed that my dad would pick up Stuart on drama club days, after he'd finished work. I collected him about seven. It gave Trevor a couple of baby free hours and my parents some regular Stuart time. He loved them both. They loved him. I couldn't fault Edith's love, even though I had to put up with her knowing what was right for him.

We were the only school in Kirkby where, a) there was a swimming pool and b) the staff were pushed in. It was a once a term event for each house. Those pupils who had taken part in the gala, had the 'pushing' honour. I'd been warned about the ritual by Susan, a member of the PE staff who also taught some dance.

"Bring in some old clothes," she'd advised.

"Why does Mr Thompson allow it?"

"It's all part of his 'humane face of teaching' idea."

"But someone like Clem would never be seen as a normal human by the kids." *The staff find it difficult enough. But to do him justice, he does allow himself to be thrown in.*

There we were, thirty of us, waiting to be pushed in, and who had I drawn out of the hat? For yes, our names were put into a hat and the winners of the various events drew them out: Johnno. The grin on his face seemed to me to shout 'power'. I was wrong. If one can be pushed respectfully into a pool, I was, for Johnno whispered, "You can jump, Miss. I'll pretend to push you. Ta for a brill lesson. You're boss, Miss."

In the changing room, I squeezed as much water as I could out of my clothes, tipped my make-up into my bag and stuffed my bra and pants into my make-up bag. Susan knocked on my cubicle door.

"You can't go home in wet clothes, Maggie. You'll catch your death. I bet they'd have something you could use in lost property."

All I could think was, *fleas*. "I think I'll pass, Susan. I shan't catch my death. Clem's offered me a lift."

"Well, if you're sure. I guess people never cease to surprise."

I didn't know whether she was referring to me, or Clem."

Clem's car was a surprise, a black E-Type Jaguar. I'd had him down as a Ford Cortina man.

"Where do you live, Clem?" I asked as we pulled out of the school gates.

"Mosseley Hill."

"Not far from me, then."

"I was wondering if you'd like to stop off at mine for a cuppa. Sybil's not back till later, she's working late and…"

Why is he telling me his wife will be out? "Thanks. I'd rather get home and get out of these wet clothes. You could have a cuppa at mine, if you like?" I didn't tell him Trevor would be there.

"Thank you, that would be nice. I've never told you, Maggie, in lots of ways you're a breath of fresh air. It's just that, sometimes, you don't seem to understand the necessity for school rules. I know you can't lead a horse to water, and all that, but school rules are there for a purpose."

"I agree."

"You do?"

"I do, if they're concerned with safety or respect."

He put his hand on my knee. "Well, outside school it's different, isn't it? Sybil and I are going through a bit of a rough patch, and…"

Creep! This is why he offered me a lift and asked me round for a cuppa. I pushed his hand away.

"When I saw you in those boots, Maggie…"

I glanced down. Clem had an erection. "I'm not going to have sex with you, Clem, if that's what you're hoping."

"I know what happened, Maggie. I had a free period and, when I saw the lads on the field, I went to speak to them: my duty, you see. Mr Thompson… I could forget about it if…" He replaced his hand on my leg.

116

I wanted to slap his lecherous face, but it would have been dangerous. "You can pull over and let me out, Clem. I'll get the bus the rest of the way."

"But…"

"There are no 'buts'. You can't take me back to yours and rape me, because I won't get out of the car. You could drive somewhere, I suppose, but I'd tell the whole world. Frankly, I don't care what you tell Mr Thompson. I'm going to have a chat with him about what happened. It turned into a very special lesson, you see. I'm proud of it."

"I…" He started sobbing. He managed to drive the car over to the kerb. "I'm sorry, Maggie. I don't know what came over me. I'm so lonely, you see. No one likes me. Sybil doesn't like me. I don't know why she agreed to marry me. She's not working late. She's left me, and…" His whole body was shaking with misery. "She's taken the children. I get to see them every other weekend."

"Oh, Clem, I'm so sorry. It's not true no one likes you. You could… " *He could what?* It was true. Clem would have had to change his whole personality for 'like' to grow. "I think you need a hug, not sex; a hug and a cuppa, eh? You got a hanky or a tissue?" He shook his head. I fumbled in my bag. "Here. Dry your eyes and blow your nose." *God, I sound like a mother. I am a mother. Yes, but not his mother.* "Can you drive now?" He nodded. "Good, I'm desperate to get out of these things." I wasn't, but I thought doing every-day practical things might help Clem to compose himself. He wasn't going to find it easy to assume his former role of a senior member of staff after this emotional collapse. I knew that I would have to help in this; act as though it hadn't happened, perhaps?

"Clem's given me a lift home," I shouted to an empty flat as I let us both in. "Oh, they're not here. Never mind. Make yourself at home, Clem. I'll put the kettle on, then I'll change."

There was a note by the kettle. *'Gone to the shops and the park. Got to think.'*

Chapter Nine
Munster Mansion

Never go to bed on an argument.

After Clem left, apologies dripping from his still teary eyes, I tried to come up with a reason for Trevor having written 'Got to think'.

Usually, when I came home, Stuart was either curled up asleep on the sheepskin rug or playing with whatever toys had taken his fancy. Angela and Dave had given him the rug for his first birthday. It was his favourite snuggle place which was lucky, as Trevor rarely remembered to pop him in his cot. And really, it didn't matter, as long as both my males were content with how they organised their time and what they did when I wasn't with them.

When they did come home, I could tell, immediately, that today had been very different from yesterday; more like the day before, in fact. Stuart's face was red and grumpy, Trevor's full of resignation. *But wait, Maggie, there's something else: determination. Why determination? I'm not sure I like determination. Determination in relation to what? Determination re our modus operandi? I bet it's something to do with that.* What else would produce the set look of Trevor's lips? There was some plan afoot. I could feel it. And the feeling wasn't comfortable.

"Tea?" I took Stuart out of his pushchair and escaped with him to the kitchen. He wriggled in my arms.

"Down, Mummy," he said.

"No cuddles?"

In an almost perfunctory manner, he laid his cheek next to mine for a second. It was hot. *More teeth?*

"Bicky, Mummy."

"Please."

"Peas."

I set him down and gave him a drink and a rusk. Stuart loved Ovaltine rusks. So did I. I wasn't sure whether I bought them for him, or me. He toddled back into the 'everything' room and climbed up onto the couch beside Trevor.

"Daddy push swings," he shouted.

"What a nice Daddy," I said as I carried through two mugs of tea. Stuart nodded and then shook his head. I looked at Trevor.

"When I told him it was time to go home, he had a tantrum. I had to squash him into his chair."

"Did you try the 'one more go' trick?"

"What do you think, Maggie?"

Oh, oh. Tiptoeing time. Diversion tactic needed. I launched into my saga.

"Not yet, Maggie. There's something we need to talk about."

Failed. I might as well hear the worst. Why do I know it's going to be something I won't like? I took a deep breath and held it. If what he wanted to tell me was too nasty, I could always go blue in the face and faint. *Drama queen!*

"That son of ours hasn't given me a moment's peace all day, so I've decided to accept the post at the tech. I mailed the letter in Allerton Road this afternoon."

It is the worst, and it's fait accompli.

"I know you didn't want me to but I can't go on looking after Stuart. He's too demanding. I don't have enough time to work. I shall, this way, and we'll have enough money to pay the nursery fees."

The air gushed with my words. "We've been through all this, Trevor. I can't believe you think teaching at the tech will be less demanding than looking after Stuart. He'll be three next May. In September he goes to nursery school." There was an issue of the fees, but we'd been putting money into a savings account, and both my dad and Katy had offered to help. "I thought we were in agreement on this? You've taken a unilateral decision."

"Yes, I have. I'm sorry Maggie—"

Why is it that people say 'sorry' when they're not? "No you're not."

The row, for that's what it turned into, lasted all weekend. On Sunday afternoon, while Stuart slept, we were still trying to get each other to agree, to see and accept a point of view, to…

It wasn't going to happen. Ever since I'd told Trevor I was pregnant we had been walking side by side on familiar pavements, yet apart. Even as that thought hit me, I wondered about the before, about people generally. Weren't we alone from birth, even with those we loved?

"Why can't you accept I've thought long and hard about this?"

"Have you? And have you thought about what happens to Stuart in April when you start at the tech? I can't give up my job."

"Why not?"

Why not? He had a point. "I—"

"Of course you could, Maggie. With me in full time employment, we'd be no worse off than we are now. But you don't have to. When I said I'd thought things through, I meant it. I've been to see the person who runs the Nursery School. Stuart can start in April." He looked at me triumphantly. "And, with both of us working, your dad and Katy won't need to help with the fees."

It was true. But his look of triumph infuriated me. "Just because you had a bad day on—"

"It's not just Friday, Maggie. There are now more difficult days than there are peaceful ones. It's not Stuart's fault. He's a demanding toddler with all a toddler's needs. I'm a composer, still trying to get onto the second rung of the musical world. Yes, I've got a small reputation here in Liverpool, but I want to have a national profile. I can't escape his noise or demands in this flat. I can't, in other words, compose. I think Stuart is ready for a more social life. I think he'll thrive in Nursery School. You know all this. Why are you making me say it again?"

"But it's not totally true. There are days when I come home and you've managed to do a lot of work. Thursday, for example. And what about when he has his afternoon sleep? You're always..." I nearly said 'plink-plonking', "...working when I come home. Then there's the weekends? I look after Stuart at weekends." *On my own. And I love looking after him. So, Maggie, why don't you want to be a full-time carer of the baby you so wanted? Because, woman, you also love teaching and you're just beginning to feel you've got to grips with it.*

"I can't compose to order. That's not the way art works."

I saw his point of view, but not his way of solving the problem. It didn't make sense. How would doing a demanding job give him more time for composing? How would snatching moments at work, at home, not be working to order? And what time would be left for Stuart and me? He'd only got to wait until... we were going round and round in circles.

"This is effing rubbish, Trevor. None of what you're saying makes sense. Teaching will drain you. You've seen what I'm like some days, and you don't have my energy. You mark my words, you won't be doing any composing, let alone your duty as a dad and husband. Stuart and I will have to play dead bears at weekends, I suppose?" Another impossibility snaked its way into my head. "You may have persuaded the nursery school to let Stuart start in April, but he'll only be there for half the day."

"Then you'll have to ask at your school if you can go part-time, do just mornings. You wanted a baby, I didn't, remember? I never hid from you that music, composing, came first. But... until now, Maggie, I've done my best to support you: at college, being a baby-minder, haven't I?"

It was true. I'd fallen in love with a composer. I'd even defended him against Edith's criticisms. But his saying it so baldly was like a punch in the guts. I hurt. I felt sick. I would have to give up full-time teaching. There didn't seem to be an alternative. I kept hearing his words, honest, cruel words, and nothing I could think would make them go away. Irony. I could have imposed Edith's person onto Trevor, for they would have been in agreement.

"Anyway, it's done and can't be undone."

"Of course it can. You write another letter, or you phone them."

He didn't reply He got up and went into the bedroom. I heard a drawer opening. He came back with some A4 sheets in his hands and thrust them at me.

It was the details of a house for sale; a monstrous house with a turret. It looked like the Munster's house.

"You're not serious are you? The mortgage will be far more than we can afford, even with two wages."

"Just have a look at the details. It's in Huyton."

"Huyton?"

"Don't say it like that. There's nothing wrong with Huyton. It's Harold Wilson's constituency."

"Huyton's in Knowsley, not Liverpool."

"That's childish, Maggie."

It was. I knew it was. "I like Lark Lane and Seffy Park."

"So do I. But there's nothing we can afford, here. I've made an appointment to see it next Friday, after you get in from work."

I felt as though I was being bullied, something I hadn't felt since I'd left my childhood home. Bullying wasn't, or hadn't been a part of Trevor's and my relationship. "I thought you said you'd sorted the nursery here? What do we do about that if we move to Huyton, eh?" The negatives in his plan were piling up around me.

"There are nurseries in Huyton, Maggie."

"Good ones? We like the one we've found? He could be uprooted, just after he's settled."

"Don't be like this, please. Looking isn't a decision."

"Isn't it? Why do I feel it is? It couldn't be because the other adult in this room has already done something without consulting me, could it?"

"Maggie," he shouted. Stuart jumped in his sleep. "Maggie," he said more quietly. "Please, stop it. Do you think your mum and dad would mind Stuart while we go to look at the house?"

I wanted to say 'no'. I didn't want to look at the big, ugly house I'd seen in the photo. I wanted to close my eyes and replay Friday; change it into a day where no husband had accepted a job that would sap his energy and make him into someone other than the man I'd married; no house for sale in Huyton, no swimming gala and no Clem Roberts. The only thing I'd keep would be the surprising lesson, which Trevor still hadn't asked about.

"I'll sound them out. But I'm not going to pretend I think it's a good idea, and I'm not going to pretend I like the ugly house, if I don't."

"Okay, but please look at the details, Maggie. The Old Vicarage has got huge potential."

I picked up the stapled sheets and read aloud: "Ground floor; two reception rooms, study, cloakroom. Basement; kitchen, utility room. First floor; four bedrooms, bathroom. Attic; two further bedrooms, bathroom." I knew, without asking him, what Trevor was envisaging up there: a music studio where he would be cushioned from toddler and Maggie noise. The kitchen and a utility room were in the basement. *Great!* You either had to eat in the kitchen or have tepid food in the dining room. Oh, there was a dumb-waiter. *La-de-da.*

The following Friday, after a week of polite distance, something neither Trevor nor I had experienced before, we dropped Stuart off at my parents' house. My dad had offered to lend us his car to save time. All the way there, I kept my fingers crossed that it wouldn't suit. I had nicknamed The Old Vicarage, 'Munster Mansion', for it reminded me of gothic horror houses.

Of course I'd bored my friends with my woes.

"Huyton's not that far from civilisation," said Angela.

"Will we have to have a passport?" asked Leila.

"Men!" sighed Einna.

"Trevor won't make an offer for it unless you like it too. He's not like that," said Debbie.

But Trevor was like that… now, and I couldn't get rid of his words, words said in anger, yes; but his truth, and so help me, mine too. I could not deny the truth of those words. 'You chose, Maggie.' You chose.

Had I? Had I been alone in that room when Stuart was conceived? No, so how was it right that I should pay now? But, to be fair, I had wanted to have my cake and eat it. Not only was Colditz day the day that threw my domestic life up in the air so high I couldn't catch the pieces; it was also the day that showed me I could teach kids who didn't want to be in school, didn't want to be taught. I still wanted to be a mum *and* a teacher.

"Hey! Did you hear what I said?"

"Sorry. Yes. You said Trevor wasn't like that."

"I thought you weren't listening. I said I can look after Stuart on the afternoons I don't work. I'll collect him, then my two."

"What? Did I hear you galloping to my rescue just now?"

"You did."

"Guess what, friend? I feel forgiven for my magic mushroom trespasses," I said.

"Der, idiot," she replied. "You'll be doing Jacob and I a favour. To use one of your expressions, Sophie loves the bones of Stuart and will stop tormenting Jacob while he's with us."

Three afternoons were sorted in the nick of time. I would not be handing in my notice. I gave her a hug.

Again I decided to eat humble pie. I asked Edith and Dad if they could have Stuart for the other two afternoons. Sadly, we couldn't involve Katy. She was a lovely granny, but not a confident driver any more. I found it odd, because she wasn't old. Whatever it was, it would have been unfair on her and us to ask her to pick Stuart up and bring him to our flat. She couldn't have taken him to Crosby as we didn't have a car to collect him. Mum's face was a picture of someone at war with herself. I suspected she wanted to 'my girl' me with clichés like, 'you made your bed, now you must lie in it'. That she didn't, showed how much she wanted to spend time with her grandson. One of the days was drama club day. My dad already picked him up that afternoon. Stuart had fish fingers, baked beans and chips followed by Angel Delight for tea, which he loved.

"And when will all this begin?" asked Edith.

"After Easter," I said. "When Trevor starts his job.

She pulled her lips so far into her mouth I thought she was going to swallow them. When I got home I couldn't help thinking what it must have cost her not to say, 'and about time too'.

In the intervening days, I'd managed to be civil to Trevor. Thanks to Debbie, I didn't feel as though I was being sucked into a black hole any more. But, as we pulled into the drive of horror movie house, my sorting of Stuart's surrogate parenting paled before the enormity of getting Trevor to realise we didn't need this house.

"Before you get out of the car, Maggie, I need to warn you that Mrs Sharpe has a speech defect. I know what a parrot you are, so don't copy her, please, and please, try to be open minded about the house."

Although I'd have liked to tell him not to be disrespectful, I couldn't because we were no longer on those sort of speaking terms, and I knew that he was right. I was a parrot. Perhaps I'd been an actress in a former life?

The Old Vicarage, Munster Mansion, was a large, red brick, detached house situated on Church Road, Huyton.

When we walked up to the front door, the first thing I noticed was that all the woodwork needed painting. It looked as though it hadn't been touched for years. I took a note book out of my bag and wrote: *1) outside paintwork and wood.*

"What are you doing?" asked Trevor.

"Jotting down things that need attention, so we don't forget."

He scowled and rang the bell. It played a tune a bit like, Ding Dong Bell. *2) Bell.*

The door opened. "Mr and Mrs Harvey?" a woman whispered.

"Yes," I whispered back.

Trevor, who was behind me, gave me a nudge.

"Yes," I said more loudly and coughed, hoping it might cover the rudeness I hadn't intended. At the same time I felt like giggling. *Think, Edith.* Thinking Edith didn't work as well as it used to do, for Edith had mellowed under Stuart's influence, and I often saw the woman who had dealt with Ian and his bluey. *Think you don't want to live in Huyton.*

But as laughter and I hadn't been playmates for some time, well not since Trevor had coerced me into looking at this house, it felt good to be on the edge of a giggle. *Laughter and tears. Love and hate. Close allies.*

"Come in," she whispered. "I'm sorry I can't speak any louder. I had a virus last winter and haven't got my voice back. The medics don't seem to be able to find out why. They say, 'it may just come back, Mrs Sharpe.' Not very helpful, really."

She seemed nice. *I don't want to like her.* She was about my height, around sixty, I guessed, slim with wispy white hair curling around her face.

Inside, the house seemed even bigger than it looked from the outside. *3) Heating.* It still sported many of the original Victorian architectural features, a stained glass window in the front door, ornate coving and ceiling roses. I couldn't deny that they were beautiful.

Debbie was right. Stuart would enjoy racing up and down the tiled hall on his horse with wheels. It was a ridiculous present, from Katy, for our tiny flat, but the moment Stuart had set eyes on it, he loved it. He called it *Don't You Stop*, after one of his favourite nursery rhymes, and along with his train set, it was a favourite toy. *Banish the picture of Stuart trundling, Maggie. The house is an ogre that will gobble us up.*

4) Hall dark and gloomy. We'd have to have the light on all the time, more expense. A porch and stained glass didn't help. But porches were very useful in wet weather and the glass was beautiful. As the house faced west, I could imagine the red tiled floor patterned with glowing colours in the evening when the sun set. *Stop! You don't want to imagine beauty. You don't want to imagine Stuart's trundles. There are to be no good points about this house.*

"I think the sizes of all the rooms are fantastic, don't you, Maggie?" said Trevor.

Silence is not agreement. 'Mmm' is only a little more than silence. "Mmm," I replied.

"Come and have a look at the garden."

"I'm afraid it's a bit overgrown," said Mrs Sharpe.

"Our son will love playing in it," said Trevor.

Will? Where's the, 'if we buy it?' Trevor was standing by the bay window in the lounge which had a deep window seat. *Hell, I also like this.* I could imagine Stuart hiding behind the curtains, then bursting out, all giggles because I'd pretended to be frightened. 'Gain, Mama,' he would say. I was constantly amazed at how many, 'gains' toddlers wanted and adults endured.

I walked across to the beautiful fireplace. It had a black marble mantelpiece, an ornate cast iron fire grate and lovely patterned tiles. Why are there so many beautiful features? *5) Three quarters of an hour by bus. 6) Three cracked tiles in fireplace. 7)Anaglypta paper below dado rail in lounge and hall.* Trevor hated Anaglypta. It was then I heard laughter. *Is a ghost laughing at us? No.* It was more like the 'ho, ho' of Father Christmas. Mrs Sharpe didn't react. Either she was used to it, or she couldn't hear it. Trevor didn't react either. Was I the only one to hear the Santa ghost? Was it directing its 'ho, ho, ho' at me alone? *Laugh all you want, ghost. You are not going to put me off writing the truth about the house. 8) Furniture. 9) More peeling paintwork. Wet rot?* Ian told me to look out for it. *10) Musty smell. Is that wet rot? Ian will know. He's a surveyor. Do I want to involve my brother?* He would probably expect me to pay for his advice. Brenda, his wife, certainly would.

11) Horrid decoration. In the dining room, below a dark stained dado rail, there was more Anaglypta, painted purple. The ceiling and rest of the walls were mushroom, the carpet dark red, the curtains beige.

"We're leaving all the carpets and curtains," whispered Mrs Sharpe.

"That'll be useful, won't it Maggie?" said Trevor.

Will be useful. He's decided we're going to have it. So much for Debbie's prediction. God Trevor, about as useful as a pain in the bum. The curtains were old and I could see stains on the carpet. It was my turn to give him a furious look. *12) Carpets and curtains. Yuk!*

The first floor bedroom walls were covered in wood-chip, another of Trevor's dislikes. But he still had a pleased look on his face.

The bathroom was astonishing. It was a seaside memorial. Bright blue tiles, with a picture of a galleon inset on the wall above a sea green bath. The other three walls were sand yellow. The basin was also sea green. Above it was a shell encrusted mirror. There were boat ornaments on the window sill. Nothing and everything was wrong with it. I wanted to sing, *'Oh I do want to be beside the seaside'.*

One of the rooms in the attic was furnished as a bed-sitting room. Against one wall there was a small organ.

"This is our son's room," whispered Mrs Sharpe. She pointed to the organ. "He's the relief organist at our local church. Liam's one of the reasons we're selling. He's getting married. Of course we're delighted. So, we don't need this big old house any longer. The upkeep's far more than we can afford."

Neither do we need this 'big old house'. We can't afford it either.

"The bathroom up here needs a bit doing to it."

The whole house needs a lot doing to it.

"But everything works. Liam prefers to ablute up here."

Ablute? What does that mean?

"Right, I think that's about everything except for the outside."

"Er, what about the kitchen?" I said. "The kitchen's in the basement, isn't it?" *Where the 'ho, ho, ho' that nobody but me seems to hear, is coming from.*

"Oh, how stupid. I'd forgotten we hadn't been down to the basement. You're right, the kitchen's there, just as it was back when the house was built. The dumb waiter still works to trundle stuff up to the dining room, although we eat down there more often than not."

As we descended the stairs to the hall, we saw a man coming in through the front door.

"Ah good," whispered Mrs. Sharpe. "I wondered where you'd got to? While I show Mrs. Harvey the kitchen, you can show Mr. Harvey the coach house, Andrew."

"Coach House?" I said. "I don't remember a coach house being mentioned in the details."

"I'm sure it was," said Mr. Sharpe, "But I suppose it might have been called a garage. We use it as a garage." He smiled. "I have a car and my son has a car, plus I have a lot of tools and machines. Really, it's my workshop. I enjoy tinkering with machines."

"I'm sure the Harveys don't want to know about your old machines," whispered Mrs. Sharpe. "He drives me mad with them.

Now, are you going to take Mr. Harvey outside, or stand here talking all day?"

"Hair on, old thing, hair on; are you fit, Mr. Harvey?"

"Wouldn't you like to see the kitchen, Trevor, after all you're the chief cook?" I wasn't sure I wanted to venture into 'ho-ho' land without him.

"I'll see it after I've looked outside. And come April, when I start at the tech, I shan't be the chief cook, shall I? I'm sure you know what we need."

Yes, and it's not this monster house with a ghost no one hears except for me.

As we descended to the basement, the 'ho-hos' grew louder. I felt like grabbing Mrs Sharpe's hand for comfort. She still gave no sign of being able to hear it.

The kitchen was large. There was an Aga in a recess opposite the door. *Bugger, another plus.* By it, in a rocking chair, was 'ho-ho'; not a ghost, a very old woman.

"Mother," whispered Mrs Sharpe. "This is Mrs Harvey. She might be going to buy our house."

"She won't," cackled Mother. "She'll be dead tomorrow."

"Mother! Take no notice, dear. Bless her, she's got senile dementia."

Bless her? Execute the demon. Chop off her head. Bless her, my... whatever the saying is? "I hope I won't be, Mrs..."

"Middleton. We often talked about making a kitchen dining room upstairs, but we never got round to it and it's cosy down here. I shall miss my Aga." She gazed at rocking 'ho-ho'. "I can't look after mother any longer, I find it too stressful. Andrew's very good with her, but he can't do all the ablutions." She sighed. "It's another reason we need to sell. Have you seen enough?"

Quite enough. I was sorry for Mrs Sharpe. I liked light playing on old tiles, a bay window seat, a genuine Victorian fireplace, an Aga but the house was a nightmare I didn't want. Why couldn't I tell her? Why did I have to wait for Trevor?

As we returned to the hall, the front door opened and in walked a very small man, followed by Trevor and Mr Sharpe. The dwarf, possibly he could be described as a dwarf, nodded at us and disappeared upstairs.

"Our son, Liam," said Mr Sharpe.

"He's shy in front of strangers," said Mrs Sharpe.

Five minutes later the house was filled with Gothic organ music. It seemed a fitting accompaniment to the 'ho, ho, ho' from the basement. I had to leave, like now.

"Trevor," I said, striving for normal politeness in my voice. "I promised Edith we'd pick Stewart up by half six."

Trevor frowned at me. He knew I had promised no such thing. "Do you want me to ring you, or should we go through the estate agents," he said.

What? My desire to laugh was murdered by those words. *Psycho and Phantom of the Opera house? No! 'Ho-ho' has threatened me with death.* I smiled. Perhaps he was making polite noises?

"I think it's best to ring the agents with an offer," said Mr Sharpe. "Keep it professional. Let them do their work, after all they get paid enough. Have you got a place to sell?"

"No, we're first time buyers. But I know we can get a mortgage."

He does? All this behind my back? I was furious. I could hardly wait to get into the car before I erupted, "How dare you. We haven't discussed anything. I hate the place."

We rowed all the way to my parents'. As we arrived, Trevor's final sally was, "I've already told you, Maggie, you started it by getting pregnant."

"It takes bloody two to tango, Trevor."

"I didn't forget to take my pill, did I?"

How dare he! Why had I been so naïve? I thought, because I'd enjoyed a carefree pregnancy, and because Stuart's birth had been relatively easy, I could be the puppeteer of our threesome. But my puppets had turned out to have wills of their own. They had ended up manipulating me.

"What's the matter with your face?" asked Edith as soon as she opened the door.

"Nothing. I'm tired, that's all. Is Stuart okay?"

"Of course he is, Margaret."

"Ball," crowed Stuart.

"He's learnt a new word. He so quick, aren't you little man?" She gave him a kiss. He wiped it away and made his goblin face. "Cheeky. He's been playing football with his granddad in the yard. It'll be good for him to have a garden, won't it, Percy? Children need space."

"We never had a garden and we were okay," I said. "In any case, we have a garden at the flat."

"But it's not *your* garden, is it? And I took you to the park every week."

She had. I couldn't deny it, wrapped up so we could hardly move.

My dad drove us home. He put the seal on Munster Mansion. "Your mother and I never gave you a proper wedding present. We'd like to give you the money for the deposit. If the house needs repairs or a bit of renovation, I can help with that now I'm retired. I'm quite a dab hand at DIY. It'll get me out from under your mother's feet."

"You've seen The Old Vicarage?"

"Yes. I drove out there yesterday. I was curious. It's a real family house."

"You didn't say." I was hurt. The two men I loved had ganged up on me.

After Dad left, Trevor said, "I'm going to ring the Estate Agents tomorrow and put in an offer. I'm so pleased your dad likes it. It's generous of them to give us the deposit."

I want to cry. I can't, not in front of Stuart. Anyway, Maggie, you don't cry in adversity. You rail. You fight. But you do have droopy bottom lip syndrome too.

I got my notebook out of my bag. "Look at my list. How are we going to be able to afford to do all this?"

"A bit at a time. You heard your dad, Maggie. He'll help."

"And what 'bit of time' will you have to do it?"

"In the hols."

From the attic? What was that saying my mother used to trot out when I told her I'd do the washing up later? 'This year, next year, some time, never.' It would not be now, or a bit at a time; it would be never.

"Okay," I said. "We'll move. Probably just before Christmas." *To a house that will eat our money.* "You'll teach, full time. And we'll see if you can be a composer as well. You and my dad will repair Munster Mansion, and we're doing it because you've decided that it's for the best. I'm writing all this down, just in case, in the future you ever say, or think, Trevor, that I wanted any of this. I'm going along with it, because I have no choice. And I'll try to make the best of it."

"I suppose you'll want me to sign it."

"Yes, we should both sign it."

Why is it, in rows, people sometimes climb beyond the point of descent? There they are stuck, waiting to be rescued, but damage once done, cannot be undone. Words said, hover in the air, waiting to swoop.

Trevor and I didn't stop loving each other but, whereas before, loving was a lane where dog-roses bloomed and yellow hammers sang, 'a little bit of bread and no cheese'; now the thorny stems of the dog roses strayed onto the lane. They tore our clothes and scratched our faces and the birds hardly sang at all.

We were changing, and the person who had been my best friend wasn't my best friend any longer. I no longer confided in him as I once had. I turned to my women friends more and more for support.

Chapter Ten
Are You Happy?

*We deem those happy who, from the experience of life,
have learned to bear its ills without being overcome by them.*

How do you know if you're happy? Munster Mansion grumbled around in my head until I thought I would go mad. So, I decided that for every grumble I must find something to be happy about. But what was happiness? I knew what unhappiness was, so why didn't I know what happiness was? Trevor and I were... what were we? Amicable, but not all of the time. Loving, but not all of the time. Thank goodness for sex. Making love was a release from whatever storms were crashing about in my head, one being that 'Ho-Ho', the prophetess, had been right. I did die on the morrow. I couldn't be the person I had been before Trevor changed our world.

Just after we moved, Angela rang me and asked if she could pop in on her way home from work.

"College mum time," she said as we were walking down to the basement. "Debbie and Einna are worried about you. So am I. You've got to try to be less negative about The Old Vicarage. It's a house with loads of character and potential."

"You'd have loads of character if you'd had Ho-ho and a gothic dwarf living in you," I said.

"You shouldn't say things like that, Maggie. I'm surprised at you."

I was surprised at myself. Was this what resentment did? "Sorry, Ange. I don't know what made me say that. I just can't like it. All I see is money we haven't got."

"I don't understand. Money for what?"

"Oh come on, Ange. Furniture, curtains. We had a one bedroomed flat with a box room."

"There are places in Liverpool where you can pick up furniture and stuff for peanuts. There's a big warehouse in Jamaica Street, for example, that's stuffed from floor to ceiling with furniture, and another in Tunnel Road. You'll be able to buy material for curtains from TJ's or Paddy's—"

"And who's going to make them? I can't sew, plus I'd have to lug all the material home on the bus."

"Fucking hell, Maggie, learn to drive. You don't need a car to go and look for the furniture, do you? They'll deliver. And you don't have to do it all at once. Furnish it gradually."

I had to smile then. Whenever Angela swore it sounded funny, not angry. But she had a point about me learning to drive, even though we didn't have a car. If I passed my test maybe my dad would lend me his? But you can't learn to drive and pass your test just like that.

"And what about Katy? I bet Katy would make the curtains, in fact, Katy would take you to buy them."

"I know she would. But she hates driving now. Obviously she still uses her car, but only for necessary stuff. I'd feel really mean asking her."

"Trevor then. You borrow a car, and Trevor drives. Solution. Or, you put up with the curtains until you pass your test."

"Put up with the frigging curtains? You have to be joking. They're rank."

"Just a thought: that odd friend of yours might teach you to drive. It's not advisable to ask Trevor. Dave started to teach me. We've never rowed before. He shouted at me to slow down. I was only going twenty, and we were on a disused airfield."

"Trevor couldn't anyway. It wouldn't be safe to have Stuart in the back, so it would mean another plea for child minding, as well as a regular commitment from the man, away from composing plink plonk. Mind you, he'll have to mind Stuart while I learn." His choice all this, so…

"Yes, he will. But, back to the house, I will admit there's an odd smell. Not rotting veg or dead animal 'nasty' but more than just musty. I wonder the Sharpes didn't notice it."

"Perhaps you get used to smells?"

"You told us about the lovely features you noticed. They're still there. You'll make yourself ill if you don't try to be more positive, friend."

I knew that she was right, and I did try. But it was hard. Drive, learn to drive. That was one positive thing to do, start with that.

Clem, who had become a needy friend, contrary to what I had imagined would happen, was delighted that I asked him to teach me. Trevor seemed to think it was a good idea. He even lightened up enough to bet me a fiver I wouldn't pass first time. I told him I didn't want to bet.

"Why?"

"Because…" *You don't pay up when you lose. Because even though I won the Colditz bet, what happened afterwards turned my victory sour.* "I just don't, that's all. It might bring me bad luck."

He frowned. "Lighten up, Maggie."

I didn't know how to respond to that. I went down to the basement with Stuart. Trevor went up to the attic. "I call you when lunch is ready," I shouted. That was safe.

I decided to ask Ian to come and advise us about the smell. Surely my brother would be prepared to advise me, gratis. I doubted that Brenda understood the word 'gratis'. I doubted that 'gratis' was a word in her vocabulary. I couldn't like the woman my brother had married. She was bossy, and mean spirited, or that's how she came across to me.

What the hell were we going to do if it was dry rot? We were mortgaged for ever, as it was. And now Christmas was upon us; our first one in Munster Mansion. I couldn't do Christmas with the more than musty odour. And I did need to make an effort, for everyone's sake. I rang Ian.

"I did notice a smell when Brenda and I came to look at the house, Maggie. But I doubt it's dry rot. Wet rot and dry rot have similar smells. You told me you had wet rot in some of the window frames. Dad's sorting them, isn't he?"

"Yes."

"I'll come this evening, after work, just to check. It's Brenda's night out with her friends."

Brenda has friends? Cow, Maggie. It's a signal that he's not going to tell her.

"Thanks, little brother." He laughed. "Do you want to stay and have something to eat?"

"Better not. Brenda always leaves my food ready for me."

Ah! Daft of me. She'll interrogate him if he doesn't eat the food she's prepared, and he daren't risk throwing it away as she probably checks the bin. If she finds out he's given us a free consultation, he'll be for it. "Well I'll get some beer in, or wine? Would you prefer a glass of wine?" *I could do with a drink. I could do with getting drunk. I could do with an army of little green frogs.*

"A glass of red would be great."

"Something like Chianti okay?"

"Chianti's very drinkable." There was a pause. "I don't need a drink, Maggie."

I almost liked my little brother at that moment.

He was right. It wasn't dry rot. I breathed five thousand sighs of relief and planned a day to get rid of furnishings. The gang, without husbands, came round. So did Clem. We stripped windows of curtains, and floors of carpets. Trevor and Clem them took to the tip. That he was now a visiting friend was more to do with Trevor than me, but I was growing to like him and Trevor got on really well with him. As characters they were very different, but they respected each other from the first moment they met. I had never told Trevor about Clem's attempted seduction. He called Clem's way of talking 'quaint,' and said he had a good mind.

It was when we took up the carpets that the reason for the smell became obvious. At some point the Sharpes must have had an incontinent animal. Instead of underlay there was newspaper and, in patches throughout the house, there were dark brown stains. While the men went to the tip, we scrubbed floors. Even though it was December, I opened all the windows until the men got back. We shivered, but the smell went.

I decided that during the Christmas holiday we would hire a sander. The floorboards looked in good condition. I saw matt floorboards, not a high gloss shine, and rugs. Rugs would have to be acquired gradually.

I was thinking about sanding floors, and Christmas presents as I waited for the noise brigade; the twenty five pupils who regularly attended drama club. Dad had suggested a set of Galt bricks as a present for Stuart... It was a possibility, but I wasn't absolutely sure. He still enjoyed his train set. He didn't need Trevor or I to set it up for him any longer. He could put the tracks together himself, arranging the bridges, the trees, the stations. But once the trains were on the rails, all he seemed to want to do was crash the engines, so I was fearful that he would hurl the Galt bricks about, rather than build with them. I would have liked to buy him a doll, encourage his feminine side but I wasn't sure whether Trevor would approve. Edith would be horrified. Dad might think it a good idea. My friends? Katy and Molly? The problem was, I wasn't sure he'd play with a doll as a doll should be played with. He might throw it about, or rip off the head, for he was an action boy, a small Maggie, all restless energy but with a touch of the macho thrown in.

A football? I might buy him a doll and a football. I bet Dad will want to take him to the match when he's older. Mind you, Bill Shankly might not be with the club then. I bet Trevor won't want to go with them and a season ticket probably costs an arm and a leg.

Luckily, the curtain material for the lounge, and ours and Stuart's bedrooms didn't cost as much as I'd feared. I bought it at one of the fent warehouses near T J Hughes. I ducked asking Trevor to take me. This was how quickly fragility had crept into our relationship. Feeling guilty, I ended up ringing Katy.

"Not a problem, I know the way from our house to the parking behind T J's. It's back of the hand stuff."

"Good," I said, thinking what a strange expression 'back of the hand' was. If someone asked me to describe the back of my hand, I'd be at a loss. "Do you think Molly would keep Stuart entertained while we look?"

"Hang on, I'll ask her." There was a mumbled conversation. "She said, 'Brill.' Her only proviso? She could check we had made the right choice before we paid."

I laughed. Typical Molly. I had done very little sewing in my life and knew nothing about what thread or machine needles would be needed. Nor did I have any clue about rufflette tape. Katy knew exactly what was wanted and it was she who suggested that we could do without curtains in the dining room and the two spare bedrooms as well as Trevor's den.

"After all, heat rises," she said. "Plus the windows up there are small; not so much heat loss. You can always buy some more material when you can afford it."

Unlike the outing to chose material for my wedding dress, Molly had very little to say about the choice I made, which was odd as she had insisted on being consulted. Stuart duty over, she was much more interested in going across the road to the new café where they made frothy coffee and served teacakes oozing with butter.

Katy and Molly were coming to stay the weekend of the college carol concert, bringing the curtains with them. I had a bet with myself that Grunt would have forgotten. 'Grunt' was now my nickname for Trevor. Einna and I had thought up names for our difficult husbands on one day of mutual moans.

"We may be the Mrs Moans," she'd said. "But they're Grunt and Groan."

"You haven't forgotten that Katy and Molly are coming to your concert and then to ours for the weekend, Trevor?" I said as we rushed through our daily morning routine. This was what Katy and I had arranged when she'd rung about the curtains. She and Molly would be able to help me hang them. "And the following Saturday, everyone's coming to ours for soup and sandwiches. Then we're going Delamere to choose Christmas trees."

"Right. Is that it for Christmas, or must I expect the whole of Huyton to invade the house as well as the gang and their families?"

I was shocked. I couldn't hide how shocked I was.

He must have noticed the look as he added, "I'm sorry, Maggie, I just can't cope with lots of socialising. I enjoy your dad and Clem's company. Your friends are all right, but they're your friends, not mine. I don't like John. Bill and Dave are okay, but I wouldn't have chosen them as friends. Actually, I don't need friends. Family is enough."

A truth. He didn't socialise with any of his colleagues at the technical college, nor fellow players at the cricket club. He didn't go out for a pint with Mac any longer. The nearest to a friend he had was Clem. They didn't go to the pub. Clem came to our house.

When we first met, he… no, even then we went out with my friends. Leila, Gail, Mac and Simon, Gail's boyfriend. But we had fun. I thought we had fun…

Okay, Maggie. You're going to have to manage the Christmas holiday like a tour guide. And try to winkle Mr Hermit out of his eerie when Katy and Molly come. Katy will sympathise. Molly won't understand. She might even get cross with Trevor. Mind you, cross and Molly don't fit.

Katy had told me that senile dementia could change a person's character, or exacerbate former traits. "Molly's always enjoyed life and loved everyone. I've never met anyone who was so uncritical of others. I feel as though I'm living with the little girl she used to be. And that's fine."

When we all got back from the concert, Katy did and didn't astonish us by saying that she wanted to give us her car. It was only about three years old and had very low mileage. The 'didn't' part was that we knew her confidence in driving had deteriorated. There were one or two moments on the curtain buying outing when I'd been very nervous. She rarely drove above twenty, and other motorists had shown their impatience. As well as astonished, I was pleased, very pleased. I had put in for my test, and Clem was confident I would pass. It was going to make sense for Trevor to use the bus and for me to use the car; well, in my head it made sense. The journey from Huyton to Kirkby was longer, the busses less frequent, than the journey into Liverpool.

"It sits on the drive because, as you know, I don't feel comfortable driving any more," she said. "There's far too much traffic. I prefer public transport or a taxi."

"So do I," said Molly. "Katy's not very good at driving now. She's too slow."

"Molly's right," Katy sighed. "I'm beeped by almost every other motorist on the road."

"You must let us give you something for it," I said.

Trevor frowned at me. "Mum wants to give it to us, Maggie. If ever she needs a lift anywhere—"

"Thank you, sweetheart." Trevor winced. He hated being called 'sweetheart'. "Molly and I enjoy going by public transport. And if the weather's bad, we can always take a taxi."

"I like sitting at the front on the bus, so I can see everything," said Molly. "I don't like your music, Trevor. Why don't you write nice tunes like in the carols. Then we could all sing them."

"My music isn't for singing, Molly. It's for listening to. The choir had to sing the carols I composed. You sang *Once In Royal*, didn't you?"

"I like singing," said Molly. "I shall sing to Stuart when I tell him his time to go to bed story. I like best *We Will Rock You*." She folded her arms to look as though she was holding a baby and crooned, "We will rock you, rock you, rock you," as she rocked.

Molly's stories were always improbable, and invariably about a puppy called Tricks. Stuart loved them. They both enjoyed creating all the noises for the various characters.

Trevor excused himself after we'd eaten, disappearing up to his eerie. He rarely cooked now, but when we were on our own, he did do the washing up.

"Shall I wash as you know where everything goes," said Katy.

"I generally leave it to drain in the rack. But there might be too many dishes to do that this evening."

Then, out of nowhere, or so it seemed to me, she said, "Are you happy, Maggie? Only you seem to have lost some of your sparkle."

Of course, it didn't come from nowhere. Nothing comes from nowhere. She'd obviously been thinking about it. For how long, I wondered?

Honesty. I had to be honest. "I don't know. I—"

"I knew it. That son of mine has railroaded you into buying this house, hasn't he? His father was a devil for making me do things I didn't want to do." She grimaced. "Before he left me, that is. Don't get me wrong, I love my son, but men like him and his dad think silence is agreement."

Now, loyalty to Trevor warred with the truth. I plumped for a compromise. "I wasn't silent, Katy. But it's true, Trevor wanted to move and I didn't. I could see the advantages for Stuart, though, The garden for a start."

I was no longer sure what happiness was. When I was younger, I thought I knew. Happiness was like a Doris Day movie.

"I don't know about you, Katy, but in any one day I experience lots of different emotions. They can range from sheer pleasure to boredom. I can be immersed in the beauty of frost on the branches of trees, and later in the day I can be bored by the conversation in the staffroom. When I pick Stuart up from nursery I feel a wave of joy envelope me. Is joy the same as happiness?" *Does Trevor feel that joy when he picks up Stuart?*

"I remember that joy when I met Trevor from infant school. Does he make you happy?"

Does he? He used to. And here a deep unhappiness threatened to drown me. He used to make me so happy before Stuart was conceived. One person's need, want, is another's drowning wave. *I can't wish Stuart away.* "Yes, but not all the time. I don't expect I make him happy all the time. What right have we to happiness, Katy? I think we people of rich nations have a great capacity for making ourselves unhappy."

141

Mrs Middleton, rocking 'ho-ho', had seemed happy enough in her dementia. Molly too. She wasn't as far down the line as Mrs Middleton. But when it began to happen, when she didn't know what ordinary things were called, and said things like, 'that thing you put stuff to drink in'; when she didn't know what a particular food was, but felt she ought to know, then perhaps she was unhappy. Of course I didn't know this for sure. Maybe dementia crept in like the morning mist on a potentially hot summer's day, or maybe it rolled in, as it did in November, like a smothering blanket.

Not even a day out with the gang was happiness all the time. We shared problems, and when we did there was rarely knickers' wetting laughter. And knickers' wetting laughter wasn't happiness, but it was good for us. If we were overwhelmed by problems, laughter could make them go away, for the time being.

As I'd suspected, maybe feared, Munster Mansion and a job hadn't given Trevor any more time for composition, and now he was creatively blocked. How did I know this? Any music he'd used for the carol concert was music he'd composed some time ago. And if I did venture up to the attic, I would catch him lying on a chaise-longue, a Katy reject, hands behind his head, staring at the dark red ceiling, listening to a record. I doubted that he heard me come in, or if he did, he chose to ignore me. I crept away.

"Does Trevor spend a lot of time up there?" Katy pointed to the ceiling.

"Yes." I changed the subject. "How are Jack and Elsie?" They were Katy's neighbours and a guaranteed diversion.

"As unbelievable as ever. I've never met anyone who courts disaster like they do. They bought a car last week. An advert in *The Echo*. They didn't notice the radiator was leaking and it overheated when they were going to Aintree to see their son. Outcome? Fifty pounds down the drain, plus they're car-less and broke again."

"Are they still grumbling about 'coloureds' coming over here and taking our jobs?"

"Yes, but not so much since I told them the country would fall apart if it weren't for all the immigrants doing the jobs Brits wouldn't do.

"'But you wouldn't want one living next door to you, or marrying your daughter, would you?' Elsie said."

"'Why wouldn't I? I can't think of a single reason why I wouldn't. We're all people. Some of us are nice and some of us aren't and they can be white, brown, black, pink or blue.' I said. They huffed off then. But I knew they'd be back. Now they don't know what happiness is."

"Maybe they do, Katy. Maybe they're only happy when they're grumbling."

"Well they're an odd mixture. 'Isms' galore, alongside kindness. Shall I tell you an Elsie and Molly story?"

"Have we time? I mean before Molly comes down?"

"It won't matter. She'll join in telling it. A couple of weeks ago, Molly had an appointment at the hospital… an endoscopy."

"I remember, didn't the appointment have to be postponed?"

"Yes. The whole saga started on Spaghetti Bolognese day. I'd invited Jack and Elsie round for dinner. One of Molly's favourites is Spaghetti Bolognese, so I decided to make it. I don't know why, I forgot it was on the cooker. I'd read that the diced veg for the sauce needed to be cooked a long time, but to forget it—"

"You forgot it?" I found that so difficult to believe, I really was open mouthed. Katy is a wonderful cook; very inventive and attentive. I suspected that it was where Trevor's skill in cooking came from. Another thing I missed: his cooking.

Katy nodded. "All I needed to do was check the water level every so often. I seem to be doing this more and more; not forgetting, exactly, flitting between jobs, like. I know we women are supposed to be able to multi-task, but perhaps I can't. The meal was ruined. It's what I did next, I still can't believe. Instead of putting the burnt mess in newspaper in the bin, I decided to flush it down the toilet. Of course it wouldn't go, would it? I was staring at it when Molly came to see where I was. 'Yuk!' she said. It was 'yuk'. I explained what I'd done, and that it wouldn't flush away.

"'I know what to do,' she said. 'I'll come back in a… soon.' She rushed downstairs and out into the garden, and returned with a twig full of bay leaves. She then proceeded to swirl it about and pump it up and down. It did look as though the burnt mince was dispersing. 'Now pull down that thing,' she ordered. It worked. 'And put smelly stuff in.'

"Molly looked after Jack and Elsie while I went to get the fish and chips. When I came back they were crying with laughter. 'Elsie's taking me to that place tomorrow,' she said.

"'The hospital?' I said.

"'Yes. the hospital,' said Molly.

"I raised my eyebrows at Elsie. But she assured me it was fine.

"'She's got a naughty puppy called Rags. Rags eats those warm things you put on your feet. Elsie's taking me out to lunch after... they do what they want to me. We're going to have pizza, chips and chocolate ice cream.'

"I asked Elsie if she was sure, as it was a longish procedure and they might be there for some hours. Elsie told me that she would take her library book.

"Anyway, as I suspected, Molly wasn't the only person waiting for an endoscopy. Elsie left her for a few minutes to go to the Ladies. When she returned Molly wasn't there, so Elsie assumed she'd gone in for the examination. She waited and waited. Then a nurse called Molly's name. You can imagine the panic. No one had noticed a chubby woman with frizzy hair, wearing jeans and a red jumper wandering out.

"Elsie rang me. I tried to assure her that it wasn't her fault and drove to the hospital. As I walked from the car park to the entrance, I noticed a porto-cabin. The sign above the door read, *Dementia Drop In Centre and Café*. I don't know why, but I got a funny feeling about it, so I went in.

"The woman behind the counter asked if she could help me. I explained about Molly. Do you know what she said? I still can't believe it.

"She said, 'Oh god! Not another escapee!' She then called her colleague and asked me to give her a description, which I did.

"'Yeh, we seen her, didn't we, Jen?' said the colleague as she began to clear away crockery left on tables. 'She asked for pizza and chips.

We told her we only served hot drinks, biscuits, cakes and scones, so she left.'

"I found Elsie in reception, and told her where I thought Molly had gone. She was beside herself, Maggie. She kept telling me it was all her fault. She should never have left her. I told her it wasn't her fault that she wanted to go to the lav. And that Molly ought to have stayed where she was. What I didn't tell her was, that where Molly's wants were concerned, what she was supposed to do flew out the window. We drove into town, you can imagine how much I enjoyed that, to the Italian restaurant where Molly had made friends with the waiters because they were all Liverpool supporters.

"She was there. We saw her through the window. She was about to tuck into an enormous slice of chocolate gateau.

"'You said we could have pizza and chips,' she said to Elsie.

"'How did you find this cafe?' I asked her.

"'Easy-peasy lemon squeezy,' she said. 'I told the man who drove the car, to go past the dancing people and straight on till morning.'

"Elsie and I looked at each other in astonishment. 'And he found this restaurant?' I said.

"'Don't be silly. I walked from the church with no windows.'

"'How would you have paid for the meal If we hadn't found you?' I asked.

"Molly looked uncomfortable. 'You know,' she said. Then she whispered. 'I'd have let them have a look. Men like that. Some like a feel as well. Then they—'"

"Take their dingle dangle out and ask you to kiss it. I don't much like kissing dingle dangles, because they spit." Molly had come into the lounge. "They're rude. They spit into your mouth. The man who came to help if you pressed the red thing where I lived before, liked me to do that so his dingle dangle could spit. I told him I didn't want it to spit in my mouth. The spit tasted yukky. I told him to let it spit in there," She pointed to her crotch. "It's nice when it spits there. Your boy's asleep now, Maggie."

I looked at Katy in horror. Had the warden in Molly's sheltered accommodation abused the trust placed in him, abused the women in his care? She shrugged as if to say... as if to say she had heard all this before and that Molly could be making it up. If she was, oh my god, Stuart. What kind of stories had she told her great nephew tonight?

"Did you tell Stuart a 'Tricks' story?" Katy had divined my thought.

"Yes. Stuart and I took Tricks to see baby Jesus and we all sang, *We will rock you.*"

Later, in bed, I told Trevor what Molly had told Katy and me.

"I expect she made it up," he said.

"That's what Katy implied. What if she didn't?"

"I don't suppose we'll ever know. Just because she has a problem with her short term memory doesn't mean she doesn't have the same appetites as the rest of us."

"I didn't say it did. What I was saying was, that if that warden is abusing women, something ought to be done."

"But what can we do?"

Yes. What can we do?

Trevor put his arm round me: a signal. He wanted to make love and, although I didn't feel like it, I didn't say no. It wasn't often that he felt like it, these days. I found it difficult to relax and I pretended to have an orgasm. I didn't want the image of that man to intrude. But he did. I'd met him. He'd seemed like a bluff, genial, caring person; a person at odds with the picture Molly had painted. Trevor didn't seem to notice. He fell asleep. I stayed awake. Molly seemed happy. She didn't seem upset by what had happened to her, if it had happened. Would she really have offered the waiters a view, a feel, fellatio? What about the taxi driver? We hadn't asked her how she'd paid for the taxi.

The next morning, the weather was beautiful. As we were breakfasting, Molly said, "Can we take Stuart to the place where they have those things that do this, today?" She mimed pushing a swing. "I like doing that, and jumping down steps. They have good steps in that garden we go to, don't they, Katy? I'm not sure about the..." She mimed again. "I bet Stuart likes jumping and swings. Boss! I've remembered the word." She jumped up and down.

"What a brill idea, Molly. We can all go," I said. I saw the look on Trevor's face. "Except for Trevor. He's got to work." Katy winked at me. Luckily Trevor didn't notice.

"On the house?" asked Molly.

I wanted to laugh.

"No," said Trevor. "I'll work on the house after Christmas, if Maggie doesn't fill my days with social gatherings. Today I have to work on a musical composition ."

"This year, next year…" I muttered.

"Did you say something Maggie?" asked Molly.

"Yes, I was thinking aloud. As Trevor wants to work, we'll walk to Court Hey Park. Are you two up for that?"

"Can I push Stuart in his chair on wheels?"

"Of course."

Molly and Stuart, years apart, but in their enjoyment of the park, as twins. Molly's laughter echoed Stuart's as they rolled down grassy slopes.

Abuse? Enjoyment? The story about Molly sucked me back in time to a young girl watching a man rub his crotch. His enjoyment, her embarrassment, and her curiosity about the tingle in her own crotch.

Chapter Eleven
The Faces of Grief

Laugh and the world laughs with you. Weep and you weep alone.

I'm convinced there are months which are filled with events that have consequences and others that sail past without a startle. The Autumn term, nineteen seventy-one held one of those months, part bombshell, part normal life.

Trevor and I had been ricocheting along in Munster Mansion. Stuart, my work and my friends helped smooth some of the bigger bumps. I had learnt to tolerate the house, and bit by bit I had furnished it.

Stuart soon grew out of the devil/angel stage and became an easy going child, who seemed to enjoy life.

Trevor's block continued to plague him; at least I could only assume it did for no musical sounds filtered down the stairs, nor did an invitation to listen to a section of a work in the making. I was proud of myself for keeping the 'I told you so' in prison.

One evening, as I was on my way to the Tennyson staffroom to pick up my coat and bag after a rehearsal for the dancers in the school pantomime, I heard sobbing coming from a box-room where the cleaning materials were kept. I knocked on the door. Whoever it was tried to stifle their sobs. I don't know whether it was intuition, but something made me say, "Lorraine? It's Maggie." Just that.

"I'm all right."

"No you're not. Can I come in?" She was standing by the electric polisher, her eyes red, her face smudged with mascara. "Is it Frank? Has Frank been horrid to you?"

Frank was a tyrant. He ruled the cleaning staff with verbal abuse and he wasn't above trying to be a dictator with the teaching staff.

She shook her head. "It's me kids, Maggie. Social's taken me kids off me."

"Oh, love." I took her hand. "Let's go into the staffroom. No one's there now. I'll make us a cup of tea and you can tell me all about it. If there's anything I can do to help, I will."

Mugs of tea in hands, we sat on the grey plastic chairs that were designed to prevent rather than give comfort.

"Will you really help?"

"Of course I will, if I can."

"Could you take me to Social Services, like? Help me talk to them. I'm not a bad mother, Maggie. And I'm a victim."

Why is Lorraine a victim? And why have social services taken her children into care? "I can. Of course I can. Their office is in the council offices, isn't it?" I looked at the staff room clock. Ten past five. I imagined they'd have gone home by now.

"Yes. Could we go tomorrow, in your lunch hour? I can't afford to lose me pay by taking the morning off work. I clean in Asda in Huyton, in the mornings."

"Okay. I'm going to give Trevor a ring, tell him I'll be a bit late, then you can take your time telling me what's happened." I went over to the staffroom telephone.

Trevor didn't pick up, Stuart did.

"Hello, sunshine. Can you call your dad, please? No, tell you what, can you give him a message? Tell him I'm going to be late, and ask him to make tea."

"Tell Daddy you're going to be late, and will he cook tea? Why are you going to be late, Mummy?"

"A friend of mine needs my help.

"Will you be back to put me to bed?"

"Of course."

Just talking to Stuart forced me to think about what it would be like to have him taken away from me.

I took my mug of tea back to where Lorraine was sitting, not drinking, somewhere far away. I touched her hand. "Can you tell me what happened, now?"

"Dinnertime this morning I got a ring from the school, asking me to go in. They wouldn't say why. I was terrified. Ryan and Loretta were in the Head's office, and there were two other people there, a man and a woman. The Head told me they were social workers.

"'We've been worried about Ryan for some time,' the Head said. 'Do you remember the incident,' she flicked through a book on her desk, 'back in April? We asked you to come and collect Ryan because he'd been in a fight?'

"I said I remembered. 'You said Ryan wasn't a fighter,' she said and I agreed. 'But since then there have been several other incidents, plus naughty behaviour in class. This morning he threw a book at his teacher.'

"You can imagine how shocked I was. 'That's not my Ryan,' I said.

"'Mrs Pearson brought him to see me. Now you know my approach with children, Mrs Dobson.'

"I do, Maggie. My kids are dead lucky. She's a really nice Head. She cuddles a kid if she sees one crying. Anyway. She told me she gave Ryan a drink of juice and a biscuit, and asked him what was wrong. At first he didn't say anything. Just sat there nibbling the biscuit, so she said, 'I know you're not being bullied.' He looked at her then. 'Ah,' she said. 'You are.' He nodded. 'Can you tell me who the bully is? We don't allow bullies in school, do we Ryan? Bullies are cowards. And sometimes they are very unhappy children.' He whispered, 'Not in school, Miss.' Then it all came out, Maggie. Stephen's been abusing him."

"Stephen?"

"Me fellah."

She started crying again. I fumbled in my bag for a tissue and handed it to her. "Every time I was out working. He'd told me he didn't mind sorting the kids out in the mornings and picking them up from school. I have to be in Asda for six and I don't finish till nine, then I'm here from half three till six so he had loads of opportunities. I did notice some bruises on Ryan. He told me he'd bumped into a table in his classroom, or had a fall. I believed him, Maggie. Why wouldn't I?" She rubbed her eyes. "Stephen hit him if he refused to jerk him off, and suck him. And he told him if he dared say anything to anybody, he'd kill him. I broke down, Maggie. I wanted to go over and hug Ryan. Social said the police were going to arrest Stephen when he came to pick the children up, this afternoon."

I was so shocked I didn't know what to say. Of course I knew abuse went on, but I'd never met anyone… I sat staring at the carpet.

"Do you want me to give you a lift home?"

"I'm scared of going home, Maggie. Stephen's part of the Wragge family. They're really bad news."

"Have you family near?"

"Me mum and dad split up years ago. I've no idea where me dad is and me mum lives with our Sylvie. There's no room for me there, even if they did want me."

"Tell you what, you can come to stay with me. Trevor won't mind." *He won't; not after I've explained, will he? Come on, Maggie, you can't predict how Trevor will react.*

"Can I? What about Asda?"

"Asda's a twenty minute walk from ours. Will you be able to ring social services in your tea-break." *The cleaners are allowed a tea-break, aren't they?*

"Yes, I expect so." She looked doubtful.

Gently, I said, "It will look odd if I ring."

"It's just that we don't always get a break. Depends how the pink dragon's feeling."

"But surely you're entitled to one, aren't you?"

She looked at me with an expression that was almost like pity, and I was jolted into the realisation that I'd moved a long way from my working class roots, Woolworths, and the rights of workers like Lorraine.

Trevor was far from happy about my offering Lorraine shelter, but he accepted that I didn't have much alternative.

Stuart was curious. I crossed my fingers and told him there was a problem with a burst tank.

"A burst tank? What's a burst tank, Mummy?"

I hadn't had time to warn Lorraine of my fib. I didn't know I was going to fib. I should have prepared myself for Stuart's curiosity. He had an enquiring mind. Thankfully, she understood and went along with my invention.

The next day, I met Lorraine in Huyton village centre. Social services were housed in the building which served as the town's offices. It was on the edge of Asda's car-park. Lorraine and I were shown into a room. There were two people in it, Mandy, a social worker and Tim, a police officer. Lorraine explained why I had accompanied her. She also mentioned that I'd offered her a bed for the night, and why.

"How are me kids?" she said.

"They're fine."

I suppose she's saying that to help Lorraine. But how can they be fine? They've been subject to abuse. They've been taken away from their mum. What explanation will they have been given for that? Fine? There has to be a better word, doesn't there? Isn't this a case where honesty's the best policy? 'They're as well as can be expected.'

"You'll be able to see them after school just for today, but only if you can take time off work."

I shall have to talk to Frank. No, Lorraine must call in sick. Will she get sick pay?

"Will I be allowed to take them home?"

"I'm afraid not. There are one or two things the police need to clear up before that can happen."

"What things?"

Tim leant forward. "Loretta told a WPC yesterday, that Stephen had drawn on her face with his 'pen'. She said she asked you to wash her face. Didn't you notice what the sticky stuff was?"

The colour drained from Lorraine's face. I felt sick. That sicko had ejaculated on a six year old's face? And Lorraine...? *Don't jump to conclusions, Maggie. Listen to what everyone has to say.*

"I thought it was sweets. It was sticky. I washed her face for her."

"The police have to be sure that you didn't collude in the abuse," said Mandy.

Lorraine burst into tears. "You tell them, Maggie. You know I wouldn't do nothing like that."

But I don't know, do I? I know the Lorraine I chat to sometimes after school. It's in a context. The conversations are fleeting.

Luckily Mandy got up, went over to her, put an arm round her shoulders and said, "I'm sorry. Whatever your friend says won't make a difference at this point. We have to be sure, Lorraine. Where children are concerned, we can't be too careful. There's another thing. You and your friend..." She gave me a look. I could have sworn it said, 'of course you don't know what Lorraine's like. No one really knows another person'. "... You and your friend are right about the Wragge family. So, we have to find you another house, not in Knowsley. We can protect your children while they're in care."

"What about collecting them from school?"

"Today we're going to collect them. After that, until we know what's what, the foster parents will collect them. Now, I have to warn you, Lorraine, all this could take some time. In the meanwhile we're moving you to Slater Court. The house you live in at present is a council house, isn't it?"

Lorraine nodded. I imagined she was having difficulty digesting everything that was being thrown at her.

"We shall arrange for the temporary change of address for your rent. Perhaps your friend could help you to sort out all the other stuff you need to do, like change of address for the post."

What have I got myself into here?

"At least you can still get to both your jobs easily. If you come here, on Saturday morning, you'll be able to spend some time with your children."

They know she has two jobs? What don't they know?

"Only Saturdays?"

"I'm afraid so. Today is an exception. Your cleaning work in the comp in Kirkby means that after school during the week isn't possible."

"I'm finished by six."

Mandy shook her head. "That's not in office hours, and in any case it doesn't take into account the bus ride back to Huyton."

"So I can only see me kids once a week?"

"I'm afraid so, but hopefully it won't be for long. The police officer will take you to yours, now, and help you pack up."

"What about me furniture and stuff?"

"That will be moved to your new address when a place is found for you. It can stay in the house in the meantime. The Slater Court flat is furnished. I think that's all."

Lorraine went off with Tim, the police constable, and I returned to an afternoon of English and Drama. Nothing we explored was half as dramatic as the events of the past twenty-four hours.

Over the next few days, I made sure I was available for chats or practical help. I asked Trevor to be responsible for picking up Stuart, who was now at infant school. Dad still collected him on Drama club day.

"You may find out about icebergs, Maggie," he said. I hadn't lied to my dad about why I was asking him to collect his grandson. I knew he wouldn't gossip.

Trevor had pulled a face when I asked him to do son duty. But five year old Stuart was very different from a two year old toddler. And I always allowed him to watch *Children's Hour*, so as long as Trevor went along with Maggie rules...

I did find out about icebergs. Stephen had been systematically abused by his father, his brothers, and his uncle. Lorraine had been abused by her grandfather. Would her children become abusers when they grew up?

I went with her to meet her new social worker, who told her that when and if she was allowed her children back, they would all be moved to Sefton. Apparently, Stephen had written to her from prison to say he was sorry for what he'd done.

"Can I go to see him?" she asked.

I don't know if my mouth dropped open, but I wanted to say, 'How can you want to see the shit?'

"Yes," said the social worker. "But just to tell him the relationship is over. If you let him into your life again, you won't get your children back."

"I don't want him back. I just want to tell him what I think of him; what he's done to me kids and me."

When she moved to Sefton with her children, I was relieved. I'd done my duty by her, but I didn't want to be involved in her life any more.

The days then bumped along without any more shocks until the Christmas holiday.

What is it about Christmas, the jolly season, the season of indulgence, that makes us feel an atrocity, a tragedy, a grief, is so much worse than at any other time of the year? Logically, it isn't. But emotions don't seem to have much to do with logic.

Dad died on Christmas Day. This year he and Edith had gone to Ian and Brenda's for lunch. They were coming to us on Boxing Day. Katy and Molly were with us, so was Trevor's sister and her family. We had just finished lunch and were opening presents when the phone rang. It was Edith.

"It's your dad. He's had a heart attack. Ian's taking me. We're following the ambulance."

"We'll look after Stuart," Katy said. "You get off. We'll sort everything out here."

Even though Trevor drove like there were no speed limits, we were too late. Dad had died by the time we got there. My first thought? Why? Why couldn't the doctors have saved him? My second? This was the man who had given me so much love and support as a child, and throughout my life. My third? No more Granddad, Grandson jaunts. My dad had worked on the railways until he took early retirement just after Stuart's second birthday. One of their first outings together was to the Edge Hill depot, to see the trains. He'd persuaded one of his mates to allow Stuart to play at being the driver. No one had told me that he had been forced into early retirement, due to angina. I must have been too preoccupied with Trevor's and my deteriorating relationship to enquire.

Dad had been an LFC supporter all his life, and had said he would buy Stuart a season ticket, the following August, so he could take him to home matches. There would be no Anfield for either of them. My dream of the pair of them singing *You'll Never Walk Alone* melted away with his death. They... I choked on thwarted future memories.

And death shall have no dominion.
Dead men naked they shall be one
With the man in the west wind and the moon...

I recited Dylan Thomas's poem at Dad's funeral. I managed to do it without crying, probably because I was numb. Numb with grief; I knew what it meant. I'd lost the one man I'd loved unreservedly, the one man I'd truly respected, the one person who, if anyone could have done, had walked the same pavements as me. Was I re-writing the history of our relationship? A little. But honesty and grief don't always go hand-in-hand.

As the coffin disappeared into the furnace, *You'll Never Walk Alone* was playing. Edith hadn't wanted the LFC anthem. She'd wanted *Abide With Me*. But, for once, Ian had sided with me.

This was his memory of our dad, for Dad, he and I had always attended the first home game of the season. In the end there was a compromise. We had *Abide With Me* at the funeral.

I felt alone in my grief. Colleagues mumbled the usual platitudes. I knew they meant to be kind, but they didn't help. My friends hugged me.

Bill said something that went a little way to alleviate the pain. I knew it, but it was good to be reminded.

"Talk about him. Maggie. Remember him through things he said, through things you did together."

Some people don't want to talk about death. They think they're being kind by not mentioning the person who's died, but really they are protecting themselves. Other people's pain is difficult to cope with.

It was to Leila and the gang that I talked; Leila, because she'd shared my childhood, and therefore knew my dad; the gang because they hadn't.

Why the Christmas period, I kept thinking? But why should it be worse at Christmas? Because of expectations? Because we are exhorted to be happy at Christmas?

It's the most wonderful time of the year.
With everyone telling you be of good cheer...

Relatively speaking, I'd been happy before Christmas, despite Einna and I having to deal with Grunt and Groan, our nicknames for our difficult men; Grunt was Trevor, Groan was John. We were able to laugh about it as we planned a gang jaunt.

From the outset that outing had us on the verge of hysteria. Angela and I had been obliged to hide in Winnowsty Court because we'd seen John phut-phutting home when he should have been at work. We'd rung Einna from a phone-box to see what was happening, and when we did meet up, we learned that she had pretended to be Debbie when, without thinking it through, she had answered the phone to John. She shouldn't have been there. She should have been in college.

Later that day, Einna, Angela, Debbie and I talked about this year's outing to Delamere Forest to choose Christmas trees. It was my turn to host lunch.

"I've had an idea," said Angela. "I thought it might be nice if we didn't go our separate ways after choosing. Dave and I would like everyone to come back to ours for something to eat, a sort of high-tea. The kids are old enough to cope, aren't they?"

"The kids are," I said. "But are the men?" Half jest, but many a true word came to mind.

"Dave will be up for it."

"So will Bill."

That left Grunt and Groan and we decided that they would have to 'put up or shut up' as Edith and Annie both said. What those two women didn't have in common would fit on a flea's back.

I decided to make a thick Mediterranean tomato soup for lunch. I'd found the recipe in a *Good Housekeeping* magazine that had been left lying around in the staffroom. There was a Jewish bakers on the corner of Penny Lane and Allerton Road. Whenever I could, I still went there for our bread. Their dense, rye bread would be a fitting accompaniment for the soup. Angela offered to make mince-pies. Debbie said she would bring cheese and biscuits, Einna fruit and a non alcoholic punch.

"But you're doing the high-tea," I said to Angela. "You shouldn't have to bring anything. I'll also make the mince-pies."

"Okay. Listen, I've been thinking about last year. We were quite late getting to Delamere. How about eating at twelve, then we can have a walk in the forest before we choose the trees," Angela said.

"Good idea, but weather dependant. There's also a grotto this year."

A crisp, blue sky day greeted me when I drew the curtains in Stuart's room. I'd left Trevor in bed. Stuart was now old enough not to disturb us before eight, at weekends and in the holidays. He had a clock on the wall in his bedroom, and knew how to tell the time. He was very excited about Christmas itself, and almost as excited about choosing a tree and seeing Father Christmas.

The children had their soup before us, and then ran from room to room, just because they could. No one, not even Grunt or Groan, told them to be quieter, or that they could hurt themselves by charging about in such an unruly manner. The house absorbed the noise, or so it seemed. By the time we'd cajoled them into going to the toilet and putting on their outdoor clothes, it was just after one-thirty.

Delamere forest is mainly coniferous, but there are areas of deciduous trees as well. The children rough and tumbled down the paths we chose to explore. They screamed through the trees. They picked up cones as though their pockets were bottomless sacks. And when it came to choosing the Christmas trees, they couldn't decide which was best. It was almost as though one child's indecision fed another's.

John got fed up with Claire's shilly-shallying and decided on a Spruce: 'less needle drop'. This was despite Einna's protestations that, in her opinion, it wasn't a proper Christmas tree. I liked the shape of a spruce but I didn't join in their discussion. I knew John would win. Einna was rarely confrontational. There was something in her character that shrank from scenes. Claire started grizzling.

"Would you like a shoulder carry?" asked Dave.

"She's too old and big for that," said John.

"I don't mind if you don't. Bill's carrying Jacob."

John shrugged. Einna smiled and said 'thank you'. Dave picked Claire up and popped her on his shoulders. She stopped grizzling immediately.

Luckily, only a small queue faced us when we arrived at Santa's Grotto, but when it was our turn to go in, Claire didn't want to get down and sit on Santa's knee. John told her she was being silly and Santa wouldn't give her a present. I could see Einna itching to tell him to shut up, and not make things worse. Luckily, Santa was a sensible chap.

"How about you whisper in my ear?" he said.

Claire shook her head. "Your hair will tickle my nose and make me sneeze. Can Mummy whisper?"

"So, it doesn't matter if I sneeze?" said Einna.

"Mummy doesn't know what you want, Claire," said John. "We shall have to go and let the others have their turn if you don't tell Santa now."

"I'll tell Santa," said Dave. "Whisper what you want to me, Claire."

"What a good idea," said Santa. "And is Uncle Dave to choose your present out of the sack?"

"No," said Claire, shaking her head. "He might choose a girl's present and I want a car. He's not my real uncle. He's a friend uncle."

Father Christmas laughed. "I stand corrected. But you've now told me what you want. I shall have to tell Rudolf what a tomboy you are."

"No, I'm not a tomboy." She turned to Einna. "What's a tomboy, Mummy?"

"A girl who behaves like a boy." She smiled at Santa.

Claire shook her head. "No, I'm not a tomboy. I want a pink car for Barbie. I like pink and Barbie likes pink, so she needs a car that's pink. Can I stroke Rudolf?"

"I'm afraid he's not here. All the reindeer are in Lapland with the elves."

Claire was disappointed up to the moment she opened her blue paper wrapped present. It was a dinky toy of an E-Type Jaguar, red not pink. "Look," she said to Einna, wriggling to get down. "It's red not pink. Princess Bethany can have it. Look, Daddy."

"Who's Princess Bethany?" I asked Einna.

"She's a princess in an ongoing, made-up story we're telling at bedtime. We have a quarter of an hour of Princess Bethany then a quarter of an hour of a book. It's the book that helps her to cuddle down and go to sleep. The made up story is interactive. Yesterday we decided that Bethany was given a sport's car for her eighteenth birthday."

"Lucky Bethany, I said. If I'm good will Santa give me a red sports car?" Suddenly I realised I couldn't see Stuart and my flippant question dropped like a stone with my stomach. "Trevor, I can't see Stuart." When had he slipped his hand out of mine? I could feel panic bubbling. A huge forest, darkness approaching.

"He's there, with Sophie, look." Trevor pointed to a big plastic model of Rudolf. Stuart and Sophie were up on his back.

"Santa's helpers said they could have a ride," said Bill.

"Your turn to speak to Santa, Stuart," I called.

Bill put Jacob on the ground and hoiked the children off Rudolph. He carried the pair over to the queue, one under each arm; not a small feat as they were big for five and seven year olds. They squealed with pleasure.

Stuart chattered all the way to Angela and Dave's house. "Which bit did you like best, Mummy? I liked riding on the reindeer; no, chasing the squirrels."

"You didn't chase squirrels, did you?"

"Yes, they didn't mind. They knew we couldn't catch them. I wish I could whizz up a tree like a squirrel."

He was still chattering later, as I put him to bed.

The following day, we decorated the tree.

"We didn't do it until Christmas Eve, last year," grumbled Trevor as he went to get the stepladder from the coach house.

"I know. But it seems a shame not to have it up for a bit longer, and I want to see what the new lights look like."

Last year we'd had the tree lights from Trevor's childhood. They were very pretty; each little shade had a nursery rhyme figure on it. But sadly, several bulbs had blown and I couldn't buy replacements.

The phone rang just as Trevor, perched precariously on a ladder, was putting the fairy on the top of the tree. He had already tested the lights.

It was Katy. "I don't know what to get Trevor for Christmas."

I told her about the masks in the shop in Ranelagh Street and, within minutes, we were giggling.

In the end, she decided to let Molly choose. "It'll be interesting to see what she picks," she said.

She chose a purple V-necked sweater. It suited Trevor perfectly. He had just unwrapped it when the phone rang.

As I sat by my dad's corpse, trying to make sense of his death. I wished I could have gone back to before Christmas, so that I could have spent more time with him. The 'never agains' piled up around me. *Why did I take it for granted that you would always be here, Dad?* No one could answer the question for me.

About a month after he died, when I was on the phone to Katy, I felt a small hand tugging at my jeans. "Mummy,"

"I'll have to go, Katy, Stuart wants me. I'll phone you back later. What do you want, poppet?"

"You were laughing."

"Yes."

"Does that mean you're happy?"

"Yes." 'Sort of' was too difficult to explain to a five year old.

"Is Granddad alive again? I miss Granddad. He was going to take me to see Liverpool play."

I miss him too. "Oh sweetheart." I shook my head. "No, he isn't. But Granddad wouldn't want us to be sad all the time. He'd like us to be happy and laugh, wouldn't he?"

"Granddad laughs a lot." *That 'laughs', not 'laughed'.* "Like you do sometimes. Nana Edith doesn't laugh much."

"No."

"I don't think she's a laughy sort of person."

Why doesn't my mother laugh? I can't ever remember her laughing. She must have laughed, surely. I must ask Einna if she ever remembers Pearl laughing? "Perhaps you should ask her why she doesn't laugh."

"Will she mind?"

I put my arms round Stuart. He cuddled in close to me. "I don't think so."

"Mummy, can you and I go to home matches?"

Interesting that he didn't say, 'Can Daddy and I go?'

"We'll see."

"When Daddy says, 'we'll see', it's 'no'."

"Well I don't mean, no." *It's true. But not just Trevor. For most adults 'we'll see' buys time because they don't want to say 'no' or 'yes'. Sometimes it is 'yes' right away.* "Not this time. I just don't know if we can use Granddad's season ticket. I'll have to ask."

"Oh." There was a pause. "Mummy, I don't want to go in a box."

"Box? We can't go in a box if we go to a match. We'll go in the Kop."

"Not football box, Mummy. A box for dead people."

"A coffin?" He nodded. "Granddad said, 'that's what a coffin is, Stuart, a wooden box.' didn't he?"

"I don't remember."

"When you wanted to bury Marmaduke." Marmaduke was Stuart's Guinea Pig.

"Oh yes, I remember."

"Marmaduke's box didn't have gold handles."

"You mean brass."

"Is brass the same colour as gold?"

"Yes."

He nodded as though brass was alright. "Was granddad's box comfortable?"

Stuart hadn't gone to the Crematorium. We hadn't wanted him to see the box disappearing into the flames. Edith had insisted on a Christian funeral service, *Abide With Me* being the compromise hymn. My dad couldn't have made his wishes clear, unless she had chosen to ignore them. Controller in much of his life. Controller in his death? It was possible.

"Yes, very comfortable. It was lined with red satin."

"Red. What's satin?"

"Shiny material."

"I'm going to do work," he said, and pottered off upstairs, a miniature Trevor. I rang Katy back.

Just before lunch, I heard, "Mummy, Daddy, come and look at my box."

Trevor, hunger I suspected having drawn him down from his studio, was already in Stuart's bedroom when I got there. Stuart had created the outline of a box with every brick he possessed. In it was his pillow and the cushions that Debbie had made for him as a welcome present when he was born; one was blue, like the sky, with different coloured balloons appliquéd on. The other was bright pink with shooting stars and his initials. On the pillow were his two favourite bedtime toys, Mr Duster, a furry monkey, and a blow-up dinosaur called Next Wednesday, both presents from Molly.

We never did discover the reason for the names. None of Stuart's cuddly toys had normal names like, Snowy, or Cuddles, or Goldie.

"See," he said as he climbed into the box, "I can fit in too. I don't have any shiny stuff but I don't mind, I like my cushions." How I stopped myself from crying, I didn't know. "Did they let Granddad have a cup of tea and a biscuit in his box?"

"Er—" *How do I answer?*

"I'd like a cup of tea and a biscuit in my box."

"You can have that this afternoon. It's time for lunch now."

Stuart liked tea. He had strange tastes for a five year old. Tea, quite milky, but no sugar. His preferred biscuits were plain, wafer biscuits, the kind you have with ice-cream. He loved brussels sprouts more than roast potatoes and asked to have mint-sauce with every meal.

As I was dishing up, I said, "I know neither of us believed in an after life, Dad so I'm talking to my memory of you. Your grandson has ritualised death for himself, so he can understand it, hasn't he? You'd have approved of that. Perhaps death won't have dominion over him now?"

Chapter Twelve
What A World

You can't judge a book by its cover.

Was loving another person a foolish thing to do because of the potential hurt? I'd loved my dad, and he had been taken from me before his three score years and ten. I'd loved Trevor; I still loved Trevor, but he wasn't the man with whom I'd fallen in love. I loved Stuart, and I quailed each time I thought of anything bad befalling him. I loved my friends. Oh, how I wanted to be a mother hen and keep all the people I loved safe under my wings. How foolish. There was only a certain amount of safety a hen could provide for her chicks and she was vulnerable to predators, like foxes.

There are so many different kinds of love: loving, caring, falling in love, sexual love, or was that lust? Friendship love, duty love; that had to be what I felt for Edith. Was infatuation a kind of love?

How many times had I wondered why my dad had fallen in love with my mother? The photo I used to look at, covertly, showed a very different person to the woman I knew. Why had she changed? Why, on the whole, was the world such a sour place for her? And why me? Why was I the one person who had to endure her bile? How long had the falling in love lasted? There hadn't seemed to be much evidence of it when Ian and I were children. Yet, my dad wouldn't gainsay her, hadn't allowed criticism. He had sighed a lot when I talked about her. But that wasn't love in the way I felt married love ought to be. But how ought it to be? What was it? Perhaps all there was, after the first flush, was loyalty and duty. Famous people threw away husbands and wives at the sniff of another. Was it that they felt it their right to be always in the first flush? Of course, they could afford to be.

In the beginning... In the far off beginning, when I was still a teenager, and Trevor in his early twenties... *My god! I was so young when we first met. Far too young to be anything other than a silly girl. Yes, I'd had ambitions, ambitions that Edith had temporarily thwarted, and they hadn't included falling in... whatever it was I'd felt.*

It certainly hadn't been love at first sight. I had been attracted to a man with floppy, dark hair who seemed so sophisticated. But looking back, I don't think I would have been devastated if he hadn't got round to asking me out. However, he had, and love had grown through weekly dates. When I knew, when I was sure, and egged on by Leila, I had allowed him to make love to me. We had been careful. Trevor wouldn't have wanted a mistaken pregnancy and I wouldn't have wanted the shame of having to tell Edith I was going to have a baby. What would I have done if...? Accepted being a wife and mother? I hadn't been seriously considering college, then, had I? Had I? If I hadn't, why had I been doing my A-levels? Whatever had been going on back then, I think my dad knew we had been up to more than chaste kissing on the doorstep.

Trevor and I used to have fun together. We used to have stimulating conversations and a fulfilling sex life. The knowledge that I loved, was loved, persisted up to Stuart's terrible twos, *no, be honest, Maggie, up to your pregnancy,* and then it changed, not all at once, but like a drip leak will mark the surface on which it drips. After I went back to work, I became a juggler. I juggled work, Stuart, a husband who had become reclusive, friends, family and Munster Mansion. I was forever thrashing around in the heart of a dark, dark wood, where the undergrowth consisted mostly of brambles and briars that tore my clothes and scratched my skin. Ahead were glimpses of fresh green, leafy boughs, dappled with sunlight that, like mirages, disappeared as I neared them.

If I tried to tell Trevor how I was feeling, all he said was, "You do too much, Maggie."

'Largely because you do so fucking little,' I didn't say. *'I carry us. You moan and groan and pass your hand across your eyes. You don't even rake your fingers through your hair any longer.'*

"I do so much, Trevor because… You used to go out with me, the cinema, theatre, visit friends. Now, I have to drag you anywhere. You don't even want to go out for a drink with Leila and Mac. Why?" *And where are your new compositions and concerts?*

"I can watch good plays and films at home, on the telly. And I've heard everything anyone of your friends has to say."

My friends? "They used to be your friends. Mac used to be your friend."

"We have nothing in common now, Maggie. I've moved on."

Moved on? Where to? An eerie in a gothic monstrosity of a house. I don't want you to have moved on. I liked – loved – the person you were.

Sadness tangled around me as I was forced to wonder if I would have married Trevor, knowing how he would change? But, no marriage, no Stuart, no Katy, no Molly, no Einna, maybe no Debbie or Angela. I was fortunate to have them in my life. It was a good thing we couldn't see into our futures.

In sunny glade moments, I enjoyed the company of the Trevor of my late teens, early twenties, but anxiety was always present, for I knew that the briars and brambles were beyond the glade.

Sometimes I wondered if Trevor would have been different if he hadn't been the child of a single mother? *No, I don't mean that. I'm sure Katy was a wonderful mother.* But, his dad leaving for work one morning, never to return must have been traumatic. From what I'd gathered, Katy had put aside her sadness and devoted herself to her children. She had never remarried. One day, she told me that from time to time she had been out on dates, and once had felt comfortable enough to invite the man round for a meal.

As they were saying goodnight, he'd told her that when he moved in, he would need to make changes. Katy was astonished.

"I'd no thought of him moving in, Maggie. I mean we'd been to the cinema a couple of times, and gone for a drink afterwards. We seemed to be getting on okay, that's all. He made me laugh. So I asked him round for a meal. He really threw me saying that, but I wasn't going to let him see I was put out, was I? So I said, 'What changes had you in mind then?'

"'Well, your children don't have very good table manners, do they? They talk while they're eating, and they really oughtn't to be allowed to get down from the table until everyone has finished. I mean I know it's been hard on you, not having a man around.'

"'They asked to get down,' I said.

"'In my opinion, they shouldn't even have asked.'

"'Thank you for your opinion. It was most helpful,' I said. And I began to close the door.

"'Hey,' he said. 'We haven't made another date.'

"'No we haven't' I said. 'And we're not going to. Your opinion helped me to realise I never want to see you again.' What an escape, eh Maggie?"

Ruth, Trevor's sister, didn't suffer from lethargic moods like Trevor. She had Katy and Molly's sunny disposition and Katy's energy. Maybe Trevor was more like his father? I used to think he was like Katy but perhaps his dad's genes had pushed to the front since Stuart… Bloody hell! Lightening struck me. His dad had walked out on his family, physically. Trevor had walked out on us, mentally. Like father, like son.

Earlier that year I'd suggested Trevor should go to see our doctor, but he'd vehemently refused, saying there was nothing wrong and I knew very little, if anything, about the creative process. *In other words, Maggie, put up and shut up.* Of course it wasn't true. I did know about the creative process, but my process was different from his. I didn't want to have a row, so I left it there.

Sometimes, when we don't seem to be able to see a way through the tangles of problems, an event, a situation can pull us out of the snarl, for a while at any rate.

Before I knew it, or that's what it felt like, Stuart was on the cusp of going to senior school.

One of his junior school friends, Neil, lived a couple of doors away. Their friendship would persist into secondary school. At weekends they were in and out each other's houses, and during the holidays, Neil spent nearly all his time at our house. It suited Eileen and Geoff, Neil's parents, as their jobs didn't include school holidays. I certainly didn't mind; I liked Neil and his parents. If they took the situation for granted, I allowed it. It had no effect on Trevor. At lunch, sometimes, he would say, "You here again, Neil?" But it was said without rancour. The boys didn't intrude upon his inertia.

One day, not long after the boys had broken up for the summer, they asked if they could go to the small park by the church to play football. Having an hour or two to myself, I decided to catch up on some phone calls and plan a day out, either to Ainsdale or Caldy, with the gang plus children. Trevor was doing whatever Trevor did up in his eerie, so it was I, not the both of us, who was interrupted by two excited ten year olds.

"Mum, Mum, look what we've found," Stuart was holding up a black leather briefcase. His auburn hair, a darker red than mine, but just as curly, danced when he was excited.

Physically, Trevor and I were an odd pair. I was short, five foot two. Trevor was tall, six foot one. I had unruly, red hair. He had sleek, dark brown. I had hazel eyes, he had blue. I had a pale skin that burnt as soon as the sun looked at it, he an olive one which tanned evenly. Stuart was a real mixture of us both. Auburn haired, tall for his age, with blue eyes that lit up when he was excited, as though a lamp had been switched on in his head. I doubt Stuart knew the effect this had on people. It made a lump come to my throat that I swallowed as I didn't want to embarrass him.

"Where on earth did you find that?" I asked.

"Under a bush in the churchyard."

"What were you doing in the churchyard? I thought you were playing footy in the park?"

"We were. Neil kicked the ball too high and it went over the wall, so we had to get it."

Stuart knew we didn't think it appropriate to play in the churchyard. It seemed disrespectful to the people buried there, and their families.

"I could see it under a bush, Mum. There were loads of nettles, so I took off my t-shirt and wrapped my hand in it. When I pulled out the ball, I saw the briefcase. Someone must have hidden it there. You can't drop a briefcase under a bush."

Neil shook his head. "It must have got there today 'cause it's not dirty or scruffy, is it, Mrs Harvey? It rained last night too."

"What do you think we ought to do with it, Mum? We tried to open it to see if there was an address or something inside, so we could take it to the person's house. But Neil said in any case we shouldn't, because if someone did put it there on purpose, they wouldn't like us looking in it, or taking it to where they lived."

"I think Neil was right," I said, though I was finding it difficult to imagine why someone would shove a briefcase under a bush. "We must take it to the police station. It's a good thing your dad decided he didn't want to go to The Walker after all, because we can use the car."

"Dad's always deciding things like that. But Mum we can walk."

We could. But somehow I felt it would be better to take the car in case the person who had hidden it, saw us. Intuition?

The desk sergeant took down the boys' statement and told us that they would deal with it from then on. He also said that the boys had behaved like good citizens and told them that he would be in touch if whoever had left the case wanted to thank them.

"Do you think there'll be a reward, Mum?" asked Stuart as we got back in the car.

"I doubt it. But you never know."

"That sergeant didn't behave like a pig," said Neil.

Stuart giggled. "But he did look a bit like one."

"Stuart! That's not very polite."

"But he did, Mum. He was quite fat, and he had little piggy eyes and a snouty nose."

The boys rolled about with laughter in the back of the car.

"I'm shocked at you both," I said. "He was an ordinary… Okay, he did look a little—"

"See?" said Stuart.

I joined them in their hilarity; all the time thinking what a cow I was and what a bad example I was setting.

A couple of days later we got a phone-call. It wasn't at all what I or Trevor had expected and we couldn't tell the boys what the sergeant told us.

"Mrs Harvey? It's Sergeant Miles. That briefcase. When we got it open, we found it contained an address book and a list of Dutch suppliers of pornographic videos."

"What?" I gasped. "How do you know they were pornographic?"

"The titles of the videos they offered, plus the blurb. I won't go into details. We think the address of the owner of the briefcase was on a letter. It's too much of a coincidence, else. He's one of your neighbours."

"One of our neighbours? Not Vincent Mather?"

"Yes, Mr. Mather. Just out of interest, why did you suggest him?"

Why did I? "Because we know Neil's parents; they live on one side, the Mathers live on the other, and Mr Mather seems…" I shook my head. "I don't really know. I just don't like him. He… he's a know-it-all."

"Right. I don't have to tell you that we don't want you to talk about this to anyone, do I? That includes the boys, of course."

"Neil's already told his parents about finding the briefcase."

"That's understandable. The DI in charge wants to come to talk to you and Neil's parents. Could we do it at your house?"

"Of course. Both Neil's parents work. That's why he spends so much time with us. So a sensible time would be around six."

"I'll let the DI know. Do you have a contact number for them? Only I know he wants to see you all ASAP."

"Eileen usually collects Neil about five. I'll mention it then. She can ring Geoff."

We neither got on nor didn't get on with the Mathers. They kept themselves to themselves, which suited us, as I knew from the odd encounter that we didn't have much in common. The wife was very thin, and on the occasions I'd seen her and passed the time of day, she had seemed very shy. The man was a different kettle of fish. He was short, stocky and in character, bumptious. He always exhibited an overweening certainty that he knew everything. If ever I happened to bump into him, he kept me talking. It was almost as though he wanted me to know how well informed he was, for whatever subject cropped up, Vince would claim knowledge of it. Chip on the shoulder? Self made man? Little man with huge ego? Any one of these labels fitted Vince Mather. If I happened to be going out, and saw him come out of his front door I would nip back into the house and wait until it was safe.

As it was raining, both boys were in Stuart's bedroom playing Monopoly. We had planned to go to Caldy, maybe walk over to Hilbre Island with Debbie, Sophie and Jacob, if the tide allowed. But that was weather dependant and it didn't look as though it was going to clear up. In any case, going to Caldy and Hilbre would have been risky with a home deadline of six. I explained this to Sergeant Miles and asked if it would be alright to tell Debbie why we had to postpone our plans.

"I'm afraid I can't give you that authorisation. It's a pretty delicate matter, as you're probably aware."

So, I've got to lie to Debbie. No, I won't do it. Debbie doesn't know Vince and she's not a blabbermouth. I'd rather lie to the sergeant. "Okay. I'll have to find another excuse. I hope your DI won't tell the boys anything about the stuff in the briefcase?"

"He won't. He'll tell them it's to do with a crime and they mustn't say anything to anyone else. I think that's all, Mrs Harvey."

The first thing I did when I put down the phone was ring Debbie.

"Bloody-hell! I remember you telling me you hadn't taken to Vince Mather, but this…"

"I'm still having a hard job believing it."

"It doesn't look as though it's going to stop raining. I may take the girls to see *The Slipper and The Rose*. Let's postpone until tomorrow, Maggie."

After I'd put down the phone, I went up to the attic to tell Trevor what had happened. We agreed that we weren't going to let Stuart be embroiled in the case after today, and that Trevor, because he was less emotional than I, would make sure no questions were asked that would upset the boys. Despite the disturbing circumstances we now found ourselves in, I couldn't help feeling happy that, for now, Trevor and I were in accord. Then it hit me; a blow that winded.

"Oh my god, Trevor, selling porn's a criminal activity."

"Yes. That's why the phone-call and the visit." Trevor sounded puzzled.

"What if Vince belongs to some gang, and because of what's happened, the boys—"

"Don't go there, Maggie. Vince is probably a small time crook, nothing more."

"I knew…" *Don't say it, Maggie. Don't spoil the oneness.*

"Knew what?"

Knew that moving to Munster Mansion would be a disaster. "Nothing. You're right. I mustn't be a worry-guts." Trevor smiled and patted my shoulder. "Right. I'm going to make some stilton and broccoli soup for lunch," I said. "It's that recipe Angela gave me. Okay with you?" Trevor didn't answer. "Trevor?"

He jumped. "Sorry, sweetheart." *When was the last time he called me 'sweetheart'?* "I've just had an idea for a composition. Bloody hell, Maggie, how long has it been since I had one? I've got to get it down before it goes." He grabbed his notepad.

I was moved by his excitement. "The soup will be ready in about forty-five minutes. I'll ask the boys to fetch you. If you're not ready to come down, you can tell them and I'll keep your soup warm for you."

DI Standing and DS Jones arrived promptly at six. Neil's mum was with us, but his dad was in a meeting. It wasn't a problem. First they told the boys that they weren't to tell anyone about the briefcase as it was connected to a crime and they wanted to catch the criminals. There were papers in the briefcase that showed Mr Mather had broken the law. "He's been doing a bit of smuggling," said DI Standing.

Clever. Of course that's precisely what he had been doing. Luckily the boys didn't ask what he'd been smuggling.

"We don't want them to be warned that we have the case. Have you told anyone other than your parents?"

Neil shook his head.

"What about Sarah?" asked his mum. Sarah was Neil's older sister.

"She wasn't there when I told you and Dad," said Neil. "She was at her friend's and… she's not very interested in what I do."

"Usual big sister stuff," said Neil's mum. "I didn't say anything to her and neither did my husband."

"Are you sure?"

"Yes. Oh, and because he couldn't be here, I rang his office to remind him not to say anything to anyone. I guessed that you'd want to apprehend Mr Mather and charge him first."

"Thank you. Stuart?"

"If it was term time, I might have told my other friends. But 'cause it's the hols, I haven't seen any of them."

"Good. I'm sure you both know how to keep secrets. We'll tell you when it's all over and you can let the secret out."

"Once it's out, it won't be a secret any more," said Stuart.

"No it won't. Is there somewhere the boys can go while we talk to you adults?" he asked Trevor and I.

"They can watch telly and we can go down to the basement."

"It's stopped raining, Mum. Can we play boules in the garden?"

The previous summer, Trevor had surprised me by agreeing to go camping in France. One of the bonuses of two salaries was, we could say 'yes' to a holiday, even though it meant postponing a house DIY job. We had found a holiday company that had tents set up and equipped. It was in Brittany. Boules had become a favourite pastime in the evenings. At the end of the holiday, Stuart had persuaded us to buy some with our remaining francs. I thought Trevor had enjoyed the holiday; he'd seemed relaxed. Luckily for Geoff and Eileen, we had all been away at the same time.

"Good idea. It will be splish-splash boules."

DI Standing told us adults that they had discovered a garage full of videos. Two uniformed policemen had stayed in the house to await Vince's return. His wife was in hysterics, apparently. She said she knew nothing about the videos. She never went in the garage because she didn't drive and Vince kept it locked.

"I felt quite sorry for her," said DS Jones.

"Fancy being married to someone like that?" I said.

"Will she stay married to him, I wonder?" said Eileen.

The court case caused quite a stir in the local papers and on *Look North*. Vince was sent to prison for eighteen months. Someone put the Mathers' house up for sale.

"He'll be out in twelve, I bet," said Angela, when we talked about it after the case was done and dusted.

I hoped not. I wasn't glad that the Mathers had moved because I felt so sorry for his wife, but I was glad because of Vince. My skin crawled at the idea of continuing to live next door to him

The boys were proud of their part in the arrest of a criminal. For days they couldn't stop talking about it. Then something else came along to take their minds and ours elsewhere. Neil's parents asked us if Stuart could go on holiday with them, and Mr Thompson, the warden of the sheltered accommodation where Molly had lived before the fire, was arrested. Indirectly, Stuart and Neil were responsible for his arrest. His name, address and phone number were in the book in the briefcase. When the police took him down to the station to interview him, he confessed. Every word Molly had said about him was true.

"When I was a teenager," I said to Katy. "I would never have believed I would know two horrible criminals engaged in similar crimes; crimes against women, and vulnerable adults who needed looking after, not abusing. What a world!"

"Molly was quite upset about Mr Thompson. 'He wasn't bad,' she kept saying. 'He was kind to me. He always brought a bottle of that red stuff when he wanted his lolly to go into my hole. Then we watched Corrie.' She meant port. 'I shall go to that place and tell the man, you know, the one who puts hair on his head, I didn't mind. It was nice. He gave me a cuddle and a kiss.' Do you know, Maggie, it made me question it being wrong. Molly was saying, quite clearly, although she couldn't find all the words, that Mr Thompson hadn't coerced her, hadn't abused her. Maybe the other women weren't abused either?"

"Why did he feel the need to have sex with the other women in his care, when Molly was willing? He was a sicko, Katy."

"Perhaps," said Katy. She didn't sound convinced.

Chapter Thirteen
Abercrombie Mansion

All good things must come to an end.

When Einna rang me up to tell me that the January coastal storms were giving her nightmares because Hunstanton pier had been swept away, I felt that, she needed more than a jaunt.

"It was like I was taken back into my childhood, Maggie, you know, when Matilda was swept away?"

Matilda, a beach hut, her sanctuary. *Counselling is all very well,* I thought. *But childhoods, good and bad, haunt.*

I rang Debbie. "Do you fancy a weekend in London soon?"

"Sounds great, Maggie. But I've got a hell of a lot of OU stuff coming up, including a weekend in York in March, so I think I'm going to have to say, no."

"Oh, you and your OU."

"I love it. Sometimes I wish I had been this old when I did my teacher training."

"You were deffo on the ball then, friend."

"Deffo? You sound like…"

Like I did way back when…

I rang Angela. She was enthusiastic. Now it rested on Einna, as we needed to borrow her aunt and uncle's flat. A hotel in London, even with our Persil tickets, which hadn't come yet, would be too expensive.

When I spoke to her about it, she pulled a face. "Great for two," she said. "No good for more, sorry Maggie. From what Aunty Ruby tells me, there's no room to swing a cat. Where did that awful… Oh, wait a mo. It's not cat, as in furry animal. It's cat, as in cat-o'-nine tails, isn't it? Anyway, you can't swing one."

"Okay. What do I think? I think you and I should go. Angela will be fine with that. She'll understand. Okay, up to you now."

"She will? I don't want to hurt her feelings."

"I'll ring her, then I'll ring you back."

Angela was fine about it. Coincidentally, Debbie had suggested that they both go to York. Angela could do her own thing, and when Debbie wasn't involved in a lecture or tutorial, they could explore the city.

Waiting. I've always hated waiting. But then the Persil tickets arrived and I managed to get tickets for *Once A Catholic*.

"All we want is a room in Bloomsbury…" I tap danced into the lounge, well my idea of a tap dance; I'd never had lessons. Was Wardour Street anywhere near Bloomsbury? I was very ignorant when it came to areas and streets in London.

"I'm a catholic and I'm okay.
There's penance by night
There's penance by day."

Trevor, who was watching the six o'clock news frowned and put his hands over his ears. "Do stop caterwauling, Maggie. What are you so pleased about?"

"I've managed to get tickets for *Once A Catholic*. And I'm not caterwauling."

"That's a matter of opinion. I hope you're not expecting me to go with you."

Would I? "Oh Trevor, I told you ages ago that Einna and I wanted to go. It's had fabby reviews. But I didn't know if the show would be booked up. It is, on the Saturday but not the Friday, still beggars can't be—'

"Maggie you're gabbling. Slow down please. The reason I miss so much of what you tell me is because you gabble."

Not true. You don't listen. I'm talking as I've always talked. "So, I've booked for the Friday." I said talking deliberately slowly.

"There's no need for that."

"It started with free Persil Tickets—"

"Persil tickets?" Trevor was looking more and more bemused.

"Einna and I both use Persil. They've had a special offer on for a few months now. Collect the tops of packets and you get return tickets to London, as long as they're not at peak travel times. Einna has asked her aunt and uncle if we can use their flat. Is Wardour Street any where near Bloomsbury?"

"Is that where the flat is?"

"Uh-huh. Abercrombie Mansion. Sounds posh, doesn't it? It's for Tory MPs, civil servants, and consultants who work for the government. Einna's Uncle Charles is a consultant on agricultural matters, so he gets the use of a flat."

"And he's allowed to loan it out?"

"I suppose so. He said Einna could borrow it, sometime."

"Right." Trevor's 'right' sounded doubtful. There was a pause. "It's nothing to do with me, but—"

"I've met Einna's uncle. He's very proper. He wouldn't do something that was against the rules."

"Um."

I suspected that the 'um' meant I was being naïve in assuming 'proper' was an adjective to be used in conjunction with anyone connected to politics. *Why am I remembering the Profumo Affair? Daft. Especially in relation to Einna's Uncle and Aunt. They were two of her guardian angels.*

"So, you and Einna are going to London to see *Once a Catholic*, when?"

"Third weekend in March."

"Right. Not a gang jaunt, then? Won't the other 'monstrous' women be upset?"

"We're not umbilically attached."

"You could have fooled me."

"I did ask them. But Debbie has an OU weekend and Angela is going with her. Even if they had been free, it would have been difficult.

The flat sleeps two, no extras possible; probably not allowed. And you ought to stop calling us 'monstrous' women. 'Gang' we don't mind."

"You are monstrous women, bossy and loud."

"We're positive, not bossy. We get things done." *Things you men would leave until the twelfth of never. As for loud, I admit I'm a bit loud, so is Angela. Debbie isn't and Einna's quietly spoken.* "I'm going to ring Einna now."

Trevor didn't reply. He was immersed in the news again. My plans would soon be forgotten in the midst of national and international affairs.

Einna sounded as though she'd run a marathon when she picked up the phone. "They've come," I said.

"What have come?"

"Oh, Einna, I know you've just got in from work, but do get your head into gear. What have we been waiting for?"

"It's a wonder I can hold the phone, my hands are so cold, let alone use my brain. The Persil tickets?"

"Yes. Why haven't you... I don't need to ask: Scrooge."

"Whatever the weather, the heating doesn't kick in until six. Claire does her homework wrapped up in my black baa-lamb coat."

"In winter I insist on a four o'clock start. Weekends and holidays it's on all the time, but I turn the thermostat down. Now, do you want the good news or the bad?"

"Bad?"

"Saturday evening's performance is full, so I've booked for Friday, which means we'll need the afternoon off work. We can't catch a train after five that'll get us to London in time to leave our cases at Abercrombie Mansion, freshen up, and make the show. Can you ring your aunt and uncle to confirm that it's still okay for us to use the flat that weekend, and give me a bell when you've spoken to them.?Abercrombie Mansion, posh or what?"

"Okay, but what's the good news?"

"That we're going. Byee."

I wanted to go to Carnaby Street, Liberty's and the just off Bond Street, street where Sandra Rhodes' shop was. I hoped I might find some cheap, wacky earrings, somewhere. I hadn't got as many as Einna, but I did like unusual ones. Soon, wants were tumbling about my mind. Mentally I rubbed my hands. A weekend in a luxury flat, in London. I wished March was next month instead of two months' time. "Dad," I said to his framed photo on the wall of the room I considered my study. "I bet you would enjoy *Once a Catholic*. It's a play that pokes fun at the catholic church."

One of the things I had to consider was, how I was going to organise time off work on the Friday? I could ask Mr Thompson if I could have the afternoon off in lieu of all the extra work I did in after school clubs and productions. I now offered two drama clubs per week and one production per term. But I suspected he wouldn't agree to that. Nearer the time, no, the day before, I'd have to feign an illness. *What will Trevor think? Don't know. I have lost the ability to decipher Trevor's thoughts.* Once we were so close we always knew what the other one was thinking. *No you didn't, Maggie. No one knows, really knows.* I sighed.

The day we moved in to Munster Mansion we had a water fight. My dad, Edith, Katy and Molly had gone home. As the door closed behind them, I felt a shiver of apprehension about what the move meant. Then, in the porch, I saw the high powered water pistols Mr Clarke had used to chase cats out of the garden. He had left them for us. I grabbed the guns, filled them with water, and initiated the water fight to stave off whatever furies were lurking behind closed doors and under floors. Two year old Stuart looked at us as though we were mad. Clem arrived in the middle of it with a moving in gift. Reluctantly, we had stopped chasing each other round the house and opened the bubbly he'd brought.

"Just out of curiosity," he said. "Why have you got two water pistols? I mean, Stuart's a bit young for toys like that, isn't he? Do you often have water fights?"

I was crying with laughter before he arrived, laughter that was near to tears.

"Cats," Trevor said as though that one word explained everything.

"Cats?"

"The previous owners said that the neighbours' cats used the garden as their toilet and Mr Clarke used to chase them off with his water pistols. A two gun toting cat hater. He's left them for us as they've moved into a flat. I don't hate cats, neither does Maggie. She hates me."

"She doesn't, Trevor. To use one of her sayings, she loves the bones of you."

"It was a joke, Clem." Trevor squirted water at him. Clem sidestepped but not in time.

"I hate you when you get water in my eyes, Trevor." *Water in my eyes. A song by Maggie Harvey.*

"All's fair in… my darling wife."

"I see," Clem said as though he didn't. He got out a hanky and wiped his face. "Well, I'll leave you to your unpacking. If you want any help with DIY, just phone me."

"No, stay for fish and chips. In fact, perhaps you and Trevor could go and get them while I get Stuart ready for bed? You can help us christen Munster Mansion." I wanted to prolong the fun.

"I would have thought you'd already done that."

Later, after showing him out, I couldn't help thinking how odd life was. That man had been so difficult during my first year in the school; picking me up on the smallest detail. He'd thought I was an easy lay. He'd broken down and told me things that I'd rather not have been privy to, and now divorced, had become a good friend to both Trevor and I. He was still a bit of a stuffed shirt, but he had a kind heart. Trevor enjoyed arguing with him. Their views on life were almost totally opposed. Clem was a church going Tory, and Trevor an atheist/Liberal.

But that was then. Fun with Trevor, now? Was before an illusion? Like words dancing on the ceiling?

I went into the lounge. Stuart was still watching the television. "Hey young man, you know you have to be in bed by nine-thirty on school days."

"But this program finishes at ten. Please, Mum."

Sometimes I gave in for all sorts of reasons. Normally Stuart didn't try to extend the time to past nine-thirty. I gave a 'Trevor' shrug. "Into bed spit spot as soon as it's over, then."

"Mu-um! I'm twelve, not six."

"When did you get to be that old?" I was only half joking. I gave him a hug which he didn't shrug off. Even in public, Stuart allowed me to hug him.

At ten-thirty I realised Einna had forgotten to, or couldn't ring me for some reason, so I rang her. I wanted to know, before I went to bed, that having the flat that weekend was possible.

"You were going to ring me," I said. I heard John's voice in the background asking who it was and Einna telling him it was me. "What was all that about?"

"Just John complaining about the late hour for a phone call. Sorry I didn't ring you back, I got immersed in preparation and then he started interrogating me about Ruby and Charles."

"Grunt and Groan. Other women don't have Grunts and Groans for husbands."

"I bet some do, and, I bet some husbands have Grunts and Groans for wives. Look at your Mother and Annie."

"Do I have to?" An image of the two women threatened to burst my happiness bubble. That Annie didn't have a husband had escaped Einna's mind, but I knew what she meant. "They'll spoil my picture of our London trip. I think my dad died to escape Edith."

"Maggie!"

"What?" *It's true. I do sometimes catch myself thinking that.* "We do shoulder burdens, don't we? No wonder we need wet-knickers, giggling sessions. What did the Roly Polies say?"

"That the weekend we want the flat is fine."

"Fabby." It was double, fabby. I wanted to put on my imaginary tap shoes and dance all round the house. "How are they?"

"Ruby's as scatty as ever, Charles, still trying to keep her feet on the ground."

"They remind me of characters in a Dornford Yates novel. I keep expecting Charles to talk about Ruby's fine grey eyes and dainty feet."

"He seems a little worried about her memory, but she's always been scatty. Anyway, I'd better ring off or—"

"Groan will moan. Am I a poet or what? Trevor will probably moan when I tell him I'm going to take all of Friday off. I'm owed, Einna, all the after school stuff I do. I'm going to see Leila. I haven't seen her since she moved to Crewe. It seems too good an opportunity to miss."

"You don't have to swamp me with reasons, friend. Is Trevor okay about looking after Stuart?"

"I haven't mentioned it yet. I shall leave food for them, and Stuart's got footy matches on both Saturday and Sunday, so he'll be out quite a bit. He might want to go to stay with Katy and Molly."

After we finished chatting, I was still feeling excited, happy. I would have liked my pre-Stuart husband to be masterful and carry me off to bed, but there was about as much chance of that as Mary O'Malley visiting Munster Mansion. Sex hadn't altogether fizzled out from our relationship, but at one time we were an almost every day couple. I decided I'd better sort out the Stuart question. Things left… I plodded upstairs.

"I know you'll be fine about being around for Stuart. But Katy and Molly would be only to happy to have him to stay if you'd like a quiet weekend? We're fortunate that he enjoys visiting them and Edith." *Why aren't I asking her? The lecture.*

Trevor looked bemused. "What are you talking about, Maggie."

Of course, our earlier conversation has flown. "When Einna and I go to London?"

"Do we have to discuss it now?"

"No, but I know how these things creep up. It's best to get things sorted early. You know what your mum's like. She needs plenty of notice. She and Molly have a very full social life."

"Meaning I don't, I suppose."

Yes, I mean that. Shall I say, if the cap fits? No. I'm too happy to be contentious. Do an Einna. A lie now and then… "No, I didn't mean that. Don't put words in my mouth. Are you marking?"

"Yes. And don't tell me it's too late and that I won't sleep."

"I don't need to. You've just told yourself. I'll alert Katy. Then she and Stuart can make the final decision."

"Fine."

I knew it wasn't too late to ring Katy. She and Molly rarely went to bed before eleven-thirty. She was only too happy to have Stuart for the weekend.

"Be better for us Saturday. Molly and I go to Bingo on a Friday Night. I'll give Stuart a ring tomorrow. What time does he get in from school?"

"Half four. He'll have footy on Saturday and Sunday.'

"Fine. No problem. Molly will want to feed him egg and chips all weekend. Last time we saw him, he told her it was his favourite meal."

"How is she?"

"Well. She's given up playing which is a blessing. I found doing twirly-whirlies very disorientating. She's now into domesticity. She'll cook egg and chips for all of us, but she won't be able to say what it is. Funny thing, memory."

"Do you think she's re-living her life, Katy? She's been the child. Now she's the young woman keeping house for her parents." *But who was she when she was having sex with Mr Thompson, a rebellious teenager?*

"I suppose it's a possibility."

"I'm going to take the Friday off school."

"Good on yer, girl. The amount of extra you do."

When I put the phone down, I went upstairs to get ready for bed. Trevor was in the bedroom already.

"You're not having the Friday off, are you?' he said.

"You heard?"

"You have a very loud voice, Maggie."

That old chestnut again. "I have to take the Friday off." I explained why.

"I understand, but I don't approve. Don't expect me to lie for you if Clem calls round."

"I'll talk to Clem. He'll have the same reaction as you, I expect."

"I don't know how you do it, Maggie."

"I don't lie very often, Trevor. I can't tell Mr Thompson the truth, can I? Katy told me to go for it. I bet you'd fabricate a story if you had to go somewhere to conduct one of your pieces."

"I would not. I'd want the college to know that they had a sought after composer for a music lecturer; a used-to-be sought after composer."

"You'll be sought after again." *In his dreams.* I suddenly felt a nostalgic yearning for… *Oh contrary Mary. Am I saying I miss his plink plonk? No. It's his being motivated you miss. It's his enthusiasm you miss. You did admire some of his pieces though.*

Time moved January and February slowly towards their ends. March did not come in like a lion. I hoped that would continue. I've always assumed it referred to March gales. I disliked wind more than all other weather. A cold wind blows straight through bodies. London in calm weather would be perfect. *Oh come on, Maggie. It's going to be fun, whatever the weather. Bombs? Am I afraid of bombs? Surely John overreacted? I don't think there have been any incidents since 1976.*

Leila met me off the train at Crewe on the Thursday evening. She hadn't changed. I wondered if she thought I had. I didn't ask her. We had a lazy, catch-up evening. Mac was out at a darts match, her children watched the television, bickered, then pottered up to bed after Leila had reminded them that they were sharing a room, as I was staying the night.

Leila was now the manager of a boutique called *Mesdames et Mesdemoiselles.* It sounded very pretentious. I wondered what the staff made of her overt scouseness.

"The shop's pretend posh," she said.

"I'm not quite sure what you mean."

"You'll see when you come for coffee tomorrow. Shall we say, eleven? You can come into town with me in the morning. I drop the kids off first. That won't be too early for you, will it?"

"I don't know what time you imagine I get up at home."

She grinned. "Well, teachers, you know!"

I hit her with the cushion. If Mac hadn't arrived home, at that moment, jubilant as their team had won, I think we might have had a cushion fight. "You two should do the female scouse greeting tomorrow," he said.

"Brill idea," Leila said. "Crewe needs a bit of entertainment. They seem very staid by comparison with us Scousers."

When I walked into the shop, she squealed, ran out from behind the counter and held out her arms. I held out mine and we ran towards each other, still squealing like stuck pigs, and hugged.

"Oh my god, it's you. How are yer, queen?"

I was so tempted to say, 'The same as I was two hours ago', but that would have spoilt the game.

"Brill, now I've seen your meffy face."

"I'll meff you, girl."

"Hey," I said more quietly. "I don't want to wet me knickers before I catch the train."

She grabbed me and turned me to face the staff and customers; they were all looking somewhat bemused. "This woman saved me life," she said. "She prevented me from having an illegal abortion."

"Leila!" I knew that sometimes I said or did things that weren't entirely appropriate. Leila could be outrageous. This was outrageous, and inappropriate.

"What? You did. You put me straight."

"Yes, I know I did but…" And suddenly I thought that she and I were alike and not alike. Two friends pregnant, but different years. Two babies wanted and not wanted, different reasons. Three fathers, for Mac wasn't Cilla's father. Luckily she was almost the spitting image of Leila, so no one thought to question the paternity. I remembered telling her about crossing bridges.

"I have three gorgeous kids, thanks to my friend here, and Mac's going to give me breast implants for me birthday."

Another bombshell. *Hey, don't start thinking about bombs. What is she like, telling the shop's world? What if someone complains to… who would they complain to? She's the manager of this kitsch boutique.*

I could see what Leila had meant by 'pretend posh'. The floor was false marble. There were ornate gilt mirrors everywhere, and plastic chandeliers. The colour scheme was crimson and gold. It reminded me of how novels described a, tart's boudoir.

When it was time for me to get a taxi, I found it difficult to say goodbye. "We mustn't leave it so long," I said. "You must come over to Liverpool. It's only an hour on the train."

"I know it is, Maggie. I do come over occasionally, to see me mum. She'd be hurt if I combined me visit with seeing any of me friends. She's like that now, you know. Dead different from how she was when were kids. Let's make a date now, or you know what will happen—"

"The months will drift by."

"Whiz more likely. Whoops, there's your taxi. Ta-ra queen. Say 'hi' to Einna for me. Have a great time in The Smoke."

At Crewe station, I saw that the Liverpool train had been cancelled. I rushed to the information desk.

"They're coming by coach. No, new information. They're on the Manchester train. You need to get on it. It's in now. You'll have to run."

I did but the guard prevented me from boarding. He shook his head at my splutters. "But my friend is sailing off to London with no ticket," I shouted. "And it's not her fault. It's yours."

He was unfazed. He looked at his timetable. "You can get the one from Leeds in ten minutes. I'll telephone the Manchester train, and make sure the ticket inspector is apprised of the situation. It wouldn't have been safe for you to board; it was moving."

I thought he was going to add, 'And you're no spring chicken.' If he had, I would have battered him with my shoulder bag. I saw the headlines: *TEACHER CHARGED WITH ASSAULT AND BATTERY.* I saw the lies I'd told being exposed.

When sorrows come, they come not as single spies, but in battalions. Only it wasn't troubles, it was problems. The train I caught was held up outside

Euston for half an hour, because of a bomb scare. *I bet Einna's calling John a Cassandra.* However, Trevor was feeling and behaving, he was not a John.

Of course, it was just a scare; perhaps a hoax even. We would probably never know. When we did meet I said, "I don't know whether I want a cup of tea, or alcohol. What a journey!"

"Charles has put a bottle of champagne in the fridge for us."

"Then why are you keeping me here talking? Let's go."

On the Underground, Einna told me we had to have a chat with Paddy before we went up to the flat.

"Who is Paddy that he demands conversation from delayed, bomb scared women in need of a rooster booster?"

"Haven't I told you about Paddy?"

"No."

"He's… I suppose he's a concierge."

"Liverpool flats don't have concierges. I knew it was a posh place as soon as you told me the name."

"Liverpool flats don't have lifts that work. We can have breakfast in bed, if we want."

"How will I be able to go back to a life of connie-onnie butties and Lambrusco?"

"Maggie, I don't want to wet my knickers in the tube."

"Why not, you wet them everywhere else?"

Oh the carefree joy of gang chitter-chat. Even if we're a divided gang.

When we arrived at Abercrombie Mansion, which wasn't as imposing as its name suggested, we saw a man, not much taller than me, standing on the pavement. He was wearing a grey uniform; a doorman's uniform.

"Paddy?" Einna said.

"I was beginning to get worried, madam. Sir Charles told me you'd be arriving at five."

"I told my uncle we'd arrive 'around' five. I'm sorry if you've been anxious. I'm Einna. This is Maggie."

"Yes, madam. Will I take your cases for you?"

Interesting. He has more or less ignored her introduction.

He didn't wait for an answer, and we trotted after him into the vestibule. "Now, all I need to know is what you'd like for breakfast, madam?"

"I don't think we'll bother with breakfast, Paddy," I said.

He ignored me and addressed Einna. "Sir Charles will be very disappointed, madam. He's paid for your breakfasts. Your aunt likes Fortnum and Mason's croissants."

"That sounds lovely," she said. "Oh, and coffee, please."

I wanted to giggle. Oh, how I wanted to giggle. But I didn't want to hurt his feelings. It was obvious that he was proud of his job and felt his responsibilities keenly.

In the lift I said, "Are we being spoilt or what? Champagne and Fortnum and Mason croissants. As for Paddy, the man's an Irish leprechaun." Einna laughed.

The flat was small, and furnished in art deco style. It had an air of another time about it. "What is this place, Einna? I feel as though I'm in a time warp, if not Berry and Co., definitely Bertie Wooster? And why is one bed higher than the other?" An irreverent thought forced a chuckle out of my mouth. "I've got it."

"What?"

"Charles' bed has to be higher than Ruby's, so he can roll on top for a bit of nookie."

"I don't like to think about Uncle Charles and Aunty Ruby having nookie."

"I've always called them the Roly-Polies, now I know why." A machine whirred into life. "Can you hear a noise, Einna?"

"No."

"Shh. Listen."

"Perhaps the flat's bugged."

"Bugs don't make a noise, they're hidden and silent."

The whirring and clicking stopped. "I bet it's the central heating."

"How disappointing, I was rather taken with the idea of someone listening to our conversation," said Einna.

"I'm glad we're going to a comedy. I couldn't cope with anything serious, I'd laugh in inappropriate places."

When I was a child, if Edith wasn't cross with me, I would be allowed to listen to *Children's Favourites* with Uncle Mac. There were several songs I always hoped he would play. Max Bygraves singing *I'm a Pink Toothbrush*, was one, and Charles Penrose singing *The Laughing Policeman*, was another. The latter had me giggling immediately. Laughter is infectious. We laughed at everything that weekend. I wanted it to go on for ever, the laughter. I think if we laughed more, maybe we would move through life with fewer burdens bowing us down. However, our chatting laughter had an unfortunate consequence at the end of the weekend, we missed not just one, but two trains.

"Are you going to wear your tart shoes and poppy earrings to work tomorrow?" I asked Einna as we plopped down in seats on the third train.

"I might. Claire and Groan will hate them."

"So will Grunt."

I couldn't help giggling at the thought of their faces and, of course, that set Einna off again.

When we were drawing into Lime Street Station, I decided I'd better make myself look more like Margaret, a responsible teacher, than Maggie, a giggling hoyden. I fished a lipstick out of my bag.

Our Abercrombie Mansion weekend was over.

I hadn't been in the house more than quarter of an hour when I got a phone-call from Angela.

"I had to ring you," she said. "I've had a zip-less fuck weekend." I was and wasn't shocked. Each one of us in the gang knew that Angela was sexually frustrated. Both Debbie and Einna had suggested a dildo, a vibrator, or both. Angela did buy them but she also said she wanted the body to body experience. I knew what she was referring to; we'd both read *Kinflicks*.

Odd. Whatever I was feeling about my relationship with Trevor, I couldn't go down the road of infidelity, even if it was a one night stand which meant nothing. However, I wasn't going to judge Angela.

"Dave's out at a pre-season cricket meeting, so I can tell you. It started on Friday evening. Debbie was engaged in the introductory stuff of her course, followed by a dinner, so I had a meal in the college refectory. I was drinking a cup of coffee and reading some bumf about York, when I became aware that I was being scrutinised. I looked up. A man was standing by the table. We appeared to be the only people in the refectory, apart from the staff.

"'Would you mind if I joined you for coffee?' he said.

"Now, I had my evening mapped out. Coffee, a bath, then bed with *Tinker Tailor, Soldier, Spy*. But the hovering man said, 'I've never had a coffee with a mermaid before.' It's been a long time since someone has called me that, or made it so obvious that they fancied me. Bloody hell, Maggie, how could I resist?"

"What was the man like?" I squeaked.

"His name was Ellis. He wasn't traditionally handsome, but definitely attractive, a bit like Al Pacino only taller and with very blue eyes. Perhaps I came with Debbie because I wanted an adventure, no strings attached?

"Bloody hell, Maggie, the sex was amazing. We fucked all night. He was the keynote speaker for Saturday and should have been at the dinner, but he'd been delayed in Peterborough, so he'd told the organisers that he'd grab something in the refectory and head off to his room. The rest is history. God knows how he managed to deliver a lecture on Saturday morning. We arranged to meet on the Saturday afternoon in my room, as he only had a room for one night.

"He was married. I was married. We had two zip-less fuck sessions and then he departed for London. He did give me his card though and said, 'If you're ever in…' I ripped it up."

"But now you've had such amazing sex, won't you want some more?"

"I don't know. Maybe not."

When I put down the phone, I was still in a state of shock. I knew that if I told Trevor, he'd be scandalised. He wouldn't want Angela in the house again. Difficult, as in a wider context the friendship was a couple friendship too. Not that Trevor had anything much in common with Dave, except for cricket. That was what they talked about, mostly. But Dave was in a different team from Trevor. I couldn't be that judgemental, could I? I was pleased for her. I wondered how Debbie had reacted. Angela must have told her. I would have to ring her, and Einna, but not immediately. *Why do I feel sad?*

Chapter Fourteen
Shocks

Actions speak louder than words.

Would it be useful if we could accept that from birth to death, life is a roller-coaster and, while we are on it, some dips are longer than others and it's more difficult to reach the top of the next climb?

After Colditz, I gradually came to realise that I should move away from teaching English, to teaching more drama and maybe link up with Susan on some dance/drama projects. I would be able to use my knowledge of literature and she would be my Debbie. One of the projects I had in mind was to get the pupils in both the dance and drama groups to work on a physical theatre piece based on *Wuthering Heights*, using Kate Bush's song.

I mulled it over for some time, and eventually got round to chatting to Susan. She was enthusiastic, so were the pupils. Many of the dancers could imitate Kate Bush's movements. My idea was that it would be a dance overture to be performed before a pupil-staff pantomime. Overture was the wrong word. It was… oh bloody hell, just something different to whet the appetite of the audience, a starter, a first course.

I was excited about the pantomime. I even got Clem involved. He played one of the ugly sisters and loved the experience. The straight-jacket came off and the Welsh performer appeared out of it. If he told Trevor and I once, how much he was enjoying himself, he told us a hundred times.

Co-directing *Wuthering Heights* and directing the play left me excited and energised in the same way Colditz had. I think it was the final spur I needed. At the beginning of the Spring Term I went to see the Head and told him that Susan and I wanted to introduce drama and possibly dance, as subjects in their own right, on the curriculum from the following September. Yes, I still enjoyed teaching English, but in every lesson I introduced a dramatic component.

I expected to have a battle with Mr Thompson, but he said, "I've been thinking for some time that we ought to include drama on the curriculum. Dance is already provided for within PE, but I'd be more than happy to offer both subjects as exam options. I've been very impressed with the extra curricular activities you do, Margaret. You and Susan work well as a team. That dance performance and the Christmas play with a mixed pupil and staff cast was very good indeed. I would have enjoyed participating myself." I left his room feeling happy and valued.

Ideally, Susan and I ought to have been in a performance arts department, with music. But I knew I would continue under the auspices of the English department and Susan would stay with PE. There would have been a problem if the Head had decided to create a performance arts department; who would lead it? Not me, because of the extra administration. Susan wouldn't have wanted it for the same reason. And we didn't get on with the Head of Music, Andy Maxwell. He was lazy and didn't appear to have any real interest in the subject. He played pop music every lesson, and only gave the pupils Beatles' songs to sing. There was nothing wrong with The Beatles; I loved their songs. But there was a world of music out there, untouched by Mr Maxwell and the kids; even plink-plonk would have been a challenging change.

The women PE staff were pro-dance, but the men! They were homophobic and sexist. They did all they could to put boys off considering dance as an option. Susan told me about one lad who had an obvious talent for movement. When he'd told Brian and Alan, the male PE teachers, he was going to do dance, not PE, they had told him he would be considered a fairy. But the lad, Martin, had guts. He chose dance anyway. The girls thought it was great having a lad in the class. I felt I'd won a small battle, even though I'd had very little to do with Martin's decision. He had discovered that Liverpool Football Club players did contemporary dance exercises as part of their training. Not surprising, really. Martha Graham's technique was based on yoga.

"I think the Head must be in love with you," Clem said when I told him of the outcome of my meeting.

"I doubt that. What about the fire extinguisher incident when we were rehearsing the Christmas play? The Arts Theatre floor had to be re-polyurethaned. I still don't think Frank's forgiven me. Every time I have a rehearsal he reminds me of it."

"I'm not surprised. Only you could sit on a fire extinguisher, Maggie."

"I didn't sit on it on purpose. I tripped over Ann's walking stick and sort of fell on it. I think she stuck it out on purpose because I'd told her off for not learning her lines.

"I thought the Head told you that the floor was due to be re-polyurethaned?"

"He did."

"You should have believed him. You didn't used to take everything to heart so… Maggie, I know you're wanting to offer O-level drama and dance, but if you'll take my advice, you'll offer CSE instead. If it's anything like T.D., it's a more practical exam."

It was good advice. When I looked at the various syllabuses, the CSE ones were right for me, right for our pupils. When I thanked Clem, he was so pleased he almost wagged his tail.

"I've had some thoughts about your personal development, Maggie," he said. "What I'm going to say isn't meant to be insulting, so don't get upset. I don't think you are management material."

I wanted to smile, no, to laugh at him. His language was so formal, antwacky, as we say in Liverpool, but he was right for the wrong reason. I knew that Clem was referring to my innate bolshiness, but I wasn't management material for another reason, a personal one; the same one that would have made me run from being Head of a performance art department. If you climbed promotional ladders you got landed with trays full of administration. My administration consisted of looking at all the bumf in my pigeon hole, having a quick sift and chucking most of it in the bin in the knowledge that someone would get back to me if it was important.

"Have you ever thought about becoming an examiner?"

"Me? Aren't I too subversive?"

"Possibly. You might have to curb some of that subversiveness, but you'd be a breath of fresh air on an examining team. Mind you, I've always wondered how anyone can examine a pupil's performance in drama. Isn't it all very subjective?"

"Not at all. There are criteria for judging performances. I imagine examining boards use them. An obvious one is, if you can't hear a performer, he or she can't have a good mark for clarity. If they shout all the time, they haven't learnt how to modulate their voice. Stillness on stage is important. A fidgety actor isn't a confident actor and detracts from the drama. Comic timing is important. I learnt this from the college drama club. Before that I didn't think about why I'd enjoyed a performance. Mind you, before college, I'd never been to see a play, only films. I can give you a lecture if you want."

He grimaced. "You did, in the Christmas production, remember? You kept reminding me not to drift about. You said, 'Only move if there's dramatic intention'. I didn't know what dramatic intention was. Do you know, Maggie, that show was one of the best experiences of my life." His face grew sombre. "I still find it difficult that you're my friend after what I did."

I too found it strange that a friendship had blossomed. It had taken a while, but I now thought of him fondly, even though at times, he exasperated me. "Oh Clem!" How many times had I said or thought, 'Oh Clem,' in the years that I'd known him? I felt like the mother and the father of the little boy whose parents owned a transport café. It had been a *Watch With Mother* programme on the television. Every week they said, "Oh Joe!" for he was always getting up to mischief. I think he was the first child anti-hero on television. Stuart had loved it. 'Joe' was one of his first words and he said it so sorrowfully.

The years continued to march on, as they must and, before I'd really taken it in, Stuart was in his O-level year, I had turned forty, Trevor forty-three. And then, this forty three year old man told me he was taking early retirement. At first, I wanted to laugh; not a belly ache laugh, a laugh of disbelief. I hadn't wanted him to go out to work in the first place. Oh how I wanted to shout it.

"The Education Authority is offering something called Crombie. It will give me quite a good pension, even though I've only taught for fourteen years. I'll be able to work on my own compositions, like I used to do," he said.

His face looked animated, hopeful and my desire for laughter drained away. Perhaps? But could he? He had been dormant for so long.

"The college management want to release their early retirees at the beginning of June, to give them the chance to reorganise. All I have to do is hope that I'll be one of the chosen few."

It was that reorganisation and Clem's suicide that forced me to consider the possibility of changing my job.

Clem dead, and by his own hand. No matter how many times I said it, I couldn't make it real. Also, I couldn't accept that Trevor and I weren't culpable in some way. We knew Clem was depressed. He had been depressed for a long time; ever since his wife had left, taking their children with her, turning him into a once a fortnight 'weekend' dad.

For me, every corridor, every classroom, was bound up in that straitjacketed man. Once upon a childhood, my father and I had talked about the use of straitjackets and the pros and cons of using them. We had decided that, on balance, they took away a person's dignity. Clem had worn one voluntarily. His stiff, uncompromising formality encouraged pupils to laugh at him. Many members of staff made fun of him behind his back, and he stood there in his straitjacket and asked for it. I imagined that the staff and pupils alike were surprised by his performance in the pantomime. But I had given him a role where he could exploit his own character. Maybe, for the first time, the laughter was with and for him rather than at him.

A few weeks after Trevor told me he was taking early retirement, Clem who was never absent, didn't turn up at school. No one phoned through from the office to tell Brian, the deputy head of Tennyson, that he was legitimately absent.

"Perhaps he's had an accident on the way in," said Brian.

"Wouldn't the police have been in touch by now?" said Susan.

"I've got his home phone number. I'll phone him," I said. There was no reply.

At break, I asked Brian if he would drive over to Clem's flat with me, in the dinner hour.

"I'm sorry, Maggie, I can't… footy practice. Stop worrying. He'll be okay. He probably had an appointment he forgot to mention."

'No he didn't,' I wanted to scream. Clem was too meticulous to forget to put in for time off because of an appointment. You had to get permission for all outside school appointments, even those that were connected to your work.

"I'll go with you, Maggie," said Susan.

Through the stained glass window of the front door, we saw what looked like legs dangling in the hall. We found a telephone box and called the police. When they broke into the house, they found that Clem had hanged himself from the banisters. They also found a note.

'I'm no good to anyone. My ex-wife won't even come to the door to say hello, when I pick up the kids. I'm only allowed to see them once a fortnight. My colleagues think I'm a joke. I can't be bothered to try any more.'

I didn't think you were a bloody joke, Clem. *Not true, Maggie. You did sometimes.*

I was so glad I had Susan with me, not Brian. She dealt with the police. I knew that if I opened my mouth I would have bawled. *I thought… I thought… you enjoyed the panto. I thought our friendship… I thought…* I didn't know what to think.

When I told Trevor, he was so shocked he couldn't say anything. When, eventually he did, he kept saying, "Why?"

All the way home I'd gone over and over that 'why' and all I could think was, that having us as friends, hadn't been enough. Having his career hadn't been enough. Being involved in the pantomime, hadn't been enough. He had been lonely in all the hours he wasn't in school, or visiting us. After all, he couldn't live with us. And, more than all that, he'd wanted his marriage back, his children back. He was like Lorraine. She'd had her children taken away from her, so had Clem. The difference? Lorraine's children had been removed in order to protect them, and then returned to her. Clem's had been removed through the breakdown of a marriage, because his wife Amanda had found him boring. And that had been that as far as being a full-time dad was concerned. I didn't know what kind of a dad he'd been, but…

The next day, one of the school secretaries, Mrs Howard, told me that Clem had phoned in that morning with a message for me: "Tell Maggie I forgot to say goodbye."

I was furious. I didn't know how to be polite to the woman. "Why didn't you get the message to me?" I asked. "It might have made all the difference. "

"I thought it odd, not urgent. It wasn't an official absentee message. And we were dealing with an unusual number of sick child calls. I made a note of it so I'd remember to tell you later, but… well it was a bit odd, don't you think?"

Later was too late. "Why odd?"

"You're not a couple, are you?"

How dare she? There's criticism in her voice. Odd fish. Odd man out. Not wanted. There are people in this world who no-one cares enough about to wonder why they go missing. Will his children care that he's dead? Suicide: one human being's act of selfishness for the burden of guilt they leave on others' shoulders.

"But he ought to have been in school. Didn't you wonder why he wasn't?"

Mrs Howard frowned. "Frankly, no, Mrs Harvey."

She's thinking she's not going to accept the blame for this.

"Management often go to meetings, don't they? I don't take particular notice of what members of staff are in or out."

Poor system. There ought to have been a book in the office where staff had to log any time they wouldn't be in school, and one in each house.

I couldn't get rid of the image of Clem dangling like some giant puppet from the banister, the unforgiving strength of the climbing rope cutting into his neck.

"I've never seen such a deliberately planned suicide," said one of the police officers. "He didn't want to be rescued. That chair was kicked away with enough force to make sure he couldn't have second thoughts."

"But didn't he choose the hall so he could be seen?" Susan asked.

Both police officers looked sceptical. "He may have done, but where else in a house could you hang yourself? You've got to have a drop."

A drop... a drop... I can't bear the way they're talking about my friend as though he's... but that's what he is, a case... a case of suicide. "He could have—" I couldn't bear to hear any more. "Excuse me," I said. "I need a bit of fresh air." And in the midst of my sadness and confusion I thought. *Why do we say 'fresh' when we live and work in a polluted city?*

For a while I talked about being transferred out of Tennyson: too many memories. It was Frank who stopped me. "No way, girl. Can't have you spilling paint over another fucking staffroom carpet." And then I saw the job at the FE college where Trevor had taught, advertised in *The Times Educational Supplement* and decided it was a bigger change that I needed. Trevor wouldn't be there, which was a blessing. We wouldn't be comfortable bedfellows in a staffroom. Another sadness. We'd had fun in Woolworths. *But Maggie, you didn't work in the same department.*

I was as astonished that I was offered the job as I had been when I'd received my college place in 1961. In September I would be the performance arts coordinator. How scary was that?

"Do they know you wet your knickers?" asked Einna when I told her.

"Of course. And I told them about the gang and our outings and how, when we're together we can't stop laughing and that's why we wet our knickers. And that I'm one of the monstrous regiment of women. They know what they've taken on."

"You are one big liar, Harvey."

"I know."

Einna too was in the process of a change. She and John had split up.

"He's gay," she said.

"I was always suspicious of those rucks," I said, trying to make her laugh.

"You don't need to jolly me out of misery. I'm fine about it. I must have always been suspicious he was gay, poor man. His dad and society forced him into an unnatural relationship, well unnatural for him."

"Don't re-write history, friend. He was a pain."

"A pain, yes, but not an abuser."

There's abuse and abuse, I thought.

In September, wearing some stripy-bee dungarees and my Carnaby Street poppy earrings, I turned up to the pre-enrolment staff meeting, where the Principal, looking, I thought, a little shell shocked, introduced me to the staff. Why was he shocked? At the interview I'd worn my red plastic mac, which clashed with my hair, and underneath, my emerald green, floaty summer dress. Trevor had told me it wouldn't do. I'd almost replied that he sounded like Clem; a hiccup had stopped me.

"They have to know what they're taking on, if they offer me the job," I'd said. "It's important I don't pretend to be someone I'm not."

At the meeting, I discovered that the performance arts department had been given the go-ahead to offer the BTEC Certificate and National Diploma in Performance Arts as an alternative to GCSE and A-level. It was a scramble to get the relevant information packs printed, ready for enrolment, but we managed it with the help of the technicians. I bribed them with the promise of a pint in the Brook House.

I hadn't been in the college long before I realised how much it suited me. I'd also done what Clem had suggested before... *don't go there Maggie...* and had applied for and been accepted to be an examiner for CSE drama and dance. *See, you straitjacketed man, I did it. I valued... Why did you go there, Maggie?*

I liked the democratic approach to work in the college. Management to lecturers, management and lecturers to students. The students were expected to organise themselves so that assignments were in on time; it helped to prepare them for higher education and the world of work. Some thrived, others found it more difficult. Stuart was the type of adolescent who would flourish at the college, as would his friend, Neil.

"What are you thinking, Mum?"

I jumped. Stuart could creep up on me without my knowing he was even in the room.

"I wish you wouldn't do that."

"I like practising walking very quietly. You have to be stealthy when you watch animals. I got to see a Hen Harrier the other day. It was boss." Stuart and Neil had joined the RSPB. "What were you thinking about? You were miles away."

"You, as it happens. I was thinking you'd thrive at my college."

"Weird! I was going to ask you and Dad if I could do my A-levels there instead of the sixth form. Neil's going to ask his parents too."

They are joined at the hip. I couldn't help thinking about a day, not so long ago when I'd asked Stuart if he had a girlfriend? His reply: "No. I don't know what it is about girls, they're so noisy. I can never get a word in. If Neil were a girl, I'd ask him to be my girlfriend."

So noisy? He is a bit like his dad then.

"You can ask him this evening." I nearly said, 'when your dad creeps downstairs'.

As it turned out, Trevor and Stuart had a fair conversation about the pros and cons of college life over school life. I did not participate. I was enjoying the to-ing and fro-ing too much. The normal pattern of meals when the three of us were present was of mother son chatter, for Stuart had not become a grunting teenager. He loved to talk. Possibly his genes from Katy and me?

"So, Dad. It's fine by you?"

"If you can cope with your mother in the same institution?"

"No problem. It's not as though I want to do Drama or Dance."

"Your lecturers may want to talk to her about your progress."

"Again, not a problem. I know what I'm aiming for, so I'll work hard. I promise, no-one will complain about me."

Trevor looked pained. "I wasn't thinking they would, Stuart. Your mother and I have faith in you."

How does Trevor know that? We never talk about Stuart. We don't talk about anything much. We may be be walking along a pavement side by side but neither of us are in tune. Odd that. Trevor's music wasn't what I would have described as tuneful. Perhaps he knew. Perhaps atonal music was about the human condition of aloneness, even when people were talking? The sadness of that thought, one I'd had so often since our move here, griped me, as it always did. *Put it in the 'later box', Maggie.* But that box was almost full.

I knew that Stuart wanted to study Law, and in 1984, he was accepted at Hull University. There, he achieved a two/one and went on to do his LPC. It was then we got the phone-call.

"Mum, I'd like to take a year out before applying to firms to be a trainee solicitor."

"Ri-ight." *What's coming and how much will it cost?*

"I want to specialise in environmental law eventually, so I thought I'd do some voluntary work at the centre for alternative technology at Machynlleth."

I'd never heard of Machynlleth. "I'm guessing, Wales?"

"Yes. They provide bed and board. Could you…?"

We provided an allowance. It was there he met Beth, the girl who would become his wife.

As soon as they walked through the front door, I couldn't help feeling her face looked familiar. She and Stuart were grinning.

"What?" I said

"Whose daughter is she, Mum?"

"No, no… you're not Lily's daughter, are you?" Lily who had been Allie's best friend. We'd met her through Debbie. She always came with the Forster family to performances, before Allie's cycling accident and subsequent death.

That had been another of those eventful years; some events positive, some funny, others so traumatic you didn't know how to deal with them. There was my magic mushroom incident, Debbie's broken ankle, her gradual involvement with Bill, the nursery man, who had driven her to hospital, and then Allie's bicycle accident, coma and death.

Afterwards Lily had become one of those people you knew for a while. Debbie had kept in distant touch, so we knew that Lily had gone to Edinburgh University to study medicine.

Beth nodded. "Oh my god!" I said. "Come here, girl. I've got to give you a big hug. Anyone who says life isn't full of coincidences talks out of their bum. Does Lily know? Does Debbie know?"

"Mum knows. I hope you don't mind, but I gave her your phone number. She's going to ring later. Debbie doesn't know yet. Stu and I felt families had to know first."

"Mind? Of course I don't mind. It's wonderful. Is it okay if I ring Debbie to tell her?"

"Of course. Mum wants to catch up with you all. Stuart's told me about the gang."

Debbie was amazed, thrilled, but I heard a touch of sadness in her voice, at the unlooked for reminder of Allie.

Catch up and plans. That's what happened in the hour Lily and I were on the phone. She and her husband Robert, Robbie, were going to come down to Liverpool for a weekend in the May half-term and we were going up to Edinburgh for a weekend during the festival. *Will I be able to get Trevor to come with me? Oh, of course I will. Beth's family will be our family.* I would invite all the gang round for dinner when they came. I knew Einna didn't know Lily or Allie, but I couldn't leave her out.

I liked Beth. Trevor said that he liked Beth, but found her a bit loud.

"You seem to find all women loud, Trevor. Perhaps you should compose a piece on loud women." He looked me strangely. "You're not writing one, are you?"

"I might be."

Well, well! I guess anything that stimulates…

I thought Stuart and Beth fitted together like a cat and a dog can do, like Trevor and I used to do before our differences niggled and set us along different pathways.

We were in the kitchen and she was helping me make our evening meal. "He seemed so unassuming," she said. "Not shy, just quiet, wanting to know, to find out. Very unlike the noisy boys I'd met at Uni; they wanted you to believe they knew everything."

I smiled. I couldn't help remembering the toddler who had crashed trains.

What goes round comes round; the phrase usually refers to retribution. This time it was good fortune. For Debbie, her parents and Lily, the union of Stuart and Beth helped heal the grief felt over the untimely death of Allie.

How was I feeling? A ragbag mixture of emotions. As though I was living in a house of ghosts, including Ho-Ho whose laughter cackled through the walls from time to time. As though I was no longer coping at work. Too often absent because of a stabbing pain in my side which scared me so much I couldn't face taking it to the doctors. It was Einna who, also plagued by ghosts who laughed at her, forced me into going by telling me it was better to know and have an early diagnosis, so that whatever it was could be treated. Einna's ghosts were Tom's parents. She felt that they didn't want her in their house. I'd never known what Ho-Ho wanted, or why she'd said, "She'll be dead tomorrow." Although, at one time, I'd felt that the Maggie I knew had died when Trevor took the teaching post and bought Munster Mansion.

"IBS, Mrs Harvey. It's treatable by diet." That's was what the doctor said. He didn't even feel it was necessary to send me to see a specialist.

But when the pain invaded my body; invasion, that's what it felt like, all I could do was go to bed with two paracetamol and a hot water bottle, until it went away; and it didn't feel like 'just anything'.

Chapter Fifteen

Ben

If life deals you lemons, make lemonade.

S tuart and Beth got married. It was a quiet affair in Edinburgh. The couple settled in Southport, as Stuart had been offered a job in a firm of solicitors there.

Southport wasn't too far away, nor was it too near.

Stuart once said to me, when I rang to ask them over for Sunday lunch, "I don't suppose Dad would care where we are. Southport, Timbuctoo, it would be the same to him. You know, Mum, he never thinks to ring me. He speaks to me if I ring. He's quite pleasant, but I never get the feeling he really listens to what I tell him. Is he okay?"

"No, not really. He's… I think he's lost himself. Before you were born and during the first two years of your life, your dad composed a lot of music. It was atonal."

"I remember, I think."

"I didn't really like it; well not all of it. When he was house husband, he used to take you along to rehearsals. I wonder…" *Would it work? I wouldn't if I did it. Stuart?* "Maybe you could ask your dad to lend you the CDs of some of his pieces, like The Liverpool Symphony. It might jog him to remember who he is."

"Okay. I don't know if this is something that happened? Did Dad tape me crashing trains?"

I laughed. "He did. Have you ever heard of Steve Reich?"

"Yes."

"One of your dad's composer heroes. I wasn't a fan, well not to sit and listen to, but I think I could have used his music in dance or drama. I'm not sure that's why music is composed though. It should stand alone, like any of the other art forms.

"He wrote an entire piece about trains. I have to be honest, Stuart, I'm an ignoramus where atonal music's concerned. I could never be a real fan, could I, not with my penchant for musicals? My heart's still with Doris Day."

"How old was I?"

"Two."

"I'll have a go, Mum."

"Great." *Would Stuart asking Trevor about his composer-self help or hinder? I don't know. 'I know nossing' said the spy, and no amount of torture made him change that statement. That's me. Or is it? Come on, Maggie. You'd spill the beans before they got out their instruments of torture.*

My sedentary and solitary husband, who if he wrote any music left it up in the attic along with his huge collection of CDs. I still socialised without him when Bozo allowed. Bozo… my name for the pain. It was my counsellor, Leif, who had suggested giving the IBS a familiar name. It was Debbie who had suggested counselling and recommended Leif. He was an acquaintance of hers from Friends of the Earth. Debbie, counsellor. Einna, doctor. Angel friends. I was beginning to go along with Einna's ideas of angels. A very comforting idea. Leif was an angel.

"I'm not suggesting your pain is psychosomatic, Maggie. It's just that I've come to believe the mind affects the body and the body affects the mind. They're inextricably linked," said Leif, on my first visit.

It made sense. Of course it made sense. How could it not? Even at the most basic level, Bozo affected how I was feeling emotionally. I hated letting people down. It depressed me. Mind body, body mind.

It was Bozo forcing me to take early retirement that pushed me into accepting Debbie's advice. Inwardly, I'd railed against giving up work. The thought of being confined in Munster Mansion terrified me. But as an employee I had become unreliable. I had to go before I was pushed.

In any relationship, some separate activities are beneficial, but I was swamped by separateness. I wondered why Trevor and I still slept in the same bed. Making love had fled when Bozo came into our lives. Even the thought of sex hurt. Not once did Trevor say that he minded.

He lived in his eerie, only appearing at meals. At breakfast he read the newspaper. At lunch he listened to Radio Four. In the evening, like many British couples, we ate our meal in front of the television. I rarely took notice of the flickering images before me. As I chewed my food, I dreamed of times gone by, or wondered if Bozo would allow me a pain free sleep.

I didn't know what to do about Trevor and I. Every time I spiralled into a 'what's the point' scenario, and decided I'd better leave, I hiccuped. The ties that bind; a love that binds. I didn't expect advice from Leif. I knew counsellors wouldn't hand out advice. Their job was to help people come to conclusions and make choices. How was I going to do that? Back in nineteen-sixty, when Trevor and I got married, I would have fought anyone who dared to say that one day…

People change. People can change. People can't change. If they change, what matters is whether it's for the worse or for the better. I had told Leif that Edith had changed for the better after the birth of Stuart. Now, I saw signs of regression. Nastiness, nearly always present when I was on my own with her was becoming the norm rather than an occasional outburst. I felt I knew why. Stuart had grown up and away, as Ian had grown up and away. Would the birth of her great grandchild bring back niceness, or was it too late? Would a grandchild pour milk of magnesia on Bozo?

When I asked Leif that, he said, "What do you think, Maggie?"

"You remind me of my dad," I said. "Sometimes he used to answer a question with a…"

Huge, gulping sobs interrupted my sentence. Crying seemed to be part of any session with Leif. If I apologised, he told me it was good to cry. I seemed to have a lot of crying to do.

Ben brought rays of sunshine into my life, into all our lives. I made sure I saw him as often as Stuart and Beth's busy lives, and Bozo would allow.

Adam followed Ben after an interval of three years. In looks and character he seemed more like his mum, whereas I thought Ben was the spitting image of his father, especially in temperament. From the moment he was born, Adam idolised Ben; you could see it in the welcoming smile when Ben came anywhere near him, and the eyes which would follow him round the room.

"Goodness knows what we're going to do when Ben goes to school," said Beth. "He'll be devastated. He's Ben's shadow. Luckily Ben doesn't mind. I did ask him, and he said, 'Sometimes I forget he's there.' I wasn't sure what to make of that."

I thought, *out of the mouths…* for I believed Trevor often forgot I was there. I felt like a housekeeper more than a wife, going silently about her business, pulled back into Maggie's world when family or friends summoned.

When I mentioned my thoughts about Adam being like Beth to Stuart, he laughed. "Beth's eyes don't follow me round any room," he said.

"She does adore you though. You both adore each other." *I so hope that adoration doesn't leak away. Don't be overly sentimental, Maggie. Love does change. What you hope is that it doesn't leak into sourness.*

The phone pulled me out of a deep sleep; the sort of sleep which occurred if I'd had a Bozo night. I'd ended up in the spare room, as I hadn't wanted to disturb Trevor. When I had a night like this, I had to take some paracetamol, drink a glass of boiled water, put a wheat bag in the microwave to warm up, and then read until the pain settled down. Sometimes it did, sometimes it didn't. On nights when it didn't, I knew I was in for a ragged day. And ragged days were days when I postponed or cancelled arrangements. Trevor must have left me sleeping and got his own breakfast, for his long-distance voice pulled me out of my stupor.

"It's for you, Maggie," he called. "Ben's not very well. I think Stuart's wondering if you can go over?"

Ben, not well? Is this a ragged day? Will I be forced to let them down? I struggled out of bed, noting, as I always did, 'I', not 'we'.

"Tell him I'm coming and don't say I've had a Bozo night, please. No, don't do that, I'll speak to him." I threw on my dressing gown and went into our bedroom.

"Are you okay, Mum?" asked Stuart when I picked up the phone.

"I'm fine; not a wonderful night; it happens sometimes."

"If I'd known you were awake in the night I'd have called you for a fellowship chat. I had to change Ben's bedding. Poor little lad was sick twice. Would you be able to come over? I wouldn't ask, but I can't not go into work today, and Beth's on a field trip in Derbyshire. She'll be home by three. She's picking Adam up from Nursery on the way back. You can stay the night if you want."

"You must always ask, sweetheart. You know that I'll come if I possibly can."

"No better then?"

"So-so." *Ben, focus on Ben.* "Did you say, stay the night?"

"I did."

I hadn't seen my Southport family for three weeks. I'd been thinking of suggesting to Trevor that we go over at the weekend. It was Thursday. If I stayed, Trevor could drive over on Saturday morning, and we could come back together in the evening; if he agreed to the plan. If he… Of course, I knew I might be subjected to the special 'Grunt' face.

"Mum, are you still there?"

"Sorry love, I'd gone into planning mode. Yes I can come, and yes I can stay, but in reality I shan't get to you before ten. Would it be a good idea…" I told him what I had in mind.

"That sounds great. We're not doing anything this weekend. Hopefully Ben will be better by then and it would be good to see you both."

"Do you think you could ring him, say tomorrow? It would be better coming from you." *He's more likely to say yes, if you ask.*

"Of course I will. Ben's looking forward to his nana reading to him. He's not been sick since eight this morning, and so far no diarrhoea."

"It can't be food poisoning, otherwise you'd all be suffering. Providing you'd eaten the same food, of course. School dinner's not a possibility. He would have had symptoms before... when did you say it started?"

"Early hours."

"I expect it's a bug he's picked up from friends."

I gave myself a mental nudge. *Little Grey Men, into my case.* I'd talked to Ben about the book the last time I visited. It had been one of Stuart's favourite bedtime reads.

Trevor gave me a lift to Central Station. Useful, but what would have been more useful would have been a lift to Southport.

Ben was tucked up in a spare duvet, on the couch, watching a Disney DVD, when I arrived.

"It sounds like a stomach bug," said Stuart. "When I rang the school to say he wouldn't be in, the secretary said, 'Not another one. We shan't have any pupils left if this goes on.' Unhealthy places, schools."

After Ben and I said goodbye to Stuart, I made myself a herbal tea and Ben a glass of ice cold water. I watched the rest of the film with him and then asked him how he was feeling. Before he had a chance to reply, an enormous fart escaped from beneath the duvet. He giggled.

"Question, Ben Harvey. Does the fart mean you need to go to the loo?"

"Excuse me, Nana." He said through his giggles. "No, I don't need the toilet."

"Einna told me a funny rhyme about farts. Your Dad knows it. Has he ever told you?"

Ben shook his head.

"Shall I tell you?"

He nodded.

> *A fart is a musical sound.*
> *It comes from the land of bum.*
> *It travels through the valley of trousers,*
> *And comes out with a musical hum.*

A fart's a mechanical device.
It gives the bowels ease.
It warms the bed in winter,
And suffocates the fleas."

I thought Ben was going to fall off the couch with laughter. Laughter is infectious. The gang members could set each other off without necessarily meaning to, and wet knickers were often the result. Now, I laughed with Ben, and whatever tension there was lingering from Bozo in the night, evaporated.

"Hey, Grandson," I said. "You've made me into a new person."

"I hope not. I like the old person, Nana."

"Enough of the 'old'. How would you like some non-Nana Porridge?"

"What's non-Nana porridge?"

"Well, Nana porridge has cream and honey on it. But that would be too much for your tummy today, maybe tomorrow. Non-Nana porridge is served with milk and honey. As you've not been sick since eight, and you've farted, I think it would be okay."

While he was eating it he said, "Tell me about the day I was born and what you did."

"How many times have I told you that story? You just want to laugh at me, don't you?"

He nodded. When Ben was happy, it was as though a candle had been lit inside him making him glow. His eyes sparkled azure blue. It made you want to stay inside the moment for ever. Stuart had been like that too. Adam was different. His eyes were chestnut brown. Brown eyes can't sparkle, but they can pull you into their depths.

Laughter. There hadn't been much laughter around the day that Ben had come into the world; it was a day full of anxiety.

There was a photo of Ben, Beth and Stuart on my bedside cabinet. He was lying in the circle of Beth's arm and Stewart was curved around them both. Nothing about that photo told the story of the trauma we'd all been through. He was looking at them. They were looking at him. His finger touched his mum's cheek as though he were saying, 'You are

213

mine. I am yours. I love you, and you love me.' There seemed to be a wisdom so profound in his gaze. Every time I looked at that photo, I wanted to cry for joy.

I gave Ben a hug. He hadn't yet reached the shrugging off stage, but then Stuart never did, so perhaps he wouldn't.

"Are you sitting comfortably? Then I'll begin. I was in the shower when your dad phoned. Your granddad took the message. The first I knew of it was when he knocked on the bathroom door." *Once upon a time, pre Munster Mansion and Trevor full time teaching, we showered and bathed together.*

"'Come in,' I shouted.

"The door opened. He put his head round the door. 'Stuart's taking Beth to the Women's now. Her pains are coming every ten minutes. He said to meet them there?'

"Ben, my heart jumped and all the breath flew out of my body."

"Like this?" Ben doubled over as though he had been punched in the stomach. "That's how I felt when I was being sick. You weren't sick though, Nana."

"No, I wasn't, and yes, it was just like that. I had to give Bozo a severe talking to in case he started whinging."

"What did you say?"

"I said, 'Now Bozo, you be good today. I usually pay you lots of attention, but this is Stuart, Beth and Ben's day.'"

"Did Mummy and Daddy know I was going to be a boy?"

"No. The doctor and midwife knew, because they had seen the scan."

"The scan was a picture of me in Mummy's tummy, wasn't it?'

"Yes."

"Did Bozo reply when you told him to be good?"

"He made tummy rumbling noises."

"You call him 'Bozo' because it sounds like a character in a children's comic, don't you?"

"Do I?" *There's a surprise.*

"Daddy told us."

Ah! "I suppose I do, then." *Odd. I have no memory of telling Stuart that. I have no memory of thinking it. I thought Leif had... does it matter?* "Anyway, I said, 'Tell Stuart I'm in the shower, and I'll be there as quickly as I can.'

"And he said, 'You'll have to get a move on, you know.'

"How fast does your granddad move, Ben?"

"As fast as a snail." He giggled. "Like this." He walked two fingers across the duvet very slowly. "Can I draw the picture while you tell the story?"

"Of course you can." *It's sad. We're not that old. Come on, Maggie, Trevor doesn't move like an old person, he moves like a man in a dream. I suppose snail could still be appropriate.*

Before I could say, 'I'll go and get your crayons and felt pens', Ben jumped off the couch and rushed out of the room. *Ah, he's better.* He was back in a tick, with a huge drawing pad and a box with a Winnie-the Pooh picture on it.

"I'm going to draw Granddad as a snail," he said.

"Good idea. Where was I? Ah yes, 'I am getting a move on.' I said.

"'I know what you're like when you get ready to go anywhere, and it's a three quarters of an hour drive, at least. Shall I tell him an hour and a half?'

"I did a quick calculation, Ben; a quarter of an hour, topside, to dry, dress and make up. I had to put on the mascara, if nothing else. You know what your Nana's like about her mascara?"

"You look like an albino rabbit without it and a panda when you rub your eyes, with it on. But Nana, albino rabbits have pink eyes. You don't have pink eyes."

"Okay, clever clogs. Anyway, albino rabbit or not, I couldn't look like a baggy-eyed old crone to meet my first grandson. That better?" Ben nodded.

"'Tell Stuart I'll be there in an hour, hour and a quarter at the most.'

"'I don't want you driving too fast. You don't want to be caught speeding.'

"'One minute you're telling me to hurry up, next you're cautioning me about speeding. Make your mind up, will you?'"

"But you did speed, didn't you?"

"Only a little. I couldn't let your mum and dad down, could I? I'd never been a birth partner before. We didn't have such things when your dad was born."

"Were you Mum's birth partner when Adam was born?"

"Yes."

"Mum asked you because Granny Lily and Granddad Robbie live in Edinburgh and they couldn't get here in time to be birth partners. I don't think Granddad Robbie would have been a birth partner, do you Nana?"

"I'm not sure. I don't think I know Granddad Robbie well enough to say that. Why do you think it?"

"Well, He's so funny. He always makes me giggle. I don't think you need someone who makes you giggle when you're having a baby."

"Probably not."

"You make me giggle too, but not all the time. I think you know when not to giggle."

And Robbie doesn't? Interesting.

"Mum asked Granddad Trevor too, didn't she?"

"Yes. She didn't want to leave him out. But your dad suspected he'd say no."

"Granddad Trevor was too… what's the word Nana?"

"Squeamish."

"Squeamish. I like that word, squ-ea-m-ish." He rolled it round his tongue. "He's got squeamish as he's got older. He was at Dad's birth, wasn't he?"

"He was." *He's got many things as he's got older. But then so have I. Have I because of him? Or has he, because of me? Or is it life and genes? Even though she's in her late seventies, Katy hasn't given up on life. Sadly, Molly is dead. She would have loved being a great aunt. Would she have told Ben and Adam, Tricks stories? Trevor couldn't bear to visit the home she was in, after Katy couldn't look after her any more. It was okay, as homes for people who can't look after themselves go. The patients weren't neglected.*

"He said he'd tremble like a jelly. I'd like to see Granddad trembling like a jelly." Ben jumped off the couch, scattering crayons and felt pens.

"Watch, Grandma."

"Wow, that's as good as Elvis the Pelvis."

"Who?"

"Don't tell me you've never heard of Elvis Presley?" I got up, made the shape of a pretend guitar and sang the beginning of *Teddy Bear*.

Ben put his fingers in his ears. "You can't sing, Nana."

"You little cheeker! In the shower, my singing sounds wonderful. My students always told me I couldn't sing. 'We'll do voice warm-up,' they'd say. But I can sing, Grandson, just not in tune. Now, do you want me to continue with your story, or are you bored with it? We could always play a game." Ben put his thumb in his mouth. "Come on, young man. You're too old for thumbs in mouths. Help me pick up the crayons and pens. I bet some of them have rolled under the coffee table and Bozo won't let me get those."

After we'd picked them all up, Ben scrambled back onto the couch. "I'm going to draw Granddad Snail trembling."

"Then Mr Bojangles?"

"Yes. Then Mr Bojangles."

In 1976, Stuart and Neil had found a briefcase in the churchyard. In 1989 Stuart and Beth had found an abandoned kitten.

"I'm sure it was the same bush, Mum. We were walking through the park and Beth heard this mewing"

The kitten, sitting in Beth's woolly hat, had been as black as night, except for four white paws. "Isn't he cute? I've called him Mr Bojangles."

"Why Mr Bojangles?"

Beth had shrugged. "I don't know, really. I like the song."

"It was Mummy who called him Mr Bojangles, didn't she?"

"She did. Anyway, back to the story. When I said goodbye to your granddad and ran out to the garage, he said—"

"He said, 'watch out for the…' only he never finished cause you trod on Mr Bojangles' tail and he yowled. He's a funny cat. He likes riding on people's shoulders doesn't he?"

"He does. I believe he thinks he's a scarf."

"A scarf? Yes, I see that, all soft and furry. How long do cats live?"

"Some can live up to eighteen. Most die around fourteen."

"Mr Bojangles might die soon, then."

"But he might not. He's only eleven."

"Was it then that you remembered it was Sunday?"

"Yes, I picked up Mr Bojangles to give him a stroke and say sorry, then I ran back to the lounge and—"

"There was Granddad reading his paper. Do you like my picture of him?"

"It's fandabidozy. Anyway, I said—"

"Very dramatically… Granddad always adds that whenever you tell stories."

"Yes, he does, doesn't he?" *Ben hasn't realised that Trevor is criticising me. Interesting. Another example of interpreting what we hear, and of never really knowing what goes on in another's head. Trevor used to enjoy my story-telling. Oh for goodness sake, stop, used-to-ing.* "Well, dramatically or not, I said, 'It's Sunday.'"

"And Granddad said, 'So?'"

"No he didn't, monkey, he said, 'Yes?'"

"And you said, 'They'll only have a skeleton staff on,' and Granddad said, 'Oh Maggie. Why do you see everything as a big drama? Surely common sense will tell you that they have to have an adequate number of doctors and nurses on duty. Instead of getting yourself all worked up for nothing, think about what you're doing. You know Mr Bojangles always sleeps in front of the back door.'"

"That's why I think he's funny, Nana. He has lots of funny habits like that, being a scarf, sleeping where he knows someone could tread on him. He slept on your head, once, didn't he?"

"He did."

"And when you woke up, you thought you had something wrong with it because it was so heavy."

"I did." *Ben's right. Bo is funny; funny odd, funny peculiar, and funny ha-ha.*

Trevor hadn't allayed my fear. Were the statistics for safe, successful births better than in the sixties when Stuart had been born? I remembered thinking, *bugger statistics, bugger numbers. Why do I even bother?* I had a flashback to the staff meeting when the Head had told us that Mrs Alsop, one of the office staff was leaving and wouldn't be replaced.

"From now on," he'd said, "You will be responsible for working out percentages for pupil attendance."

I'd felt all the blood leave my face. I couldn't, in all fairness, ask Trevor to help; he was struggling with his expected work-load and his mistaken belief that he would have time to compose. So, I'd improvised. I looked along a line of pupil ticks and absences and decided on a figure. In all my years of teaching, no one had ever questioned my results. I suspected the registers were never looked at, let alone checked. If a pupil had a lot of As, I did ask Trevor to do the sum. To be fair to him, never once had he suggested that I learnt how to do percentages myself.

Had I been overly dramatic about statistics and safe births? I just knew that they would only have a skeletal staff on duty on a Sunday. I'd heard of women being given caesareans, when they'd opted for a natural birth, to make sure babies didn't arrive at an awkward time, like a weekend or a bank holiday.

"Come back, Nana?" Ben tapped my arm.

"Sorry love. My head's chocker with memories."

"What does 'chocker' mean?"

"Full."

"Chocker. I like that word. You know lots of interesting words, Nana. When Mum says, 'Eat your greens, Ben.' I'll say, 'Sorry Mum, I can't. I'm chocker.'"

"You are a scamp, Ben Harvey. When I gave Bo to your granddad he said, 'Remember not to drive too fast and ring me when you know what's happening.' And I said, 'I will if I can find a public telephone.' I gave him a hug, said bye-bye and rushed out. When I started the car, I noticed that the petrol gauge was on empty, and the warning light was on."

"You swore."

"I did."

"What naughty words did you use?"

"You won't catch me out, young man." It was a game we played when I told the story.

"You didn't really need to go to the petrol station, did you?"

"Well, for my own peace of mind, I did. But no, not according to your granddad. I pulled into the petrol station at the roundabout and as I was expecting there to be a lot of to-ing and fro-ing over the next week or so, I filled up. I don't know what made me glance up at the booth, after I'd paid and got back in the car, but I did, and saw the cashier gesticulating at me. I frowned. I couldn't have left my card in the booth, I'd used cash. Had I forgotten to pick my up my purse? No, it was in my bag. I was holding the car keys. It was at this moment that I was interrupted by a knock on the window. A man was standing there. I wound it down.

"'You can take my car if you like, queen,' he said. 'It's older than yours. But I don't think you'll be able to start it up without these keys.' They were dangling in his hand. He had a big grin all over his face.

"For a second, I didn't understand what he was saying. I looked at the seats, they were the wrong colour. 'I'm so sorry,' I said. 'I'm all over the place this morning. My first grandchild's on the way, and—'

"'That's all right, queen. You get off,' he said. 'But take care now.'"

"I've finished Mr Bojangles, Nana, but I don't think his ears are right, do you?"

"I think he looks great. You're spot-on with his fur colour. Time to draw the hospital, I think."

"It was an old building, wasn't it?"

"Oldish."

"What colour was it?"

"Light grey."

"You did go a bit too fast, didn't you? But there were no policemen with gun cameras, were there?"

"No. I parked the car in Myrtle Parade and ran round the corner."

"I bet you looked funny. You always look funny when you run."

"Well, thank you for that. I can't sing and I can't run properly. What can I do?"

"Tell good stories and make yummy porridge."

"I suppose that will have to do. When I got to the maternity wing and found the room where your mum and dad were, your dad said—"

"'I don't think Ben wants to come out yet.' I didn't. I didn't get born for ages."

"I decided I'd better ring your granddad. So I asked your dad if there was a public phone nearby that I could use. He told me that there was a public phone booth near reception. The next half an hour was a bit like a dream, and as dreams sometimes do, Ben, it turned into a nightmare."

"You didn't have a mobile phone did you?"

"No. Not so many people did have them then."

"Phone boxes get vandalised now."

"That's a big word for a seven year old."

"I don't remember when I learnt it. Maybe the Head Teacher talked about it in assembly. I know quite a lot of big words, some of them are pretend words."

"Pretend words?"

"Yes. Like that one you said. Fandabidozy. What happened then?"

Usually I glossed over this part of the story. Today, although difficult, I decided not to; perhaps Ben and his big words told me he could cope. "You needed to be delivered by forceps."

"I've seen pictures of them. They look like things you hurt people with. I had to be given blood and oxygen," said Ben proudly.

"You did, sweetheart. We were very upset at what had happened to you and your mum. She was exhausted."

"What was the name of the ward where she went for a rest?"

"The post delivery ward."

"She didn't get much sleep, did she?"

"No. but that bit comes later, doesn't it? There we were, Ben, and all we knew was that our little scrap—"

"Me."

"Yes you, were in the intensive care baby unit having to be given oxygen."

"And blood, Nana. Don't forget the blood. Now tell me what Granddad said to you when you got home."

"He said, 'Goodness, Maggie, you didn't go out like that, did you?' I didn't know what he meant. 'Look at yourself. You've been walking round all day with your jumper inside out.'"

"I had, and it was obvious. There were two huge labels, one on the back of my neck, and one on a side seam. I was so ashamed of myself, first the petrol station fiasco and then this; what must everyone have thought of me? When I rang your dad to see how he was, I asked him why he hadn't said anything. He said. 'I didn't notice. I can't tell you what anyone was wearing.'

"The next day when Granddad and I went to the hospital, both your mum and dad were in tears. 'Ben's still in an oxygen tent,' your dad said. 'They keep saying it's just to make sure.'

"I asked them if they'd like me to try to find out. They both shook their heads. 'We've got a growing list of complaints,' your mum said. 'You won't believe what happened to me last night. A fire alarm went off, a nurse rushed in and told us that we needn't worry, as it wasn't on the maternity wing, it was in the baby unit. I've had no sleep, Maggie. And I was told, over an hour ago, that they'd help me to have a bath, and change my sheets.'

"So I said, 'Now that is something I can sort, one way or another. I'll go to the nurses' station and see what's happening. Sometimes you have to be a squeaky wheel.'"

"And Mum and Dad didn't know what a squeaky wheel was. It's someone who keeps asking until whatever it is they want, gets done. Then you and dad helped Mummy have a bath, didn't you?"

"Yes, and that, Grandson, is the end of the story."

"No Nana. The end is, I'm here and I'm okay."

He was right. It had taken a month for the specialist to pronounce Ben fit; to say he was suffering no permanent damage from his traumatic birth. And by that time, we had calmed down and were simply relieved to learn that the hospital would be keeping an eye on him for a couple of years. It didn't make what had happened right, but it was something.

"I'm starving," I said. "Shall I make us some lunch?"

"Can we have pizza?"

"Are you sure your tummy's up to it?"

"I think so. I'm going to draw a surprise picture for Granddad while you make it."

The picture turned out to be one of me getting into the wrong car, in clothes with labels all over them. I tried to picture Trevor's face when he gave it to him. Would he smile? Would he remember? At lunch, Ben told me he was going to recite the poem about farts at the end of golden time.

"Is that a good idea?" I said. "Is your teacher going to be happy for the class to listen to a rhyme about farts?"

"Oh yes. Miss told us a story about her uncle trumping louder than a trumpet. It was because Kenny had let off a loud one in sharing time. She said, we all needed to trump. It showed that our bodies were working properly. We giggled. I mean, it's dead funny a teacher talking about trumping."

"Goodness me," I said, thinking that I would like to meet his teacher.

"So, if I say trump, not fart, it will make Miss laugh. If she laughs, I might get a gold star."

Very wise, grandson. "Will you be disappointed if you don't?"

"No. I'll have made everyone laugh, like you do."

"But not like Granddad Robbie does?"

"A bit like Granddad Robbie. Wait a minute. It wasn't because he makes people laugh. It was because he was the wrong sort of doctor."

There's a thought. General versus special. "I'm not sure about that, Ben. I think it's going to have to go down as a 'don't know'."

"Okay," said Ben. "I'm still hungry Nana."

Chapter Sixteen
The See-Saw

What goes up must come down.

The very nature of a see-saw is that it goes up and down. Sometimes so fast that you jar the bottom of your spine on the descent. That was how I felt when I heard Angela's news; or I should say, Angela and Dave's news. "Let me off," I was begging, but no one heard, no one saw. They were all too astonished, excited. Well, that was what the expressions on their faces told me. Even Trevor looked interested. The shock. It was the shock, the not being forewarned. Why hadn't Angela said anything to her gang friends before their holiday? But Debbie and Einna's faces didn't look as mine felt. *And to be honest, Maggie, would it have made any difference when you knew?*

I wasn't in when Angela rang to invite us for dinner. I was surprised when Trevor told me he'd accepted the invitation.

"She was mysterious," he said. "She told me she and Dave had something important to tell us and she wanted to try out some French recipes. I like French cuisine"

Was it as simple as food? Was Trevor being lured out of Munster Mansion by the prospect of French cuisine? Where had 'your friends have nothing interesting to say' gone? "I hope the food won't be too rich." *Herbs are okay, but wine and cream, no.*

I saw the fleeting look of exasperation pass across Trevor's face. Any reference to my condition brought the look.

"I'm sure I'll find something I can eat." *Angela will have thought about Bozo. All my friends are so careful of me. It's touching. It's sad. Trevor is impatient with me. Looks more than words. But then I'm impatient with him. Not in words or looks. It's all squashed inside my mind.* "I wonder what the news is? Perhaps he's going to run his own business? Perhaps they're going to go into business together? Of course that would mean Angela giving up work. No, I know. They're going to adopt a baby."

"Why must you make up stories, Maggie? What would they want to adopt a child for at their time of life?"

"You used to—" But Trevor had turned from me and begun to ascend the stairs. "Enjoy my stories," I whispered to his retreating back. But perhaps he never had? Perhaps it was just the first flush love?

The phone rang as I watched him walk away from me. "Ah, you're in. Where were you? It was nice talking to Trevor though. I feel very honoured that he's gracing us with his presence. I forgot to tell him that I'm making some simple, wholesome dishes as well as richer ones, so Bozo won't raise his ugly head."

I was right. "Thank you, friend," I said. "I was taking Edith shopping"

"You are good to the dragon. And there's no need for thanks. We've always been there for each other, haven't we? No matter what. And we always will be."

Odd! Why did she feel the need to say that? So much said. Is it so much unsaid? Unaccountably, I shivered as I put down the phone.

This would be the first social occasion for the gang for a long time. There were so many reasons for this. Bozo, and Einna's relationship with Tom were just two.

I could see why Einna had been attracted to him. He was good looking in an unconventional way and he was funny, entertaining. But there was something about him that made me uneasy. An occasional frown when a frown seemed out of place, jagged gestures, a sense that he wasn't quite comfortable in his skin. *Me being fanciful? Don't know.*

"Dave and I have some news," said Angela as we were tucking into mushroom and tarragon pate with melba toast. "We're in the process of buying a place in France. We've signed the compromis, so we can't back out. If we do, we lose the deposit."

"Wow!" said Bill.

"A holiday home?" said Einna.

"No." Dave looked at Angela "We're going to live there."

Live there? Move to France? That will mean… It came back to me, that shiver, and I understood it.

"It's partly your fault." A gesture embraced us all. "You keep telling me I should be a restaurateur not a teacher. I do love cooking, and I'm growing to love teaching less and less. We can't afford a suitable property in the UK. We can in France. But it's not going to be a restaurant per-se. It's going to be a gîte where the holiday makers can eat with us if they want to."

"My main role is the renovation of the property we've bought," said Dave. "It's part house, part barn. The house, such as it is, needs modernising. And we can develop the barn into two, two bedroomed gîtes."

Dave sounded excited. I hadn't seen him this excited since he'd been made redundant. *I ought to be able to applaud that excitement, but I can't. Oh, ungenerous friend.*

"What about cricket and rugby?" said Trevor.

"I did have to think long and hard about cricket. I haven't played for the County side for some time, and I doubt that I'll get into the club's first team now. Maybe it shouldn't matter, if you love a sport, but it does. I gave up rugby a while ago. The scrum and a sixty year old body don't make good bedfellows. There are other sports in France that I can enjoy, like pétanque. New challenges. That's what I want."

Like speaking French.

"Phil Collins is the name of the estate agent. I have to admit, I took an instant dislike to him. We told him what we wanted to pay, which was a mistake. To begin with, he only showed us properties above the sum, on the assumption that we'd lied. When we said we weren't interested in any of them, he asked us if we were serious about wanting to buy. Did I tell him what I thought of him? Talk about a scouse tirade. You'd have been proud of me, Maggie," said Angela.

I was too shocked by the news that they were proposing to move to France to remind them that they weren't bona-fide Scousers; an ongoing tease. I was the only Scouser in the gang. *The gang. The gang is being broken up.* I tried to smile.

"He then showed us properties we could afford," said Dave. "As for his sales patter. We were both convinced he'd told us there was a bathroom."

"You mean you saw properties without bathrooms?" said Tom.

"Quite a few. Anyway, the details he gave us said this property had a bathroom. But it certainly wasn't in the house. We couldn't have missed it. There was a large kitchen, living room, a scullery, a bedroom, a storeroom and a two good sized empty rooms at the back which we'll develop into a sitting room and our bedroom. This was all ground floor. There's a grenier above."

"Grenier?" asked Debbie.

"Grain attic" said Angela, "'Where's the bathroom?' I said. 'It says there's a bathroom in the details you gave us.'

"'Sharp, your missus,' creep said. 'She cut herself often? Come with me.' He led us into the barn. There, still swathed in plastic, was the bathroom suite."

"Oh my god!" said Debbie.

"So it will be sink washing until we install it." Angela laughed. "But we got the property for a good price, and when we've sold our house and paid off the mortgage, there'll be enough for the renovations. So, what do you think? Exciting isn't it?"

Gang Maggie would have said something to make everyone laugh, but Bozo Maggie couldn't. *No, it's not exciting, it's… it's… I can't bear it. It's another death I have to cope with. I can't.* 'Drama Queen,' I heard Edith hiss.

I couldn't speak for fear of bawling at the picture of Angela and Dave eating croissants, camembert and singing the *Marseillaise* and… Of course, I wanted her to be happy and to be happy for her, but I was filled with so much sadness for me there was no room for positive emotions.

A couple of days later, when I felt I could talk without crying, I rang Debbie. "I bet Dave has pushed for this," I said. "I bet they could have found a place in Wales."

"Wales is still a distance, not round the corner, Maggie."

"It's not across a sea."

"I think it would have been a joint decision."

"A joint decision motored by Dave."

"I don't think so, Maggie. Don't forget, Angela's parents sent her to France for a month, every summer, from the age of eleven to sixteen. She loves France."

"We can't have gang jaunts in France. We could have managed them in Wales." *How will I get Trevor to France when I can't get him to go...* "We have such fun, when we're together. Whenever I think of our jaunts I start giggling."

"Yeah, me too." We sighed at the same moment.

"I'm going to have to go now, Maggie. Bill's just come in for some sandwiches. He's got to go back into work again. The nursery's demanding a lot of its staff now it's being developed into a garden centre." She rang off.

Five months, that was all it took, and they were gone. No more Angela, no more Angela and Dave. We had been a gang for over thirty years. Stuart, ringing to ask if Ben and Adam could come for the weekend as he wanted to take Beth to London for her birthday, saved me falling.

"Of course they can come." It was just the distraction I needed. "I've invited Einna and Debbie for coffee on Saturday morning. Are either Ben or Adam playing in footy matches?"

"No. Neither of them have got games this weekend."

After Stuart and Beth had dropped them off, Adam asked if he could watch the telly.

"Just for a little while," I said.

"Can I go and find Granddad?" Ben asked.

"You know where he is." It came out bitterly. Ben didn't seem to notice and ran off up the stairs.

"I want to play chess," he called back. "Last time, Granddad beat me."

Good luck sweetheart, I didn't say.

Einna arrived, and we went down to the kitchen to wait for Debbie. She took off her coat and pushed back the settle so she could slide in. She hadn't seen it back in situ since Tom had repaired it. She stroked the arm. "Tom's made a good job of the repair. You can't notice the join." There was pride in her voice.

Her head was bent so her dark hair fell like a curtain across her face; dark, with the odd silver strand gleaming in the light. The basement of Munster Mansion was so gloomy we always had to have the light on.

"I've never noticed your white strands before. Why don't you dye your hair?" I said.

"You don't."

"No I suppose I don't. *But my hair has faded, not begun to turn grey. Is faded red hair more attractive than grey strands?*

"I don't mind the strands."

What I felt she didn't say was, 'Besides, Tom wouldn't like it.' Tom didn't like make-up. Tom didn't like Einna's earrings. It seemed that, in her middle age, Einna was less in control of her personal life than she had been when she was married to John. Was she less in control than when Annie had bossed and bullied her?

To dye or not to dye? How many times had I asked myself that question. But then I was in my late-fifties, what else could I expect? I was no longer a pre-Raphaelite woman, a Lizzie Siddal woman.

I'm Maggie Harvey, naked now, and with a pain that scares me despite all the reassurances.

When I looked at my face, I didn't think that dying my hair back to its former colour would suit me. I always wore make-up, but, only a little. I tried not to hear Trevor saying, 'You look washed out, Maggie. Why don't you put some rouge on?'

Rouge, the man was stuck in the dark ages. He ought to have looked at himself in the mirror, occasionally. He was grey all through. Einna and I used to joke about that. It was a Christmas phenomena. John turned into Scrooge and Trevor into the Grey Man. The Grey Man often looked like the Green Man all crunched and grumbly.

I'd hoped Trevor would become the man I'd met and subsequently married, when he took early retirement. He had appeared briefly. He had even tinkered about on the piano, for a few months. Then the morose expression had returned and settled. I knew that when I got in from college, his day would have been spent listening to music. Apparently, he and Tom met, occasionally, in the Central Library, always coincidence, never planned. They had music but not taste in common. Trevor would have ordered something by a contemporary composer. He particularly liked Harrison Birtwistle. Tom was a Mahler, Richard Strauss, and fifties/sixties popular music fan. Einna liked Richard Strauss. Or at least she used to, before Michael. There were a lot of 'befores' in Einna's life. There was a similar list lurking in my life. And what would we two have been like without those 'befores'?

"Debbie's very late, isn't she?" said Einna.

"Yes, it's not like her. I think I'll put the coffee on."

Adam materialised as if by magic. "Can we have coffee please, Grandma?" he said. "And some of your chocolate shortbread?" He slid onto the bench beside Einna.

"We?"

"Ben said Granddad didn't feel like playing chess at the moment."

"Where is Ben"

"In the lounge watching CBBC.

Flash anger. How could he? To me, yes. To his grandson? I subverted my feelings into a question. "How do you know there's chocolate shortbread?"

"You always make it when we come."

"Are you allowed coffee?"

"Yes, if it's milky."

Ben clomped down the basement stairs, no fleet of foot Mercury, unlike his brother. "I'd like——"

"… A hot chocolate with a marshmallow in it."

Ben grinned. "You're a witch, Grandma."

"No, psychic, not a witch. It's not too difficult, grandson. When have I ever made you anything different? The wonder is that you never get tired of it."

"It's not you that's a witch, it's Einna," said Adam. "Can I have a hot chocolate too, please?"

Mercury is right. A quicksilver change. "If you tell me why my friend's a witch." I put the drinks and the tin of chocolate shortbread on the table.

"I must admit, I've never thought of myself as a witch. Am I a good witch or a bad witch, Adam?" said Einna.

"Well, you're not a bad witch. I wouldn't sit next to a bad witch. But you're not a good witch either. If you were a good witch, you and my nan would have loads of money."

"Ah! Let me get this straight, Adam. If you're a good witch you make lots of money?"

"Yes."

"What about helping people?"

"Money does help people. You'd tell people they had to give some of their money away."

"What about turning toads into princes?"

"Or pumpkins into amazing sports cars. I'm going to have a sports car," said Adam.

"Why do you think I'm a witch, Adam?"

"Because your hair's long and black with white streaks and you're very, very old."

Einna and I glanced at each other. Years ago, a smile would have been catching and members of the gang would have succumbed to giggles. Today we smiled.

"What about your grandma?"

"She's been a witch forever. She's a lovely witch, but not a good witch because she keeps telling me she hasn't got any money."

"I don't have any money when you go on about wanting things, Adam."

"But I like things."

"So do we all," said Ben. "Drink up, Adam, then I'll let you shoot goals at me in the garden. Is it okay, Grandma?"

"Just be careful of the plants, love."

"We will," said Adam.

Plants? What plants? Weeds. Nettles, cleaver, lemon balm, buttercups; that's what grows in our garden.

When they'd put their mugs in the dishwasher and disappeared outside, I looked at the clock. It was eleven and there was still no sign of Debbie. "Shall I give her a ring?" I said.

"Good idea, or, I could put a spell on her and magic her here," said Einna.

"Do you remember your childhood spells?"

"There was only one, I think. And yes, I remember that one.

"Changing pearls into rubies is very hard to do.
It's as hard as killing a croc
and flushing it down the loo.
Pearl, ruby, pearl, ruby
Annie down the loo."

"Impressive." I let the phone ring and ring. Debbie and Bill didn't have an answer phone.

"She must be on her way. I don't know about you, Einna, but I'm a bit worried about Debbie. She seems to have been very distracted lately."

"Not herself, certainly. But none of us are the women we used to be. Look at Angela, moving to France without a, by-your-leave. Did you warn her that we were going to ring?"

"No, but they'll be there at lunch time, won't they?"

At midday, there was still no Debbie and, having thrashed about in our surmising of what might have happened to her, Einna said something so outrageous that we did almost giggled ourselves into wet knickers.

"Bill's upped and left her."

"Bill? He'd be lost without Debbie."

Little did we know... Little did we imagine... that our joke...

Debbie had arrived home on Friday evening to find a note from Bill to say he'd left her. Sophie knew about it. Bill had called round to Sophie's on the Thursday and told her what he was intending, but asked her not to say anything until he had thought through how to tell Debbie.

Still in ignorance of all this, Einna said, "I'll go home via her house. I must go now. Tom will be expecting me for lunch. I said I'd pick up fish and chips, a treat."

She rang me as soon as she got in. "Tom's popped the fish and chips in the oven," she said.

"Is Debbie ill?"

"No. Yes. Sort of." And then she told me what had happened. "Sophie was at Debbie's when I got there. Obviously she's very upset too. Apparently Debbie's gone to the garden centre to find Bill. She hasn't taken it in. She thinks he's had a funny turn. Bloody hell, Maggie, I almost feel I am a witch."

"Why? Because you made a joke which we nearly wet our knickers over? We couldn't have known. What does Sophie think? I mean Bill, our perfect man? I'm inclined to believe Debbie's right. He's had a funny—"

"No, he hasn't. Sophie said he's been having an affair with a colleague for years. He told Sophie how much he'd been enjoying sausages and bacon."

If we weren't so appalled, I think we'd have laughed again.

I didn't want Ben and Adam to see that I was in a state of shock. *Bill, adulterous? Bill leaving Debbie for a carnivore? It had to be a mid-life blip.*

"What are you shaking your head for, Nana? We haven't broken anything," said Adam, running in from the garden. "Can I have one of your home-made orange-juice lollies, please?"

No you haven't broken anything, Bill has. "Yes. You know where they are." Time bought, for he went off to the garage where the spare freezer was. *Bill? But Bill and Debbie were happy. They were happy, weren't they? But Maggie, how often have you said, you can never fully know a person. And, what is happiness?' Would anyone be surprised if you left Trevor, or he left you? Would they?*

233

"Oh," I called after him. "Einna told me to tell you that she's fallen off her broomstick, and Tom—"

Adam ran back. "Einna's boyfriend? Ben and I don't know him."

I'd forgotten that the boys hadn't met Tom. "No, you don't. I think, perhaps, partner's a better word for someone Einna's age."

"Not husband. Not like Granddad's your husband and Daddy's Mummy's husband."

"No, Tom and Einna aren't married. Anyway, Tom had to carry her into the house and put a plaster on both her knees." *Bill, how could he?*

"If she was a good witch, she would have made her knees better herself. She didn't really fall off her broomstick, did she Nana?" said Adam.

"You know she didn't, dozy. Nana made it up, didn't you, Nana?" said Ben.

"Yes. Only one lolly, Ben, Adam. Lunch will be ready in half an hour." *Lunch, what am I going to give them for lunch? I want to go to Debbie's, tell her it's…*

But it wasn't and in the ensuing months I, Sophie, Einna, Debbie's grandchildren, and other friends all did our best to help her, but we only ever saw a sad, lost ghost.

"Do you know what my dad said?" said Sophie, one day when she, Einna and I got together to plan something for Debbie's birthday. "He thought it would make his action more understandable if he told me and Mum he'd been having an affair with Carol for years, since before that concert Mum couldn't go to because I was ill. He wasn't at Green Fingers doing overtime at all. I don't think I've ever felt so angry. I mean Dad, my dad. How can any woman trust a man? How can I trust Charlie?"

"It's people, not men," I said. "People betray other people." *Angela and her zipless fuck. Okay, Dave didn't know but…*

"Yes, but I'd like to bet that more men are putting it about than women."

"I think, biologically, their sexual urges are greater,"

"You are too compassionate, Maggie."

Not always.

Then, Debbie disappeared. One moment she was in a grey fog of misery, the next, gone. In a frantic quandary I telephoned Angela.

"Zero deux, quarante et—"

I cut her off. "Ange, it's me."

"Hi you, what are you ringing me for this early in the morning. It must be only eight at yours."

"I knew you'd be up. I've had a bad night worrying about Debbie. She's disappeared." I said it as it was. No drama queen stuff.

"What do you mean, Debbie's disappeared?"

"Just that. One day she was in Liverpool, the next she wasn't. Sophie's no idea where she's gone. She has a key to the house and she found a note, propped up against a tin of organic tea bags. It said: *'Can't stay in the same city as your dad, any longer. We'd planned to go away for my birthday. I feel so betrayed. I know you were planning something to take its place, but I can't face any sort of birthday stuff. I'll let you know where I am when I get there.'* What kind of a note is that? One that makes everybody sick with worry."

"One that shows us just how miserable Debs is. Dave and I are still in shock over what Bill's done."

"But where can she have gone?"

"She'll let us know when she gets there, like her note says. But if you want my guess, The Beara Peninsular."

"The where?"

"Ireland, the south west, near Bantry. She'll have gone to stay with Chrissie."

"Chrissie who lived in their house? CND Chrissie? You think so?"

"Yes, so stop being an old worry-guts. You're at it again, aren't you?"

"At what?"

"Trying to solve everyone's problems."

She's right. But you can't switch off thoughts. Clear as a crystal, I could remember the day Debbie had met the bastard.

"Do you remember when she met Bill?" I said as ghosts from college floated out of my eyes and danced about the room.

Angela laughed. "How could anyone forget?" There was a pause. When she spoke again her voice was sombre. "Debbie's had to deal with a lot of trauma in her life."

She was right. Her early childhood and the teasing, which was, after all, a form of bullying.

When she was at college, Allie being killed by a drunk driver; the tragic irony of that when Debbie's intentions had been to teach in a school for handicapped children so they could have a challenging education, not the kind that had been offered to Allie. Bill had helped her live again. And now he had deserted her and taken away a whole chunk of her life.

"So, you don't think it advisable to ask Sophie for Chrissie's number and give her a bell then?"

"No I don't. I think Debbie needs space and time from everything and everyone that reminds her of Bill. Sadly, that includes us. But the ties are strong. When she heals, she'll come back to us."

"And to think he wanted to be part of the gang, come on jaunts with us." I couldn't help thinking that we too were Bill's victims. I changed the subject.

"How are you two getting on?"

"I've a notebook full of stories already. It would send your phone bill through the roof if I started. Suffice it to say, it's a mixed bag. Some things are okay, others not. But on balance, there's more okay than not." She whispered, "I find having to translate almost every word for Dave really tiring. He ought to have had French lessons before we moved." She spoke normally again. "Hindsight is wonderful. The French for that is so much prettier: *Sagesse retrospective*."

"How will you mix the French experience with the English recipes?"

"I shan't. I've decided to write a series of short stories, loosely based on my life, which has a recipe at the start of each one. So, the recipe has to be relevant to the story."

"On your life? Isn't that an autobiography?"

"This won't be. At least I don't envisage an autobiography."

"It sounds amazing."

"Don't know about that. I'll have to go now, Maggie. I've a meeting at the Mairie at ten. I'll ring you at the weekend. And Maggie, try not to worry about Debbie."

How can you turn off worry?

Chapter Seventeen
Why Would They Believe Me?

Faith will move mountains.

When Angela lived in Woolton. When Einna wasn't as caught up in her relationship with Tom. Before Debbie fled to Ireland, face to face help was no more than half an hour away. We women talked our problems out. We even laughed them away, sometimes. Now, all my agony aunts were far away physically or mentally.

Not long after Dave and Angela left, I signed a contract with a phone company to enable me to have free, any-time calls, national and international. Of course they weren't free. The consumer paid an upfront charge. But it meant that I could spend up to an hour chatting to my departed friends.

However, phoning or sending an email didn't have the same help factor built in. Phones are fine for arrangements and light-hearted stuff. For problems or heartache? No. You couldn't give someone a hug down the phone, hence Dr Clarke: Leif. Leif wasn't just a counsellor. He was a holistic healer. He became Einna, Angela and Debbie rolled into one. But, of course, he wasn't my friend. I paid him to listen.

Phone-calls did bring sound, other than the music percolating through the floorboards from the attic, or the voices of doom from the television news. For that brief hour there could be laughter in otherwise people silent rooms. I hoped I didn't over-burden my friends with the chatter of loneliness. I was the one who, on the whole, did the ringing, filling in each friend with news of the others in the disbanded gang.

One morning, I had no sooner put down the phone from ringing Angela, when it rang again. It was Stuart, a very upset Stuart. My mind began jumping racecourse fences.

"I can't talk about it on the phone, Mum. Can you come over, please?"

I was packed and ready to leave the house before Trevor could tut or Bozo could snarl.

I asked Trevor to order a taxi if he couldn't give me a lift into the city centre. Still tutting, he agreed to drive me.

"Couldn't you have insisted Stuart tell you what was wrong on the phone?"

"No, I couldn't," I said. "You didn't hear Stuart's voice, Trevor. He needs a hug."

Once the train had left Central Station, I made for the toilet. After I'd had a wee, I took a good look at myself in the mirror. There were bags under my eyes, and lines at the corners of my mouth which made me look discontented.

"When did you get to look this old then?" I said to my parrot reflection.

"When you stopped caring girl," the parrot squawked. *I'm beginning to sound like Einna. She told me ages ago that she talks to herself.* The other day I asked her if she still did and she said, yes, because talking to Tom was often so difficult. *Me, what excuse have I got? Trevor, who rarely does anything but grunt, and Bozo. Am I going to dye my hair?*

"Can't be bothered. Can't be bloody bothered."

'Wash your mouth out, Margaret.' *Why do I always go into Maggie and Edith mode? It's bloody pathetic.* "There, I've sworn again. I'm an elderly woman, Mother, and I'll swear if I want to."

Lipstick? No, Stuart won't care what I look like, will he? He's far too upset. You can't let yourself go, queen. Why is Stuart upset?

"Just come," he'd said. "I really need to see you, have a chat, see if it clears my head."

I started worrying immediately. Something was wrong, had to be. Stuart wouldn't have rung me otherwise, well not like that.

"Oh, Maggie," Trevor had said. "What do you want to go rushing over there for? You're always rushing about, and you know it brings on your IBS."

No, you and Edith bring… Don't be unfair, Maggie. Leif said, stress. This is stress, is what I'd thought. And 'We're Jack Sprat and his wife,' is what I'd wanted to say. 'Me doing. You sitting on your arse contemplating your navel. Why don't you come with me? Our boy's in trouble.' But I'd known what the answer would be, so I'd kept the frustration locked away with all the other frustrations and stresses, where it festered. Maybe it was all that rotting stuff that caught the nose of Bozo, carrion feeder that he was.

God, Trevor is so like Tom. Einna helps Claire. Tom questions it. He won't go with her. Actually, that is a 'used to be'. Einna doesn't leave Tom now he's got leukaemia, poor man. And Tom isn't Claire's father. Trevor is Stuart's father.

After I'd packed a bag, I wrote out a list of prepared dishes that I'd stashed away in the freezer; they were ready to heat up in the microwave. If Trevor chose to ignore them, and live off takeaways, that was his prerogative.

As I was about to leave the toilet, my stomach growled, a little throaty growl, not the 'ow, side clutching growl' that had me reaching for a packet of painkillers; a growl that said, 'have a cup of something and I'll be good.' That's how I thought of Bozo, as a potentially good or naughty two year old. *Whoops, someone is knocking at the toilet door. I've no idea how long they've been there. Too bad. There are other toilets on the train.*

"You shitting a brick in there?" a voice, crude with impatience crashed through the door.

I would have liked to answer, "This is not the only toilet on the train, you know." The old me would have done so, but this me was more cautious. I pressed the button to unlock the door, and rushed past the man who was waiting. I refused to look him in the face, or apologise for monopolising the toilet. I would have done so if he'd been polite.

In the seat across the aisle, a woman was chatting into a mobile phone. I soon realised it was not one of those inane, 'we're just leaving Crosby', conversations.

"I'm telling you Arthur, it's wonderful. I can't think why we haven't tried it before… The seats are very comfortable. Someone's told me that on longer journeys there's a buffet car, and a trolley service. I never imagined there would be anything like that; fancy being able to have a cup of tea while you're travelling. You can't do that in a car, not unless you stop." There was a pause. "Yes, I know we've seen restaurant cars in films and on the telly, but that's not real life, is it? I always thought that was the author's imagination, so that someone could be poisoned."

I could hardly believe my ears. The woman was chattering away into a contemporary communication device, a mobile phone, but had never travelled on a train before, nor had the man to whom she was talking.

"Yes, they have a toilet." She began to whisper and I had to strain to hear what she was saying. "The woman across from me has just come back from using the one at the end of our carriage. I could ask her what it's like.

"I'm sure it will be clean, Arthur. Of course I can see it might be a problem from your point of view; I don't think of things like that… You could always use a paper towel to hold the door handle, when you came out."

What a good idea. I shall do that whenever I use a public convenience. There are still people who don't wash their hands, particularly men. I bet it was other men Arthur was referring to. What about the man who used the toilet after me? He was so impatient and rude, I bet he wouldn't have bothered to wash his hands. He probably thinks, because he doesn't have to wipe a fanny, just hold his cock – sorry Dad, penis – that he doesn't need to bother.

The woman was still chatting on her mobile phone when the train pulled into Southport station. As I opened the carriage door to get out, I heard her give a little squeak. "I shall have to go, Arthur, we've arrived. I'm quite glad you couldn't give me a lift. I wouldn't have ever been on a train, otherwise. No, of course it's sad you're not with me. I'll speak to you tomorrow from Helen's… yes of course I'll give her your love." As she got up out of her seat she said, "Men, what else would I give her, his hate?"

On the platform, away from the diversion of the ingénue train traveller, the worry about why Stuart needed to see me in such a hurry, bounced back like a tennis ball on elastic. Was he ill? He didn't sound ill, he sounded worried. He wasn't ill when we last saw him. When was that? A month ago, he'd brought the boys over; they all looked well. He and Beth, my stomach gave a lurch, and Bozo growled again. Not Stuart and Beth; I was very fond of Beth. In so many ways she was an ideal partner for Stuart. *Not Stuart and Beth; Not separation, divorce, please not that. Surely they are rock solid? We all thought Bill and Debbie were rock solid.*

I began to massage my side. I had another three quarters of an hour of worry before meeting Stuart at the café opposite the Arts centre. "It's not too far from the office and the coffee's good," he'd said. *Comfort.* Surely someone with a life-threatening disease or marriage break-up wouldn't be thinking about good coffee?

I window-shopped for a while, but as Bozo was still grumbling, I decided to find the café and grab a table. I would order a herbal tea while I was waiting for him, but which one? Mint for Bozo, or chamomile to calm me?

It was in the middle of a street full of little shops, none of them chain stores; the sort of street that was rare now, in British towns in the twenty first century. I went in, found a table and ordered a cafetiere of coffee, quite changing my mind as I thought that an injection of caffeine might be what was needed before I was told which imagined scenario was the... *None of them. I don't want it to be any of them.*

He was twenty minutes late; he looked grey under his fading tan. *Oh god, he's got cancer. Beth's got... Ben, Adam? Would he look this grey if it were a split? Yes.* I got up. He threw his arms around me and clung on, as though to a mast on a ship in a storm.

"I'm sorry," he said when eventually he managed to let me go, and stand without looking as though he was going to fall.

"Sit down, sweetheart. I'll go to the counter and order another cafetiere."

I could see him in the mirror behind the coffee machine. He was staring into space. When I returned to the table, I decided to say nothing, recognising that he needed time to crawl back up the precipice of his emotions.

He lifted his head. "Oh, Mum," he said, and then was silent again, staring down at the scrubbed-pine table top. *Is it a fear I haven't dared think about? Beth and the boys… dead? No he would have told me on the phone; no he wouldn't have been able to; someone else would have rung. Stop this, Maggie.*

"It's Ben."

Oh god. A picture of Ben flashed behind my eyes. One of my favourite R S Thomas poems, *Farm Child*, described him perfectly. He had an unruly red, gold thatch and harebell eyes. The farm child's hair wasn't red-gold exactly, but it was untidy.

"The police took him and his friend, Ryan, in for questioning, yesterday morning."

I was so startled I didn't know what to say. In none of my imagined scenarios did an arrest of anybody feature. Was it an arrest? My next thoughts were, *thank god, he's alive; he hasn't got an incurable illness; this isn't as bad as I'd feared.* It was bad though. "What did…?" I shook my head, trying to clear the mess that was accumulating.

Stuart reached across the table, his hand begging. I took hold of it. "He, and one of his friends, Ryan, have been growing marijuana in a greenhouse in Ryan's garden. His parents don't use it; they have no interest in gardening, apparently. It's stuck away at the bottom. They don't venture further than their made-over patio and grassed area." Stuart's voice was resentful, almost as though he blamed Ryan's parents for not using their greenhouse. "There were so many plants in it, the police are suggesting that the boys intended to sell the stuff. Ben, a drug dealer…" He couldn't continue.

I'm falling… help! And there was no rope or jutting piece of rock to grab hold of. *Slow down your breathing, Maggie.* I took a slow, deep breath, held it for a count of three and let it out again.

"Ben wouldn't sell a drug to anyone, let alone his fellow pupils, Stuart. We know him. His teachers know him. When has he ever been in trouble at school?"

Stuart shook his head. "The evidence, Mum."

Evidence versus knowledge. *Has Ben been duping us? Is the boy we know a fake?* "Have you talked to him?" Of course he and Beth will have talked to him.

"He's clammed up. He's in shock. We're all in shock. We don't seem to be able to find the words to say anything to each other. Beth and I start a sentence, and can't finish it."

I stroked his hand. "I suspect that's normal." There were so many questions racing around in my mind that I couldn't catch them. *Order. They need to be in some sort of order.* I gave up. Why should I be any different from other people who had to deal with the unexpected? And before I could stop it, there was the image of Clem Williams, dangling from the rope in his hall.

"How did the police find out?"

"A neighbour's daughter, Janine; she could see the greenhouse from her bedroom window. The plants were huge; she recognised them."

"Why did she...?"

"I imagine she felt she had to. Her parents are friendly with Ryan's parents, but..."

But what? They don't want to know them now? Friends support you, if they're good friends. If they don't, they're not friends. Mind you, I shall have to be careful. My friends might get sick of Bozo tales; no, they'll stick by me, and still ask how I am, knowing I probably won't be able to resist telling them. Stop it, Maggie. How can you...? Self centred, that's what you are, thinking that.

"Have you asked one of your colleagues to represent him?" *There has to be an explanation. There has to be, otherwise we'll fall over the cliff edge.*

"No. That wouldn't be wise," Stuart shrugged.

How do I interpret the shrug? Not wise because of his job? Not wise because a judge, or magistrates would see it as nepotism? "But you have got Ben a solicitor, haven't you?"

"We rang one of Beth's friends; she works for the CAB. She gave us the name of a solicitor. She was very direct."

"And?"

"If the CPS decide to prosecute, and they're found guilty, they could be sent to a juvenile detention centre."

"For how long?"

"She couldn't say... months, years if they're convicted of dealing."

I fell, crashing onto the rocks below. How were we all going to bear it? How would Ben cope? He would be unavoidably changed, damaged.

"She doesn't think they will get a custodial sentence, more likely community service."

"Why?"

"Apparently, it's as simple as the amount being grown. There were only fifteen plants and it's his first offence."

Only fifteen, it sounds a huge amount. "Why did they do it?"

Ben was an intelligent boy. His reports and grades year on year were excellent. He read newspapers, and watched the news. They had PSE in school. Stuart and Beth didn't shirk from having difficult discussions. He would have known all the pros and cons of smoking marijuana.

"We don't know. Ben wouldn't even talk to the solicitor. That's why I've asked you to come over. Will you see if you can get him to talk? Both he and Adam have a special relationship with you."

"They do with you and Beth. As a family you've always discussed issues."

"Yes, I know...but... oh, I don't know why he can't... guilt that he's let us down? Will you try, Mum?"

"Of course I will." *I will... will he?*

"And to Adam? He's clammed up as well. Beth thinks he knows something but is afraid to open his mouth for fear that he might further incriminate his brother."

I squeezed his hand, trying to push hope through his skin, then I looked at my watch. "We ought to eat, Stuart."

"I can't..."

"You can, we must. Facing difficulties on an empty stomach isn't a sensible idea, and you have to work this afternoon, don't you? Have you told anyone in the practice?"

"No. Outside the police, the solicitors, and Ryan's neighbours, no one else knows. After we've been back to the Police Station on the sixth, and see what the charge is going to be, we'll tell everyone who needs to know. He and Ryan will be automatically excluded from school, no matter what the sentence is."

"What about the girl?"

"Ryan's parents have asked the Davis family to warn Janine of the consequences of telling any of her friends or the teachers. Apparently it was unnecessary. The police had already done that. Everyone will know if it comes to trial."

The ripple effect. Oh god! What will Edith think? Why am I thinking about her? I don't care what she thinks. She adores Ben as she once adored Stuart and Ian. Adoration can change.

"I'll go up and order," I said. I couldn't cope with any more words like 'trial' and what sprang to mind afterwards. "Could you manage soup? It's ham and pea." Comfort food was what we needed. The menu offered an imaginative selection of salads, and in other circumstances, providing Bozo was behaving, I would have been tempted, but today it seemed like unnecessary hard work, all that munching and chewing; the very smell of ham and peas combined seemed to bring solace.

"Do you want any drinks?" asked the waitress.

"Tap water, please."

The waitress didn't look pleased.

"Is there a problem?" I'd encountered this reaction before when asking for tap water. "Is water off today? Has the café got a policy about customers drinking water? It's the best thing to drink, you know. We're all supposed to drink… It doesn't matter." I suddenly became aware that I was taking my anxiety out on this girl, for she wasn't much more than that. In any case, I could have misread her expression. *Misread… misunderstood. Clem had misunderstood my attempts to befriend him as flirtation. We misunderstand all the time. Of course Ben and Ryan weren't growing marijuana to sell as a drug. They'd had another plan. I just needed to find out what. But then fear kicked in again. Whatever the reason, who would believe them? You needed proof to be believed.* "Sorry, love. I'm a little bit out of sorts today." *Not a lie.* "I shouldn't have taken it out on you."

"That's okay. Where are you sitting?"

"By the window."

Later, after Stuart had gone back to work, I rang Trevor to tell him that I would be staying in Southport for a few days, and I told him why.

I quite understood the lack of response. This wasn't one of the times when I felt aggrieved by his silence. He was in shock. Eventually he said, "Do you want me to come over?"

What to say? The Trevor I'd married would have known how to help, but... He answered his own question.

"I'm not sure I'd know what to say. I'll let you deal with it. I'll ring you tomorrow morning."

I looked at my watch, two fifteen; I had three and a half hours before Stuart would be ready to leave the office. We had arranged for me to go to there, so that we could travel home together.

Normally, I would have enjoyed pottering around the shops, especially if I was feeling fit, but today I decided to go to the library. I was going to prepare myself for the chat with Ben by looking up marijuana, making sure I knew about it, and its effects. What I discovered was very interesting, especially about the family of plants. I made notes. Now I had knowledge, I realised I would have to be careful not to put ideas into Ben's head, words into his mouth.

When we walked through the front door, the first thing I noticed was that the house was unnaturally silent. Stuart didn't alert the family that he was home; as far as I knew, a normal practice. Beth didn't come to meet us. The boys were nowhere to be seen. The house seemed to be wrapped in a bubble of misery. How I hoped I would be able to burst it.

Stuart looked at me. "This is how it's been since yesterday," he said. "Cup of tea?"

I would have liked to say that I was overflowing with tea, and would prefer something stronger – a little brandy, Bozo tolerated brandy – but that didn't seem appropriate and I intuited that Stuart needed to make one, to be busy.

Beth was in the kitchen. Her eyes were red. She'd been crying. Stuart went over to her, put his arms around her; drew her close. They stood, statue still. I hovered in the doorway.

When we were sitting at the table, Beth said, "Jean told me again that she doesn't think the boys will be sent to a centre for young offenders."

"Jean?" I asked.

"Ben's solicitor."

I couldn't help thinking that maybe Jean ought not to have set up a hope, an expectation, but then a second thought chased the first: they needed chinks of hope.

"I wish Ben would talk to us."

"Beth, are you sure you want me to have a go?"

"Oh yes, Maggie. Stuart and I..."

Wits' end. End of tether. Emotionally bankrupt. "Is he in his room?"

"Yes."

"I'll take him up a cup of tea." I didn't add, 'shall I?' having decided, during my time in the library, that no-nonsense Nannying skills were needed. When people were in shock, or distressed, as my family was now, choices were straws that could break backs. I poured out another mug of tea and took the two upstairs.

The Harvey house was a cusp, Victorian-Edwardian semi. It had always had a pleasant atmosphere, but today, the stress seemed to have seeped into the walls and I shivered. I decided not to bother to knock at Ben's door. I didn't want to give him the opportunity of not responding.

Ben was lying on his bed, staring at the ceiling. From the state of his room, it looked as though he'd been lying there for days. Clothes had been left in a pile, as had his school bag, which was open. Ben had always been a tidy child. I put his mug of tea down on the bedside table.

"Give your old Gran a hug then," I said.

Ben, pre-arrest Ben, would have rolled off the bed, given me a bear-hug, and told me I was forbidden to say I was old. This Ben didn't move.

I stroked his hair. "Tell me," I said. "Whatever you want."

He mumbled something. I leant closer. "Sorry, sweetheart, I didn't catch that."

"What's the point?" he said, a little louder.

"When I was at college, I bet Angela she couldn't drink a pint of beer in one go." *To get my own back for her teasing me about the magic mushroom episode. Can I tell Ben about that? Maybe not today.* "She drank it and was promptly sick in the union bar. The manager made us clear it up."

No reply. "I bet you're feeling that it's not the same, that lots of young people do that?" No reply.

"Your great uncle and one of his friends were arrested in Boots." Ben frowned. *Ah, a reaction of sorts.* "They stole a record. Your great grandfather had to go to Garston police station to pick him up."

"Uncle Ian?"

Good. He's spoken. "Yes, Uncle Ian."

He rolled over on the bed so he was facing me. "What happened?"

"The arresting officer read them both the riot act and told them they were now in the book."

"Uncle Ian has a record?"

"I suppose so. I'm not sure if you do, after a warning." *I'd forgotten that episode in Ian's life, until now. And I can't remember how Edith dealt with it. He certainly didn't have to leave school and work in Woolies.*

Ben almost managed a smile, then his face grew sombre again. "Shoplifting isn't as bad as what Ryan and I are being accused of. Everyone's going to think we've let them down."

Interesting. Language is so important. Listening to what people say even more so. Ben said, 'what we're being accused of,' not 'what we've done'. Hold onto that Maggie.

"We all let people down, sometimes. We're human beings, not gods. What you're being accused of doesn't stop people loving you."

"No one will love me if I go to a detention centre."

"Why not? I shall still love you, so will everyone else."

"I bet Granddad Trevor won't," said Ben.

"He will." *Will he?* "I don't think you'll be sent to a detention centre."

249

"You can't know that, Nana."

"That's what the solicitor has told your mum and dad. You should try to believe her."

"But no one knows what we've done. They've all assumed something. They all think we're guilty."

"No one can know, unless you tell them. I have a theory, Ben. While I was waiting for your dad to finish at the office, I did some research in the library. Now I want to see if my theory's correct. In fact I've had a bet with myself that it is. I'd like you to stop me if I'm wrong. You see, Granddad and I can't believe that you smoke pot or grow marijuana plants because you want to make money." I mentioned Trevor because of what Ben had said earlier. That it was a lie didn't matter; it was a necessary lie. "You don't have an acquisitive nature. Adam does. But he wouldn't do anything wrong, to make money, either. Why? Because you both have a strongly developed sense of what is right or wrong. You're interested in all sorts of ethical issues, aren't you?"

Ben looked at me for the first time. "Yes. Mum and Dad must think I'm into drugs though."

"It's difficult for your mum and dad to know what to think, because you haven't talked to them. They're probably thinking, why grow it if you're not intending to smoke it? You must have known that growing it was illegal. Young people do experiment with drugs of some sort; if not marijuana, alcohol. Your dad once smoked pot when he was at university. He told me about it and said it had made him feel sick and dizzy. I ate magic mushrooms when I was first married to your granddad. But that's a long story which I'll tell you another time." *There I've told him.* "Nobody has stopped loving your dad, and nobody has stopped loving me."

"I've never smoked marijuana, nor eaten it in a cake or biscuit," he said. "Smoking's disgusting. It can give you all sorts of cancer. Why would anyone want to risk that? Marijuana's got side effects as well. It can cause depression. I'd never… Oh it's useless." He flung himself on his back again. "No-one will believe the truth."

"Ah, the truth? How about a mistake being the truth? I told you to stop me if I was getting it wrong. Your go now. I'd like to see if I've won my bet"

"Yes, we made a mistake," he whispered.'

"I thought so. I've won my bet. Eco warriors?"

"How did you know, Nana?"

"I didn't. I know you and I've met Ryan. That and the info I got in the library helped me put two and two together."

"It was an experiment."

"But why didn't you tell the solicitor that?"

He shrugged. "Police, people in authority, they believe the worst, don't they?"

"But your solicitor's job is to look after you."

"Yes," said Ben. "But all she could talk about was mitigating circumstances. We're innocent of what we're being accused of, Grandma."

"Of course you are, so let's start from there. But you have to remember the fact that there were marijuana plants in the greenhouse. The police have them. You can't deny that." I would have loved to have another bet, that some leaves had been harvested and taken home for police use. "The mistake was that you and Ryan ordered the wrong plants online, didn't you? So, what we need to do is find a way of telling your story so that you will be believed."

"Adam was right, Nan. You are a witch."

"Wasn't it Einna who was the witch?"

"And you. You knew what we did without me saying anything. In science we've been looking at environmental issues and climate change. If we don't find solutions, lots of people will die. Look at all the increased flooding, for example. Ryan and I went on the Internet, and we discovered that the plant hemp could provide us with loads of things, like a bio-fuel, hemp seed foods, oil, wax, cloth, paper, resin, rope… it's a really cool plant. We wanted to do some experiments with it, and send the environment minister the results; we knew we wouldn't be believed unless we had proof. We wanted to tell him that Great

Britain could help save the planet. I know we couldn't have made a bio-fuel, but we thought we might have been able to make some of the things. We sowed the wrong seeds. No one will believe that; why should they? It's stupid. We were stupid. But then I wouldn't have known the difference between a hemp seed or a marijuana seed, anyway; neither would Ryan. I've never seen them. Some idiot must have put them in the wrong packets."

"Have you got the seed packet, Ben?"

Ben shook his head. "No, Grandma. You see, I told you no one would believe us."

"I do," I said. "Come on. We've got to try to sort this out. You're heroes, not villains. By the way, why did Janine tell her parents?"

"I think it was because I'd told her she couldn't be in the debating society any longer; she wouldn't obey the rules. I think she was getting her own back."

"Ah!" I was so tempted to say 'little bitch'. I held out my hand. "You coming?"

"If you think I should."

"Yes I do."

We walked downstairs together. Stuart and Beth were still in the kitchen. Adam was slumped in front of the television.

"Adam," I called. "Do you think you could forsake the programme you're watching and join us in the kitchen? We need everyone's brain working."

"Do you want to tell everyone what you've told me, Ben, or shall I tell them?"

"You please, Nana."

"Okay, but if I get anything wrong, you correct me."

Apart from Ben, whose stance didn't change, I noticed that the others seemed to grow, as though they were gathering strength. Ben didn't correct me, even though I wasn't sure I remembered all the various uses of hemp.

When I'd finished, several things happened. Stuart, his voice cracking, said, "You duffer, you wonderful duffer." He rushed out of the room. "I'm going to phone the solicitor." Within two seconds he returned. "I can't, can I? It's well after seven. First thing tomorrow."

Adam punched the air and danced around the kitchen table shouting, "I knew, I knew Ben wouldn't, but I couldn't say, 'cause I didn't think anyone would believe me."

Beth got up and put her arms round Ben. "We'd have believed you, Ben."

"I was so mixed up. I thought all adults would think the worst."

What a world, where three boys, Ben, Adam and Ryan feel that adults won't listen to them, won't believe them, even those who know them. But, hopefully, their tilted world will soon be righted.

Stuart rang Ryan's parents. He was the sort of lad who, if there was a bully around, might have been a target. He was small for his age, not at all sporty; in many ways an unlikely friend for Ben. But I was glad they were mates. They complemented each other and Ben looked out for him.

When the families saw their solicitor, she was confident that the police wouldn't take the matter any further.

"The boys may get a telling off for being naive," she said.

And that was what happened.

I had rung Trevor to tell him all was now well. But as I let myself into the Old Vicarage, the grey atmosphere threatened to suffocate me, and Bozo, relatively quiet during my stay in Southport, growled. All may have been well with my family there, but it was far from well here.

Chapter Eighteen
How Will I Survive?

Don't let the bastards grind you down.

In the weeks that followed, I had to prod myself to remember how effective I'd been in helping

Ben and Ryan. I was almost the Maggie I used to know.

The two boys had been gently castigated, for their naivety more than anything else. Stuart told me that the police sergeant who interviewed them said he had bought a mislabelled packet of seeds once, and he didn't believe the boys could have concocted the story. Of course, the glowing reports from the school helped.

They also had an interview with The Head. She told them that they had been foolish, but she understood their motive. She also told them that Janine had done the right thing in telling her parents, even if she had done it for the wrong reasons. I wasn't too sure about that. What about honour among fellow pupils?

Prodding myself didn't work. In a world where the rich were getting richer, and the poor, poorer, where some people still didn't have clean water and lived in filthy conditions, where climate change was spiralling towards world disaster, I was fixated on the personal and how much of a wimp I was in my dealings with Trevor, Edith and Ian.. How pathetic was that? But however many times I castigated myself with: you're comfortably off, Maggie, you have heat, clean water, sanitation, light and food, Maggie; the silence in Munster Mansion, a phone-call from Edith, Ian's lack of support had Bozo in a paroxism of delight.

"Everything's relative," Leif said.

And it was. My problems were real. The world's problems wouldn't go away if I ceased to be concerned about my own problems.

There were many times in my life when I'd felt my mother hated me. I never knew what I had done to deserve her hatred, any more than I knew what Ian had done to deserve her love. I didn't hate her, nor did I hate Ian. I wasn't sure what I felt for them.

Edith claimed that, as children, Ian and I were close. This didn't tally with my memory of our childhood. I was three years older than my brother, and yes, sometimes we'd played together but that had been forced, not because either of us had looked for it. During the school holidays she had often said "I want you to look after Ian today, Maggie. And mind you don't get into any mischief. I know what you're like."

But, what had I been like? Surely, on any one day I'd been a kaleidoscopic pattern, changing according to circumstances and whoever I'd been with.

My dad used to say I was a rebel who made him laugh. My mother used to say I was a naughty, disobedient nuisance. *The way she speaks to me now shows she doesn't have a much better opinion of me.* Teachers in school said I was a chatterbox and a daydreamer. Leila said that I was her best friend. It wasn't difficult to be all these different people, but Edith couldn't have known the all of me, because she only saw maybe a couple of my many patterns.

No. Leila, Gail and I hadn't wanted Ian tagging along with us. Looking back, we must have given him a dreadful time. We used to take the tram or the bus, whichever took our fancy that day, and stay on it until the end of the route. We loved the feeling of not knowing where we were, of being scared but safe, because all we had to do was wait for the next one back. Edith would have had an apoplectic fit if she had known what we were up to. Ian was sworn to secrecy, with the threat of dire consequences if he dared to say one word.

On one such journey Ian, who had been chattering non stop about how one of his classmates had been sent to the head for spitting into his inkwell, suddenly stopped, and clutched his crotch.

"What do you want, nuisance?" I said.

"I need to do a wee and a poo, Maggie."

"Shh!" I hissed, looking round to see if any other passengers had heard what he'd said. "You can't, not till we get off the bus. Why didn't you go before we left home?"

"I didn't want to, then."

"You'll have to do it in a back alley. Leila, Gail and I'll keep guard."

Ian looked as though he was going to cry. "I can't go in an alley, Maggie. How can I wipe me bum? Me pants'll have skiddies in them, and me Mum'll kill you."

I glared at him, then turned to Leila and Gail. "She will too," I said. "She won't blame him. We'll have to find another way."

"Tell you what," Leila said. "Make him promise not to say anything, and we'll knock on the door of a house, and ask if he can use their bog."

"What, a stranger's house? We're not supposed to talk to strangers," said Gail.

"It's a daft rule," I said. "The bus conductor's a stranger, isn't he, and we have to talk to him." The bus stopped. "Right, we'll have to get off here instead of going to the end of the line. You stay with Leila and Gail, Ian. I'll go to a house over there and ask if you can use their toilet. What mustn't you do?"

"Tell Mum. Hurry up, Maggie, I can feel it coming."

"Squeeze your bum cheeks together," I said. "You can keep it in if you try."

The look on his face, squeezing his brow into furrows, and pursing his lips was worth the embarrassment of asking the lady who answered the door if my brother could use her toilet. Oh, the lie I created. We were on our way to visit our aunt and uncle, a lie, and my brother had been caught short, the truth; and their house was a good ten minute walk from the bus stop, a lie, and he couldn't last till then.

I was a little worried that she might ask me for the name and address of the pretend aunt and uncle, but she saw the look on my brother's face.

A lot of terraced houses didn't have an indoor toilet in the fifties. The lady, whose house we knocked at, told us to go through to the back yard.

Trust. The lady had trusted us to be telling the truth, not playing a stupid game. We hadn't been telling the whole truth, but it hadn't been a game. Necessity, need. I'd responded to the need.

No, Ian and I were not close, had never been close, indeed we were poles apart. He was a successful businessman, and I was an early-retired drama teacher. He voted Conservative and I voted Labour. I could have coped with the business aspect of our differences if I didn't find some of the practices reprehensible. I'd tackled him about them, one day; though I wasn't sure what I'd hoped to achieve. Understanding? A change?

"You are so naive, Maggie." Was what he'd said. "Of course we don't point out all the faults in a house. We'd never get any business if we did. It's not lying, it's an omission. People can always pay more for the truth."

I couldn't accept that this was an ethical way to do business and had said so. His reply? "You don't live in the twentieth century, Maggie. This is how businesses are run. My business is successful. I am successful." Had that way of looking at the world started when he'd attempted to shoplift as a fourteen year old? Not, 'I came, I saw, I conquered.' Rather, 'I wanted, I couldn't afford, I stole.' Had I ever really believed he would find time to help me with Edith? I'm sure his friends thought he was running around after her all the time. After all, Edith often told everyone what a caring son he was.

As for Brenda, every time I forced myself to get on the phone to tell him about a problem, and she answered, she would make no effort to hide the sigh. "Can't you sort it, Maggie? Ian's very busy." So much for the caring son.

Then came the evening phone-call that did do a little to alleviate the February blues. Angela and Dave were coming home. It was difficult to know whether it was what they wanted or not. Would they have chosen to come back if Angela's parents hadn't needed help? I suspected not, even though Angela had once said, "I am no more than a welcome stranger in France. It's not my land."

The following morning seemed to be a morning full of promise. I was in the garden, refilling the bird feeders, so I didn't hear the phone. Trevor answered it.

"Your mother says she's scalded her hand, making herself a cup of tea," he called out of the back door. "I'm not sure how bad it is, Maggie. She wants you to go round."

I groaned. "Did you ask her if she'd run it under a cold tap for ten minutes?"

"Yes. She said that my suggestion showed that we weren't on a water meter like she is. Shall I tell her to go round to Ian's?"

What a question. Should he? Would she? She lived in a terraced house whose garden backed onto Ian and Benda's property. Ian had bought it and had it done up for her so that he could be on hand in an emergency. *So he could steal some of the garden for a conservatory.* Brenda called it an orangery; what was that if not pretentious snobbery?

"No. Tell her I'm on my way."

"And what about our lunch?"

"We'll turn things round. There's some soup left over from last night. You can heat that up, can't you?"

"But why you, Maggie? Why don't you ring Ian?"

"I tell you what, Trevor. You ring Ian. He—"

"I couldn't do that, Maggie."

"No?" Glancing at my watch, I relented slightly. "You know Ian, he might have gone into work." I believed my brother went into the office on a Saturday morning to escape Brenda; I would if I were him.

As I put on my coat, I caught the shrug. *'Come with me,'* I'd nearly said. *'We could go out for a pub lunch after we've dealt with the burn.'* The shrug shut my mouth. I knew that as soon as I left the house, he would heat up the soup, cut himself a piece of bread and, sloth-like, repair to his den for the afternoon. But he would have done that if I'd been at home. Indeed the telephone call had provoked him into a conversation, which was more than I ever could.

I got the car out of the garage, and set off for Woolton. I found a parking space not too far from the house; sometimes I had to park in the next street. When I rang the bell, there was no answer. I rang again, still no answer. I fumbled about in my bag for the key; it wasn't there. I felt in my coat pockets; sometimes I did slip keys into my pockets. Trevor always said, when I was hunting high and low, "Why don't you put them in the same place, Maggie?" Did he think I didn't mean to do this? Every person who has lost keys and spectacles means to do this.

Ring Trevor? Why? What good would that do? It wouldn't.

Then I remembered I'd lent my key to Ian, so that he could get a copy made; he'd lost his along with the keys to their house, when he and Brenda had gone to Spain, a month earlier. Both claimed it was the other's fault. As I walked down the street to their house, I felt a Bozo grunt in his sleep.

I rang the bell. Our bell was programmed with a simple ding-dong; not Ian and Brenda's. It played the first line of Cavatina. No one answered. I went round the back. I could see Brenda in the kitchen. The look on her face, when she saw me tapping at their kitchen window spoke irritation. She didn't know why I'd come round, yet her unguarded reaction said, 'Oh no, what does she want?'

"Brenda, is Ian there? I need to have a quick word with him." I called.

She disappeared. I was left, feeling like the unwanted ghost at a wedding. Five minutes later, Ian came to the front door. I knew it was five minutes because I kept checking my watch.

"This isn't a good time, Maggie," he said. "We've got friends coming round."

"Actually, brother, it's not a good time for me either, and thank you for leaving me standing about on your doorstep. I suppose I should feel lucky it wasn't raining. Mother's scalded her arm, and she isn't answering the door. Could you let me have my key back, please?"

"Mightn't she have gone up for her afternoon rest?"

"Oh, for goodness sake! At lunch time? She rang me for help."

"Maybe she decided she didn't need any help, after all."

"Stop imagining scenarios and—" *What am I saying? It's what I do all the time. Doesn't stop it being true, Maggie.*

"You could go through the garden gate."

"I thought you'd locked and barred that. Besides, I wouldn't be any better off, I don't have a back door key. Just stop faffing and give me my key, so I can be on my way and you can do whatever job Brenda has lined up for you before your guests arrive." Suddenly the look on Ian's face seemed shifty. "You've lost my key, haven't you?"

"No. I just can't put my hands on it. And there's no need to be rude."

"Ian, I know two wrongs don't make a right, but you were rude to me keeping me waiting on your doorstep. Either put your hands on that key now, or phone a locksmith."

"There's no need for that." Brenda came into the room. "Here's the back-door key, and this is the one for the gate."

I felt like shaking the pair of them. Instead, I snatched the keys and marched out of the house into their garden without saying goodbye. Bozo growled.

"Bring them back after you've sorted her out," Ian called after me.

"No, tomorrow," yelled Brenda.

I carried on walking. They could whistle for the bloody keys. I could still hear Ian saying, "I'm so glad I bought number forty-eight for Mum. She's been very lonely since Dad died. Being just round the corner means I'll be on hand to help her, if she needs it." I'd nearly choked then and I still felt like choking now. Ian, Brenda, helping? Pigs would... As for Grizzle being lonely, that was her own fault. She drove potential friends away with her sharp tongue, said that the neighbours were busy bodies and refused to join any clubs.

When Stuart was little, before Dad died, she became a person I quite liked. Even after he died she was softer, somehow. But as soon as Stuart became a teenager and I started to suffer with what I believed, at the time, were bouts of indigestion, she reverted, and over the years got progressively worse. She gloated when she rang me to tell me of Ian's plans to move her to a house in the next street. "My garden backs onto theirs," she said. "At least I've got one child who wants to see me."

Ten minutes round the block, two minutes through the two gardens. Why Brenda had ever agreed to Ian's crazy idea for the connecting gate, I would never know. She must have realised that Grizzle would be tempted to use it indiscriminately.

One Sunday, when I called to return her washing and give her the tea loaf and scones I'd baked, she said, "Lets have a wander in Ian's garden. It looks beautiful at this time of year."

"Do you think it's a good idea? It's Sunday, Mother."

"I know it's Sunday, Maggie. What's Sunday got to do with anything?"

"Only that Ian and Brenda are probably at home. They might not..."

"Fiddle-faddle. Are you implying that they won't want to see me?"

"I... well..."

Edith put on her cardigan, a shapeless, green garment that ought to have been consigned to a jumble sale years ago.

"Come on," she said.

Ian came out of the back door as we were walking past the conservatory. "Mother, Maggie, how nice." I felt the insincerity dripping off his tongue. "Cup of tea?"

Edith gave me a 'see?' look. He pottered off into the kitchen. Unexpectedly, we had a pleasant half an hour. Ian seemed relaxed. I began to think I'd imagined the insincerity.

"Where's Brenda?" Edith asked.

"Inside with her feet up, reading the Sunday papers, I expect. We won't bother her. Have you ever been to Bodnant Gardens?"

"Several times," Edith said. "I was just thinking about Bodnant only yesterday. I'd love to go again." She gave me a meaningful look.

"Then you've seen the Laburnum arch there. I'm recreating it here, although it won't be as long. I wouldn't have been able to do it if we hadn't stolen a little of your garden," he said, giving her his 'impish son' grin.

"Well I don't need it. I don't want the bother of a big garden. I have a little wander round your garden, most days."

He showed us the fledgling creation. It would run from the gate alongside the, orangery. "Laburnums grow quickly do they?" she asked.

"Quite quickly. There'll be a little show next year."

I looked at the sticks, for that's what they were and wondered about time left to any of us. It prompted me to say, "I think we should be going. Or it's time I was. Trevor will be wondering where I've got to." *He won't, but they aren't privy to that.* "Of course you can stay as long as you like, Mother." Trevor never wondered where I'd got to; he rarely noticed when I went out. It was only when I was at home that he noticed me, and then he made it obvious that he did not like what he was noticing. I clattered, apparently.

"I've got some work to do before tomorrow," Ian said. "Not like you, Maggie, all the time in the world to enjoy yourself now you've taken early retirement. But it was lovely to see you both. We must do this again."

"I'll pop in the house and say goodbye to Brenda," I said.

"I wouldn't bother, she might have nodded off.

The next day, Grizzle phoned me. I was not often in sympathy with my mother; today I too felt the insult.

"I went to have my constitutional round Ian's garden, and the gate was locked.

I expect it was a mistake," she said. *I expect it wasn't.*

I was right. She rang Ian, and was told that they had not thought things through carefully enough. "We work hard, Mother," Ian said. "And at weekends Brenda likes a bit of time on her own; you know, to chill out."

We hadn't stopped her 'chill'.

"I told him I didn't want to be a nuisance," said Grizzle. And of course he said, 'Oh Mother, you're not that, never that.'

I intuited that it was Brenda who had bullied him into doing it.

The laburnum sticks had grown, but they were nowhere near being an arch yet. Still seething, I marched between them, unlocked the gate and out of cussedness left it unlocked. When I let myself into Grizzle's house, I found her lying on the kitchen floor, an ankle at an awkward angle under her other leg. I knelt down beside her, wondering which to do first – phone for an ambulance, or make her comfortable. *Make her comfortable.* I fetched a cushion from the lounge and a rug from the chest in the hall. Then I rang for an ambulance. That she didn't say, 'can't you take me?' was an indication of the pain she must have been in.

"Trevor told me you'd scalded your hand?"

"I did. I boiled up some water for the sweet peas I'd picked earlier; they last much longer that way. I can't have put the lid of the kettle down properly. I did immerse my hand in cold water in a basin. It felt a bit easier so I decided to get the green vase out of the cupboard, and lost my footing when I got down from the chair."

The green vase. The story of the green vase. One day, accidentally on purpose, I would smash the green vase. If she had used the crystal vase on the mantelpiece in the lounge she wouldn't be lying on the floor in the kitchen.

She winced. "Would you like a paracetamol?"

"Yes please."

"The paramedics should be here soon."

"Why were you so long?"

Should I tell her? Yes. What will she say to exonerate him? I told her the story, fact without feelings.

"He was always losing things, as a child."

"I'll give him a bell, after we've been to the hospital, to tell him what's happened," I said. *Why am I relenting?*

Her ankle was broken; I'd suspected as much. I took her back home with me after she had been plastered up, for I knew she couldn't manage on her own. She stayed with us for eight weeks.

"Wouldn't it be better if you went to stay with her? I can manage perfectly well on my own?" grumbled Trevor.

"Mother hasn't got a downstairs lavatory." I felt as though I was talking to a toddler who couldn't think things through for himself. "She can't get up to hers, or to bed just yet."

Ian came to see her once, during her stay with us. He didn't invite her to their house.

Six months and three falls later, she, my brother, Brenda, and Trevor had me frazzled to the point where I was attending counselling sessions for support.

Ian mentioned, several times, that the best solution would be Edith coming to live with Trevor and I. "Your house is far too big for you and Trevor. It makes sense."

Of course it does, for you. "No, Ian. That can't happen. You and Brenda couldn't live with Edith; neither can Trevor and I." *We can barely live with each other. We waft about like ghosts most of the time. The Old Vicarage looks like a neglected horror movie house; truly Munster Mansion. And I've lost myself among the monsters.*

The very thought of this had Bozo twanging.

Chapter Nineteen
Daffodils

A woman's work is never done.

To leave or not to leave? I was one with Shakespeare re the tragedy of indecision. And where did love come into leaving? Would Trevor care if I left?

I was sitting in the lounge staring at the three piece suite. In the gloom of the grey, March morning it looked as faded and dingy as I was feeling.

"New covers is what you need," I said to the not-quite silence. The Old Vicarage was never totally silent for I could always hear strains of whatever CD Trevor was playing. "I should go to Abakhan Fabrics. I wonder if Angela would come with me?" It would depend on any supply work she might have, and how her parents were faring. "Well, sitting here won't find out, will it woman? Get on the phone." Phoning out to a friend rarely brought a twinge.

"Hi, Ange. You busy today?"

"Well, Dad's having one of his good days, and Mum's coping, so I'm not needed at home. But I've just this minute told the agency I can work today. Why?"

That means she can't come with me... pity. "I was wondering about a gentle jaunt."

"You feeling okay today then?"

No. But when do I feel okay? Bozo is doing an occasional snarl. That's as good as it gets. "Not too bad. I want to see if I can get some fabric to cover the three piece suite."

"A, T J's and Abakhan jaunt, then. What a shame."

"Yes." *Question. Am I up to going on my own?* "So, things aren't too bad your end?"

"Not too bad at the mo. I don't really know how senile dementia progresses. I mean you can look things up on the internet, but... I guess every case is different. Some days Dad doesn't seem any worse than when we arrived back. Other days he struggles, memory wise. We all struggle because the man we knew isn't there. He goes to a day centre now which gives Mum some respite. He seems to enjoy it which stops her feeling guilty."

"That's good."

"You got any further with Edith and sheltered accommodation?"

I waited for the pain twinge. Bozo stayed still. "No. I daren't even bring up the subject."

"Why don't you take her to see Katy, show her how content she is?"

"Because she wouldn't go." *Because she and Katy aren't from the same planet.*

Angela asked how things were in Southport, and I asked her how Dave was enjoying his part-time job? He was working as a, well sort of general handyman and groundsman for Liverpool Cricket Club.

"He loves it. It's only one day a week until the season starts. Then it's a couple of days. More when there are county fixtures. The DIY skills he picked up on our French project are serving him well. He's been painting the pavilion with the aid of some pupils on work experience. It was his idea to see if Calderstones Comprehensive would be interested in having a relationship with the club."

"Do you know if you've got any bookings for the summer for les Peupliers?"

"The two gîtes we created in the barn, are full from the end of April through to October. Our house, no. If my dad's no worse, I may take him and Mum out in August if we don't get a booking. You and Trevor ought to come too. There's room."

Trevor and I go to France? A suggestion that ought to excite, but doesn't. Too much in the way of anxiety, too many pressing problems, too many questions about Trevor's and my relationship.

We said goodbye and rang off. I was pleased, in a way, that I hadn't burdened Angela with how I was really feeling. Leif was the only person who understood, or seemed to, what Bozo was like. How pain-killers provided temporary relief in what seemed like an unending battle in my intestines. And they had side effects, like constipation, and once a person was on the side effect slide, the remedies mounted and soon, like Tom had been with leukaemia, he or she would be rattling, I would soon be rattling. Crying with Leif. Rattling at home, was that really all I had to look forward to? *Oh, you sorry for yourself wet nellie. What are you like?* Chastising myself sometimes helped.

I knew that even going out and looking for material could be a waste of time. I'd spend quite a bit of money but there was no guarantee that I'd have the energy to sort out someone to make the covers. In former years, Katy would have made them. She had just turned ninety and was amazing for her age. But make covers? No, not in a residential home. After Molly died, without any fuss she had decided the move to Albermale, was what she wanted.

"I don't want to be on my own," she'd told us. "And it will be nice having someone else cook my meals."

I told Einna and Angela, at the time, that I suspected she would be organising everyone into having jaunts and doing activities, in no time.

Jean Paul Sartre was half right. Hell was relations, not people per se. *Is a husband a relation? He's not, blood, so I suppose he's an 'in-law' relation. My dad was a relation and he was a lovely man. Stuart is a relation and he's lovely. My dad was a bit 'anything for a quiet life' with Edith, but… Perhaps the saying has to be 'some people'? Hell is some people. Hell is some relations.*

I wish Claire would come to The Old Vicarage and bully Trevor into moving like she did Einna. But she would also need to have a go at Ian about Edith. I'm not sure she did bully Einna. I shouldn't even think something like that. Einna needed to move after Tom died. She would have rattled round in that house. Besides, she told me she never really felt at home there. Just like me here. It had been a home of sorts while Stuart was with us, but after?

Claire and Einna have as lovely a relationship as Stuart and I. Funny we both have just one child. Same and different reasons: husbands. One who did his duty, the other… what did Trevor do? Stuart was a drunken accident. Trevor did another kind of duty, acceptance duty, at first. Ow! You've woken up have you? Good thing I'm seeing Leif next week. I bet he's right. I may have IBS, but it's exacerbated by unresolved anger issues, stress and grief. Because I'm used to suppressing my anger and grief, they fester inside me.

At my last appointment, he had placed his hands on my head then my neck. "You are very tense. Can you feel how tense you are? All the anger, stress and grief is imprisoned inside you."

"Grief? Do you mean for my dad and Clem?"

"More than for them, Maggie. You are grieving for the loss of yourself."

"And that's contributing to Bozo?"

"Almost certainly, yes."

I believed him. I think I've been angry with Trevor ever since he took a job and bought Munster Mansion. I've certainly been angry with my brother for not pulling his weight with

Grizzle. As for her…

I guess I've never known what to do with the anger, so it made sense that I internalised it thus the anger became pain. Leif had suggested that I ought to find some way of expressing it, but he didn't know the three characters concerned. I told him that his massages were helping.

As Angela couldn't come with me, I decided to make the trip an afternoon one, and take it easy for the morning. I didn't ring Einna to see if she could come. She'd begun to create a garden at the bungalow and wanted to dig beds so she could start planting before spring became too advanced. Would the Maggie before Bozo have asked her?

The fabric warehouse was as it sounded; an enormous characterless building with bolts of material from floor to ceiling, and remnants, jumble sale deep, on huge counters. It was an Aladdin's cave where, for a snip, you could buy the fabulous fabrics of Liberty, Sanderson,

Laura Ashley, and other well known brands, or glitzy lurex, tasteless fur fabrics of all hues and any sort of trimmings you could imagine. It was needlecraft paradise.

Why can't I remember what happened? Why am I sitting in the car, in the car park near the lake in Sefton Park, staring at a carpet of daffodils? The last thing I remembered was being overwhelmed by the choice of furnishing fabric. I must have had a panic attack in the warehouse. Did I buy any material? What triggered it? Ian's phone call? I looked at the car clock: four-thirty.

I should have been home by now. Would Trevor have noticed that I hadn't yet returned? Suddenly a load of 'used-tos' bundled through my mind. Trevor used to cook. Trevor used to socialise. Trevor used to compose plink-plonk. Trevor used to laugh at my stories. He was a 'used to' man. And what would the 'used to' man be doing? He would be up in his eerie, sitting in the armchair facing the window that still needed repairing; staring at the garden without seeing it, listening to music he would never write. He would not be wondering what had become of his wife. *What has become of Lizzy Siddal? What would my dad say if he could see me now?*

All the windows needed attention. The whole property, including the garden, needed attention; it was overgrown with ground elder, nettles and cleaver. If we could have eaten them, we would have had greens for the whole summer. I did attempt nettle soup, once. I put on gardening gloves, picked a colander full, stripped off the leaves, cooked them as the recipe suggested, but the soup wasn't worth the effort; it was bland.

What CD will he be playing, one of his plink-plonk, atonal ones? Probably. Although of late he had borrowed some less minimalistic ones from the library: Berlioz, Poulenc, Schoenberg.

Sometimes I wondered if the man I knew as Trevor was a figment of my too fertile imagination. Perhaps I'd dreamt the first few years of our relationship and marriage.

When we first met, he had been so energetic, so ambitious. Now, he had about as much energy as a snail, no, less than a snail; at least a snail travelled with some natural purpose. Snails made me think of Ben and the picture he had drawn of Trevor when he was... about eight? Then we had laughed. Now, I couldn't laugh. All I could think of was, what purpose was there in Grunt's life? Was it purposeful to stare out of a window, day after day, listening to music? Once I'd queried this lack of activity. He didn't get angry; Trevor was no Tom. He just sighed and said "Too many people rush about with no thoughts in their heads except for personal gratification. We need to take time to reflect."

Thinking all day? What's that if not personal gratification?

All those years ago, I'd told him he wouldn't be able to do a full time job and compose. How little pleasure there has been in being proved right.

The daffodils nodded their heads as though they agreed. "Hey daffs," I whispered. "I need some help. Trevor and I can't go on like this. Edith and I, Ian and I. It's all... I used to enjoy phone conversations. Now, more often than not, I walk past the phone in the hall and the one in the kitchen thinking, *don't ring.*"

The phone rang as I was doing the washing up, after we'd had lunch. Washing up was another source of irritation. Why didn't Trevor ever think to do it? Okay, we had a dishwasher, but I only used it when visitors came. I suppose he thought it was stupid not to use it all the time. But he didn't offer to fill it. He just melted away as soon as he had finished eating. Today, I really didn't want to do the dishes as I needed to get to Abakhan Fabrics before Bozo told me I couldn't go.

I didn't hear the phone at first, as I was day-dreaming about what material I might buy. Should I opt for blue and cream stripe or rose and cream stripe like I'd seen in Laura Ashley, in Wilmslow; the latter would be a change from the faded, plain blue, and would go well with the stone coloured walls.

I lifted the receiver, hoping it might have been Angela with a change of mind, but heard instead, my brother's voice telling me that he wanted to talk to me about Edith. The material question floated out of my grasp.

"She's had another fall, Maggie. She refused to ring you because you were so nasty to her the last time, telling her she had to consider moving into sheltered accommodation."

"I did no such thing, Ian. You should know me well enough to know that I wouldn't do that."

"Well, Brenda said that she thought you'd become quite impatient and crotchety recently."

"What?" *How dare she?* I wanted to scream. "I don't know what you're talking about, Ian. When have I seen Brenda, recently?"

"It was that time I mislaid the key. She said you were rude to her."

I took a deep breath. "I was not rude to Brenda." *I'd like to have been but...* "And all I said to Mother when she had her third fall was, 'it would be a good idea to consider...' I got no further than that. She had a tantrum." *And Bozo kicked in so when I got home I had to go to bed with a billy and a couple of pain-killers.* "Can you ring back this evening, Ian? I have to go out now." Grumbling, Ian agreed.

So that's what a panic attack does. It makes you irresponsible. How scary. How bloody scary. I could have had an accident. I could have killed someone. There are limits on drink driving now; too late for Allie. Should there be a law against panic attack driving?

I felt as though Bozo was growling at a golden company of dancers. I could see the choreography, but I couldn't hear what music they were dancing to for the wind howling around the car. I put a hand on where I believed the source of the pain was.

"If I sit still for a few minutes, you might quieten down, mightn't you?"

Odd, all this mind/body stuff. Anger, stress, equals mind, but that gives the body pain. In Einna's case, a prickle band headache; that's how she describes it. In my case a stabbing pain I call Bozo, in my side. People don't know I talk out loud to you, do they?

Words from childhood made me start, and glance across to the passenger seat. *'Mind over matter, Margaret, mind over matter. Pull yourself together. Only babies cry.'*

"This baby's in pain, Mother, and I'm not crying, not yet." I massaged my side as Leif had taught me, and stared out of the window at the dancing flowers.

"I wonder how long it took to plant all those bulbs, Bozo? I read in *The Echo* that there are over a million."

As soon as I'd said it, the image of a woman on her knees, digging holes and planting bulbs in the autumnal turf, then straightening her back, and rubbing her neck with a grubby hand came into my mind. She stood up and looked about her as if to say, 'where now?' As she moved towards the car I caught a glimpse of her face. It was me. It was me out there on my own doing all the work. Where were the others who had promised to help me? I didn't even have a dibber. I closed my eyes against the dismal picture. *It's not fair. I do everything, Trevor grunts, Edith Grizzles, and as for my brother and that wife of his…*

"Why? What have I done, hey daffs?"

A patchwork of pictures flickered behind my eyes. Trevor improvising at the piano, immersed in his latest composition. Me rushing in from work, eager to amuse him with stories about my colleagues and the students; holding back because I could see that he didn't want to be interrupted. The birth of Stuart. It was okay, to begin with, then… Stuart turning into a volcanic toddler, all charm one minute, a tiny tyrant the next. Trevor smacking him for drawing on a manuscript. Stuart screaming. Me trying to remonstrate with Trevor, trying to get him to understand that Stuart didn't know the difference between manuscript paper and scrap paper. Trevor accepting the post at the college and buying The Old Vicarage without consulting me, knowing that I didn't want to move, knowing that I hated the house. Me being bludgeoned with reasons: we needed more space, he needed a room of his own away from toddler noise, toddler mess, and – he didn't say it – from me.

"How many times did I warn him, daffs? You tell me that instead of nodding at me."

Trevor had told me I was a Cassandra filling the flat with doom and gloom before he had even tested the water of teaching.

"I wasn't strong enough, Bozo. I was as weak and feeble as a wibbly-wobbly Kelly-man." *Hey idiot. Kelly-men bounce back up. You didn't, did you? You still don't.*

A weakly sun appeared and disappeared behind grey clouds. It was as wan as any hope I might have had of enticing Grunt out of his den to help me with the Edith/Ian problem.

So it goes. That's the way it is. What can you expect?

How dare Ian say, "Mother has to move, Maggie. She can't look after herself. Brenda and I are worried sick."

What a joke. The only thing Brenda and Ian were worried about was that their comfortable life might be disturbed; that they might have to do something. Did they even think about me? Who was it who rushed over and took her to the doctors? Who was it who rang for an ambulance when the fall was serious? Who went to A and E with her, and stayed for the hours that it took to sort her out?

I went to see Grizzle twice a week. I did her washing, made her tempting dishes, took her on little outings and to the shops. I put up with her complaints and ill humour. What did that brother of mine and his wife do?

Anger, coursing through my veins nudged Bozo again. He growled. He barked. He bit. I opened my bag, took out a strip of pain-killers, and a small bottle of water. I popped a couple of tablets in my mouth, and took a sip from the bottle.

"Who'd have thought that you could reduce me to being a pill popper, hey Bozo?

And tomorrow morning out will come the lactulose."

I glanced in the car mirror. *I look pale and old. I look worse than that watery sun. Grunt will look at me and wince. Get your make-up out, Maggie.*

I opened my bag again, and took out my make-up purse. I dusted blusher on my cheeks, and covered my mouth in lipstick. "And is that better, Bozo?" I sighed. "Not really. I used to be attractive, once." I put away the cosmetics.

Trevor had grunted about me going back to the doctors. What was the point? Now Leif had put forward his theory, I didn't need to go. I'd be wasting their time.

273

I needed a strategy and a decision, not 'You have irritable bowel syndrome, Mrs Harvey. Many people have it.' And what was the inference? Put up, and shut up. Those doctors and 'ologists', didn't have to put up with Bozo, Grunt, Grizzle, Ian and Benda. *Odd, no nicknames for my brother and his wife. Why?*

"Do you know what I'm going to do when I get home? I'm going to make a nice cup of tea and a billy. Then I'm going to bed. That'll calm you down, won't it, Bozo? Trevor can heat up some soup, and my brother can whistle for his conversation about Edith."

Einna told me she sang when a tension headache assaulted her. Perhaps singing would calm Bozo? "No students here to put their hands over their ears and tell me they'll take vocal warm-up." *Are the corners of your mouth turning up, Maggie? No. The joke's worn thin.*

"*Rub, rub, rub the pain*
till it goes away.
Round and round, and up and down
all the livelong day."

I used to sing songs from Doris Day films, not made-up words to toddler songs.

"Once I had a secret pain, that…"

There are daffs in that song. "Even told the golden daffodils…" *Those flowers are a wonderful colour, against the grey sky; intense. They'll lift the spirits, if you let them.* "Grey skies are gonna cheer up…" *But are they? No not unless you stop shilly-shallying.* "I shillied and I shallied. I shallied and I shillied…" *How do you stop though?*

A young couple appeared. They were so deep in conversation they didn't seem to notice that their dog, a red setter, was creating an erratic pathway through the daffodils with its scattered energy. Sometimes it paused, shoving its nose deep into a trumpet, as if to smell the flower's scent. Then it would jump backwards as though it had been stung, and career off in another direction; it was a mad March dog.

Full of rude health. Rude, rude. Two words, spelt the same but with different meanings. In this instance, rude seems right in both senses. That dog is bouncing with health and it's being rude to the daffodils. The couple ought to have it on a

274

lead. *But they look troubled. Maybe they're having relationship problems, or discussing a difficult parent, or whether they should start a family?* 'Creating stories again?' 'Yes Trevor, I am.'

The young woman sighed, and looked down at her feet. Unconsciously, I sighed with her, as if the sigh was drawn, like a catching yawn, across the yellow carpet.

"I shilly and I shally. I shally and I shilly…" *What am I to do about Grizzle? Stuart agrees with me that it's time for her to go into sheltered accommodation. 'After all, she is eighty-seven, Mum.' Perhaps I could get him to come over to help me persuade her. The sun shines, as it does with Ian. Eighty-seven isn't too old if you're still physically stable enough to live on your own, with no on-hand support. If Edith didn't keep having falls, she'd be fine.*

"I'm not going into an old people's ghetto, my girl. You can't bundle me out of the way just to suit yourself. You have a duty to me; a responsibility. Two words that have never meant much to you." *That's what she said the last time; the time she told Ian I tried to bully her.*

And what does Ian keep suggesting? The Old Vicarage. Does he think perpetual mentioning will wear me into acceptance? It's out of the question. It would drive me to commit myself. I can't put up with Grunt and 'nobody comes to see me, nobody cares' Grizzle, under one roof; it's bad enough under two.

"Do you know, Bozo; if it wasn't for the people I love, I'd be happy to commit suicide. I can really relate to that line in *Ode to a Nightingale*.

'Darkling I listen, and for many a time
I have been half in love with easeful death.'"

A few tablets, several gin and tonics, and no more Grunt, Grizzle, and Bozo.

"That's the way to do it. If it only were, Mr Punch."

But who do I love? That is the question. And I think again of how I felt when we found Clem. Could I do that to… well, anyone?

A little girl, tiptoeing through the daffodils, stopped about five metres from the car. She looked around, and then crouched down. I sat up straighter so that I could see her. She picked some flowers. I raised my hand to tap the windscreen, and let it fall again. The few flowers the child was picking wouldn't make any difference to the golden carpet. She was taking such care with her choice, looking at each one she picked.

'Are they for your mum?' If they are, I hope she appreciates them. Not like Edith. Not like Mothering Sunday, last year. What a fiasco; is that the right word for something pear-shaped that hurts? Why did I bother to ask Trevor to accompany me? I knew what his answer would be. Does hope spring?

I'd set off, as I usually did for any occasion, social or otherwise, on my own. Edith's first words to me were, "You're late." She snatched the bunch of daffodils out of my hands, hustled me inside, and threw them in the sink.

"What did you go and buy daffs for? You know they bring me out in a rash." I didn't know that. As far as I was concerned, Grizzle didn't have allergic reactions to anything.

"Well, now you're here, you can put the washing machine on for me. I had a nosebleed in the night. I didn't know what to do to make it stop."

"Did you try a spoon down your back?" I asked.

"Don't be stupid," said Grizzle. "How could I do that? I'm not double jointed."

Unvoiced anger. Bozo snarled. I spoke calmly. "Please don't speak to me like that, Mother. It's disrespectful. It isn't difficult to tie a piece of string to a spoon, and slip it down your nightie. You have a lot of nose bleeds; you could always keep a spoon on a string in your bedside drawer." And before she could reply, I gathered up the bloody sheets, pillowcases and duvet cover, and put them in the washing machine.

"I've thrown the duvet in the bin. I shall have to use the one from the spare bed until you can buy me another."

"I'm going to put a handful of soda crystals in with the washing powder," I said. "That should shift the blood stains."

"I hope it doesn't make me itch," said Grizzle.

After the bedding had been washed and hung out to dry, I baked Grizzle a cake and listened to her diatribe against her neighbours, over a cup of decaffeinated coffee. Then, I thought I'd done my duty so I got up to go. So did Grizzle.

"We are going out for a spot of lunch, aren't we?" she said. "I fancy the Philharmonic Dining Rooms. I haven't been there for ages. They do a lovely steak and Guinness pie, or they used to do; after all, Mothering Sunday only comes round once a year."

I opened and closed my mouth like a goldfish hoping for word food. 'Trevor's expecting me.' He wasn't. 'Stuart's taking me out for a Mothering Sunday lunch.' He wasn't. We didn't bother with Mothering Sunday.

I was prevented from saying anything by the doorbell. Grizzle opened it. There, with a bunch of tulips in his hand, and a smile on his face, was Ian.

"Oo tulips, my favourites," cooed Grizzle.

"Can't stop, Mum," puffed Ian. "I've left the motor running. Brenda and I are on our way to Chester for a spot of lunch. Maggie taking you out, is she? Who's a lucky woman then?"

Brenda.

"I wish I was coming with you," said Ian.

'So do I' and 'I bet' warred with each other.

Ian gave Grizzle a peck on the cheek, and ran down the path to his BMW, and his waiting wife.

Later, much later, I arrived home like a wrung rag that had got so twisted in the wringing, that it had become knotted. Bozo loved knots.

A cry interrupted my thoughts. It rose and fell over the daffodils. At first I thought it had erupted out of my own mouth, but as the vision of Grizzle, purring over Ian's tulips, faded, I saw a woman, smacking the little girl; the flowers lay, discarded, on the ground beside them.

It would be dark soon. I knew I ought to be getting home, home to Munster Mansion, Grunt, and a telephone conversation with Ian. The mother and the wailing child had gone. The young couple and their dog had gone. The daffodils were fast losing their colour as night fell. I was alone, alone with Bozo. As I rubbed my side for the pain that continued to spiral in spasms, I wept. The sky wept with me. Tears splashed onto the car as tears splashed onto my cheeks. The daffodils bowed their heads with the weight of water. Their dancing was over for the day.

I sniffed, took a tissue from my bag, wiped my eyes and gave my nose a good blow. "I bet I look a right mess. Tell you what, Bozo. I have you as an excuse for looking pale, wan and lined. What excuse does Grunt have? He looks grey because his skin only gets fresh air when he takes it to the library to borrow some new CDs."

I put the sodden tissue on the floor and continued to sit in the car, staring out of the window, at a lake and flowers I could no longer see. Then the moon appeared from behind scurrying clouds, a full moon, turning the daffodils silver, and I was wrong: they were still dancing.

Chapter Twenty

A Silver Light at the End of the Tunnel, Perhaps

Attack is the best form of defence.

How many times, on the journey back to Huyton, did I think of a golden field of daffodils disappearing in the dark black sky and then turning silver as the moon peeped out from behind a cloud. The sheer beauty of it made me feel ashamed of my weakness. Silver power, that's what some people said pensioners had, and that's what I'd got to tap into. *If I can. Don't say 'if I can'. You can, okay? Bozo grumbled.*

'Dad, you would have been ashamed of me over the past few years.'

Take off the gloomy mask of tragedy,

It's not your style…

Not my style… It's been my style for so many years.

I was a feisty child, a feisty teenager and a feisty young adult. *'Feisty'. I shouldn't really use that word, now that I know what it means. Why would anyone want to be likened to a farty, smelly bitch, and a small one at that?*

I held on to my, what shall I call it? Spikiness? Too sharp. Spunk? Sounds rude. Oh the difficulty of words. When did spunk become another name for semen? Odd that. Feisty used to mean a smelly bitch and spunky used to mean brave, didn't they? Gutsiness? Yuk! Intestines. Boldness? Yes, boldness.

My dad said I was fiery; that redheads were known for their fieriness. I bet that originated with the Tudors. They were a red headed, fiery lot. I held onto my boldness until… until… I lost it and lost me.

A loss connected to ego is rarely sudden. I didn't lose me just like that, and I wouldn't be able to find me again, just like that. Had I the energy? Gold to silver… Gold to silver… With gold, I had been one with the storm, then swamped. The silvery light made me feel as though I had been bathed in hope…

What a chicken and egg situation. The more Trevor shut himself away in his eerie, the more he grunted rather than talked, the more stressed I felt. The more difficult Edith became, the worse I coped. And of course, the opposite side of that was the less I was able to cope with Edith, the nastier she became, the more Bozo affected me, the more Trevor shut himself off.

Stop right there, Maggie. Trevor started shutting himself away as soon as we moved into Munster Mansion. Or… No, he couldn't do it in the flat. Shit Maggie! A thought had just seeped into my mind. I wasn't just angry at Trevor and Edith. I was angry with the one man I thought I had loved unreservedly: my dad. If he had been a stronger character? *But Maggie, genetics. Isn't that why you're not as strong as you should be? And, okay, he didn't stick up for you all those years ago, but look at all the people you now have in your life because you weren't allowed to stay on at school. And it's no good you saying you could do without Trevor. No Trevor, no Stuart, Ben and Adam.* What would Leif say? Probably something about forgiveness. Can I forgive my dad? Leif would add, 'do you want to?' *I have to. I have to forgive them all. I have to forgive me.*

After I'd put the car in the garage, I went straight upstairs to Trevor's eerie. He was listening to a recording of one of last year's promenade concerts. I gave him a kiss on the top of his head. He looked startled.

"You're home late. It's almost time for the seven o'clock news."

"Yes it is. If you come down and put it on, I'll get us a glass wine."

"You're going to have a glass of wine, Maggie? When was the last time you drank—"

"I know. I feel like one."

"What about—"

"Bozo?" I shrugged. "I'll risk it." *Don't say too much; prattle on.*

"Maggie I—"

"Don't know what to say? I know." *Why did I say that? But I did know. He has years of thought stored up in his mind, just as I have.* "We need to talk. We will, after the news, while we eat. Okay?"

"We need to talk? Why do we need to talk? And, I've eaten. I hope this isn't about--"

"Ah." *This isn't going to plan.* "It's about us, our life. I mean… Trevor, do you still love me?" *Why did my mouth say that?*

He looked away. "I don't know."

"I thought you'd say that. Do you know why? Because I'm not sure I love me, or you. Do you love yourself?"

"I've never thought about it. Have you been drinking already?"

"Only moonshine, and I mean moonshine as in the moon." I did feel a bit drunk. "Come on, you'll miss the news."

I walked out of the room and downstairs, trusting that Trevor would follow. I poured two glasses of wine, put some cheese, water-biscuits and grapes on a plate and carried them through to the lounge. Trevor was sitting in one of the blue armchairs. The TV was silent.

I handed him a glass and took a sip from mine. *Nice. Maggie a long time ago nice. The senses play such an important part in memory.* "Do you know what I've been thinking about today? Why we stay together. When I look at you, I feel… sad. You look so grey and… do you know how many times you run your fingers through your hair when you talk to me?"

"About the same amount of times you massage your side when you talk to your mother on the phone, I imagine. What's the point of this, Maggie?"

What is the point? "Maybe if we can be honest about the way we're feeling… I don't want to get into a slanging match. It won't help, will it? There are things we have to sort out, Edith for one." Oh, how I wanted to say, 'Look at your face now. It's crunched.' "And us."

"I won't live with her."

I hesitated, but only for a second. "Neither will I. So that's two of us." *But do you still want to live with me? Not exist with me, live with me?* "Do you remember when you first met her? You told me you'd got her measure. I hope you still have, as I need your help. I believe we can get the Edith problem sorted if you help me. I seem not to be strong enough to do it on my own.

"Ian is the only one she listens to. He has to get her to agree to move to sheltered accommodation. Ian won't help if I ask him. He needs to say no to one woman. I'm that woman. Besides, he keeps on at me about us sharing Mun... The old Vicarage with Edith. He won't say no to you. When he rings I'm going to tell him I'm not prepared to discuss Edith's future over the phone and invite him and Brenda for lunch this Saturday."

"Ah, b—"

Be strong, Maggie. There are no 'ah buts.' "Don't you think the time for 'buts' has passed? I, no we, can't go on like this. You've become a hermit and I've become a martyr to Bozo. Yes, I know you don't like the fact that I personalise the pain; it's a coping strategy. I've also learnt, from my counsellor, that it has mental and emotional exacerbations, like stress. We can begin to sort one stress this week. But..." *Now I'm using the word 'but'.* "I suppose I can only expect you to help if you think our relationship's worth saving." I picked up my glass and took a large sip. "Do you?" *Don't you bloody dare react to this wine, Bozo.*

"I..." He shrugged. "I don't know. I spend so much time on my own."

"Would you like to spend less time on your own?" *I want to say are you happy on your own, but what is happiness? I've considered that question so many times.*

"I don't know. I'm used to it."

Used to. I'll try a 'used to'. After all, it's the truth. "I love the Trevor I used to know. I would like to believe that you love the person you used to know. Maybe we can grow to love the people we are now, but with some changes?" *There do have to be changes. We can't be in stasis.* "How about we see what happens after we get Edith sorted. Could that be a plan?"

Trevor didn't look at all confident. "I'm not sure Ian will be prepared to talk to Edith."

Neither am I. But I have silver magic on our side. Even as I think it I say, 'Crap Maggie. Magic?' My Doris Day self replies, 'Why not? Dafter things happen.'

But, Life isn't a Doris Day film. When Ian rang I felt Bozo stir. Hand to side. Pain-killer. Bed with billy. 'Down boy!'

"Ian."

"We need to talk about mother, Maggie."

"Yes we do. But not now. It's too late to be sensible."

"It's no good putting it off. You did that this morning. I know what has to happen, it's the only—"

"So do I know what has to happen. But I'm not prepared to talk about it now. I want you and Brenda to come to lunch on Saturday. We'll talk then, Goodnight, Ian." I put down the phone.

I didn't have another glass of wine. That would have been too risky. I put the kettle on and poured myself a mug of boiled water. Trevor was watching the ten o'clock news.

"I'm going up now," I said. "I didn't wait for an answer to the invitation."

"So we don't know if they're coming or not?"

"No. But I think they will."

Trevor frowned. "How can you plan a meal if—"

"I can't. Ian or Brenda will phone in the morning and, if they don't, I shall phone them."

I slept better than I'd done for weeks. The next morning Ian rang to ask if they could come to Sunday lunch instead of Saturday? I said yes. It meant I had to change my day for visiting Edith … *sharp pain. That's what it is, not a growl. Okay, calling it a growl doesn't matter as long as I recognise it for what it is. Stress, pain. Deal with it.*

"Mother, I'm going to come to see you on Saturday, not Sunday this weekend."

There was silence at the other end, then, "And what about my Sunday lunch?"

"I shall bring it on Saturday and you can heat it up in the microwave." *I'll get one of the supermarket ones when I go shopping tomorrow.* In my head I was already planning what I would give Ian and Brenda.

"I don't want one of those supermarket ones. They don't taste of anything."

You can fool some people some of the time… who said that? I have given you quite a few ready-made dinners when… a variety of reasons. You've never guessed because you always plaster everything with sauces.

The only time we had any sauce on the table when we were kids was when we had fish and chips. Then it was vinegar and tomato ketchup. I would micro-plate her meal up as I always did when I resorted to subterfuge.

"I'm not sure it's convenient for me on Saturday."

"That's okay. We can give this weekend a miss if you like." *That's pleasantly assertive, Maggie. I know full well she won't like.*

"I'll just have to put up and shut up, won't I?"

Wow! She's turned one of her favourite sayings on herself. I want to giggle. Giggling is good. I mustn't giggle.

Saturday came and went. I managed to stay calm by telling myself that I wasn't at fault here. I did my duty by my Edith. I would switch off and let the tempest rage around me as the storm had raged around the car. *Those daffs were bowed, but not beaten. They raised themselves up and shone silver.*

However, no buttons had been pressed that morning. Edith was in as good a mood as her nature would allow. She wanted to go shopping, so I took her into Huyton Village. She then decided it would be nice to have lunch out. So we went to the café in the supermarket where she enjoyed grumbling about the food.

"What have you made for me for tomorrow?" she asked as I took her shopping through into her kitchen and helped her put it away.

"Pork, apple sauce, mashed potatoes, cabbage and carrots."

"I was hoping it would be roast beef. It's my favourite. It's Ian's favourite too."

"I know," I said. "But it's nice to ring the changes, isn't it? You had roast beef last week. Right, I'm off. I'll pop in to see you on Wednesday." *Maybe.* It would depend.

Brenda would be elegant; she always was. I could honestly say that I did admire my sister-in-law's dress sense, but her character epitomised her figure: thin and taut. Like a bow string, I half expected her to twang when she spoke. The last time I'd seen her was the garden gate incident, when she had been swathed in an apron and as I was only going to see Edith I'd made no effort with my appearance. Today I dressed for the occasion.

Green was one of my favourite colours; a cliché maybe, green with red hair, but I felt comfortable in green and I loved my bottle green velvet skirt. With it I was wearing a copper silk blouse and a lighter green velvet jacket I'd bought in a nearly new shop in Knutsford, many years ago, on a gang jaunt. It had a peplum which, with my now, slightly chunky figure, was flattering.

"Don't forget to wear your apron while you cook, Maggie. It would be a shame to get anything on that skirt or jacket," said Trevor.

"I prepared the main course yesterday morning before I went to Edith's and the dessert yesterday evening. We're having a chicken and apricot tagine. But I will wear it when I cook the rice and dish up."

"A dessert? I doubt Brenda will eat dessert." *The food is another experiment, like the wine. I want to see if Bozo reacts? I guess it might depend on how the Edith discussion goes.*

"Claret jellies and red fruit salad? I think she might."

"Do you think they'll have suspected why they've been invited?"

Trevor is saying more in one morning than he has for months. But he's forgotten I told him I'd mentioned the reason for the lunch to Ian. Don't show him up, Maggie.

"Maybe."

"When shall I broach the subject?"

"What about when we have coffee." Trevor's face suggested a doubt. *Maybe he won't be able to enjoy the food if...* "Or you can broach it while we have a pre-dinner drink, if you want. That gets it over with, doesn't it?" *But it could mean Brenda and Ian will walk out before they've eaten. I guess we'll have to risk that.*

He nodded as though confirming it. "I'm just…" Without finishing what he'd been about to say, he left the kitchen. I heard his footsteps climbing two sets of stairs. *Little steps, Maggie. Rome wasn't…*

I was right, Brenda was elegance personified. After a grudging greeting she said, "I always think it brave of people to wear full skirts when they've put on weight."

"I feel about the right weight for my age, Brenda. Drinks everyone?" *Cow!* I hoped my voice wasn't wobbly.

"Bitter lemon for me, please. I never drink alcohol during the day."

"Have you a beer?" asked Ian.

Brenda looked disapproving. "I don't want to drive home, Ian."

"Don't worry. I'll only have one."

"Trevor?"

"I'll join Ian. Er… Should I…?"

"No, it's fine Trevor." I wanted to say, you have a job to do. Instead, head high, I hoped, I left the room, pausing outside the door before descending to the kitchen. I wanted to know if Trevor would start the conversation that had to happen. But, what would I do if he didn't? I had become so used to Grunt, the inactive. I needn't have worried, he got straight to the point.

"Maggie and I feel that you are the best person to talk to Edith about moving, Ian…"

Brenda interrupted him. "Maggie should deal with it, not Ian."

"Why?" Trevor asked.

"Because she's the eldest."

"That's not a good reason," said Trevor. "Ian is Edith's preferred child. To put it crudely, Brenda, the sun shines, it always has. If Edith will listen to anyone, it's Ian."

This is amazing. Trevor sounds like… well Trevor.

"I'm with Brenda, Trevor. Maggie's the one to do it."

I didn't hear any more until I returned with the drinks. The voices were edgy.

"After all, the most sensible solution is—"

"No, Edith is not coming to live with us. You wouldn't be prepared to have her, would you?"

"We would," said Ian. "If our house were big enough. Yours is."

You wouldn't have her, even if it were, liar. I walked through and put down the tray of drinks down on the coffee table. "Help yourselves," I said.

"There's a strong possibility we might be downsizing soon," Trevor said.

What? This was to have been my next important chat with Trevor. I was going to brave the grey-faced reaction and tell him we had to stop rattling round in a house that was too big for us. If we were going to stay together. If not, we would still have to sell Munster Mansion, anyway.

"Obviously news to Maggie," said Brenda, who must have seen my expression.

Whoops! Guard your feelings, woman. You know you've always worn your feelings on your face. That's what you told yourself before you saw Edith, yesterday. Oh my god! I was hurtled back to the girl who had plotted herself out of the house to watch *The Pyjama Game;* who had enjoyed playing a role. How could I have lost that girl?

"It isn't news to Maggie, Brenda." said Trevor. "We've been discussing it for weeks."

A lie.

"The place is too big for us now: a) we rattle around with the ghosts; b) It eats up money—"

True. But I'm shocked that Trevor is admitting it.

"You'd have extra money if —"

"Over my dead body," Trevor said pleasantly. "You know well enough, Ian, there's never been any love lost between your mother and I. Things improved a little when Stuart was a baby, but once he became a teenager, they deteriorated. Even with the addition of great-grandchildren, her attitude to Maggie and I is belligerent. You would be asking us to live in a war zone, so no. Besides, think of all the stairs, her falls. It wouldn't be fair on her. Edith needs to move into sheltered accommodation. I've been doing a bit of research on my computer. I can show you, if you like.

Clamp your mouth shut, Maggie. Is that why Trevor went up to his eerie this morning?

"She'll refuse to look, let alone move," said Ian.

"Not if you tell her she has to, for her own sake as well as everyone else's. I bet, once she's seen the Stowe Lodge development, she'll fall over backwards to move in. Maggie, can I borrow your laptop?"

"Of course. I'll fetch it." *And take a gulp of fresh air before I faint.*

The pictures of Stowe Lodge looked lovely. I wouldn't have minded moving there myself.

"The pros of the place are numerous, and as far as I can see there aren't any cons. All the inhabitants are over fifty-five, and there's a warden on call twenty-four hours," said Trevor.

"It looks expensive," said Brenda.

"It's not. One bedroom properties go for about a hundred and ten thousand. Two bedroomed ones, a hundred and fifty thousand. With the sale of the bungalow, no problem, and there would be some left over. It should be enough to redecorate and cover the yearly service charge; that pays for the warden and gardener."

"Well, it certainly looks in good order," said Ian.

"There's a two bedroomed bungalow for sale opposite the little pond, look."

I was drowning in amazement, but I didn't need to wave.

"Who's selling it?"

"Brogdens."

"Right. I know Simon Brogden. I'll check with him re the condition of the place. If you could come with me—"

"Tomorrow?"

What the hell has happened to the snail?

"We were going to Altrincham, but…" Ian looked at Brenda. She shrugged.

I let out the breath that it seemed I'd been holding for the past ten years. "Lets eat," I said, hoping it didn't sound like a squeak. *I'm going to have a hell of a lot to tell Leif.*

The conversation at the table was perfunctory. I didn't care. I gave myself up to the food, which was delicious. I'd blended the spices to a taste I found almost erotic, and the naturally dried apricots weren't too sweet. *Why did I cow-tow to you, Bozo. The specialist said, 'No one diet suits IBS sufferers, Margaret. I'm afraid it's a matter of testing foods.'* Even Brenda, sour-puss, complimented me on the wine jelly. She did have some.

"Lovely flavour, Maggie," she said. "It doesn't matter that it's cloudy."

It's odd. I've made fun of men. I've been in despair over Trevor. But the only people I want to kill are women.

They left at three o'clock. Brenda was one of those people who thought it wasn't polite to stay longer.

What a puzzle, that my dad and my brother should have married such difficult women. What had they seen in them, way back when…?

"Are you going back up to your ee… studio?" I said as the Volvo purred down the drive.

"It's okay, Maggie. I know your nickname for my room. Adam told me, years ago. No, not yet."

Scallywag. He would have teased his granddad. "A cup of tea?"

"That would be nice. I'd like some Darjeeling, if we have any."

"We do."

Leaf tea, a pot, a strainer, china cups and slices of lemon. *No, I won't risk the lemon. Maybe one step too far with acidity?* I poured. I handed. We sipped. "I can't pretend you didn't astonish me, Trevor, and I have to say, delighted me. You reminded me of my pick-n-mix man. I just hope I can be your pick-n-mix woman. Do you ever look back and think of the fun we had?"

"No. It's not what I do."

"Well, I do." I looked into my cup, for tears were pricking my eyelids. "Did you mean what you said about selling the house?"

"I'm very fond of the house."

"I'm not sure you are." He frowned. "You're fond of your eerie. You must have a den wherever we move to." Too fast. Change the subject. "I wish I'd put some cyanide in Brenda's claret jelly."

"That was a leap I can't follow."

"The house and her..." Implying that I was fat. "Oh just her. She's such a cow."

"You wouldn't survive prison."

"No I wouldn't." *But I think I might survive it better than I would you, Edith and I, under the same roof. I don't have to think of that now. Edith will turn into an obedient puppy with Ian.* "Do you remember Debbie telling us about visiting a fellow CND member in prison? Her description of admittance procedures was enough of a crime deterrent for me."

"Debbie surprised me when she became so ferociously political. She was such a quiet little—"

"Mouse? Mice have sharp teeth, you know."

If I said that everything was back to nineteen sixties married bliss, I'd be lying, but it was different from recent Harvey history. Just before I went to bed, I checked my emails. There was one from Debbie saying that she was coming to the UK on a visit. Could she stay with us during the week as Sophie worked? She would stay with her both weekends, as she would be here from Friday night for ten days. I scribbled off a reply, but not before I asked Trevor if he could cope with that. Two days ago, Maggie wouldn't have asked. Two days ago, Trevor would have looked pained and grunted. Now I got a fleeting frown, followed by, "Fine by me." It was enough.

To: debbie23@serviceprovider.co.uk
Cc:
Bcc:
Subject: You coming home for a visit.

Hello Friend, it will be grand, more than grand, to have you to stay. Can you let me have some set in stone dates so that I can alert Angela and Einna, please? We have to keep the week, or however long you're coming for, free.

My news? I think I've begun to find myself again. A road to Damascus experience in Sefton Park, a few days ago. March the sixteenth at five-thirty. I never want to forget the day or the date.

I'm going to try to become the Maggie you first met in college, the Maggie who told Macker to take a running jump.

I stopped typing.

Macker, college, those were good times. Were all the good times before Stuart? There were bad times in college too. Some of them really bad, like Allie's death.

I know what I want to happen and I'm determined to achieve it. I've consigned the Bozo terrorised Maggie to another time zone. I can't pretend she didn't exist; sadly you all had to put up with her, but now I've accepted what sets Bozo off. I believe I can change that, in fact I started as soon as I got home from the park.

I've no idea how those storm swept daffodils worked magic, bit I felt as though I'd been transformed by the silver power of the moon. Don't laugh.

See you soon, xxxx

I pressed send and the email whizzed off: more magic. I didn't understand any of it, science, technology. It was all magic. I suspected very few people did. It was a magic we accepted, unlike thinking I had been saved by moonlight on daffodils. That was magic a step too far, but...

Of course I knew there would be repercussions from Edith after Trevor and Ian's visit, and of course Bozo played up because change hiccups along. What did alter was, after I'd endured fifteen minutes of being told I was the worst daughter any mother had had the misfortune to raise, Trevor, coming in on the conversation mimed, cut her off. So I did. Three times I cut off the rant and then there was blissful silence. Three days of it. Maybe Edith worked in threes? Then she rang me to ask if I would be coming to see her at the weekend. There was no apology, that would be asking too much, but she was polite.

Houses can take time to sell. But in this we were blessed with Ian's expertise as an estate agent. A young couple made a sensible offer for Edith's house which he accepted on her behalf as she had given him power of attorney. She would be moving into Stowe Lodge as soon as all the legal business had been sorted.

I suspected that The Old Vicarage would take longer to sell. But one step at a time. The next step was Debbie's visit.

Chapter Twenty-one
No Wet Knickers

A good laugh recharges the batteries.

We were a gang, a monstrous regiment of women, who laughed at our husbands, our jobs, our children, and ourselves. We laughed so much we wet our knickers. Later, the laughter began to crack our faces. The tears ran down the fissures and the salt hurt the raw flesh.

Debbie arrives. I meet her off the train at Huyton. Trevor did offer to accompany me, but I wanted to get the shock of change out of the way, alone. I didn't tell him this.

Same clothes, same hair, same Debbie. Is it only I who have changed? But she doesn't say anything. Maybe the make-up has filled in the years.

She puts down her case so we can hug. How is it that I've never noticed we're a similar height, before? She is still slim.

"Plans," she says once we are in the car. "Tell me what the plans are for my visit. When am I seeing Einna and Angela?"

Her voice is alight with expectation.

"The only fixed plan is for tomorrow," I say. "We're going to Chester. How's Sophie?"

I know how Sophie is, I have a chat with her every so often. It's one of the reasons I know about Bill and how life after Debbie hasn't been all that he'd hoped. The other, Dave meeting Bill for a weekly drink, I can't mention and I need to know if Sophie has said anything.

"Sophie's fine. She told me you and she ring each other occasionally. That's nice, Maggie. She told me…" Her voice loses its edge of light. "She told me about Bill. I don't know if I feel it serves him right, or if I'm sorry for him."

Ah, she knows a, but not b.

By the time we go to bed, we've caught up, more or less. The less part is to do with Trevor. We talk more about general matters over the evening meal. There will be plenty of time for intimate conversation when the gang's together. What will it be like, the four of us together again?

I wake to a feeling of well being. I'm fit, no Bozo pain. My knee's aching a little, but it won't prevent me from enjoying myself. Suffering joint aches and pains as we get older is understandable. It's the ones we can't explain that are daunting.

After I shower, I give my knee a good rub with Glucosamine gel so that by the time we've had breakfast it will have eased off. But I shall give Einna a ring and ask her if she'll drive. I'm sure she won't mind. Chester is about twenty seven miles from Huyton, so if we all give her three pounds, that should cover the petrol.

Memories, strong and full of friendship flood in. That's how we organised our jaunts if we went by car anywhere outside Liverpool. In town, we created chattering, laughing mayhem on Mersey rail or buses. We would gravitate towards Paddy's market and jumble sales like flies to jam, but they aren't the same as they used to be. Now I prefer charity shops to jumble sales, and Paddy's market has succumbed to the sort of stalls you find in any market: training shoes' stalls, acrylic sweaters' stalls, fleece stalls. There used to be stalls where you could find second-hand designer dresses at prices that didn't make you flinch. I once bought a pair of silver and red, mock crocodile shoes with heels that made my toes cry.

"They're for the drama cupboard," I said.

"For if you ever do Cinderella?" asked Angela. "Which you won't; well, not unless you give it a feminist slant. I bet you wear them."

I feel sad for a moment, as I remember. Where have my feminist beliefs gone? I don't think I was a rabid feminist. I don't remember any man having to have anti-rabies injections because I'd bitten him, but I tried to uphold feminist principles.

Of course, Angela was right. I did wear them, once, to a party in Fulwood Park. It was a haven behind wrought iron gates for middle-class professionals.

Not only a feminist, Maggie. An inverted snob. You wanted to dislike the people from the park and you found you couldn't.

My feet took days to recover.

At breakfast, Debbie compliments me on my choice of clothes, a deep blue flounced skirt, a lilac blouse with a mandarin collar, and a blue and mauve patchwork jacket with a peplum. I don't seem to have any jackets without peplums. Once, in a charity shop I tried on a short, Chanel-style jacket. It made me look like a rectangular box.

"You don't think I look fat? Brenda suggested that I was brave wearing a full skirt."

"Since when have you taken notice of Brenda?"

"Since…" Bozo? "I don't know."

"You don't look fat, does she Trevor?"

Trevor looks startled at having his opinion sought. As usual, he's brought the paper to the table, but today he hasn't opened it. Nor has he turned on the radio. "Er, no," he says.

I'm glad Bozo hasn't managed to destroy my enjoyment of clothes. I know some people think my choice of colour can clash sometimes but I don't care. I love vibrant colours. In my opinion, most people dress dowdily. It's odd though, Debbie likes earth colours, but she never looks dowdy. It's her style. Today I am colour coordinated, although I'm tempted to wear a dark red necklace or my amber beads; they are rose amber.

If I wasn't looking forward to our day out, I might have had a little weep, for I keep catching glimpses of the man I fell in love with and married; it's unnerving. Goodness, we might fall in love with each other all over again. We might have a world of conversations without grunts, moans and Bozo. Then, of course, we might not. Have either of us got the energy to separate?

"I'm going to ring Einna," I say in the space filled with sips and munching. "I want to make sure she's up. She keeps on telling me that if she forgets to put her alarm on, she can sleep in until ten."

"That's odd," says Debbie. "When Tom was alive, I remember her telling me she woke, no alarm call, at six every morning."

"She did. But in the last few months of Tom's leukaemia she snatched sleep whenever, as Tom was often in such pain both their nights were disturbed. As soon as he died, her body told her she needed to catch up, is my guess. I'm also going to ask her if she'll drive. I don't know why I didn't before; she's a much better driver than me." I feel anxious about telling them my knee's playing up so I decide not to. "And if I don't use the car, Trevor, it will be free for you, if you want it…" Shall I, shan't I? I toss an imaginary coin up into the air and it's 'shall'. "You know you said you didn't understand how to de-clutter your computer? Ben knows about all that stuff. I bet he'd love to come over and help you, if he's free. If Einna doesn't want to drive," I shrug. "I shall leave the situation as it is."

"It's not a problem, Maggie. Let's see what Einna says, shall we? We can't presume, as you offered. If she can do it, I might just give Ben a ring and give him a break from AS Level revision. The computer stuff is called de-fragging, I think."

Trevor has remembered that Ben's doing his AS levels. Not unaware then, just… just what? Apathetic, or depressed, and like many men refusing to do something about it? Maybe not even recognising that he was depressed? If he's depressed, will a new start be the cure? Or, as with many people, will the depression have to be managed? Oh don't start thinking about another potential problem, Maggie.

"Angela drives." says Debbie. "An 'in case' if Einna, for some reason, can't."

Bloody hell, I'm beginning to spin webs like Einna. "As she thought I'd be driving, she told Dave he could have the car. He's dropping her off here before... before he... does whatever he wants to do." He's meeting Bill. "Debs, will you make another pot of coffee while I make the call?"

"I'll do it," said Trevor.

"Great," said Debbie. "I like being waited on."

I get up and go up to the hall.

Einna's bungalow is in Woolton, near her family. Like me, but for a different reason, she's been stuck in a grey place since Tom died. It was a difficult relationship, but she loved him. And he was charismatic, no doubt about that, well on a good day. He had rather a lot of bad days.

I don't like the bungalow. Will Trevor and I buy a bungalow? There are attractive bungalows. Einna's isn't. It's a box. But then she has never been that interested in her living surroundings. It isn't fully furnished yet. She's an odd one about decoration and furniture. She knows what she doesn't like, but not what she does like; except for Thomas Gardner, her grandfather clock. But that's got nothing to do with taste and everything to do with sentimental attachment. The garden's a very different matter. She designed the garden, in her mind, before she moved in.

I hoped that selling Roby Road might have opened a curtain and let in some light. Her voice, in recent conversations, has seemed brighter. She told me that Zac popped in to see her most days; good for her, good for him, a happy symbiosis. Einna was laughing when she told me. She said that he came for her jam tarts and flapjacks. We didn't graduate to a knickers' wetting conversation, as we would have done in the past. But it takes two to tango into giggles, and I wasn't in a place for wetting knickers either.

Flapjacks remind me of the marches we used to go on to support Debbie in her CND and Friends of the Earth, years. There was this wholefood shop, *Kirklands*, in Hardman Street, They sold flapjacks that were mouth wateringly scrumptious.

Einna is lucky to have Zac living nearby. Southport is too far away for Ben and Adam to drop in for love of jam tarts and flapjacks. I don't begrudge her the pleasure; I merely wish it could be the same for me.

And maybe it will now that there is a possibility of moving to Southport.

I tap out Einna's number. My grandsons think I'm a dinosaur for not programming my phone.

"703 8431, no... oh bugger! Hello Maggie, if it's anyone else, sorry, I don't know my new number yet."

"You'll have to write it on a post it and stick it on the wall by the phone. How are you? Becoming a bungalow person? Did I just say that? What the hell is a bungalow person? Debbie hasn't changed a bit; well in character anyway. Obviously she looks older, but still beautiful. We're all beautiful." I say this to convince myself.

"Are we?"

"We are."

"I don't know about beautiful, but I'm looking forward to our jaunt."

"So am I. Remember our song, *Time Off For Good Behaviour?*"

"How could I forget? But that was after Rock Follies became the TV show we had to watch, wasn't it? Before that, it was, *These Boots Are Made For Walking*, because of our trip to London."

"While Debbie's here, we're going to have lots of that, time off, I mean. She's in love, by the way."

"Coffee's ready." I didn't hear her coming up the stairs. "I shall never fall in love again. Love's for naïve idiots. Once bitten... I'm in lust and like, that's enough for anyone." Debbie shouts so Einna can hear.

"That's brazen, Einna" We're teasing each other as we used to do, quick repartee conversations. If I look in a mirror now, will I see my thirty-plus self. Probably not, but I might see a woman, who isn't looking grey, smiling at me.

"Shall I bring yours up?"

"No, ta. I'll be down in a mo." I wait until I know that she's out of earshot. "I'm a beautiful woman who needs a favour. Could you drive? My knee's playing up." Einna doesn't reply. That's two things I've hidden from Debbie; omission lies. We can't always tell the truth. Would Leif agree? Need, Maggie. You don't want Trevor to know.

What's going on is too fragile. You feeling that… Does it mean you want to save your mar… of course it does, dozy. That's what all the days since daffodils have been about. "Are you still there?"

"Yes, I thought… oh it doesn't matter. Of course I don't mind driving. What time shall I pick you up?"

"Angela's coming for ten."

"Is Trevor in the attic?"

"No, he's talking to Debbie. He's quite animated for Trevor. He's been grunting less and less since daffodil day."

"I think all men need Super Nannies for partners. J M Barrie was right. They're all Peter Pans, Mr. Darlings, Captain Hooks, or a mixture of all three."

"I hope I've helped Stuart to grow up."

"You'll have to ask Beth that."

"Maybe I will, one day. I do hope Beth and Stuart stay together. She is such a darling. It's going to be wonderful, us four together again, isn't it? We're going to try to persuade Debbie to come back so we can reform the knickers wetting gang."

Back in the kitchen I tell Debbie what the rest of us in the gang will try to do.

"I don't think that will suit Debbie, Maggie. From what she's told me, living in Ireland suits her. It's difficult to recreate the past." says Trevor.

A warning?

"Even if I could come back to betrayal city, Mitey would never leave his farm." Debbie says.

"You would want Mitey to come? It must be serious then," I say.

"No… sort of… it's difficult. Trevor's right about Ireland. I love Ireland and the way of life there. You and Trevor must come over, soon."

"Ye-es." I hear the doubt in my voice.

"We've a lot to sort out first," says Trevor.

Sort out? Yes. Well, I'd sorted not driving so Trevor didn't know about my knee. Then I remember I didn't tell Einna to put spare knickers in the bag. We mightn't need them, but… And wouldn't it be great if we did. "Debs, can you ring Einna back while I splodge some make-up on? Remind her to put—"

"… A spare pair of knickers in her bag? Will do."

"You're not hoping you will—"

"Wet our knickers?" says Debbie. "If we do, it will probably be more to do with age than hilarity."

Trevor's looking more like Grump. Is it monstrous regiment thoughts, or just distaste? He used to laugh when I told him wet knickers' stories, didn't he?

"Is she going to take her car?" he asks.

"Yes."

"So I can have ours?"

"You can."

"Good. That's sorted then."

Upstairs, as I put blusher on my cheeks, I think about the past few weeks. Our house is on the market. We've already shown people round. It brought back so many memories; a whispering Mrs Sharpe, me writing anti Munster Mansion notes, 'Ho-ho' and organ crashing music from the attic. Edith will soon be settled. She's moving to Stowe Lodge at the beginning of June. She told Ian that she liked the warden, Mary. She met her when she went to look round. Am I surprised? Not really. She has always taken instant likes and dislikes.

"She runs some clubs for the people who live there. I might join a couple. I like the fish and chip one, and the cinema trips one. But I'm not joining a housey-housey one for anybody," she told me.

If Edith joins anything, Mary will have accomplished what I never could. I wonder why she has taken to her?

Suddenly I see Ian's shadow hovering in the mirror behind me.

'I don't know why you always make such a fuss about the way Mother behaves, Maggie.'

'Because she's rarely reasonable with me. She is and has always been the, 'Stay still, Margaret.' The brush yanking my hair. The fingers plaiting or scragging back

so that every curly strand is pulled so tight my head hurts. 'She reserves pleasantness for you.'

"Do you often talk to your mirror?" Debbie has come into the bedroom without me noticing. "And there was I thinking I was the only fey gang member."

"I have my moments, so does Einna. Can you remember if she was potty about angels when she was younger?"

"I don't think so."

"Well she is now. Are you ready?"

"As I'll ever be."

"You look great," we both say and laugh.

I take a last look in the dressing table mirror, run my fingers through my hair. The colour may have faded but it's as unruly as ever. I never confine it with brush and bands. No scrunchies when I was a child. When I took the band off at night, strands of hair would get pulled out of my scalp.

On one morning of hair-scragging torture, I remember saying to Edith, "You're going to make me go bald before I'm old enough to do my own hair."

She replied, "Don't be silly, Margaret. Everyone's hair grows again."

I knew this to be a lie. Uncle Charlie was almost bald. Lots of men were bald or nearly bald. If she had said women's hair grows again I might have believed her, except for Mrs Huddleston. She had lived next door to Danny Murphy. Her hair was so wispy thin you could see her scalp through it.

"Do you remember our jaunt song of the seventies, Debbie, *Time Off For Good Behaviour?*" I say as we go downstairs.

"Yes, but unfortunately, when I think of those times I think of Bill, and how we were all duped by him. It still hurts, Maggie."

"Oh Debbie, it's so sad if you can't remember the laughs we had." What am I saying? Earlier I was wondering if enjoyment was linked to before Stuart? "But I do understand. Until very recently, I found it difficult to remember the Trevor I fell in love with. No, that's not quite true. I did remember him, but he'd become so different I, began to wonder if I'd imagined him?" I give her a hug. "No men today. We love them, but we need time off."

"Those outfits!"

"What outfits?"

"The *Rock Follies* ones. A friend of Chrissie's has the two DVD's. The clothes are amazing."

Trevor was still in the kitchen where we'd left him, immersed in his newspaper.

"We shall be off in a minute," I said.

"I think you've got a nice day for your gang outing, if the forecast's correct. Where did you say you were going?"

Fleeting irritation. I'd told him where we were going.

"Chester," said Debbie.

"I haven't been to Chester for years."

You haven't been anywhere... Stop it Maggie.

"Well have a nice day." He folds up the paper. "I think I'll go upstairs and write a list of questions I need to ask Ben. But I suppose I ought to phone him first, make sure he can come over." He gets up.

Angela and Einna arrive at the same time. Dave must have dropped Angela at the gate, for we see her walking up the drive as we greet Einna.

"You sit in the front, Maggie, as your knee's playing up," she says.

"What about your back?" Angela asks Debbie.

"What are we like? Courageous Crocks, not a monstrous regiment, any longer," says Debbie.

"Crocks? How dare you? I'm not a crock, courageous or otherwise," says Angela. She stretches up to the sky and stoops over to touch her toes without bending her legs. "You're still pretending to be a Scouser, then?" she adds, looking at Debbie through her knees.

We laugh. It feels good to laugh. It feels good to be together. The last time we were together was a sad occasion, saying goodbye to Angela, a few days before she and Dave left for France.

I've always felt completely safe when driving with Einna. I'm not an especially good passenger; I'm tempted to back seat-front seat drive.

But I don't feel the need to comment when I'm out with her. She's not a fast driver, preferring to tootle along motorways at an average of sixty; doing her bit for the environment, and her purse; I know this because she's told me.

In the car, our conversation revolves around serious topics. I wonder what our thirties and forties selves would have thought of the people we are today? Did we talk politics back then? We must have done, especially when Debbie became involved with Friends of the Earth and CND.

Today, we talk about taxes, present day laws, the plight of women the world over, especially where fundamentalists of any religious persuasions are concerned. I am against interference politics. I believe we go into situations when we have something to gain, not because of inhumanity, or injustice and too often the innocent get hurt. Debbie feels the same as I do.

We are all in agreement about the terrible example set to young people by adults who ought to be good role models, like politicians, sports' stars, pop stars and actors. As for the celebrity culture, it appals us all. How anyone can watch reality television is a question constantly in my mind. It seems to me that one of the criteria for participating is being an 'any age' brat who can cry in public; even the judges cry on programmes like *The X Factor.* Why? Because, it seems, that it's what Joe Public wants them to do. So, why is it that I and my friends find it nauseating, sentimental, and finger down the throat? I can't believe that we're the only ones, but we're obviously in the minority.

As for the money floating about... I find I'm shaking my head. How can anyone justify earning those sums when all round the world people are starving, drinking filthy water and living in slums not fit for cockroaches? There aren't just bag ladies and bag men, everywhere. There are bag children.

But, in regard to the celebrity culture and the huge fortunes stars earn, I know you can't turn any clock back. Football clubs will continue to search for icons from all round the world, rather than nurture the future Gerrards and Carraghers, and silly money will go on being earned and spent.

Turning clocks back applies to me, too. I can't resuscitate the marriage I had before Stuart.

I realise I've missed some of the conversation because Debbie is now talking about the impact of capitalism on the environment and ultimately our planet.

"Do you know what puzzles me?" says Debbie. "All the people we're talking about have, or will have, children and grandchildren. This money-ridden society is making the world spin faster and faster towards catastrophe, because of consumption, greenhouse gasses and depletion of the world's resources. And they don't care. If they did, they'd change things. But firms aren't allowed to stand still. Bigger profits have to be made each year. Shareholders, bonuses and on and on. Do they hope their grandchildren will escape to another planet?"

"Maybe," says Angela. "Then they can ruin that one."

"We're never going to wet our knickers if we carry on like this," I say "We should have stuck to what men think we talk about... them."

"Then we'd be in danger of committing suicide," Einna says.

"Never," I say. "We have to beat the buggers." But my bugger could be becoming a person I like. Will love follow like?

Our conversation is organic. Suddenly we're talking about people not voting and how our grandmothers might have fought for us women to have the right to vote. I can't say that they would have been a part of the suffragette movement, for I don't know, and not all women fought or believed in the movement. Queen Victoria was adamantly against these rights for women. She said, '*This mad, wicked folly of women's rights with all its attendant horrors on which my poor feeble sex is bent, forgetting every sense of womanly feelings and propriety.*' Would Edith have joined the suffragettes? I doubt it. I bet Katy would have.

None of us are content with the way things are in Britain. New Labour, huh! That's how I feel. If I were a man, I'd spit on the floor. As I've always thought that Tony Blair dripped charm, rather than sincerity, I wasn't surprised at the way he and New Labour politicians behaved. The few dissenting voices were outnumbered and the gulf between the poor and the rich widened. How they squared what they did or didn't do with their consciences I couldn't fathom and, in my opinion, many of them behaved as badly as any of the brats on the reality television we had been discussing.

Yes, I'd been a bit of a rebel when I was a teenager, but, in the main, we had a healthy respect for adults. As for the police… the Bobby on the beat knew all the likely miscreants and ruled the streets with a firm hand.

"Are there Freds in Southern Ireland?" I ask Debbie when she suggests that we should all move to Ireland to be near her.

Fred was a Panda car policeman who had come into our lives through Lena, a friend of Einna's, well all of ours, at The Teachers' Centre. We women weren't exactly pro the police, Debbie more than Angela, Einna and I. She'd had several run-ins during her CND activity.

Fred was special. He was our laughing policeman and… not an alcoholic, exactly, someone who drank far too much when he was off duty. He always claimed he could handle alcohol, but he died of cirrhosis of the liver, nevertheless.

Debbie tells us that Mitey's nephew is a cadet in the guarda. "He's the kind of man you think ought to try for another profession, because he's gentle. He told me, in front of Mitey, he was glad his uncle had met someone special, someone who might be able to keep him in order. You should have seen the look on Mitey's face. He was grinning from ear to ear. I half expected him to start clapping."

"Why?" asks Angela.

"Because he's considered the black sheep of the family"

"No, why are you smiling now?"

"At Charlie saying I was special. Policeman aren't known for saying things like that, are they?"

I hear something in Debbie's voice that tells me her smile has vanished. I know how she feels; how easy it is to think you are without value. Angela lifts our mood by telling her she's a special nut-case. But I feel I need to point out that in all societies, victims can feel they are to blame. It's often the reason abusers get away with bullying control, or worse. I know it's not major abuse that I've experienced, but nevertheless it is a form of abuse and too often I castigated myself because I believed that somehow I'd been culpable.

"In bleak moments I did wonder if you lot thought I was to blame? After all, you often said I fed Bill on too many pulses." She blows a raspberry. She laughs. We laugh with her, but the laughter is tinged with sadness.

As I'm wondering if she will ever be able to put Bill and her first marriage into a locked box, she says, "Mitey wants me to move in with him. Trouble is, I've got used to a bit of space. I like it, even though the space is just a caravan. And there's the other thing." She pauses. "Mitey likes to wear women's clothes."

Wow! I don't imagine any of us were expecting this. Her new fellah a transvestite? Is this why he's considered the black-sheep of the family? But would they know? I have no idea how I would feel about it. Logically, women wear trousers so why shouldn't men wear skirts or dresses? Why shouldn't men wear make-up, if they want. Not so many centuries ago they did. Grayson Perry, unashamedly dresses as a woman. I try to put myself in the position of a woman who knows that the evening is going to lead to sex and when you tear off each other's clothes you find that, he's wearing a bra and women's panties. Would the discovery be a turn on or a turn off?

"Not all teenagers grunt," I say after what seems like a long dramatic pause.

"You've butterflied again," says Angela.

"No I haven't. I've just gone back to what we were talking about before Mitey."

Grunting teenagers. I suppose it was a butterfly. Was it because I found it too weird to continue to talk about Mitey being a cross-dresser? I'd have to ask her later what she felt when she found out, and how she dealt with it. I can't remember when Debbie met Mitey. Was it at Chrissie's wedding? If so it took them a while to get together.

I tell the gang what I remember of my teenage years, and how any grunting would have been followed by a clip round the ear. It would have been the same for Einna. Annie and Edith were both clip round the ears merchants. Einna reminds us of how much of a drama queen

Claire was when she was an adolescent. It was what Edith had always thrown at me, and not only when I was a teenager. I could be dramatic. Trevor thought I was dramatic. My being dramatic often used to end in sex. It wouldn't now.

"John still behaves like a teenager," she says.

"I saw him the other day," I say. "He's put on a lot of weight. He would have passed me by if I hadn't grabbed his arm. He said he didn't recognise me. He's got to have a hip replacement operation." Why didn't he recognise me? I recognised him. He's changed. I've changed. But... oh he was always a difficult man. He blamed me for Einna gradually becoming assertive. That assertiveness didn't last though. She was a rolling over dog with Michael and... I'd almost say a doormat with Tom. How can I talk? My assertiveness went mat-wards didn't it?

"Trevor wasn't doing much grunting this morning. I was almost flattened by his civility," says Debbie.

When did Einna and I first start calling our men Grunt and Groan? I can't remember.

I remember the laughter though, and how it helped.

Einna then says something that confuses Angela and Debbie, but I know what she's referring to; the difference between relationships. Lena and her daughter, who will cope well living together, as did Katy and Molly. But Edith, Trevor and I? Never. I explain and insist that I'm not going to spoil our outing by talking about the dragon. Even though the her removal to Stowe Lodge is accepted, I know that I will be at the but-end of any future grumbles. That leopard isn't going to change her spots. I never did ask Trevor and Ian why it's called Stowe Lodge. Stowe Lodge sounds like a residential home, not sheltered housing.

"I'm going to butterfly deliberately. How are you getting on at Saint Benedict's, Angela?" says Debbie.

"God it was dreadful. I wish I knew why I have to fill in for absent language teachers, just because I've lived in France? On the form I put that I was prepared to teach English and at a push, drama."

"There's a shortage of language, science and maths teachers," I say.

"I know that. But surely knowing a subject's important, isn't it?"

Debbie points out that Angela must know more French than the majority of people, having lived in France for, how long? Does it matter that I can't remember exactly when she and Dave went to France, or when Debbie went to Ireland? Perhaps it's selective memory. After all, a post sixty head has a hell of a lot of memories and facts in it. I bet any brain has to choose what to remember.

None of us have her facility with languages. Okay, I can see her point about not being perfectly grammatical. I imagine conversations with French friends would be very stilted if you were corrected all the time. But school work? Well certainly for exams you need to know the grammar.

Angela then tells us a story about her first lesson in a comprehensive in Bootle. I was shocked. Year ten pupils telling a teacher to 'fuck off', and then disappearing. What has happened to kids since I took early retirement? I don't think B3 was as bad as that, and it was my bête-noir class. In fact I didn't experience any class as bad as that. Kirkby and Bootle are similar, deprived areas. Is it because parents don't discipline now? Is it because teaching is so stressful now that staff are absent more and continuity for pupils is lost? The 'is its' begin to pile up.

I can hardly believe what the Head of Languages said when Angela told him what had happened. "Par for the course!" How can a school accept that behaviour like that is, par for the course?

The way the girls behaved in Angela's class did remind me of the B3 girls. Apathy personified until Colditz.

"I couldn't teach now," I say. "Not even in the primary sector."

"If I wanted to earn some pennies, teaching, in Castletown Bere, I'd have to pass an exam in Irish."

"It was the same for me in France," says Angela. "So much for let or hindrance."

"What?" I say.

Angela explains that 'let or hindrance' is supposed to mean that a European citizen can work in any EU country.

"Mind you, the EU was just a theory according to Madame Tatry."

"Madame Tatry?" We speak as one.

"One of the bureaucrats at CPAM where we had to go to get our cartes sociale. She said we couldn't have them without cartes de sejours. It's bollocks."

"I see France hasn't improved your use of language," says Debbie.

"Okay, Miss Prude. You didn't used to be, did you?"

"No, and I'm not now. I was trying to be ironic. Why are you doing supply? You're past retirement age. You have your work and state pensions, don't you?"

"We do. Dave and I need an excuse to be out the house so we don't feel overwhelmed by Mum and Dad. Does that sound cruel?"

It didn't sound cruel. It sounded normal, especially as they were living with her parents, temporarily. They couldn't buy any old house. They needed to find one they could afford near to Angela's parents. That, after all, was the reason they came home.

"Have they considered sheltered accommodation?" I say. "The one and two bedroomed bungalows are lovely at Edith's place. The one Edith's having looks out onto a duck pond. At the back is a large, communal courtyard, with beds, tubs of flowers, and benches to sit on."

But Angela says that they dare not even mention it. On the one hand her mum cries out for help, on the other, she won't consider useful suggestions. I sigh. Are we going to be a problem for our kids in the same way our parents are a problem for us? I do hope not. We ought to write something now to the effect that when it becomes necessary, they can sort out sheltered accommodation or a residential home. Edith has almost cost me my marriage, health and sanity. How can I tell Angela not to let it happen to her? And telling somebody is one thing, them being able to act mis another.

She told me, soon after they moved back to Liverpool, that Dave knew all about *Kinflicks*. It was one of the reasons he'd wanted to move to France. He partially blamed himself because of his low sex drive. She said he'd told her that a sexual fling wasn't something to get worked up about, but he'd been scared that she might have been tempted to see her *Kinflicks* man again and then she might have fallen for him. That, apparently, was his straw. He loves Angela and couldn't bear the idea of losing her.

Suddenly I think how daunting a life without Trevor would be. I do hope that we find we want to continue on into old age together.

Chapter Twenty-two
The Mirror in the Cathedral

Life always offers you a second chance. It's called tomorrow.

Parking in Chester is always difficult, and very expensive. Just as I'm about to suggest that she uses the park and ride, Einna drives past the first Chester turn off, thus making for Chester Zoo where it's situated. We see a bus waiting. I know we're not going to run for it. In our carefree, no physical ailments, thirties we would have skedaddled over. Now, we take our time.

Angela struggles to get out of the car. She chides Einna for not having one that is easier on older bodies. Debbie helps her out. She and Angela stretch as though their bodies are trying to remember the contemporary dance exercises we used to do.

Einna suggests that we all join a Pilates class and Angela tells us that it was almost the first thing she did when she set foot on Liverpool soil. We don't have access to each other's lives in the way that we used to do… I pause my thoughts. Another 'used to do'. But I'd already thought about this. I can't remember when, exactly. My conclusion? We don't really know anyone. We may do stuff, physically, in tandem, but what is going on in our minds?

"You could sign up for it too. I don't think Annette's list is full," she says.

"I'm not sure Bozo would allow me to." But is this true, now? Less stress, less Bozo. Learn to manage stress, because everyone experiences it, less Bozo. Maybe I could? Maybe it would be beneficial? It probably would be beneficial. Would Trevor see it as a continuation of trying to 'chockablock' my life and having to cancel or postpone engagements?

"I've never asked you why you call the IBS 'Bozo', Maggie?" says Angela.

"Dr Clarke, Leif, suggested that giving it a name, like Bozo, might help me to deal with the pain. I could talk to it, swear at it if I felt like it. I thought I might as well adopt that name. It sounded like a cartoon monster." I don't tell them that he also said he thought it was related to emotional pain. I don't want to talk about Bozo today.

"Are we fit?" Einna asks.

"Fit for anything," says Debbie.

"You speak for yourself," says Einna.

Angela makes a comment about the contradiction between what Einna has just said and her appearance. I can see her point. The red lipstick and feathery winged angel earrings do make a statement. I'm not sure she looks brazen, though. I think she looks more like the Einna we used to know. I wonder why Angela thinks she does? I'm about to ask when I remember the story Einna told me about slipping earrings into her make-up purse when she went out on her own, so that she could take out the silver violins Tom had given her, early on in their relationship and replace them with earrings that called to her; that's how she described choosing what ones to wear. Another web spin. Apparently he used to get upset if she didn't wear his gift. What we've had to do to survive.

"These are my Zac earrings. I'm in the process of putting together a new Einna," she said.

What an odd phrase 'putting together', but I rather like it. I wonder if she will be able to be more assertive when she has put herself together? If one has spent most of one's life cow-towing and spinning webs, can one reconfigure oneself?

Einna wants to be a new person, I want to be an old person; not old, as in years, old as in the person I used to be. I think Einna saw flashes of the self she could be, when she was with us, Fred and Lena, and when she was working as a peripatetic music teacher. If she can rediscover those pieces and build new ones, she could become… become who? We are all our experiences, aren't we? Yes, the good and the bad. Shit! I have to be a new me. I can't be the Maggie before all the experiences. I mean, where did that Maggie start? Before Trevor? Before Stuart, before Ben, before Adam, before Clem, before my dad be… Stop! You'll fill your mind with 'befores' and they'll turn to ashes.

Debbie asks Einna if Annie Grizzle still lives in Chester. Einna explains that she had changed her mind and bought a flat in Hunts Cross instead. I say, "It wasn't just the expense, Einna. Chester was too far away to be able to bully you. She was in a cleft stick: live in vulgar Merseyside and be able to bully, or live in a city with social clout, and not be able to bully."

Einna is insistent that Annie no longer bullies her. "There's bullying, and bullying," I say.

But Einna denies it. She tells us that Annie is sad and lonely. So was Edith. They are both bullies. They both grumble about others. If Edith does avail herself of the social activities at Stowe Lodge, she may become less lonely. But why would she? Experience has shown me she hasn't involved herself with any community activity where she has lived up to now. We shall see, when she moves in. There's talk and there's action.

Is Einna rewriting her history? Will I be able to be that generous when I talk about the removed Edith, in the future? People do change what has happened to them in the past. I think it's a coping mechanism. Sometimes the past is too difficult to deal with, as it was.

"We shan't risk bumping into her then," says Debbie. "That's good. Sorry, Einna, but seeing Annie would spoil the gang outing."

"Have you lot noticed any physical changes in your bodies over the last few years, apart from lines and age spots?" Einna has changed the subject. I'm glad. Talking about Annie is depressing.

"Not sure what you mean," says Angela.

"Well, I take ages to have a pee, now. I think I've finished and then more dribbles out."

"That's me," says Debbie.

"I haven't noticed it," says Angela.

"My body seems to have let me down every which way," I say. Stop that, Maggie. That is you pre those silver daffodils. Quickly, I add, "But no more. I'm in control." Blow me, can it really be that simple? There I was. Here I am. Why the hell couldn't I cope before? Anyway, 'I'm in control' sounds assertive. As if to contradict me, Bozo gives a little snarl. To massage or not to massage, that is the... Ah! He's settled down again, interesting. Residual stress, Maggie. And if you start worrying about why the snarl, it could get worse. Stop thinking about potential problems and concentrate on the present, your friends, this day out.

When I come back into the conversation, Einna is talking about the fact that she doesn't want to be a burden to Claire if she becomes senile. Angela says she doesn't understand why she is thinking along those lines and tells her that making lists of likes and dislikes won't be any good if her dad's senility is anything to go by. I agree with her. In any case, surely there would have been signs by now?

"Annie told me that my maternal gran went senile and my great grandmother, so genetically, it is possible. I shall go into a home because I don't want to spoil Claire and Andy's late middle age."

"Annie probably told you that to upset you. It's the only way she has of punishing you, now," I say.

Will Edith find new ways to punish me once she has moved? Oh for goodness sake, Maggie! You've only just admonished yourself for not concentrating on the gang jaunt. After this week, when will there be another one? Truth? Not for some time. Truth? Yes, Edith will find new ways to punish you, but you will cope because you won't allow yourself to be abused any more. Bloody hell woman. You are sixty-five. You take that on board.

"How has the dementia changed your dad's personality, Angela?" asks Debbie.

"If you remember, he was a very gentle soul. He had a wonderful sense of humour. Now, he's often aggressive and never jokes. He doesn't like things he used to like, for example sausages. He says he doesn't know what they are. When we persuaded him to taste one, he said it was disgusting, and spat it out. If he makes a cup of tea, he always leaves the tea-bag in the mug and gets angry if you suggest removing it."

I feel sorry for Angela's mother. It must be so hard to cope… and with her four children spread round the world, except for Angela who has returned to the nest to help. But that's what you've been trying to cope with for… almost forty years, Maggie, the change in Trevor's character and the cementing in of Edith's. Look what it's done to you. Angela does seem to be managing. Her mother is a very strong character, perhaps too strong. I bet she doesn't deal well with Angela's father's health problems. I seem to remember Angela saying she keeps telling him he does know x or y, as though that will kickstart his memory.

"We do so much now with technology, but we still haven't got to grips with diseases like dementia and Alzheimer's," says Einna.

"Nor with arthritis. What's the point of living to a grand old age if your mind's gone and you're in pain?" If Bozo isn't connected to stress, and becomes a permanent fixture in my guts, would I want to carry on living? Pain wears you down. It incapacitates.

Einna says it's why she can't understand why celebrities have so much cosmetic surgery. I agree. Physical pain doesn't go away under the beautifying knife or botox.

I think we haven't been able to find cures or really alleviate pain because the body is a far more complicated machine that any of those mankind has invented.

There is a mutual sigh. "Come on, gang women," says Angela. "Enough of this. New challenges, that's what we all need. They say it keeps the brain healthy."

Leif keeps telling me that bodies and minds are intertwined and we can't untangle them. So if a new challenge helps the brain, it also helps the body. Helping Edith pack up and move will be a challenge. *Snarl.* Down monster. My family is going to help. Stuart said he would hire a van, and we'd make a day of it. Apparently you can hire a van up to

7.5 tonnes without an HGV licence. When we also sell our house and move – is it if, not when? The if would be to do with Trevor regretting his decision – it will also be a challenge. It could free up some capital, which would be good. Holidays. Maybe I would be able to persuade Trevor to come on some holidays with me, France or Ireland; there's another challenge. I wonder if Ben and Adam would like to help us choose what we should keep and what we should charity shop or take to the tip?

Chester's a bit of a tip now with litter flying round the streets as it does in Liverpool. Yet it's heaving with tourists for the history and the architecture attracts as it always has. Perhaps tourists don't notice litter. We all know Chester. It was a jaunt haunt, so we don't need a tour of the sites. We're here to window shop, bargain hunt and have comfort stops. But gone are many of the individual shops we used to enjoy. They have been replaced by ones you can see on any high street. If it weren't for The Rows, we could have been anywhere. Yet another sign of the chains taking over. On our way to the vegetarian bistro where we always lunched, I have to cover my nose and mouth and stop breathing as we pass *Lush*. The smell of chemically scented soap is so strong I feel asthmatic. How anyone can bear to work in the shop, I fail to understand.

The vegetarian café has vanished, or that's what it feels like. Where once you could order spicy lentil soup, or a wonderful medley of salads, you can now pig out on charred jacket potatoes with various fillings. Is it the final straw for Chester, our café being transformed into one of those fast food jacket potato cafés? Without even discussing it, we turn back. We all know we don't want fast food. We decide to make our way to the Cathedral restaurant. It isn't what you could call warm in there, but we don't know where else to go. There is a soup and sandwich deal. It seems a sensible choice.

Nobody mentions the chill. I suspect we don't want to put a damper on the day. It is being together that's important, not the place.

It's when we're on our way back to the park and ride that I realise it's still early. Chester hasn't been able to capture us for the whole day.

We could do something else. What? There's a stained glass window exhibition in Paddy's Wigwam. I'll suggest it.

"Hey women, it's only two. There's an exhibition on of contemporary, stained glass in Paddy's Wigwam. Shall we go? We could have a cuppa and a cake in The Bistro, afterwards." Something extraordinarily tempting, not Hobson's choice. Angela and Einna say 'yes' immediately. Debbie is more reticent. I'm not quite sure why. After all, Bill is everywhere in Liverpool, not just the city centre. Indeed, the city centre is probably... Ah, you've forgotten, Maggie. It's where much of their courting took place.

Bill. What a let down. He was our perfect man. He wanted to come on jaunts with us because he liked us all so much. We weren't a monstrous regiment to Bill. None of us could believe he had always been prone to looking outside his marriage for sex and friendship. Debbie used the word 'betrayed'. Was betrayal too strong a word? I'm not sure it was. We had certainly been thrown out of kilter. We thought we knew him and we found he was a figment of our imaginations.

"Would you prefer not to risk Liverpool?" I say, meaning the city centre now I've remembered why it almost certainly does hold memories she would rather leave in a locked box.

"Yes, but I can't. Anyway it's stupid. I'm being stupid. It's people, not a place. I shan't bump into Bill, his new partner, the girls who tormented me, or the man who killed Allie, and I shall be able to enjoy a scrummy cake."

But will the ghosts try to escape from the box and flit about down Hope Street?

Einna seems to understand that, for she holds out her arm to be linked. "I've read about the exhibition in *The Echo*. There's an angel window."

"What is it with you and angels?" asks Angela.

"I like the idea of them. I don't believe in God, but I'd like it if angels were real. In stories and films they're always helping people."

"Some angels are vengeful. Michael was a warrior angel."

"I wonder if he's the angel in Epstein's sculpture?" says Einna.

Angela tells us facts about aspects of the Jewish faith and practice that aren't in the story. I'm with Debbie about not liking the idea of eating sinew. I wonder, could I be a vegetarian? No. Every time I think about it I come up against lamb. I love the taste of roast shoulder of lamb, lamb chops, leg of lamb. I always buy free range meat, and sometimes, if it's not too expensive, organic, free range.

Debbie then points out that being a meat eater is another hitch to Mitey's moving in with her. He obviously couldn't understand her abhorrence of the practice for, soon after they had met, he asked her if he could use her car to take his sheep to be dipped as his truck was off the road. I have to say, it made him sound a bit thick. I mean, how many sheep can you get in a small hatchback?

As for this brawny man wearing women's clothes… Our laughter rolls round the car, but still it isn't hilarious enough for us to wet our knickers.

"He can't have thrown an Irish paddy or you two wouldn't have got together," Angela says.

"No, he didn't. Mitey's not like that. He was abjectly apologetic. So much so, I had to shout at him to stop."

"You? Shout?" says Einna.

"I've changed quite a bit since Bill. I was more assertive before I met him, wasn't I?

Remembering dance club, yes she was.

"Anyway, my friend Ben--"

"Ben?" asks Angela.

"Didn't I mention Ben in any of my emails?"

Einna and I know who Ben is, why not Angela? Benedetta. She hates her name, apparently so she insists on being called Ben. My Ben has always been just, Ben.

"He's a her," says Debbie. "Her full name's Benedetta. She has a nearly new shop in Castletown Bere, with a café attached. She's a fantastic cook."

"That Ben. You sent me her apple amber recipe. I used it on the Committee des Fêtes. They loved it and then said, 'Ah!' when I told them it was an Irish recipe, as though that explained everything. Not

318

English, you see. The fact that I was English, and I'd cooked it, didn't enter their heads."

It's the mention of cooking apple amber that leads into a discussion of how Debbie could organise Mitey's house so that meat cooking would happen without Debbie having to see or smell it? No conclusion is arrived at and the more I think about it, the more I see difficulties in their living together. And that's without the cross dressing issue.

"I hope there isn't a strong smell of incense in Paddy's wigwam," Einna says. "It makes me nauseous."

"Now you've butterflied," says Angela.

"Yes." Einna doesn't elaborate on her butterfly.

"Most things to do with religion make me nauseous," I say. "Especially the hypocrisy of some church goers. They're every 'ist' under the sun." I can still remember the way the shop keepers had reacted to... Arthur? Arnold? What name had I given him? And had I really wanted to call Stuart, Arthur or Arnold? Ah, I have it. I'd called the old man Albert and his real name was Henry.

Debbie sticks up for religion, Mitey's influence? No. I believe she told us he was a lapsed Catholic. Still what do they say? Once a catholic. And she's right. There is no harm in taking comfort from belief. It's when religion, any religion, is forced on people that it's wrong.

Einna tells us an amusing Zac story with a grain of truth in it for the four of us, I imagine.

It's about God sending his only son to earth to be tortured and killed. Not much fatherly love shown there.

We're silent for a few minutes, then Angela says, "Tea and cake sound fabby. Is the food as good as ever in The Bistro?

"Yes," Einna and I say in unison. Although I'm not sure as I haven't been to The Bistro for several years. Mind you, I assumed the food was still wonderful when I recommended that Einna met Annie there instead of Lewis's. After all, it was owned by the same people. It still is, unless something has happened recently to change that. Mistakenly, I thought the change of scene and the scrumptious cakes would have a softening effect on the curmudgeon. But it didn't and Einna ended up with a migraine because Annie was spitting feathers the whole time. See Maggie, yet more evidence of a physical effect from stress.

"I'm not sure I'll be allowed in Paddy's Wigwam. I'm a lapsed Catholic," says Debbie.

"Edith always said she'd be excommunicated if she put one foot inside," I say. I'd forgotten that Debbie's family are Catholics. She and Mitey have that in common.

"I took Claire and Annie, once, some time ago. Claire was three or four. It was probably on one of Annie's Christmas visits. As we were looking around, a nun appeared out of a chapel. Claire took one look at her and started screaming. Annie told me I ought to smack her if she didn't stop. I can hear her now: *'You spoil that child, Einna. She'll never know what's right or wrong if you don't punish her. This maybe a Catholic church, but it's still a place of God, and Claire should be taught to be respectful.'*

"*'She's scared of something,'* I replied. *'Children don't cry for nothing.'* Later I discovered Claire thought the nun was the Hooded Claw."

I can't remember what the Hooded Claw looked like. I can remember Dick Dastardly and Muttley. I can't even remember if Stuart watched them, what was it called? Wacky something.

Some people love Paddy's Wigwam. Others hate it. I don't have feelings either way about the exterior, but on a sunny day the interior is stunning. The stained glass windows in the tower, with its crown of thorns, throw rainbows around the cathedral. One day, years ago I overheard a conversation on a train about stained glass windows. One woman was telling her friends about a visit to Cambridge and Kings College chapel. She said, "I bet the architect knew, that at sunset, the light coming through the windows mirrored the pictures in the stained glass on the columns. Ordinary people then, might have seen that as a sign of God's presence." I remember thinking, did he? Would they? But, whether the intention was as clear as that, nevertheless, the effect is awe inspiring.

I'm not sure what I expected of a contemporary stained glass window exhibition. I enjoy it, but end up feeling I prefer the ones of the cathedral itself. The angel window itself is disappointing. I can see wing shapes, but they could have been birds just as well as angels.

"It's a perfect day for looking at stained glass," says Angela. "But my neck's beginning to ache."

"Look, in front of the choir, there's a mirror, for little old ladies," I say.

"Enough of the 'old'," snaps Angela.

"Enough of the 'ladies'," says Debbie. "I may be little but I'm not a lady and men get sore necks too."

The mirror does help us to see the windows in the tower but unfortunately we also see a view of ourselves that clearly shows the ravages of time. I hope Trevor never sees me from this angle. But if he does, I'll be seeing him at the same time. I step back. So do my friends. A salutary experience. Perhaps the cunning catholic church also wants to teach people a lesson about vanity?

Debbie must have also been aware of the effect for she says, "The windows will retain their beauty, whereas we must turn to dust."

"Then, let's have a cup of tea before we do," I say.

"A nice cup of tea," says Angela.

"Oh, I think I'd prefer a nasty one," says Einna. "The real question is, meringue roulade, chocolate orange mousse, almond and orange cake, or…?"

"Oh god, I can feel my belly expanding and Bozo… No. No Bozo today." I smile. "Bozo will not control me any more. I shall control him."

"Tomorrow?" says Angela.

I'm not sure what she's talking about. That I shall control Bozo tomorrow, not today? That wasn't my intention. I meant, stuff Bozo, I was going to enjoy a cake treat.

She notices that I'm confused and explains that she means what's planned for the next day as she's told the agency that she won't be available for the whole week.

"Debbie's going to see Sophie tomorrow."

"Ah yes. I forgot. Isn't she working?"

"She's taken the day off," says Debbie. "I was just going to see her at the weekends, but it will be good to see her without the children.

They are darlings, but they do tend to dominate any time we have together."

I can still remember what Ben and Adam were like when they were that age, wonderful but tiring.

We decide that we'll go to Knutsford the day after and maybe have a look at the daffodils in Tatton Park. Snowdrops and daffodils have become a feature of public spaces now. They cheer up gloomy late winter, early spring days. But, however beautiful they are, I doubt that they'll turn from gold to silver and put a spell on me.

"Ten-thirty at yours, Maggie?"

"I'll drive if I'm up to it." Stop the 'if', Maggie. You will be up to it.

"Bozo isn't connected to your knee," says Angela.

Is that a criticism, a fact, or a question? I can't tell from her face. "I've been a wreck, haven't I?" My friends don't answer. They smile and give me a hug. Perhaps a question then? I know they are saying 'yes' but they still love me.

Einna waves goodbye as she disappears out of the drive. Dave comes for Angela about ten minutes later.

"Would you mind if I looked at my emails?" Debbie says when we're alone.

"Help yourself. When you've finished come through to the kitchen. I'm making a pearl barley and pistachio casserole for our evening meal. Good farting food." As soon as I say it, I wish I hadn't. It used to be a running joke about Bill. But then Debbie did refer to it earlier. Perhaps that's why it came into my mind just now. I change the subject. "I expect you're still logged on."

"Sounds wonderful."

"Being logged on?"

"No. The casserole, Muppet."

I wonder why it is that close friends can insult each other without the insulted taking offence? 'Muppet' isn't a big insult, I guess. Although it does suggest stupidity. Throughout her life, Einna kept being called stupid, first Annie, then John, then Tom. She is far from stupid. 'Stupid woman.' I can hear the bitterness in her voice. Were they trying to put her in the place where they wanted her to be? Was it a control technique? If you are called 'stupid' often enough, you become afraid to open your mouth. You are gagged. You only speak when you are spoken to, and then tentatively. I don't think that Debbie's implying that I'm stupid, so her calling me 'muppet' doesn't hurt. Being called 'stupid' hurt Einna. Answers. Wouldn't it be lovely to have answers. But what would we do with them?

When Debbie is settled at the dining table, I potter through to the lounge. Trevor is asleep in his armchair. I wonder if Ben was patient enough to be able to help him with whatever he wanted to know about his computer. I see an A4 sheet of paper on the coffee table beside his chair. He's written 'Maggie' at the top, so I pick it up.

1) Spoke to Ian this afternoon. That young couple who came round at the weekend have made an offer for our house. It's not quite what we wanted but… No changing his mind, then?

I lay the piece of paper down again. It looks as though he'd started to write a list before he fell asleep. I'll let him give it to me when he's ready.

Maybe we will be moving…

Maybe the people I see walking along a pavement that stretches away into the distance are side by side, physically, at any rate. And perhaps that's enough for me.

Made in the USA
Charleston, SC
03 August 2016